BYRON

A Man Of No Country

A Biographical Novel

Gretta Curran Browne

SPI

Seanelle Publications Inc.

First Published 2018 by Seanelle Publications Inc.

ISBN: 978-1-912598-05-2

Cover Design by Melody Simmons
Cover image by permission of Mr Alain Delon
Painting of Villa Diodati Cologny Switzerland: Meyers 1824.

Dedicated with love to my son-in-law

ANDREW SOUTHERN

a superb actor who, some years ago, in the presence of HRH the Prince of Wales and some 400 diplomats within the British Embassy in Rome, gave a memorable performance of the English poet Percy Bysshe Shelley, whose story in part is told in these pages alongside Byron's.

The Man ... The Poet ... The Legend

PROLOGUE

'It saddens me that Lord Byron, who has shown such impatience with the fickle public, is not aware of how well the Germans can understand him, and how highly they esteem him. With us, the moral and political tittle-tattle of the day falls away, leaving the man and the talent standing alone in all their brilliance.'

GOETHE

Dover, England
April 26th, 1816

Fletcher, the valet, had gone below to the cabins of the ship, as had all the other servants and passengers. All had worn a shade of grief on their faces as they had taken their last look back at the land of England.

The huge white cliffs of Dover now looked smaller in the distance and, apart from a few sailors heaving on the mast ropes, only two young men remained standing on deck. They stood apart and alone in their separate silences, but one was keenly watching the other.

John Polidori, being twenty years old, was the younger of the two men, and he did not feel sad at all about leaving England, he felt joyous and exhilarated.

Although half-Italian and born and bred in England, Polidori had studied medicine in Scotland and had recently scraped through to his graduation, but that was not the impression he had given to Mr John Murray in London who had hired him to accompany his lordship abroad as his personal physician. It had all been arranged in such a hurry that Mr Murray had not been allowed any time to seek references.

John Polidori could not take his eyes off his new employer as he watched him staring across the sea at the white cliffs of his country. A young man, just turned twenty-eight, handsome, slender yet masculine, romantic-looking, with the most beautiful blue eyes Polidori had ever seen. He was also dressed severely in black, as if he was a politician or a preacher, or just a young man in mourning.

Still watching him, John Polidori smiled, and it was almost a lover's smile, for the fact that his new employer looked so young and personable was an added bonus to his joy. The man's obvious sadness did not touch him at all. And why should it – when it had led to his own great opportunity and personal triumph.

Oh, how he wished all those other students at his medical college in Scotland could see him now – hired as personal physician to an aristocrat, and the greatest poet of the age. A poet who was proudly bragged about by the Scots, because although Lord Byron's father had been English, his late mother had been a true Scot of the clan of Gordons and a direct descendant of King James the First of Scotland.

Still revelling silently in his own good fortune, Polidori wondered if his younger sister, Fanny, had received his letter yet. If so, he knew she would either be shrieking with joy or crying with jealousy to read that her annoying brother was here on a ship with *him* – yes *him* – the famous idol of all her romantic dreams.

Fanny had seen him once, just for a minute, coming out of a house and stepping into a carriage in Piccadilly, and the effect on poor Fanny was catastrophic – moping and sighing and unable to eat for days, and then she had written an admiring love-letter to the poet, which had never been answered – causing such devastation to his silly starry-eyed seventeen-year-old sister. Poor Fanny, how proud she would be of her brother now, and how jealous.

And the *cachet* of this appointment as personal physician to Lord Byron was not his only triumph. No indeed, because Mr John Murray, Lord Byron's friend and publisher, had also made a secret and hush-hush agreement with him, promising him the magnificent sum of five hundred pounds if he would write a book giving an exact eye-witness account of Lord Byron's journey and experiences abroad.

"*No matter what it is, or how small and insignificant the detail,*" Mr Murray had said, "*as long as it is about Lord Byron the public will grab it and devour it.*"

Which was somewhat puzzling now to John Polidori, for during the short time after his arrival back in

London, he had heard all the rumours about the scandal of Lord Byron's separation from his wife of one year, and although many of the upper class and aristocracy still adored him, those of the middle and lower classes had turned viciously against him.

Polidori's sudden sniff was condescending. Now that he was in the employment of one of the aristocracy he considered himself to be above those middle class *bourgeois,* all so greedily materialistic and righteously opinionated in their humdrum little lives.

As for the *lower* classes, the best thing to do with them was ignore and avoid them. But the middle-class *bourgeois* – who were they to voice their opinion on the greatest poet of the age? Pretentious riffraff always gossiping meanly about the behaviour and morals of others. He knew them well.

And because he knew them well, and knew that many of them were wicked and mean, he was not surprised when they readily believed and accused others of being wicked and mean.

He had heard their gossip about Lord Byron, the slanders, the innuendos, the slurs. He was suspected of lax morals with low women of the theatre while his poor wife sat righteously at home; but none knew anything for sure; so they guessed and hinted, and their slanderous hints caused heads to nod in agreement at the undoubted truth of it.

And so the cacophony of slanders, as well as the vitriol being spread by his shrewish wife, had all succeeded in driving Lord Byron to make the decision to leave it all behind and go abroad. That must have been the cause – all the whispering rumours – John Polidori was sure of it, because on the night before they had left London, he had overheard Lord Byron saying to his friends – "*If all they say of me is true, I am not fit for England. If false, England is not fit for me.*"

Polidori agreed with that. In his own opinion, Lord Byron's greatest crime was that his sensational poetry and handsome looks had made him *too* famous, *too* adored by the literati and the reading public, and too much loved and lionised by those at the top of society, including the Princess of Wales.

Few of the upper class believed all the rumours, but then they all knew Lord Byron so well. He was one of their own. How dare his parochial wife and the lower classes slur a member of their aristocracy in such a common way?

And based on his own first impression, Polidori now knew that Lord Byron, in reality, possessed a kind of classic grandeur about him, despite his reserved smile and manner. He also possessed a natural grace in his person, despite the slight limp when he walked – the latter being the reason why Polidori had been hired, due to his lordship often suffering great pain in his leg from the affliction of being born with a semi-paralysed right foot.

Yet all the rest of him was perfect, so John Polidori could foresee little trouble or inconvenience in their journey abroad. A dab of ointment now and again to soothe the leg muscles, a powder in some water to ease the pain – and the pay was so good, so generous – *three hundred pounds* a year – as well as the secret bonus at the end from Mr Murray. Oh yes, this journey abroad could be the making of him; and if he wrote his secret book well, then one day John Polidori might become even more famous in England than Lord Byron.

Unfair or not, and despite what his publisher Mr Murray had said, Polidori was certain that Byron was now finished in England, no longer famous but *infamous*, accused of every scandal known to man. His star was falling fast ... yet Polidori had an exciting conviction that his own star was about to rise and shine into a beautiful glow of fame.

And why not? If Lord Byron could write from the heart, so could he. If Lord Byron was handsome, so was he. His ambition had always been more for *literary* distinction than medical – for when did anyone ever applaud an underpaid doctor in a country town, or a mere medical lackey in a hospital?

No, from his boyhood, his burning wish had always been to be greatly admired, to be distinguished, to become famous, and now his chance had come.

~~~

Still gazing back at Dover, Byron was deeply grieving, not for the country he was now sailing away from, and not for all the good friends he was leaving behind; and certainly not for that pious monster his wife, a woman capable of real malice towards people, most people, and especially the people *he* liked – judging them jealously and disparagingly after only one meeting – all had faults to be criticised as soon as they had left the house. Yet in herself she saw only virtue and perfection. He was glad to be done with her, glad it was all over, glad to escape the house of horrors that had been his marriage to Annabella Milbanke.

Yet his sadness consumed him. His heart felt as if an elephant had trodden on it. While the storm in London had lasted, it was bad enough; but now in the peace it was worse, for his freedom had come at a high price ... the loss of the love of his heart, his little girl, his first and only child.

He continued to gaze at the cliffs of England while seeing again his baby daughter whom he had loved and adored every day and every night for a full four weeks after her birth, before her mother had taken her away into the fortress of her own mother.

Ada ... my Ada ... or as he so often smilingly called her "*Miss Byron*"... When would he see her adorable little face again?

Ada, sole daughter of my house and heart,
When last I saw thy young blue eyes they smiled,
And then we parted – not as we now part
But with a hope –
~~~

His sorrow was so heavy that despite the fresh breeze of the sea, his throat tightened until he felt he was suffocating.

"Lord Byron, are you unwell?"

Dr Polidori was at his side, peering at him anxiously. "I saw your hands grip the rail as if you were feeling faint."

"I breathe lead," Byron whispered. "Every moment I think of her, I breathe lead."

"Your wife?"

"No, my child."

"I think you should retire to your cabin now, to rest," said Polidori.

A sudden flock of gulls cried piercingly overhead as they swirled excitedly above the ship. The sudden din of their screeching jolted Byron out of his thoughts and into movement, turning away from the land and walking along the deck towards the stairs down to the cabins.

Polidori quickly followed him.

At the top of the stairs Byron paused and looked at him. "May I beg a favour, Doctor?"

"Oh, anything you wish, my lord."

"The captain has asked me to join him for breakfast in his cabin. Will you tell him I am indisposed."

"Certainly."

Polidori waited until Byron had descended the steps and then made his way towards the stern of the ship and the captain's cabin.

The door was opened by the captain's steward, an older man with white hair. Polidori immediately got the tantalising aroma of a good blend of coffee.

"The captain is still up on the bridge," said the steward, holding the door only half open. "May I help you, sir?"

Polidori was instantly offended by the half-closed door, knowing it would have been flung wide open to receive his employer.

"Yes, you may," he replied haughtily, "I am Dr John Polidori, a companion of Lord Byron. Will you inform the captain that with regard to his breakfast invitation, we regret that we are indisposed, and we will not be able to attend."

"Very well, sir."

The steward closed the door and turned back into the cabin, a puzzled frown on his face. He had been preparing breakfast and laying out the table for only three people; the captain, the first officer, and Lord Byron. And not once did the captain say that Lord Byron would be bringing a *companion* with him – that would have meant setting the table for four – but the captain has definitely said for *three.*

He moved across to the table and began removing cutlery from the table to reduce the three place-settings to two, feeling mightily disappointed. He had been looking forward to seeing Lord Byron up close, because they said he was a young man worth seeing. Some of the sailors had often come back from London telling of his great reputation up there. They said he was the cause of at least two divorces and all the women in London were dying for him.

The steward smirked ... so his lordship must be a very different type of man to the individual who had just knocked – short and stocky and big-headed in his style of talking – and the owner of two of the heaviest black eyebrows he had ever seen ... at least, not since the last time the ship had docked at the Egyptian port at Cairo.

~~~

In London, Lord Holland, the leader of the Whig Party, returned home to Holland House full of exasperation while complaining to his elegant American wife – "It was bad enough before Byron left, God knows, but now I am not even safe from it in the House of Lords."

"Safe from what, dear?" Lady Holland put aside her book, but left a finger inside the page she had been reading.

"Yes, even in the *House*," her husband insisted. "Men coming up to me saying their wives had heard *this* about
~~~

Byron, and the wives of others had heard *that* about Byron, and was any of it true? And my reply is always the same – how the devil should I know?"

"Yes, it's all becoming quite excruciating," agreed his wife, discarding her book. "Why can't they leave poor Byron alone?"

"Why can't they leave *me* alone? Surely they know I would never indulge in scurrilous gossip about a friend."

Lady Holland frowned. Like herself, she knew her husband was very upset about the increasing onslaught against Byron, and she also knew exactly just *who* was to blame for it all.

"Lady Byron," she said contemptuously, "is seen by all those who do *not* know her – as some forlorn flower of virtue now drooping in the solitude of sorrow; but I am acquainted with her well enough to know different. I'm now convinced that woman is either mentally unbalanced, or totally indifferent to the truth."

"Indeed." Lord Holland nodded agreement as he poured his usual evening glass of brandy. "She writes letter after letter to me hoping I will take her side, but my reply to her is always the same – I am not disposed to involve myself in other people's controversies."

"And *yet* ..." said his wife, becoming so annoyed she had to stand up, "only the other day I heard Fanny Kemble lauding Lady Byron for her *'beautiful gift of silence'*. It was too much, I had to protest and tell Miss Kemble that it was all very clever for Lady Byron to have people believe she is remaining virtuously silent throughout – while at the same time writing daily letters to her confidential friends and using *them* to communicate and spread her so-called 'facts' against Byron."

Lord Holland had heard enough. He now believed that Byron's wife was a tiresome and perpetual grievance-monger who should be ignored.

"I know," he said, "that she was utterly shocked when she was told that he had upped and gone and had left

England. She told John Hanson she was completely *torn* by the news"

"And now the little witch is doing everything possible to save herself from blame and *justify* her bizarre accusations and behaviour," said Lady Holland. "But she will never succeed in justifying herself to *me,* nor to Lady Jersey or Lady Melbourne."

"Nevertheless ..." Lord Holland sat down, "my own recommendation to you all is for complete silence on the matter. Lady Byron will feel it more if no notice is taken of her; and if she is treated with contempt by Byron's friends, instead of being regarded by most as the innocent victim of the separation."

Lady Holland looked at her husband. "*We* would find no difficulty in remaining silent on the matter, but will *she*? Can you stop her? Can you stop all her letters of secret gossip to her few special friends?"

Sighing wearily, Lord Holland shrugged, "I can try."

During the following week, while Lord Holland attempted to persuade Byron's wife to stop stirring up all the gossip she pretended to find mortifying, Lady Holland wrote a letter to one of Byron's close friends, her son Henry.

> *"Your Papa is doing his utmost to quell her restlessness, but in vain. I am afraid she is a cold obstinate woman."*

And then, on a lighter note, she added another fact that she knew would amuse Henry –

> *"Yet, despite everything, so many of our younger women are still frantic about him, especially now that he is legally separated from her. Some are even talking about taking a holiday in Switzerland,*

if indeed it proves to be true that Switzerland is his intended destination."

PART ONE

"I was young and vain and poor. He was famous beyond all precedent – so famous that people – and especially young people, hardly considered him as a man at all, but rather as a god. His beauty was as haunting as his fame, and he was all powerful in the direction in which my ambition turned."

Claire Clairmont

Chapter One

~ ~ ~

Sécheron
Switzerland
May 23rd 1816

In her room on the top floor of the *Hôtel d'Angleterre*, Mary Godwin opened the shutters wider to let in more air. Baby William had been irritable and sick, but now he was settled and asleep in his crib.

From this high open window Mary smiled at the sunshine warming her face and, one hand shading her eyes, she gazed upon the lovely Lake Leman spread out in front of her and stretching into the distance; as blue as the heavens which it reflected on its water, and sparkling with golden beams.

The opposite shore was sloping and covered in pine trees. Benches for gentlemen were scattered over the banks, behind which rose the various ridges of black mountains; and towering above them, in the midst of the snowy Alps – the majestic *Mont Blanc*, the highest and queen of all.

Such was the view reflected by the lake, a bright summery scene; and such a relief after escaping the gloom of winter and London.

She gripped the ledge of the window and leaned out to gaze down on the hotel's garden where her beloved Shelley was strolling around the path while reading a book.

Her eyes followed his figure tenderly. Words could not describe how much she loved him. He was not handsome in the way of other handsome men, but he possessed a wild beauty in his person, a heart that was always kind, and the pure spirit of a true poet.

She saw him pause and look up from the book, staring towards the lake as if anxious, or baffled, and he was probably both.

Even from here she could sense his impatience, his annoyance with Claire, and knew that he had positioned himself in the garden so he could intercept Claire on her return from her ramble down to the lake. Something had to be decided now, something had to be done; yet Claire was so insistent on having her own way most of the time that it was very hard to reason with her, and extremely difficult to oppose her.

~

Down below, from the window of his office on the ground floor, the proprietor of the hotel, Monsieur Jacques Dejean, was also watching the Englishman as he walked around the garden path ... a tall and lean fellow who always had a book in his hand, sometimes reading, sometimes carrying it, but one never saw Monsieur Shelley without also seeing a book.

Dejean continued to watch. Most of the guests here were typical of the English, but this one was different. He was young, and his clothes were of good quality but he wore them as if he had no interest in clothes or the fastidiousness of style. His hair was light and wavy and he wore it long, almost down to his shoulders. And worse – he rarely wore a hat when outdoors, which was quite outrageous for a gentleman.

Dejean shrugged woefully ... No hat, no care, no respect for etiquette ... but what better could you expect from an Englishman who wore his hair like a French revolutionary? And what better to expect from an Englishman who had unflinchingly signed his religion in the hotel register as '*Atheist*'.

Dejean tutted his disgust, wondering if such a disgraceful statement was true, or just a young man's wish to shock? In the hotel register, Monsieur Shelley had also written his occupation to be "Poet", and Dejean was certain that was *not* true, because he had never heard of an English poet named Percy Bysshe Shelley, and nor had any of the other English guests.

~

On the top floor of the hotel, Mary was about to withdraw from her position at the window, pausing when she saw Claire returning from her walk. Minutes later she heard Claire cooing to Shelley and saw her running towards him in the garden.

Mary sighed deeply and closed her eyes, suddenly depressed. Would Claire ever leave herself and Shelley alone? Even when she and Shelley had run away to France two summers ago, Claire had insisted on going with them, and continued to live with them on their return to England, attaching herself to them like a barnacle to a ship.

Perhaps if Shelley had not always been so kind to Claire, things might have been different; but then Shelley was kind to most people, especially to someone who made so many heartfelt appeals to him as Claire did.

Mary turned back into the room and sat down on the bed. She had not wanted to come to Switzerland, but Claire had, and so Claire had persuaded Shelley to come here by brazenly telling him an enormous lie. Or was it a lie? Who could ever know anything for sure with Claire? She was a law unto herself, and she had a way of usually getting whatever she wanted.

~

In his office, Monsieur Dejean was drinking coffee at his desk, turning his head when he heard the cheerful voice of an English girl in the garden.

He quickly stood up and moved to the window to look, and saw it was the sister of Madame Shelley, the one they called "Claire," ... the one he did not like, because she was a liar. What else? – when she had signed her name in the hotel register as *Mrs Clara*

Clairville, even though her name in her passport was Mary Jane – *Miss* Mary Jane Clairmont.

He frowned at the deceit of some of the English. That sister was no more a married woman than Madame Shelley was. She, too, had lied in his register, signing her name as Mrs Mary Shelley, even though her passport recorded her as *Mary Wollstonecraft Godwin,* and she also was a 'Miss'. Passports did not lie, even if people did, because all their details were based on documents; birth, marriage, true names.

The only one of the three who had written the truth in the register, in replica of his passport, was the Englishman, the atheist, Mr Percy Bysshe Shelley, aged 23.

Madame Dejean came into the room to collect his coffee tray and smiled knowingly when she saw him at the window. "Who, Jacques? Who are you spying on now?"

"Two of the *ménage à trois*. See now, the sister, she has her arms around his neck, kissing his face."

"Eh?" Madame rushed over to the window and stared at the sister, a busty brunette, yet slender and of medium height, with long black hair that was coiled up at the back. She appeared distressed, close to tears, pleading with him for something."

"You know, Jacques," said Madame, her voice low and confiding, "the other English guests, they have a new name for those three ... *the incest group."*

Jacques looked at her. "Incest?"

His wife nodded with certainty. "What else? One man, two sisters – he sleeps in the same room, same bed, with one of them, and that other sister – that one out there, is shameless – *même vulgaire.* Look at her now with him? The way her hands are clutching at his arms – has she no care for his wife, her own sister?"

"I do not believe she is his wife, and I do not believe they are sisters."

"Not sisters?" After a moment of surprise, Madame paused to think about it. "Perhaps," she nodded, and said slowly. "The one with the baby is very fair in her colour, but that one there, with her flashing *black* eyes ... but that does not mean ... " She looked at her husband. "What makes you think this, Jacques?"

"The passports," he replied. "Passports never lie, because they are based on legal documents, and the *dates* in legal documents. Now, the one who calls herself Madame Shelley, she was born on 30th August 1797, so she is still eighteen, and will not be nineteen for another three months, in August."

"So young." Madame Dejean pursed her lips. "And already she has a child to care for."

"And the sister, the one who calls herself Madame Clairville," Jacques continued, "she was born on 27th April 1798, and she became eighteen one month ago."

Madame Dejean stared. "So they are *both* eighteen?"

Jacques nodded. "I made the figures, more than once, and always they came out the same – less than eight months between their birth dates."

"Less than eight months? Then they *could* be sisters. One could have been born premature, at seven months, but ... so soon after the other, it seems unlikely."

Madame Dejean stood contemplating, and then made a decision. "No, Jacques, no – you must not speak and spoil it for the other English guests. Allow them to continue enjoying all their daily gossip about the atheist and his *ménage à trois*. It is all they know to talk about, apart from the weather."

~

Mary was still sitting on the bed when Shelley entered the room. Claire, he said, had gone to her own room and was refusing to join them later for dinner. "When I said we should leave Switzerland, she became distraught."

"Perhaps she has told us the truth and it is not a lie after all," Mary said fairly.

Shelley was not convinced. "If it's the truth, then why is he not here? He left England before we did. And now we are almost two weeks in this damned hotel and still no sign of him. And where else would he stay upon his arrival in Geneva but the Hôtel d'Angleterre? No, now I am sure it was all one of Claire's fantasies and nothing more."

Shelley lay down on the bed and closed his eyes, knowing it was his own hero-worship of Byron that had made him so readily agree to divert to Switzerland instead of going direct to Italy as planned.

Yet, in truth, he could not blame himself, nor even Claire; because, like so many young people in England, all three of them had been mad about Byron; not only for his poetry, but for the radical way he had continuously and publicly criticised the corrupt ruling government on their sadistic treatment of the English people, especially the lower-class workers.

And then there were his daring attacks on the fat-bellied bejewelled Prince Regent, who was known to eat five large meals a day while the majority of his people lived a near-starving existence.

Such public attacks coming from a common radical would have been recklessly dangerous, but coming from a Lord – a *Peer of the Realm* – was heart-thumping in its magnificence.

But that was then, and now was now – and now was the time to stop being foolishly star-struck and return to reality. If it was really true that the sadistic hypocrisy of "Public Opinion" had forced Byron out of England into exile, then so had *he* been forced into exile, so had Mary, so had Claire. And now he was being *forced* to find a cheap way of living in a cheap country abroad – and yet here they were in costly and high-priced Switzerland !

"Switzerland is too expensive for us, and so is this hotel," Shelley said. "Italy will be a lot cheaper."

"So did Claire agree? Are we leaving here tomorrow?"

"No. She begged for one more day, until Saturday morning."

Shelley suddenly turned his head and looked at Mary, his blue eyes bright with curiosity. "What made *you* believe her?"

Mary shrugged. "I was with her when she met Lord Byron. I liked him. So I suppose I *wanted* to believe her."

Mary paused, hoping she had not betrayed her true feelings about Claire, which always must be kept from Shelley who was so fond of her. He did not see Claire as she did, for always Claire had been *his* sweet consoler, not hers.

Mary's mind drifted back to that year in England after their short period abroad, remembering her happiness when her first baby had been born, a daughter, whom Shelley had named Ianthe. It was a gloriously happy time, for a full two weeks, before the night she had risen to feed her child and found she had died in her sleep.

"*Found my baby dead,"* she had tearfully written in her journal.

Desperate and heartbroken as she had been then, thinking about her little girl all day, and dreaming about her at night, Mary knew she would never forget how Claire had chosen to console Shelley in his loss, becoming his constant companion, going off with him for long walks while Mary was left to grieve alone. Nor would she ever forget Claire's tactless hilarity upon their return.

And Shelley, sensitive to her depression and grief, had agreed to send Claire away, but Claire had soon come back to them, complaining that the rages of her mother were unendurable.

Mary said now: "Claire needs a man of her own, Shelley. She can't spend her life trailing after you."

"Us," Shelley corrected, "trailing after *us*."

No, it had always been Shelley, Mary knew that. Claire had always loved Shelley, but never in the way she now seemed to feel about Byron; fanatical, desperate.

Shelley was thoughtful. "Tell me again about that meeting with Lord Byron."

"I have already told you."

"Yes, but not in any detail. How did Byron respond to Claire? Did he appear interested in her?"

"Not really, no; but he was very polite."

Mary lay down beside Shelley, turning on her side and linking his arm. "I don't think Claire would have gone if she had not heard the rumours that he was separating from his wife. She asked me to go with her as she could not go to a theatre alone, not without a chaperone. She told me she had an appointment with him, but now I think she was lying because he did not seem to know her at all."

Mary thought back to that afternoon at the Drury Lane Theatre with some discomfiture.

"Claire knew that Lord Byron was one of the directors on the Theatre Committee," Mary went on, "and as soon as we were shown into his green room, Claire told him she was seriously considering a theatrical career as an actress, and was seeking his advice. I simply stared at her in shock but she seemed blind to my presence."

Shelley half-smiled at the audacity of it. Claire had always been a forward young miss; and bold, extremely bold.

"'Is it absolutely necessary', Claire asked Lord Byron, 'for one to have to go through the intolerable drudgery of provincial theatres before commencing on the stage in London? And did one have to have very fine manners and a good figure to be an actress, or was talent enough?' Lord Byron listened politely, but he seemed amused. He told her he could offer her no advice or help, other than to introduce her to Mr Kinnaird, another member of the Drury Lane Management who dealt with the actors. His own role was solely to read and find a good script amongst the many scripts sent in by the playwrights.'"

Mary sighed at the embarrassment of it all.

"Claire then remembered to introduce Lord Byron to *me*, and I have to admit, I found him quite charming. He offered to take us down the hall to introduce Claire to Mr Kinnaird, but Claire started gabbling all sorts of nonsense, finally telling his lordship that, in truth, she really would prefer a *literary* career, and had already written half a novel. Would he be kind enough to read her manuscript if she were to bring it to him?"

Shelley was quietly laughing. "Only Claire would have the nerve."

~

In her own room, Claire was pacing up and down in a state of high agitation. If Shelley left Geneva now, all hopes of seeing Lord Byron again would be gone. She would have to leave too, because only Shelley had any money.

She stopped pacing and put a hand to her brow, her mind in a whirl. Had Lord Byron lied about leaving England for Geneva? Had his servants lied? Had the newspapers lied?

She went to her portmanteau and lifted out her letter book, deciding to read again the rough copies of all the fair-hand letters she had sent to Lord Byron. It would give her pleasure to read them again, even though he had not yet replied to any of them – except this first one – he had replied to this one with a short note.

She sat on the bed and lifted her first letter to him to read it again, her eyes scanning past her opening pleasantries to read on –

> *It is not through selfishness that I pray something might prevent your departure from England. Mary is delighted with you, as I knew she would be. She entrusts me in private to obtain your address abroad that we may, if possible, have again the pleasure of seeing you. She perpetually exclaims 'How mild he is! How gentle! How*

different from what I expected!'

Since you disappointed me last evening, will you see me tonight? Pray do. And don't send me away with that little smile on your lips when you say, "Now pray go – Now will you go?"

This is the very last evening I shall see you, as I myself am going – to somewhere where you least expect. I have a letter to show you, and a plan of my own to lay before you – a plan which your advice, whatever it may be, shall not be rejected.

Any advice he had ever given her had been rejected, but that was of no consequence. She was passionately in love, and all passionate lovers were allowed to be determined.

She placed the letter down beside her on the bed and lifted her second letter to him.

You bid me that when I write to you, to write short, and yet I have much to say. You also bade me to believe that it was only a fancy which makes me cherish an attachment to you.

When you read this letter you will say in that most gentle tone of yours "poor thing." Now do not smile complacently and call me a "little fool" when I tell you I weep at your departure.

Pray write and answer of when you go. I assure you nothing shall tempt me to come to Geneva since you disapprove of it. If you do not go on

Monday may I come and see you in the evening?

If not, let me wish you every happiness; may your journey amuse you; may it cause you to forget the home which calumny and folly have deprived you of, but above all may it dispose you to believe in my sincerity, and if we meet in a foreign land, to greet me with kindness.

And then the third letter, which she had written to him from Paris, from their lodgings on the Rue Richelieu, asking him if he had reached his destination, and whether he ever thought of her.

I know not how to address you. I cannot call you friend, for though I love you, yet you do not feel even interest in me. Fate has ordained that the slightest accident that could befall you would be agony to me: but were I to float by your window drowned and dead, I know all you would say would be "Ah, voilà."

I half thought to begin my letters with "Honoured Sir" because I honour you; and because your coldness allows ought to prevent my expressions from anything but reverence. A few days ago I was eighteen; people of eighteen always love truly and tenderly.

Farewell my dear Lord Byron. I have been reading all your poems and almost fear to think of you reading this stupid letter, but I love you.

She was about to lift the next letter when she heard the baby screeching next door, and Mary trying to pacify him, without much success ... Poor little William had been suffering from colic for days, but Mary was not very good at soothing him. Yet as soon as Shelley took the child from her, all the crying would cease, as if by magic.

Minutes later, silence returned, and she knew Shelley had taken the boy from Mary. She had seen him do it so often, she could see it now ... Shelley walking up and down the room with the child in his arms while softly singing a song to him – a song which seemed to entrance the boy into a state of calm, although it ran on a repetition of one word of Shelley's own creation ... "*Yahamani... Yahamani ... Yahamani*".

~~~

Claire did not join them for dinner that evening, nor was she anywhere to be found the following morning. Her room was empty, and Shelley's search of the hotel and its grounds proved futile.

"She has probably gone for one of her long walks alongside the lake," Shelley decided. "You know how she loves to mystify us."

Mary agreed, although as much as Claire often mystified Shelley, it was not so with her. She knew Claire too well. Wherever Claire had gone, she would stay there and continue with her sulks until she knew they were fraught with concern; and then she would appear, full of smiles and innocence, her eyes wide with amazement that they had spent a moment in worry about her.

Yet by late afternoon, when there was still no sign of Claire, even Mary started to worry. Shelley, too, was now extremely concerned, wondering if she might have fallen into the lake.
~~~

"I think I should go and look for her," he said, and immediately began to walk down the path that would take him to the lake.

Holding William in her arms, Mary watched him go, following his every step and hoping frantically that Claire had come to no harm.

She turned, about to take William back into the shade of the hotel when she suddenly heard Claire's voice cooing loudly to Shelley.

Mary turned, and saw Shelley emerge from the path to the lake and walk back to join Claire on the road. It looked like he was speaking to her quietly and sternly, but Claire appeared too excited to heed him.

"Claire!" Mary called out in exasperation, "Where on earth have you been?"

Claire waited until she had reached Mary before encompassing them both in one great big happy smile. "I've been into town," she said, "to find *le bureau de poste."*

"The post office? Why? We are not expecting letters from anyone."

"Not *you*, perhaps, but others might ..." Claire then explained that after awaking that morning she had looked through the window, saw a cart coming down the road towards the hotel, and remembered Madame Dejean saying the groceries and other orders from the town were always delivered on Tuesdays and Fridays.

"And with today being Friday, I knew the delivery man would be returning to town, so I determined to go with him.

Mary was shocked. "You travelled all that way alone with a delivery man?"

Claire smiled. "He was extremely obliging and as well-behaved as any gentleman. And as my French was almost as good as his French, we had some enlightening conversations. He very kindly took me all the way to the door of *le Bureau de Poste* and there we said farewell."

"But the town is four miles away," Mary said. "How did you travel back?"

"On my feet, of course. With no money I had no choice but to *walk* back, but I didn't mind doing so, not a step, because I now know that he *is* coming to Geneva. Lord Byron *is* definitely on his way here."

Shelley gave her an amazed look. "How do you know that?"

"In the bureau I asked the clerk behind the counter if any letters had arrived from England for Lord Byron, and he said yes, quite a few had arrived, *poste restante* and asked if I had come to collect them on behalf of his lordship. I said no, I was merely enquiring, but don't you see – we *cannot* leave here now, not before he arrives."

Mary was about to speak, but Shelley had the same thought and spoke first, as if vexed with Claire: "So when he left England, he must not have known exactly *where* he would be staying in Geneva – not if he arranged for all his mail to be sent to the Geneva post office – hence, you don't really know, do you, Claire, that he intends to stay at *this* hotel?"

"Of course he will be staying *here*," Claire said. "All the best English people stay here, because it is outside the town walls. Why do you think it is called *L' Hôtel d'Angleterre?"*

"When Shelley and Mary remained silent, Claire insisted, "You should look through the hotel's register and you will see the names – Lord and Lady Holland, Lady Jersey, Lady Dalrymple-Hamilton – all have stayed here in the past, and all are friends of Lord Byron. So of course they would have recommended it to him – how else would he know the best place to stay in a country that he has never before visited?"

Mary could see the sense in that, but Claire misread her look. "I don't care," she said with a defiant lift of her head. "Think what you will, but I'm tired and my feet are sore. I'm going to soak them in a bowl of warm water."

Mary watched her stride away, and then turned round and stared as Shelley, who appeared puzzled.

"What is it?"

"Byron left England a month ago," said Shelley. "So if he is truly coming to Geneva, I wonder why it is taking him such a long time to get here?"

Chapter Two

~~~

If Byron had known that his new doctor was a hopeless hypochondriac, he would never have employed him. The man was always unwell, or upset about one thing or another, delaying their journey at every turn.

At *Ostend* he was discommoded into a vapour at the news that he would be expected to share a carriage with Monsieur Berger, a Swiss servant, insisting that, as a doctor, he should be allowed to travel in the same carriage as his employer, which finally was allowed.

At *Antwerp,* inside the inn where they had lodged, the doctor's continual complaints about the "smell of fresh paint" in his room had rendered him so unwell, their journey was delayed again.

At *Cologne,* it was the tea that had left him so nauseous and unable to travel. Dr Polidori was very particular about his tea, apologising profusely to his lordship while insisting that it was "the scented variety" of tea that he "simply could not stomach".

Then through the Rhine country, while travelling over high hills and through pine forests, Polidori suffered an attack of *vertigo* and fainted, forcing them to halt at the nearest inn, where he had dosed himself with lemon acid and stewed apples, but remained weak.

At *Lausanne,* when the pained expression on Dr Polidori's face told Byron that another complaint was about to arise, he interrupted the doctor's grumbling with a question – a question he should have asked at the outset: "Dr Polidori, pray may I ask, in what field of medicine do you specialise?"

"Specialise?" Polidori stared at him. "I am a certified doctor, that is all you need to know."

"Yes, but in what area do you *specialise* and have the most medical knowledge? At your college in Edinburgh, on what subject did you write your paper in order to get
~~~

your medical degree?"

"Somnambulism."

"Somnambulism...?" Now it was Byron who stared ... before turning and taking himself outside to the inn's rear garden. His valet, Fletcher, quickly followed him, and found his lordship quietly laughing.

"My lord?"

"*Somnambulism,* Fletcher! As if my fortunes over the past few months were not bad enough, *now* I find myself saddled with a doctor whose only certain medical knowledge is the condition of sleepwalking. Have I ever walked around in my sleep?"

"Not as I've ever known, my lord, and I've known you since you were a boy of ten."

"And sleep-walking is a condition of the *brain,* not of the body."

Byron began quietly laughing again, ironically, because now it all made more sense. "Polidori must have chosen to study the brain because he knew there was something wrong with his own."

"And the rest of him," Fletcher grumbled. "He may be twenty years old but he acts like a spoiled child. Not a man of the world at all. And he's also driving me and poor Mr Berger mad with all his haughty ways – but you, my lord, you always just laugh and let Doctor Dori get away with it. Why so?"

Byron shrugged. "You should know by now, Fletcher, that I consider laughter to be life's sweetest medicine."

"Even so," Fletcher grumbled, "with a man like the doctor your –"

"*Even so,*" Byron snapped, "with a man like the doctor, my laughter is the only escape from my anger, otherwise I fear I may lift up my pistol one day and *shoot* the good doctor into a peaceful eternity and release him from all his continual tedious complaints!"

Fletcher smiled, satisfied now to know that his lordship felt the same about Dr Dori as the servants did. The man was insufferable.

"And I have enough worries of my own to contend

with," Fletcher said. "What with Annie turning around at Ostend and deciding to go back home, telling me she was too frightened to go any farther abroad to mix with strange foreigners."

Byron was surprised. "I assumed you had sent her back."

"Me? No, not me. She's a good wife is Annie, so why would I send her back?"

Byron looked at his valet, a man who was less than ten years older than himself; a good man, and yes, Ann Rood had turned out to be a good wife to him.

"Was it my fault then?" he asked. "Something I said or did?"

"In a way it *was* your fault, my lord, though not intended. It was that cottage on the land of Newstead that you put in my name for when I get old ... and well, you see, Annie has always wanted to have her own home, her own nest. And so on the ship she begged to be allowed to go back to England and the cottage, and wait there for me there until I get back."

Byron thought back to the odd behaviour of Fletcher's querulous wife on the ship, speaking as if terrified at the thought of leaving the familiarity of England for the unknown.

"I told her," Fletcher went on, "what Mr Hobhouse had said to me, that we would probably be back in a few months. Was Mr Hobhouse right, my lord?"

Byron did not answer, knowing "a few months" was merely wishful-thinking on Hobhouse's part.

"I have no idea of how long, or how far," he said finally, "but you do know, Fletcher, that you are free to leave my service and return to England whenever you wish."

Fletcher stared, startled. "Leave you, my lord? Why would I ever want to do that?"

"To go back to your wife and cottage perhaps? I may be away from England for a long time."

Fletcher paused to think about it. For the past twelve years his entire life had been centred around Lord

Byron, being his valet and looking after him and going everywhere with him ... and truth to tell, he was deeply devoted to his lordship.

"When I went with you and Mr Hobhouse to Greece," said Fletcher, "we was away from England for almost two years, and that did no one any harm, did it? People back home knows that travelling takes time."

Byron shrugged, and turned back to the door of the inn. "Well, I have told you that you are free to go back at any time, so any decision is up to you."

"No," said Fletcher, quickly following him, "I'm too young yet to be settling down in a cottage. That's what women do. But a man must always attend to his work."

Byron was no longer listening, his mind miles away as he calculated how much longer it would take them to get to Geneva ... forty land miles to Sécheron, so a journey of about five hours ... If they left here now, they would reach the hotel very late at night. Would the proprietor be discommoded by travellers arriving at night? Should they risk it? He was now utterly sick of stuffy inns with their small rooms, low ceilings, and narrow beds. At least the Hôtel d'Angleterre was known for its luxury.

Returning to the salon he found Dr Polidori standing at the window, a smile on his face as he gazed back at a small crowd of sightseers trying to peer inside.

"Look at them!" said Polidori sniffily. "Everywhere it's the same. As soon as the word gets round that the famous Lord Byron is in the vicinity – out they come running like a small swarm of beetles."

"I think we should journey on," Byron told him. "If we leave now we could reach Sécheron by midnight."

"Leave now?" Polidori's face flushed as he sank down in a nearby chair. "But we have travelled so far already today."

"And when we get to Sécheron and the hotel you can rest for as long as you like."

"Yes but, dear God, I am so very *tired* now from travelling and –" A loud and sudden clap of thunder made Polidori jump with fright.

Moments later the rain came belting down. A flash of lighting lit up the sky outside, followed by another roar of thunder.

"We cannot journey on to anywhere in weather like this," said Polidori.

Byron had to agree, gazing up at the sky through the window as more lightning flashed. "If nothing else, it would be unfair to the horses. Lightning terrifies them."

"Milord ..." the innkeeper came rushing up. "Milord Byron, do not be concerned. Storms like this, they do not last long."

"Storms?" Byron frowned. "Is it a storm?"

"Oh, yes, it will rage for an hour or two, and then it will cease and all will be peaceful again."

"An hour or two? Oh, then no, it would be cruel to force the horses out in a storm, even for an hour or two."

The innkeeper smiled. "So, you will stay here and sleep very tranquil after the storm, but first you will take dinner of some fine cuisine? My wife is an excellent cook."

His wife was indeed an excellent cook; and later in his room, his stomach replete with satisfaction, John Polidori sat down to write a letter to his sister, Fanny, for he had a great deal of exciting things to tell her – certainly enough to make her cry with jealousy again.

It still amused Polidori that Lord Byron had left England to travel incognito and get away from scandal and his own fame, only to find his own incredible fame waiting for him on the Continent of Europe. Within a day of their arrival in Ostend, his arrival was announced in the *Ghent Gazette.*

Polidori was so impressed, he had cut out the article and sent it to Fanny for her to show to the family and all their neighbours and friends.

But now, dear God, he had enough articles to fill a paste-book, since Lord Byron had been instantly recognisable wherever they went, due to all the copies of his numerous portraits which filled the pages of European newspapers. Some hinted at scandal; others praised his poetry and genius. Lord Byron refused to read any of them.

He had also refused to go anywhere near France, stating he had no wish to see a once-proud degraded France, now back in the hands of the Bourbon monarchy after Bonaparte's defeat.

"The streets of Paris may be thronged with triumphant English," he had said, "but I want no part in their victory."

He had chosen instead to go to Waterloo, where he had stood gazing over the battlefield, which was more like a playground now – curious tourists walking over the field and small French boys selling souvenirs of the battle – mainly silver buttons that had come from the tunics of fallen French soldiers.

An excited young English lady accompanied by a gentleman who might have been her brother or husband, had suddenly recognised Lord Byron and rushed over to him, dropping a curtsy, and then taking a small book and blue pencil out from the reticule hanging from her wrist, opened the book at the flyleaf and begged his lordship for the kindness of his signature.

"Here, on the battlefield of Waterloo," she had gushed excitedly. "Oh, it would be so wonderful to show everyone back home."

Byron silently took the pencil and Polidori watched his hand as he wrote: *Stop! – for thy tread is on an Empire's dust!*

~~~

The following morning, in his office in Mayfair, the publisher John Murray was at his desk, frowning in confusion at the first instalment of the secret journal sent to him by John Polidori.

"This is all rubbish," he finally said to his editor, William Gifford. "I'm not paying him five hundred
~~~

pounds for this!"

William Gifford had always thought it a rather deceitful thing for John Murray to do; and very unfair to Byron; as well as being an enormous amount to pay an unknown amateur.

"I told Polidori that I wanted him to write an account of Lord Byron's journey abroad, all his activities, because that's what the public wants – more news about Byron – but most of what Polidori has written so far is all about *himself.*"

John Murray was shaking his head in disbelief. "And in those few sentences where he *does* refer to Lord Byron, he merely refers to him as 'my companion' – *my companion and I'* ... and as for the rest of it, well, it is all mundane nonsense! Here, read it for yourself."

Gifford, a hard critic even in his mildest moods, took the pages and began to read ...

> *"April 28th. – We set off at 8 this morning to go to Anvers; but, after proceeding some way, one of the carriage wheels refused to turn. I rode off in a passing caleche to Ghent. My horse was particularly fond of the shade; and a house being near one of the barriers, he kindly stopped there to cool me. It being Sunday, we saw some of the women of the village – all ugly.*

Gifford read on to the following day, but it was more of the same –

> *"Having eaten, I issued forth in search of the Promenade, and found the canal with walks. Many ladies, all ugly without exception – the only pretty lady being fat and sixty. The men are also short and bad-looking.*

Gifford read to the end, to where they had reached

Brussels.

> *After dinner, having dressed, I went, having written two letters, to the theatre. Mounting a voiture, I was soon there. Mounting some stairs, I came to a door where, after knocking, a man took my money and gave me tickets, and brought me to the first row of boxes. The first look at the lobbies was sufficient to give me an idea of all the rest – misery, misery, misery, wherever one turned – to the floor, to the ceiling, to the wall.*
>
> *Curtain up – a farce: no – it did not make me laugh. How call that a theatrical amusement which only –*

Gifford could read no more, and he was laughing. "It serves you right," he said to Murray, "for using a vain amateur as a snoop."

John Murray was not listening, for he had taken another package of papers from the pile of post, and these pages in his hand were from Byron himself.

Gifford was surprised to see raw emotion pass over Murray's face as he intently read a page.

"What is it?"

"Byron ..." Murray said slowly. "I should have known he would document his journey himself – in poetry – just as he did in Childe Harold's Pilgrimage when he went to Turkey and Greece.

Gifford stared, doubting that he had heard correctly. "You mean, he is *writing* again?"

Murray nodded. "The beginnings of the next Canto of Childe Harold's Pilgrimage, and he has been to the battlefield of Waterloo ... Now, on this page, listen to how sadly he describes that field after all the bloodshed of the dead on both sides ... although he's getting a dig in at Wellington and King George too."

John Murray read aloud:

Stop! – for thy tread is on an Empire's dust!

An earthquake's spoil is sepulchred below!

Is the spot marked with no colossal bust?

No column trophied for triumphal show?

None: but the moral's truth tells simpler so,

As the ground was before, thus let it be; –

How that red rain hath made the harvest grow!

And is this all the world has gained by thee

Thou first and last of fields! – a king-making Victory?

Gifford shifted uneasily in his chair, but remained silent, feeling emotional. He took off his spectacles and sat twiddling them in his fingers ... his nephew had bled and died on the field of Waterloo, along with thousands more ... fifteen thousand young English soldiers slain, and thrice as many French. All dead. A field of bloody slaughter ... and yet now ... now less than a year later, someone had said the daffodils were blooming there again

Huskily, he said to Murray, "Only Byron could so masterfully write a venomous line like that ... *'How that red rain hath made the harvest grow'.*"

~~~

Inside the carriage rolling towards Geneva, Byron was reading a book, lost in another man's mode of thought.

It is not possible for us to know each other except as we manifest ourselves in distorted shadows to the eyes of others. We do not even
~~~

know ourselves; therefore, why should we judge a neighbour; Who knows what pain is behind virtue and what fear behind vice? No one, in short, knows what makes a man, and only God knows his thoughts, his joys, his bitterness, his agony, the injustices committed against him, and the injustices he commits.

God is too inscrutable for our little understanding. After sad meditation it comes to me that all lives, whether good or in error, mournful or joyous, obscure or of gilded reputation, painful or happy, is only a prologue to love beyond the grave, where all is understood and almost all forgiven.

Sitting on the seat opposite, Polidori had spent some time intently watching Byron. "It is a long time since I was so engrossed in a book," he piped up. "Who is the author?"

"Seneca."

"May I read it after you?"

Byron looked at him. "Do you normally read Latin literature?"

"Latin? The book is in Latin?" Polidori hesitated. "Is it a Holy book?"

"No, Seneca lived long before the birth of Jesus and Christianity. He was a great Roman philosopher, a great statesman, and the author of *Medea."*

"Of course he was." Polidori scowled petulantly. "And of course I can read Latin. Am I not a doctor?"

"A doctor, yes," Byron said, half smiling, "I had forgotten that."

Chapter Three

~~~

There had been no rain up in Sécheron, no clouds at all, just continuous bright sunshine.

Monsieur Dejean looked on happily as some of the English ladies and gentlemen came back into the hotel from their daily sightseeing excursions through the snow-covered mountains, noticing the red blotches on their cheeks and noses due to the blazing sun and the frosty air on their unseasoned English white skins.

The atheist, Monsieur Shelley, accompanied by the two sisters, had taken one of the rowing boats out onto the lake to go exploring. For two Swiss Francs their child had been placed into the care of the hotel's nurse.

Dejean's face changed, became tight, his eyes dark with disapproval. Today he had heard some wicked things about Monsieur Shelley from some of the new English guests, very wicked things.

One guest said that when a boy, Shelley had tried to blow up his school at Eton.

Another said he had been excommunicated from his college at Oxford for being an atheist and a political revolutionary.

The last did not worry Dejean, considering it of no consequence. Had not the great Jean-Jacques Rousseau been a great political revolutionary? Had not everyone? But now all revolutions were over, peace had returned, and hotels could charge high prices again.

"Is that why," Dejean inquired curiously, "why so many of my English guests dislike Monsieur Shelley when told who he is, his name?"

"Probably," said the young man who had spoken about Oxford, "but added to that, his flaunted atheism, and even worse –"

Dejean could hardly believe the bad thing he was now also being told about Monsieur Shelley, a terrible thing,
~~~

and very shocking behaviour from any young man still aged only twenty-three – his early marriage to a girl of sixteen, and then deserting his wife and their child to run away to France with Mary Godwin who had a child by him outside of marriage.

"Terrible! A disgrace!" Dejean had declared indignantly, deciding he must immediately preserve the good name of his hotel by requesting Monsieur Shelley to leave – but then one of the Englishmen commented that it was indeed surprising and disreputable behaviour from the son and heir of Sir Timothy Shelley, a baronet.

Dejean had been silenced abruptly, staring at the two Englishmen, and then needing clarification. "A baronet? His father is one of the English aristocracy?"

"Indeed. And yet, by all accounts, Sir Timothy is a good and decent man."

"And rich?"

"Oh yes, rich."

Which left Dejean baffled as to why Monsieur Shelley had chosen to reside in the very cheapest rooms in the hotel? Up on the fourth floor? Perhaps he had sent for more money from his rich father and it had not reached Switzerland yet? That occasionally happened with the English, but the money always came in the end. And perhaps then Monsieur Shelley would move down into the more expensive rooms?

Dejean's eyes narrowed. Despite his prejudice against atheists, he had never permitted anything to interfere with the *financial* health of his hotel; deciding he could not embarrass the son of an English baronet by asking him to leave the Hôtel d'Angleterre.

In any event, he now reasoned, it would be a risky thing to do, because despite all their tattle and bickering and gossiping against each other, when push came to shove the English *always* closed ranks and stuck together in the end. The devil got into them when any 'foreigner' appeared to be ordering one of their own around.

Dejean knew from his own experience, God knows, and he also knew that in this one respect, the English will never change.

~~~

Geneva's *Lac Léman* was the largest lake in Western Europe, and Shelley knew that its green banks and wide vistas held a lot of fascinating history.

It was somewhere here, on the banks of this lake that his own political hero, Jean-Jacques Rousseau, had been born and lived – Rousseau, the author of the *Age of Enlightenment*. Rousseau, who believed that no government should have the power to rule, unless it be by the will and vote of the people.

Shelley gazed around him as he rowed, enjoying the vast silence of the lake, broken only by the slow and rhythmic splash of the oars. He had always loved being on water, although he had never yet learned how to swim.

He turned his gaze to Mary, lying back on the cushion with her eyes closed, dozing under the sun, a picture of contentment.

Not so, Claire, who was huddled on her seat, staring into space. It was as if she could not bear the hours as she waited mournfully for the arrival of her hero. Occasionally she pulled absently at the collar of her dress, as if feeling too hot, and then huddled deeper into herself as if cold.

Shelley sighed, knowing that Claire was a girl ruled by her passions, but never before had she been so singularly determined to get her own way.

It worried and sometimes irritated Mary, the way Claire now appeared to be "making herself cheap" by recklessly "chasing Byron across Europe".

Shelley had shrugged, unwilling to agree. He had always refused to follow the herd and taken his own path, fervently believing that others should do the same – choose their *own path* in their route through life.
~~~

And now, in truth, he harboured no regret or fault against himself for his own attempt to meet Byron, certain that if he had lived in the time of his other hero, Jean-Jacques Rousseau, he would have scrambled up mountains and down ditches solely to meet Rousseau in person. Even now, in his opinion, there was still none greater than Rousseau, and before Rousseau there was Voltaire; and now there was Byron.

Back in England, Shelley reflected, Byron's fame as a poet was unprecedented; but here in Europe Shelley had been shocked to discover that Byron's fame was *phenomenal* – all his works in every bookshop, copies of his portrait in every newspaper and magazine – and especially in France, whether it be an inn that one entered, or a shop of any kind, as soon as they had heard Shelley's English voice, the first eager question to him was always the same – "*Vous savez Lord Byron?*"

And his answer – No he did not know Lord Byron – always led to an expression of dismay.

In one bookshop, the shelves containing books in various languages, Shelley noticed that the main supply of offerings on the shelves were French editions of Byron and Goethe.

The bookseller, a young man who spoke good English, shrugged carelessly when Shelley asked him why he stocked no editions by Wordsworth. "Oh, to us, he is a woman's poet. His writings of lonely clouds and daffodils have had no influence here."

"And Byron?"

"Ah ..." a smile, "a *man's* poet. To us, he is the most like Rousseau. Byron has great influence here because he is daring and his writings are so *political.* We are very political in France."

Shelley was political too, fanatically so – and his favourite quote about the common lives of ordinary men also came from Rousseau – "*Man is born free, and yet everywhere he is in chains*"– but Shelley also loved the poetry of Wordsworth and he resented the French bookseller's dismissal of his work.

Shelley came out of his thoughts and saw that the sun above the lake, which had been so high and bright when they had first come out onto the water, was now dipping lower.

He paused to lean on his oars, gazing about him at the silent beauty of the scenery all around the great Lake of Geneva ... Geneva, where Rousseau had been born, and yet it was the poetry of Wordsworth that now flowed into his mind – "*It is a beauteous evening, calm and free ...* "

"We should go back now," Claire murmured.

"Not yet," Shelley said, content to remain at this peaceful distance between land and sky. "Soon, but not yet."

Chapter Four

~~~

"*Jacques!*"

Madame Dejean, who had been giving instructions to one of the calèche-drivers in the stable block at the side of the hotel, came rushing indoors excitedly – "Jacques, there is a large four-horse closed carriage coming on the road?"

"A four-horse?"

"And a two-horse calèche following behind carrying baggage and two servants sitting on the box behind the driver. I think it must be one of the English *milords!*"

Dejean stared at his wife. "A milord?"

"It must be." Madame nodded her certainty. "In the sunshine, Jacques, I think I saw the shine of a gold crest on the side of the coach when it turned the corner of the hill."

Dejean beamed and clapped his hands, delighted to once again have an aristocrat arriving at his establishment. Why, *L'Hôtel d'Angleterre* – without an illustrious English aristocrat residing in one of its suites – would completely lose its salubrious and enviable reputation.

Unaware that most Englishmen who had stayed there in the past, now fondly referred to his establishment as "Dejean's Inn"– Monsieur Dejean proudly stepped outside as the large carriage with its four horses and a golden crest on the door came to a halt.

"*Ah, voilà!*" he cried, smiling broadly as the carriage door opened. "*Bienvenue, milord, bienvenue* – welcome to Sécheron!"

A young man stepped out, heavy-browed and haughty. Dejean instantly disliked him.

"Milord?"

"I," said the young man, "am Dr John Polidori, physician to Lord Byron. We will need a suite of at least
~~~

four rooms. Can you accommodate?"

Dejean stared, in shock. "Lord Byron? The *famous* Lord Byron?"

"As I said." Polidori nodded. "Do you have a suite of rooms available?"

Dejean was still staring at Polidori, unable to believe whom it was that was seeking to reside at his establishment, "*Lord Byron*" – the best known name in Europe, after Napoleon.

"Lord Byron ... he wishes to come here?"

"He *is* here," Polidori turned his head as another man stepped out of the carriage, smiling at Dejean as he carefully carried a small black kitten in his hands.

"I presume, M'sieur, that you have no objection to the accommodation of a few small animals?"

"There is more?"

"Just a dog, but a very well-behaved dog."

Dejean instantly liked this young man on sight. He had black-hair, was uncommonly handsome, and wearing a perfectly-tailored fawn velvet jacket with brown piping on the lapels, dark brown knee-breeches and brown boots. But was it really *he?* – It was said that even Napoleon had greatly admired him.

"You are ... Milord Byron?"

Byron nodded. "Your servant, sir."

Dejean doubled into a low bow.

~~~

Later, when Shelley had moored the boat and they returned to the hotel, Claire exhaled a sigh of huge relief as she inspected the register – something she had done every day since their arrival.

She swung round to Mary and Shelley. "He is here! At last! But he must be feeling exhausted ... Look – he has entered his age in the register as being *one hundred* years old."

Shelley and Mary moved closer, smiling as they peered at the register and saw that, under "Age", Lord
~~~

Byron had entered the figures of *100*.

"Dejean will think we are all crackpots," Shelley laughed; and then went to retrieve baby William from the hotel's nurse.

Mary's anxiety had returned. "Lord Byron does not know we are here," she said to Claire, "so how do you know he will even speak to us?"

"Don't be silly, Mary. He may be a lord, but he is also a gentleman, so of course he will speak to us ... if we speak to him."

Claire smiled. Now Mary would see that she, too, could capture a poet, and not an obscure poet unknown to the world, like Shelley, but the most talked-of poet in England and Europe.

As soon as Mary had left her to follow Shelley to the nursery, Claire rushed up to her room and wrote a note to Lord Byron in her usual brash way:

> *I am sorry you are grown so old, indeed I suspected you were 200 from the slowness of your journey – I am so happy.*
>
> *Claire Clairmont.*

~~~

Less than half an hour after arriving at the hotel, and without Byron making any request for such, Monsieur Dejean had arranged for the best and most beautiful writing desk in the hotel to be carried up to his lordship's apartments.

Byron instantly recognised the desk as a 16th-Century Louis XIV *Bureau Mazarin,* lavishly-adorned with Boulle engravings. It was beautiful, yes, but hardly practical for him, due to the *eight* ornate legs which took up most of the knee-hole space. He knew that this style of desk had been named after Cardinal Jules Mazarin who had ruled as Louis' regent in the 1650s. So, yes, more suitable for a Cardinal in his robes or a lady in her gowns sitting sideways. Still, he was touched by the
~~~

gesture, and thanked M'sieur Dejean with an appreciative smile.

He was at the desk making further notes for the Third Canto of *Childe Harold's Pilgrimage* when Fletcher handed him the note, which had been slipped under the door.

Reading it, Byron was appalled to learn that Claire Clairmont was here in Switzerland – and *here* in this hotel. Her persistence in England had been bad enough, but now he had travelled eight hundred miles only to find her here waiting for him. Was there *no escape* from that odd-headed girl?

Her note served only to make him angry – angry with her, with himself, with the world.

He had left England and travelled to the pinnacles of Switzerland in the hope of finding some peace, and being able to live an inconspicuous life without his every step being trailed by one deluded female or another. Fame was a terrible thing. It turned you into public property and exacted a high price.

And yet he had never sought fame, not on this scale. All he had ever sought for himself was recognition as a poet. Impulsively he picked up his pen and began to scribble furiously –

With false Ambition what had I to do?

Little with love, and least of all with fame!

And yet they came unsought and with me grew,

And made me all which they can make – a Name.

A name which was still respected in Europe, but had been stamped into the mud in England, and all due to the spite of two women and their lying tongues: the first, that maniac Lady Caroline Lamb, and the second, his wife.

For Caroline, he had no anger left to waste on her; she had done what she had done in the hopes of separating him from his wife and returning to her, as if that was ever remotely possible. She was the daughter-in-law of Lord Melbourne, and as mad as the winter winds.

But his wife, his very *jealous* wife, who suspected the motives of everyone, no matter how good and true they might be. Even now he was still at a loss to understand what had driven Annabella to such cruel and sadistic behaviour.

True, she had quickly bored him, and she had known that she bored him, although he thought he had hidden it well, but clearly not well enough; which should have alerted him to the vengeance that lay ahead, for he truly believed in the old adage that "We can endure the people who bore us – but never those that *we* bore."

The ultimate insult, that few could tolerate; and vain Annabella the least of all.

He stood up, and wandered over to the window and its open blue shutters, gazing for a time at the evening sky which was already beginning to burn with white stars ... just as his mind was beginning to burn with rage against the woman who had been his wife. She had driven him out of his country, and deprived him of all his friends, and now for the first time since leaving England, now that all his travelling had stopped, he felt extremely homesick for those friends, and lonely.

He wandered back to his desk and consoled himself in writing a letter to the only woman he now trusted, his half- sister, Augusta.

My dear Augusta,

I hope most truly that you will receive my letters, not important in themselves, but because you wish it. It would be difficult for me to write anything amusing. If you hear anything of my child let me know.

As for me, I am in good health, though unequal in

spirits. I have written to you several letters and I have broken my resolution of not speaking to you of Lady Byron – but do not name her to me. Of her you must judge for yourself, but do not forget that she has destroyed your brother. Whatever my faults may have been, SHE was not the person marked out by Providence to be their avenger.

One day or another, her conduct will recoil on her own head – mark – if she does not end miserably.

She may think, talk, or act as she will – but woe unto her, because the wretchedness that she has brought upon the man to whom she has been everything evil, will flow back into its original fountain one day. I do not think any human being could endure more mental torture than that woman has directly and indirectly inflicted upon me within this past year.

She has (for a time at least) separated me from my child – but I must turn from that subject and not relapse into the dismals. Tomorrow I will go –

"Beg pardon, my lord, but Monsieur Dejean is at the outer door, asking to see you."

Byron looked up at Fletcher. "Did he say why?"

"He said it was of the utmost importance."

"Then show him in."

Dejean entered the sitting-room holding a large open book in his hands. "Milord, please to forgive me, but my register, it must always be correct. The Swiss Authorities, they insist, you see?"

"Is something wrong?"

"Oh yes, very wrong." Dejean laid down the book and pointed to Byron's age of 100. "The Swiss Authorities, they will not believe this. Even in the good air of Switzerland, no man lives to that age. So pray be kind, milord, and correct."

"Of course." Byron grinned as he crossed out the age of 100, and replaced it with his correct age of 28.

~~~

Receiving no reply to her note, Claire's determined fight for Byron's attention resulted in her sending him two more sentimental letters at intervals later that night; but, like her first note, they went without any reply.

Claire was utterly dismayed, and even more alarmed the following morning when she made inquiries to Monsieur Dejean, only to be told that Milord Byron had left the hotel and gone into the town of Geneva.

"Left the hotel?" Claire almost collapsed, her mind frantic, certain that here, now, in Switzerland – away from his admirers in England – this was her only chance of securing Byron's attention.

"Is he coming back to the hotel?"

Dejean shrugged, unwilling to give her any further information.

"It is most important that I know," Claire insisted. "I have a very urgent communication for him."

"His physician, Dr Polidori, remains here," Dejean replied in an offhand manner. "He is taking breakfast in the dining room. Perhaps you may entrust the communication to *him?"*

Claire sought Polidori out, and found him in a bad mood, stating that he had not been informed that Lord Byron would be rising early and going into Geneva. He also made it clear that he considered it unfitting for her to be questioning him about his employer.
~~~

Claire thought him very young to be a doctor. "How old are you?" she asked him curiously.

"None of your business," he replied, airily flicking the napkin in his hand and sitting down again to continue his breakfast.

When she had gone, Polidori mused on her appearance ... she was not beautiful ... her face *could* be called pretty, although her nose was slightly irregular.

He dug his fork into one of the fried eggs on his plate. It was a damned cheek though, for her, a stranger, displaying such poor manners – no better than those of a tradesman's daughter! No half-decent young lady would come and brazenly approach him and question him during his breakfast.

PART TWO

"Very few young men have been so run after, and so spoilt by women, as Lord Byron has been."

Lady Frances Shelley

Chapter Five

~~~

In London, Lady Frances Shelley, the beautiful 29-year-old wife of Sir John Shelley, a distant relative of Percy Bysshe, was diligently getting her private diary up to date, having little else to do.

As Sir John had decided they should go abroad for the summer, she had not made any arrangements for the London Season, and she was glad of it. The social life of London's *beau monde* had lost all its verve since Lord Byron had quit the country in April, and within weeks Beau Brummell had also set sail for the Continent. The two young lions had shocked them all by leaving the greatest city in the world.

And now ... now London was just the usual round, the usual sounds, and nothing much of interest to write about.

Frances had just lifted her pen to write a new entry in her diary when Maria Edgeworth, the novelist, was announced and shown in, followed by a maid carrying a tray of tea.

"I ordered it as soon as I arrived," Maria said smiling. "You don't mind, do you, Frances?"

"No, not at all."

"My goodness, the *crowds* in Piccadilly! Tea is the only reviver after such an excursion."

"Then pray relax and revive at your ease," Frances urged. She liked Maria, although a visit from her was like a visit from a political warrior.

And true to form, within minutes Maria had quickly turned their conversation of pleasantries to her favourite subject of the fight for the self-realization of women, and their being allowed to participate in politics.

"We *cannot,"* Maria insisted, "continue to satisfy ourselves with that namby-pamby little missy phrase of
~~~

'Ladies should have nothing to do with politics.' They should be equal in all ways; and boys and girls should be educated equally and together."

Frances was not sure about that: mixing boys and girls together at such a young age was just *too* radical.

"Oh, before I forget ... I received a letter from Mary Leadbetter," said Maria, fishing inside her bag to find it. "They know so little in Ireland about what goes on here, so Mary sent me a letter that *she* received from Melessina Chenevix Trench – about Lord Byron – asking me to read it, and then to tell her if what Melessina says is true or not."

Lady Frances asked, "And is it?"

"I know *my* answer, but now you tell me what *you* think?" Maria held up Melessina's letter and read out –

> *"I have seen, but am not personally acquainted with that prince of modern poets, Lord Byron. It is said he has behaved unkindly to his wife. I doubt his having been much to blame, because her friends and partizans have, in my hearing, brought forward the most vague and pitiful accusations."*

"I completely agree," said Frances; and Maria continued reading:

> *"I believe his faults have been cruelly magnified by those who lead the world; first, from the desire of lowering such pre-eminent genius; next, because he wrote verses satirizing the Regent, and blaming unnecessary war; and thirdly, because he is of a reserved disposition, eats no meat, and enters not warmly into the pleasures of this dinner-loving age."*

"Most of that is true," Lady Frances agreed. "He says he loves animals too much to enjoy eating them, and he has discommoded a number of London hostesses by partaking of only the first course of fish, and leaving all the following courses untouched."

"No meat?" exclaimed Maria. "Why, there is nothing more good for man or woman than a nice slice of beef."

Maria returned the letter to her bag. "So, Frances, may I tell Mary Leadbetter that you concur with all Melessina has said about Lord Byron?"

"I do, so you may."

"Oh, and I *must* tell you," Maria went on, "I recently accepted an invitation to go to the Lushington's for dinner."

"*Stephen* Lushington?" Frances asked with some surprise. "*Lady* Byron's lawyer?"

"The same – although it was Mrs Lushington who invited me."

Maria shrugged carelessly, "I only went in order to finally meet Lady Byron, and I must confess I was *not* impressed. I did not like her at all – cold – and dull – and with a flat-looking face."

Lady Frances almost choked on her tea, and quickly put down her cup and saucer. "Oh, Maria, is there really any need to be so –"

"Dull!" Maria reiterated. "I found her to be formal, pedantic, ill-looking, ill-dressed, and ill-mannered. An inflexible and dogmatic saint! And later, when we found ourselves quite alone in her dressing-room, Mrs Lushington enlightened me on my vexed question about Lady Byron. She told me she was an only child who had been born late in her parents' life, and so she was treated like a toy pet and idolised by them. Consequently she grew up believing she was very special and is still generally disliked by her country neighbours. She is said to have ruled her parents, her servants, her pastor; and no doubt she even tried to rule Byron."

"No wonder the marriage ended so badly."

Maria shrugged. "Have I not always said it is better to

marry someone who is most suited to one's self in character, temper, and understanding. Have I not always said that?"

"You have," agreed Lady Frances, "and I am sure that is why my husband and I are so very well suited."

"Remaining single and unmarried is far better than an incompatible union. That is what I think, so why do not others think it also? Surely it is basic common sense?"

Frances could not help thinking sympathetically of all the young ladies now preparing for the coming London Season, out to catch a husband of any kind, whether his character or temperament suited or not. *Money,* and the secure lifestyle it provided, was the main requirement.

"I presume that she bagged herself a good settlement from Byron?" Maria asked.

"I believe she did," Frances answered. "Rumour has it at three thousand a year, as well as half of the proceeds from his Newstead estate when it is sold."

"Three thousand?" Maria's eyes were wide. "What a *clever* little pixie she is then – three thousand a year for herself and now no need to brighten up her clothes or attempt to make herself likable!"

When Maria finally took her leave, Lady Frances had found herself thinking that it was very fortunate for London society that Maria Edgeworth now lived for most of the year on her family's estate in Ireland.

Still, it brought back to mind Frances's own first meeting with Lady Byron. She had not known then what a spiteful and ungrateful young woman she could be – as proven now by her whispering rumours about Augusta Leigh, Byron's half-sister.

Augusta Byron Leigh, five years older than Byron, and a mother of three children, was not only Frances's friend, but also a half-sister to the Duke of Leeds, and a Lady-in-Waiting to the Queen at St James's Palace.

Frances knew Augusta to be a sweet and gentle-natured person who had always been very kind to her brother's wife, and had done everything to befriend and help her new sister-in-law in every way possible.

Frances searched through her private diary to find where she had a made a note of that first and last meeting with Byron's wife ... it had been a year ago, sometime in April ... Finding the correct section in her diary, she read the entry again:

April, 16th, 1815, – At Augusta Leigh's request I yesterday accompanied her to Piccadilly Terrace to call on Lady Byron. As I had not previously made her acquaintance, I feared that, perhaps, my visit might not be welcome

On the way, Augusta spoke a good deal about Byron, to whom she is much attached. She is by no means insensible to her brother's faults, and hopes that a good wife will be his salvation. Very few young men have been so run after, and so spoilt by women, as Lord Byron has been, and marriage will, she hopes, have a steadying effect on him.

We mounted the stairs, and were about to be ushered into the drawing-room, when the door suddenly opened and Lord Byron stood before us. I was, for the moment, taken aback at his sudden appearance; but I contrived to utter a few words by way of congratulation. Lord Byron did not seem to think that the matter was adapted to good wishes. At least I thought so, as he received my congratulations so coldly.

Lady Byron received us courteously, but I felt, at

once, that she is not the sort of woman with whom I could ever be intimate. I was not sorry when the visit was over. I felt like a young person who has inadvertently dipped her finger into boiling water.

Reflecting back on that day of her visit, and knowing what she now knew, Frances could not prevent herself from thinking it so very sad that a child had been born of that unfortunate union ... sad for Byron who had clearly adored his little daughter, and was now separated from her ... but not quite so sad for Lady Byron, a young woman who appeared to spend all her time concentrating on the faults of others in order to further her own purposes. Yet how she was now managing to blame the collapse of her marriage upon the sweet and kind Augusta Leigh, was grossly wicked.

As Lord Holland had once said of Lady Byron – "*Not even a priest could live with such a woman.*"

Lady Frances read over the page in her diary again, and then dipped her pen in the inkpot to add a further note to the entry:

NB:– Looking back upon that day, the words I have written read like a premonition of the dark days that followed. I had, of course, no reason to think that Lord Byron would not be happy in his married life. But the preposterous accusation which has lately been brought by his wife against his sister, seems to me, who knows her well, to be the height of absurdity. She is what I would call, a religious woman, and her feeling for Byron was that of an elder sister towards a wayward child.

~~~

Later that day, Lady Frances made another entry in her diary.

Shall we never hear the last of Lady Caroline Lamb and her vagaries! She has published a novel which has made much fuss, and has revived the story of her wild enthusiasm for Byron. I hear that Lady Byron is furious. What a strange being is Lady Caroline, first to run all over London after Lord Byron, and then spreading all kinds of stories about him, good, bad, and indifferent. Holding up her folly for all men to see.

Frances was annoyed, very annoyed, because now it seemed that most of the slander and ridiculous rumours against Byron and his sister, which his jealous wife had spread throughout London, had been fed to her by that equally jealous young woman, Lady Caroline Lamb.

Poor Augusta! An innocent and unwitting scapegoat used by those two vain and unscrupulous women in order to hide the truth of Lord Byron's increasing dislike for both of them.

And yet, the irony of it all, was that those two women were cousins who, according to Lady Melbourne, had in the past always detested each other.

During dinner that evening, Frances said to her husband, "Do you know, John, as sad as Augusta Leigh feels now about her brother's departure to the Continent, I believe that in Switzerland, Lord Byron will find himself much safer there; at least, from the pursuit of scandalous women.
~~~

Chapter Six

~~~

Determined to leave the Hôtel d'Angleterre as soon as possible, Byron had gone into Geneva in the hope of finding a private house to rent. His two closest friends, John Hobhouse and Scrope Davies, had promised to join him in Switzerland for the summer, so here he must stay, at least until they arrived.

In the town of Geneva he went to his Bank of the Corraterie where he changed money, and then asked the banker, Charles Hentsch, if he could advise him. "I don't suppose you have any idea of a property that might be available to rent?"

Charles Hentsch, a cultivated young Swiss in his late twenties, was only too happy to oblige. "What kind of property?"

"Somewhere very private, but not in town. Somewhere on the banks of the lake, if possible, as I like to swim."

Charles Hentsch hesitated, thoughtful. He had taken care of numerous leases for properties in the area, but since the end of the war, and with France now open again, so many of the rich English were flooding across France into Geneva. It was the new place to go – for the air, the peace, the Alps.

"I can look through those leases I have in my files and see if there may be anything suitable, my lord, but I will need a little time. Do you have any other business in town?"

"Yes, I need to collect my mail from the Geneva Poste."

"Then perhaps I will have discovered an available property by the time you return. Maybe so, I don't know, but I will do my best to help you."

"Thank you."

In the post office, Byron collected his mail and then
~~~

stood by the window reading his letters for some time, for longer than he had realised, dwelling on the encouraging and cheerful words from his friends in London, and feeling more homesick than ever.

He left the post office and made his way back to the bank, rather doubting that Charles Hentsch would have any good news for him so soon; but if not, where to then? A hotel in town was out of the question, too restricting. One of the main reasons why English people always recommended the *Hôtel d'Angleterre* in Sécheron as the best, was because it was outside the walls of Geneva, which were locked from 10 p.m. to 6 a.m. each day. Who could bear such imprisonment? Locked inside a small town of high houses and narrow streets?

Charles Hentsch greeted his return to the bank with a dubious smile. "There is one house, named *Maison Chapuis,* which stands above the small harbour of Montalègre – but I fear it may be too small for your lordship's requirements."

"May I see?"

Byron took the lease and read through the number of rooms and their proportions, finally nodding in agreement.

"Much too small. I have a physician and two servants with me, and I will need to hire a cook and a few domestics."

"As I thought," Hentsch nodded, "too small. However, there is another property which I think would suit you admirably, but the rent is outrageously high. The owner insists he will take payment of no less than twenty-five gold louis per month.

Byron became thoughtful. "But does it have –"

"Great charm," said Hentsch. "I own a property not too far from there, so I know. The Villa Diodati is at Cologny, on a hill above the lake. It is a seventeenth-century mansion which still belongs to the descendants of Dr John Diodati, the eminent Swiss theologian. You must have heard of him?"

Byron looked blank. "Forgive me, but no."

"Never mind," Hentsch said soothingly, "there is nothing to forgive, because I know you will certainly have heard of your own Englishman, John Milton."

"Milton?" Byron stared. "The author of *'Paradise Lost'*?"

"Yes!" Hentsch smiled, pleased at his lordship's surprised reaction. "It was at the Villa Diodati, inside the house and wandering out in the gardens, that Sir John Diodati entertained John Milton in the year 1639."

"At this house which is vacant – Milton lived there?"

"For several months, yes. Does it not make you wonder what conversations those two men must have had there? What agreements and disagreements about religion that may have influenced Milton when writing his great work years later?"

"Indeed." Byron's distant air had disappeared. He even grinned now. "Can we go there? Just to see the place?"

"Of course." Hentsch smiled. "We can go now, if you wish, in my carriage."

Outside the Bank, Byron spoke to the driver of the calèche he had hired from the Hôtel d'Angleterre, sending him back, and then joined Charles Hentsch in his carriage.

During the journey Hentsch pointed out every hillside house and villa to Byron and named the occupants who had arrived for the summer. "You probably know them all," said Hentsch. "They are all English."

Byron sighed his dismay. "I came here to escape the English and their gossip."

Hentsch's expression was sympathetic. "And you may do that, my lord, at the Villa Diodati. Live your own life, and ignore them all."

Byron looked at Charles Hentsch, liking him more and more by the hour. "And you say that you too have a house near the Villa Diodati?"

"Oh yes, and near also to the Hôtel d'Angleterre. It

would be a great honour for me, Lord Byron, if you were to visit at any time. Just ask anyone to direct you to the villa of *Mon Repose."*

"Mon Repose?" Byron smiled. "Is that its true name – My Rest?"

Hentsch shrugged. "In Geneva I work hard every day. I meet a lot of tiresome people ... small-mannered and unimportant people who question and insist and demand, and then know not how to say thank you ... very tiresome."

Hentsch suddenly brightened and settled down more comfortably in his seat. "But not today, because *today* I am happily helping one of the most celebrated Lords of England."

Byron shook his head. "No, not any more, M'sieur. Now I am certainly the *least* celebrated lord of England."

"Ah, we are here ... the Villa Diodati."

Byron took his time inspecting Diodati: it was a pretty villa in a vineyard, with the Alps behind, Mount Jura in front, and the lake below.

It had a large grand salon on the first floor, with long windows and French doors opening onto a balcony that surrounded the house on three sides.

On the same floor there was a dining room and three more rooms, and another floor of four bedrooms above, and some attic bedrooms above that. The ground floor contained the kitchen and pantries and dining quarters for the servants.

But it was not a mansion – nowhere near as large and as spacious as Byron's own mansion at Newstead Abbey.

"It is a *small* mansion." Hentsch said. "And yet big enough for you to lose your guests in it if they call; so many rooms."

"I'll take it," Byron said. "May I move in immediately?"

"I regret, no. The family are having some work done to the villa, some minor repairs and improvements, so it will not be available until June 10th."

"June 10th ... two more weeks at the hotel? Oh, well, as there is nowhere else, I will take it. Will you see to the lease?"

"Of course," said Hentsch, "I will take care of everything, and when it is done and confirmed, I will contact you at Hôtel d'Angleterre. Now come, and I will show you the quickest way back there."

Byron was surprised when Hentsch led him over the lawn and down to the lake, where two boatmen had their rowing boats moored to the bank.

"For a few napoleons," said Hentsch, "one of these boatmen will row you back to the hotel and you will be there in seven or eight minutes."

"Seven or eight minutes?" Byron looked around him. "Are we are that close to Sécheron?"

"By boat, across the lake, yes. The journey by road is much longer, but as you are here now in Cologny, a boat across the lake is the shortest way back to Sécheron."

Byron took his leave, very impressed with Charles Hentsch, and certain that he now had a friend here in Geneva.

~~~

Mary was relieved to get away from the Hôtel d'Angleterre for a while, linking Shelley's arm as they strolled down towards the lake. Claire trailed behind them, her face a portrait of gloom.

All knew that they were now being frowned upon and gossiped about by the English guests at the hotel, whispering God knows what about the threesome. Mary suspected that Monsieur Dejean knew that she and Shelley were not married, and if so, then no doubt she was being scandalised by all as a scarlet woman.

They turned down the small path that led to the jetty and Claire emitted a sudden choking sound. Mary turned to her and saw that she was staring at the lake.

"It's Byron," Claire whispered. "I would know him anywhere."
~~~

Now that she looked, Mary recognised him too. He had disembarked from one of the rowing boats and was paying the boatman. He turned, and saw them, and without any change of expression, he began to walk along the jetty boards towards them. Mary saw that his limp was very slight, barely perceptible.

"Lord Byron, we meet again, at last!" Claire gushed, hurrying towards him, and then busied herself in a bustle of introductions.

Mary watched it all like an interested stranger, seeing the reluctance on Lord Byron's face as Claire tried to take his arm in a proprietorial way, but most of all she wanted to watch Byron's reaction when Claire introduced him to Shelley.

"A fellow poet," Claire said.

Mary knew that Shelley was always shy with strangers, but he seemed to instantly relax when Byron said with interest, "Shelley – the author of *Queen Mab*?"

The shyness of one, and the reluctance of the other, seemed to vanish once the subject turned to literature. The afternoon sun seemed to shine on them both, the light-haired Shelley and the dark-haired lord.

Perhaps, based on Claire's description of him, Mary wondered if Byron had expected Shelley to be a brash young poet chasing fame, but if so, he saw now that Shelley had the politeness and good manners of his own aristocratic class, and none of Claire's boldness.

Nevertheless, their conversation was that of strangers, cordial and guarded.

Yet still between his Darkness and his Brightness
There passed a mutual glance of great politeness

And throughout it all Claire kept interrupting, furiously trying to make an impression, as if auditioning for a central role in a drama, while Byron was visibly indifferent.

"How do you find the other guests at the hotel?" Byron asked Shelley, and Shelley looked blank, having paid no attention to the other guests at all.

Mary smiled. "We do not go into the society of the hotel," she explained. "They appear to whisper and gossip suspiciously whenever they see us, and Shelley never wastes a moment of his time on people who behave like that."

Byron was puzzled, due to knowing very little about these three people, and asked, "Why should they whisper and gossip about you?"

"Because Shelley wrote his religion as *atheist* in the hotel register," Claire said.

Byron smiled at Shelley. "Now I remember ... you once sent me a pamphlet entitled *The Importance of Atheism."*

"The *Necessity* of Atheism," Shelley corrected. "That little piece got me sent down from Oxford, but I have no regrets. The various tribes of all the different religions have caused too much hatred and too many wars in our world."

"Indeed," Byron agreed. "Although I think that even without any religion, mankind would find something else to war about."

Byron took out his watch, glanced at it, and then looked towards the lake. "You were on your way down to the water?"

Shelley nodded. "For an hour or so. We enjoy being on the water."

"As do I," Byron said, and then seemed to find it difficult to put his watch back into the small watch-pocket of his waistcoat. "But now I must be off. We will meet again, Mr Shelley."

Shelley smiled. "As we are all residing at the same hotel, Lord Byron, I would say that is a certainty."

"Yes, undoubtedly ..." the watch was finally tucked into the waistcoat pocket, "but if we are to become even the remotest of friends, then pray leave out the 'lord' and 'my lord' business, and call me Byron. Just Byron."

Once they were out on the lake, and Shelley was rowing easily, lost in thought, he suddenly started laughing in amusement.

"What is it, Percy?" Mary asked curiously. "Why are you laughing ?

"Just Byron," Shelley said. "As if he could ever be anything as commonplace as *just* Byron."

Mary smiled in agreement. Lord Byron had enchanted her from the first moment she had met him in London. He had been so different to what she had expected, so unlike all the rumours about him. She had been so determined beforehand not to like him, but she could not help doing so. At that time he had a reputation for being charmingly wicked, and yet she had found him simply charming.

His looks, she reflected, were as described; beauty sat on his countenance. But at that first meeting, what had struck her most was his voice – an unusual voice – low and winning, gentle, like soft rain with no thunder behind it – a voice once heard, never to be forgotten.

He was also reputed to be capable of great sarcasm and comic wit, but if so, she had yet to hear it. Would she hear it? Would he become friends with her beloved Shelley? She dearly hoped so. What Shelley needed now was a calming voice, a calmer mind to guide him, instead of all the zealous praise heaped upon him by his band of revolutionary disciples.

~~~

In his rooms at the hotel, Byron was still trying desperately to overcome his dark depression; yet to the face of the world he remained outwardly cheerful, his dignity intact. But his heart was bitter, and inwardly he continued with an agonising struggle. That cursed marriage to Annabella Milbanke had caused him to lose everything. He longed to be back in England, with his friends, with hope, with his child. How could such a tiny being have such a powerful effect upon him, drawing all the love out of his heart for her alone.

Sitting at his desk, he read the letters from his friends again, writing back to just one, Thomas Moore, a friend whom he knew he could be totally honest with –
~~~

"I would, on many a good day, have blown my brains out, but for the recollection of the pleasure it would give to my mother-in-law; and, even then, only if I could be certain of coming back to haunt her in her frightful face – but I won't dwell on these trifling family matters.

When does your Poem of Poems come out? I hear that the Edinburgh Review has cut up Coleridge's 'Christabel', and declared against me for praising it.

He continued writing and conversing in the usual way, from one poet to another, and it cheered him.

It also reminded him of that other poet he had met today, Mr Shelley. Of course he had heard of Shelley, from political radicals such as Leigh Hunt and other firebrands.

He shrugged, thoughtful. His plan had been that the outer world of people and their passions would no longer be of any interest to him. That was why he had come to the mountains of Switzerland, to lose himself. But was it really possible, at the age of twenty-eight, to live a life of isolation without friends or social intercourse?

He had hoped so, but damn it, meeting Shelley had brought his old life and the old world flooding back to him. That clear English voice, a man of education, dressed in clean linen and good clothes – not an unkempt bohemian after all.

~~~

Returning to the hotel, driven by her obsession and vain fury, Claire hastened up to her room where she wrote yet another letter to Lord Byron.
~~~

I have been in this weary hotel this fortnight and it seems so unkind, so cruel of you to treat me with such marked indifference. I am sure you can't say as you used to do in London that you are overwhelmed with affairs and have not an instant to yourself.

If you go straight up to the top of the hotel this evening at half past seven, I will infallibly be on the landing and will show you to my room. Pray do not ask any of the servants to conduct you, for they might take you to Shelley's room which would be very awkward.

As Fletcher was in the room, and Byron was so irritated, he showed the letter to Fletcher.

"Oh, heavens, it's shameful," Fletcher said, shocked.

Byron was silent, feeling dully disgusted. In London his interest in the girl had been extremely slight, and it was her very brashness and forward manner that had inspired his aversion to her. And she *knew* he did not particularly like her – her own words in her letters were proof of that – '*I cannot call you friend, for though I love you, you do not feel even interest in me.*'

Yet still she kept following and harassing him with letters.

She reminded him of his wife.

Annabella, too, had plagued him with regular letters, insisting that her only desire in living life at all was to be able to fill *his life* with happiness – but once she had got her finger into the marriage ring – the mask came off and her only desire seemed to be that of making his life a misery. She had proved to be no tender-hearted kind angel, as she had led him to believe. Once she had achieved the title of "Lady Byron", her manner to all had become proudly cold and repulsive. Before the marriage all her letters were, she claimed, a response to his poetry and the wondrous effect it had upon her heart; yet even before the honeymoon was over she was advising him not to give himself up to the *"abominable trade of versifying,"* urging him to abandon poetry and, instead, to take his rightful place in the House of Lords and become one of England's legislators.

Fletcher handed back Claire Clairmont's note. "Who is she, my lord?"

"An uncommon nuisance," Byron replied, remembering the stage-struck, odd-minded pest that she was then and now.

"Is she a harlot, perhaps?" Fletcher wondered.

"No, but she is one of the daughters of Godwin, so that may explain it."

"Godwin?"

"What irritates me beyond measure," Byron said, picking up the note and staring at it, "is her tone of *entitlement,* as if she possessed some right of tenure in my life ... what if every female I knew briefly in London was to come along to Geneva with the same entitled approach? Who does she think she is? Her vanity is absurd."

"Absurd," agreed Fletcher supportively. This was all very disturbing, though not unusual. How many times had they endured this kind of thing back in London before his lordship had married? Countless times. Unknown females finding their way into the apartment at Albany to hide themselves inside his lordship's closet or pantry? Lady Caroline Lamb attempting to gain entry by disguising herself in male clothes and cap in the pretence of being a messenger-boy delivering a packet.

"Absurd," agreed Fletcher again. "As if we had not suffered enough of such nonsense."

Byron sighed, feeling truly despondent. "Now I regret giving that letter to Polidori to take up to Mr Shelley. Perhaps Shelley will decline, and that will be the end of it. He did say he and his party would be leaving in a few days or so."

~~~

In response to the knock, Shelley opened the door of his room expecting to see Monsieur Dejean or one of the hotel staff, and was surprised at the sight of an absolute stranger.

"Mr Shelley?"

"Yes."

"From Lord Byron," said Polidori, holding out the sealed letter. "His lordship requested me to personally hand this to you."

Shelley unsealed the note and read it there and then, a smile coming on his face.

"Your reply?" asked Polidori.

"My reply is yes, of course. It will be an honour and a pleasure."

"In that case, Lord Byron begs to know, do you eat meat?"

"No, never."

"Very well. We will dine at seven."

Polidori turned up his eyes as he made his way back down the stairs. Dinner with one vegetarian was bad enough, although in truth, Lord Byron always made sure he was supplied with whatever victuals he wanted. But dinner with *two* vegetarians would no doubt spoil his relish and enjoyment of whatever meat he chose to savour tonight.

Claire and Mary stared curiously when Shelley closed the door, holding up the letter. "It's from Lord Byron. An invitation to join him for dinner this evening in his rooms."

Claire clapped her hands, exultant. "Oh, how gloriously and marvellously wonderful! Now we can all talk and dine and become closer friends."

Shelley shook his head. "I'm sorry, Claire. He asks if I could come alone."
~~~

"Alone?"

"Then you *should* go alone," Mary said, knowing it was the convention for men to seek to know each other better personally, before becoming familiar with their wives or women. If the men did not get along, the womenfolk were not involved; if they did get along, then all became friends.

Claire was furious with jealousy when Shelley had left to attend his appointment, but Mary succeeded in sensibly calming her. "If you would just pause to *think*, Claire, then you would realise that this is all for the best."

"How?"

"Well, if Lord Byron had shown no interest in any further communication with Shelley, then you know our proud Shelley would remove us from Switzerland very swiftly, if only to move on to Italy where living is cheaper."

"But why did he ask Shelley to go *alone?* Was that not odd?"

"No, not odd at all. Women usually enjoy the company and conversation of only women now and then, and gentlemen are the same. Men can talk in a more relaxed way when it is one gentleman speaking to another, without women present. And you must remember, the Swiss are very correct about these things."

"What things?"

"Everyone in the world knows that Lord Byron is married. And the people here in this hotel, know it too."

"Then they must also know that he and his wife are legally separated," Claire retorted.

Mary was silent, until Claire added resentfully, "And may I remind *you*, Mary, that Shelley is married, and *not* legally separated; but that consideration did not stop you from running away with him and having his child."

"I was sixteen, Claire, *sixteen* ... and if you recall, *you* insisted on running away with us. You could not leave

Shelley and I alone, even then, even *then*."

Mary sat down, hunched up her shoulders and put a hand to her brow. Claire had been the bane of her life for so long now, so long.

Seeing Mary so upset, Claire, as usual, suddenly tried to make everything appear normal again. She said brightly, "Mary dear, shall I go down and bring us up some tea? And perhaps a pastry or two? Would you like that?"

"Go away, Claire. Go back to your own room."

"Are you sure you want me to leave you, and not wait with you until Shelley's return?"

"No, I want you to go."

Claire looked at her anxiously. "It has been a terribly tiring day for us all, and Shelley probably won't be back until late, tired out and thinking only of his bed. So I hope, Mary, that you won't spoil his evening and worry him about this little squabble of ours."

"No," said Mary, and wondered why Claire always managed to make herself sound like the older sister, instead of the younger brat that she was.

Chapter Seven

~~~

There were moments during dinner when John Polidori felt he was supping with the gods – or two of them at least – so high above his head was their conversation: *Spinoza, Kant, Plato, Pantheism* ... and all without one piece of iron-filled nourishing red meat being eaten by either of them.

Mr Shelley was not only a strict vegetarian, he had also refused wine, brandy, and any other liquor drink that was offered to him.

"How abstemious of you," said Polidori, and deliberately filled his own glass almost to the brim with glistening red claret.

As the evening progressed and he drank more and more claret, Polidori's face began to turn red, but not as red as his ears which were aglow with shock at some of the things said by Mr Shelley.

Without any shame, and with what seemed like true honesty, Shelley admitted that he believed in communal living, free love, and supported the view that "marriage" was a state of degradation for any man or woman.

Polidori, a devout Catholic, wondered if he should protest; but he was so slow in considering whether he should or not, Shelley's conversation had moved on to the Prince Regent and his barefaced hypocrisy.

"He lectures us all on good Christian living, and yet how many illegitimate children has he had with his mistress, Mrs Fitzherbert? Certainly more than the one child he has had with his wife."

"I met her once," Byron said, "At least I was told it was her, the mistress, Mrs Fitzherbert, posing as one of the guests. She had a long nose and loose teeth."

Shelley grinned. "How did you know her teeth were loose?"

"Because she kept sucking them back with her
~~~

tongue, as if fearing one or two might fall out."

"They could have been false teeth."

"True, but they were still loose. Eventually I became as nervous as she, dreading one might drop out onto the floor – *then* what would I have done? I could hardly have picked up the tooth, handed it back, and carried on conversing as if nothing unusual had occurred. Even I am in incapable of being that blasé."

"Bad gums," Polidori said. "People with loose teeth usually have bad gums."

"They do, certainly," Byron agreed.

"Still," Shelley sighed, "a woman with decaying gums is more preferable any day, than a man with a decayed soul."

And he was back to the Prince Regent again. Polidori felt insulted that his participation in the subject should have been so quickly dismissed by Shelley.

There was a knock on the door and Fletcher entered carrying a tray of desserts as well as fruits, nuts, and various cheeses.

His lordship rarely ate dessert, but Polidori's eyes feasted on the chocolate puddings. Chocolate was a novelty only for the rich, and when it was boiled with milk and thickened with beaten eggs and sugar and then mixed with cream over biscuits, it was delicious.

Shelley frowned and sat back in his chair when the dish of dessert was placed in front of him. "No, thank you," he said politely to Fletcher. "None for me."

"No?" asked Fletcher, astonished that such a delicious chocolate dessert would be refused by anyone. "You don't want any dessert?"

Shelley shook his head. "To me, eating a dessert is a crime."

Byron, in the process of cracking a nut, paused and stared at his guest. "A crime? How can eating a dessert be a crime?"

"It is made with sugar, is it not?" Shelley looked at Fletcher for confirmation. "Is it not?"

"I'm sure it is," Fletcher nodded. "Most desserts are

sweetened with plenty of sugar."

"And that is why I won't eat them, on principle. Not as long as free men and women are captured and stolen from Africa, and then shipped to the West Indies to work as slaves on British sugar plantations."

Byron smiled, somewhat cynically. "Or is it that you just don't like sugar?"

"No, I *love* sugar," Shelley insisted. "But how can a man march and protest against slavery, while at the same time eating the very sugar that the plantations produce, keeping them rich and thriving and needing more and more African slaves to work and whip."

"I never thought of sugar in that way before ..." To Byron, Shelley was a revelation; a man who truly did live in accordance with his conscience and principles.

He said to Polidori. "We will ban sugar from our table in future. Slavery is a human obscenity, so why should we support it, even through innocence or ignorance, by eating sugar?"

Polidori hastily scraped up the last few spoonfuls of his chocolate dessert before nodding his agreement – as if he really had any *choice* in the matter – and a devil's damn to Mr Shelley."

He put down his spoon and dabbed his napkin to his lips, deciding that if his lordship believed that he, Polidori, would now be going through life without any sugar on his stewed apples in future, then his lordship was woefully misguided and mistaken.

Misguided by Mr Shelley, who was now drawing his lordship into a very serious conversation about William Wilberforce, the leader of the movement to stop the slave trade.

Fletcher was busily renewing some of the candles, and now they were glowing in their sconces around the room. The candles on the table flickered brightly between the two poets.

Polidori silently watched them, wondering when they were going to speak about something more interesting than the greatness of Wilberforce. He knew nothing whatsoever about the slave trade, and so was unable to participate. He could ask questions, of course, but he was warily reluctant to show his ignorance on the matter.

Sitting silent, he studied Mr Shelley with intense scrutiny. Tall but slight, fair and boyish in his looks, but with the mind of a scholar and the conversation of an outright revolutionary.

The two poets were speaking to each other as if Polidori was not even in the room. And now Mr Shelley was speaking in admiration of Jean-Jacques Rousseau and his immense influence on the American and French revolutions.

His lordship was not inclined to agree. "America, yes; they succeeded, and all glory to them. But France ... poor France ... and now with a Bourbon back on the French throne, it makes you wonder what was gained by their revolution after all? Nothing but the loss of too many lives."

"That is why the next one, in Britain this time, must be a *non-violent* revolution," Shelley said. "It can be done. By the will of the people, it *can* be done."

Fletcher finally opened the door to carry out his tray, and immediately began to remonstrate with someone, which distracted his lordship who looked ... and then smiled, "Ah, my little pet!"

Shelley turned his head to look ... and saw a tiny black kitten skipping between Fletcher's feet in an attempt to enter into the room; a tiny little thing, no more than a few weeks old.

"She's been crying for you, my lord," said Fletcher, "running all over your bed trying to find you. I could do nothing to calm her."

The kitten found a way in and ran straight up to Byron, who pushed back his chair and lifted the little kitten, nuzzling it lovingly.

"This is Jade, my new *amoureux*. Isn't she adorable?"

Shelley, who also loved all animals, stood up to get a closer look at the kitten's cute little face and sleepy eyes.

"Adorable," Shelley agreed, "but so young. Where did you get her?"

"Oh, from the banks of a river just outside Lausanne. She was about to be dropped in the river and drowned by an old witch of woman, until she was stopped by a sharp smack on her arm from my cane."

Shelley sighed. "Humans can be so cruel to poor dumb animals, especially little defenceless ones like this."

"The woman had already dropped one kitten into the river, dropped it like a stone," Byron said, nuzzling the tiny kitten, "but I was able to reach her in time to save this one. That is why I named her Jade."

Shelley was perplexed. "Why?"

"In France, Jade means 'a special stone.' So as this little one was not dropped like a stone, but saved, I would say she is special."

"In England," Shelley grinned, "the word Jade means 'worthless' or 'worn out', and sometimes a disreputable female."

Polidori decided to take his leave. Even Wilberforce was better than this. And would his absence be even noticed? He disliked cats, almost as much as he now disliked Mr Shelley.

He rose from his chair, begged all pardons, made his bow, before strolling to the door, where he suddenly stopped, turned, and said curtly – "Tell me, Mr Shelley, is it true what I heard in the dining room this morning, that you once tried to blow up your school at Eton?"

Surprised by the question, Shelley looked irked. "Oh that old rumour? It was a *chemistry* experiment that went wrong, very wrong. For reasons of safety I took the experiment outdoors, and the unexpected explosion sadly damaged a tree."

"And now the incident has been blown up out of all proportion and honesty." Byron was looking reprovingly at his physician. "You should never play pass the parcel with gossip, Poli, not gossip."

"How was I to know it was gossip?" Polidori shrugged

airily, and left the room.

"Although," said Shelley, seating himself down again when Polidori had gone, "I would not have been adverse to blowing up Eton back then. I hated every day at that school."

Byron stretched out a hand to lift his wine glass. "Are you of a violent disposition?"

"No, on the contrary, I am a pacifist. That is why I did not fit in at Eton. If anyone challenged me to a fight, I always walked away."

Byron frowned. "So they must have thought you a coward?"

"I am a coward," Shelley agreed. "Most people are, but I have never been anxious enough to hide it."

"And if it was a fight for your life? Would you walk away then?"

"No. If it was a fight for my life, I would not walk away. I would *run*, as fast as I could."

"And if it was the life of your wife that was in peril from an assailant, or the life of your child ... what would you do then?"

"Oh, then I would fight to the death – the assailant's or mine."

Byron smiled. "So, a pacifist with a murderous temper."

~~~

In his bedroom John Polidori was sulking. So many annoying things had blighted him today.

First, that bad-mannered girl accosting him in the breakfast room this morning.

And then, this afternoon, even more exasperating, Lord Byron asking him to take a letter up to Mr Shelley, as if he was a servant. Why could he not have asked Fletcher to take it, or Mr Berger? Either one of those lackeys would have been a more appropriate choice than himself.

The most vexing event of all was Mr Shelley joining them for dinner. Within minutes Polidori was alarmed
~~~

to see the two poets relax into easy conversation and become friends. They spoke like two soul-brothers who had found each other in a foreign wilderness. Both spoke the same intellectual language and understood each other perfectly.

"And sitting between them, there was I," Polidori wrote resentfully in his journal – *"like a star in the halo of the moon – invisible."*

~~~

Mary was awake when Shelley returned to their room. A candle was still burning in one of the sconces above the dressing-table.

He smiled. "You need your rest. You should have slept."

"I have slept, for hours. William woke me to feed him. Now he is back in dreamland again."

"Do babies dream?"

Mary lay back on the pillow. "Our entire lives are just a dream, Shelley, One long dream until we finally wake up again."

"It's too late for metaphysics," Shelley said, and Mary smiled.

"You must have enjoyed your time with Lord Byron, to stay so late. Tell me about him?"

Shelley sat down on her side of the bed. "Lord Byron is everything I expected him to be, and yet he is none of those things, no, not at all."

"I don't understand."

"Lord Byron the Legend is very different to Lord Byron the man."

"And which one do you prefer?"

"Oh, the man, certainly." He then told her about the evening and how Dr Polidori disapproved of his refusal to eat meat or drink wine. "He accused me of being consumptive because my skin is so fair. I was very glad when he quit the room."

Mary frowned. It always hurt her terribly whenever
~~~

anyone said anything even remotely disparaging about Shelley.

"Tell me more about Byron."

"Byron, well ... his character is like a puzzling maze. As soon as you start to believe you are getting to know him, he does or says something that confounds you utterly."

Shelley stood and walked round to his side of the bed, beginning to undress "I reciprocated his invitation by inviting him to join us for dinner tomorrow evening, on the terrace."

Mary half sat up. "Did he accept?"

"He did accept, very politely. But are *you* agreeable to that?

Mary smiled. "Very agreeable. And Claire, I'm sure, will be over the moon."

~~~

As the night moved on, and Shelley slept soundly, Mary lay wide awake. Her earlier sleep was now preventing her from dropping off, and she blamed Claire. But for that quarrel with Claire, she would never had gone to bed so early in the evening. Why did that girl always upset her so?

Claire was not even her sister; no blood relation at all. Probably that was why they were so different in every way. Her own mother had died giving birth to her. Three years later, her father, William Godwin, had married a woman who called herself Mrs Clairmont, although Mary now knew that *Mrs* Clairmont had *never* been married.

Mrs Clairmont, a vulgar commonplace woman, loud-mouthed and argumentative. Nothing at all like the intellectual lady that Mary's mother must have been.

Mrs Clairmont, a horrid woman whom Mary had been forced to call "Mama". And worse – Mrs Clairmont had brought along her own three-year-old daughter, Jane, and since then that girl had been the bane of Mary's life in every way – so vain, so greedy, so full of herself – she would never share a toy.
~~~

And yet now, all grown up, she insisted on sharing everything Mary possessed, including her life with Shelley.

It was impossible to fight her; she was so aggressive, so wheedling; whatever worked to get her what she wanted: as sweet as syrup with Shelley, and as sour as vinegar with everyone else.

And then there was her name ... oh, her *name* ... Upon her sixteenth birthday she announced that 'Jane ' was too plain a name for herself; and henceforth she must be referred to as "Claire". And wild blew her temper if anyone forgot, and referred to her by her old unsatisfactory name.

And now they had all got used to it, and knew her only as Claire. Mary *had* hoped that her change of name would also bring a change in her personality; but no, Claire was still Jane underneath.

Jane, the vain. Jane, the greedy. Jane – Claire – who had jealously fought her tooth and nail for the love of Shelley, causing such unhappiness to all three of them.

Now, though, they were in Switzerland, living at a higher altitude, under a clearer sky and in fresher mountain air. And thank goodness Lord Byron had come along to distract Claire –and, in consequence, eased the pressure and the pain for herself and Shelley.

Chapter Eight

~ ~ ~

Claire was buzzing with excitement; but now she had decided to change her tactics. She would stop pursuing and allow herself to be pursued. Her manner would be quiet and gentle and feminine at all times, just like Mary.

For too long she had been a daily witness to the romance of her stepsister and Shelley. Of course, *she* loved Shelley too; but then, who could not love Shelley? He was the kindest, truest, most unpretentious man in the whole world, and in his own way he was beautiful. At least, she had always thought so ... until she had met Byron. Now the four of them were going to dine together this evening and it was all going to be wonderful.

It was horrible – due to small crowds of the other guests who gathered around every window and open door to stare at Lord Byron on the terrace.

Byron finally stood up to apologise to Shelley and depart. "If I leave now, the rest of you may be able to enjoy your food without being gawked at."

"We can eat later," Shelley said, and came up with a solution. "As the weather is so warm, why don't we go down to the lake and take out a boat?"

Mary thought it an excellent idea. "It would be so much more enjoyable than returning to our rooms. Do come, Lord Byron. The lake is so peaceful."

Byron hesitated, and then agreed. "Anywhere would be better than here."

Monsieur Dejean came out to the terrace, carrying his most expensive bottle of wine to recommend to his lordship as the perfect addition to his dinner – standing in confusion and staring at the empty table – until he saw the party of young people walking away down the slope.

A maid approached and whispered to him the reason; delicately pointing to all the staring faces at the windows.

Dejean plonked the bottle into her hands and furiously marched back into the dining-room waving his arms for the guests to return to their seats. "*Monsieurs! Mesdames*! Some respect, *s'il vous plaît!* Pray show some respect to my noble milord guest!"

~~~

Down at the lake, once they were all settled in the boat, Byron finally relaxed. "I shall be very glad to get away from that hotel."

"We do not like it much," Mary said, "Particularly now that we know the other guests are referring to Shelley as 'the man with two wives'." She looked significantly at Claire, but Claire's head had turned in alarm to Byron. "Are you leaving Sécheron?"

"No," Polidori replied, "*we* shall soon be moving into our own private villa."

"A villa?" Shelley was surprised "Where?"

Byron looked behind him. "We shall pass it, I think, the Villa Diodati."

The evening sun was shining on the water of the lake as the boat reached Cologny where they paused to gaze up at the Villa Diodati.

Shelley leaned on his oars and gazed dreamily at the land around the villa. "It's so peaceful here," he said. "Perfect for poetry."

And then his eyes dwelt on a smaller house further down the bank. "That house looks empty ... no doors or windows open to the fresh air and sunlight ... I wonder if it is?"

Byron looked down the bank at the small house, and recognised it from the sketched picture that Charles Hentsch had shown to him. "If that small harbour there is Montalègre, then that house is '*Maison de* something or other,' and yes, it is empty."
~~~

"Available to rent?" asked Shelley.

"I believe so. At least it was a few days ago."

"I wonder if it is expensive?"

Byron shrugged. "If you are interested in staying longer in Geneva, it would certainly be cheaper than the hotel."

Polidori abruptly sat up on his seat. "But you are leaving in a few days, are you not, Mr Shelley? Last night you said you would soon be moving on to Italy."

"We have no definite destination," Mary said to Polidori. "Nor do we have any exact timetable."

"And we are free spirits," Claire added. "So we can go or stay where and when we choose."

Polidori sank back on his seat. He did not like this at all. It was *his* role to be Lord Byron's friend and companion, the man always at his side. Now he could see his position being endangered by Mr Shelley.

"I don't believe an *atheist* should stay too long here in Geneva," he said warningly to Shelley. "They tell me in the hotel that all the Genovese are very religious, all devout Calvinists."

Shelley shrugged. "You can't generalise. All religions are intolerant of the others."

"My mother was a devout Calvinist," Byron said. "And she was extremely intolerant of others, whatever their religion may be. If they were not Scottish like herself, then they were all kinds of everything, and nothing good."

Shelley laughed, although surprised. "But *you* are English?"

"My father was. All my Byron ancestors were. And I was born in London; although the first ten years of my life were lived in Scotland." He gazed around him. "I thought these mountains might remind me of the Scottish Highlands ... but no."

"Nor the Scottish people," Polidori said, and began to talk scathingly about all the gawking and spying behaviour of the English guests in the hotel, refusing to allow a man to dine in peace, solely because he is famous.

Byron was not listening, gazing down at the glassy surface of the blue water and lost in his own blue thoughts ... Fletcher and Mr Berger, in their mutual bond of indignation and fury, had already told him some of the stories they had heard circulating about him in the hotel – discreditable rumours and untruths which the residents had been only too happy to believe, without ever questioning the reliability of such scandal.

He leaned over the side of the boat and let his fingers skim through the water –

And Folly loves the martyrdom of Fame.

The secret Enemy whose sleepless eye

Stands Sentinel – accuser – judge – and spy.

The foe, the fool, the jealous, and the vain

The envious who but breathe in other's pain –

Upon returning to the hotel, Monsieur Dejean greeted his lordship with many apologies and an avowed assurance that many of the guests had agreed to afford him more respect in future. Dejean nodded his head emphatically. "*Oui, plus de respect!*"

And yet in the following days Byron was persecuted by guests waylaying him here, there and everywhere, begging for his signature in their journals. And then he was afforded even less respect from those guests who bribed the chambermaids and servants to go into his rooms when he was out, and steal any little book, ornament or trinket belonging to him that they could take back to England as a memento.

Other bribed servants pillaged his travelling carriage for even the smallest scraps of paper that could be termed as 'souvenirs' of the 'famous Milord Byron', so admired by such men as Johan Wolfgang von Goethe, and even Napoleon.

Byron haughtily rose above it all; struggling to

maintain his anger; until the night he tiredly turned down the coverlet to get into bed – only to find that his bedsheets had been stolen.

PART THREE

Albè

"Albè -- the dear, capricious, fascinating Albè -- Can I forget our evening visits to Diodati? How we saw him when he came down to us, and always welcomed our arrival with a good-humoured smile. Can I forget all our excursions on the lake, when he sang the Tyrolese Hymn, and his voice harmonised with the winds and waves?"

Mary Shelley

Chapter Nine

~~~

On the tenth day of June, upon entering the spacious and private residence of the Villa Diodati at Cologny, Byron could feel an exalted rebounding of his spirit, now that he was free from all the spying, stealing and constraints imposed upon him at the hotel.

He stood in the centre of the grand salon, smiling at Fletcher and Berger as he spread his arms out wide and said – "Freedom!"

"Aye," nodded Fletcher, "free from all the robbers. And at least in this place your sheets will remain safe on your bed."

Standing by the French doors that opened onto the balcony, Polidori made no comment, still upset to some degree at the news that Percy Shelley and the two sisters had decided to stay on in Switzerland with 'Lord B' as they called him; and had now rented the empty house above the small harbour at Montalègre, no more than a few minutes walk through the vineyard, or up from the side of the lake.

He stepped out onto the balcony which looked down onto the lake, and there paused to peer down towards the curving harbour of Montalègre and the Shelley house.

Yes, he nodded to himself, a few minutes walk up through the vineyard would bring the Shelley group *here* in the evenings; and Shelley would then capture his lordship in intellectual conversation. Two poets together, while he was left to sit as mute as a ventriloquist's abandoned dummy.

Dear God, what was he to do about this unsatisfactory situation? He had been hired to assist and advise Lord Byron on his health, not on his choice of friends.

To those glancing at him occasionally from inside the
~~~

salon, it appeared that Polidori was gazing down on the lake; but it was inwards he was looking, inwards at his own dilemma.

What could he do? How could he fill his journal with interesting Lord Byron stories for publication if Percy Shelley was always on the scene? Another poet, yes, but completely *un*-famous and unheard of. And besides all that, who in England would want to know or read anything about an avowed atheist?

Byron stepped through the doors and joined Polidori at the balcony balustrade, and he too gazed down at the lake for some moments, his head tilted slightly to one side.

"Do I disturb you?"

"No." Polidori shook his head. "Not at all."

"You seem to have something rather heavy weighing on your mind."

"Perhaps that is due to my not possessing the power of a great intellect as you and Mr Shelley do. Perhaps I should not have come to Switzerland at all."

"For pity's sake, Poli, what's surling you now?"

"I, as you know, my lord, am a Catholic, a *devout* Catholic, and so it is hard for me to show respect to Mr Shelley, an avowed atheist."

"Shelley is not an atheist," Byron said. "He may think and say he is, but really he is not. He does not believe in churches or dogma and he refutes Deism, but he *does* believe in God."

Polidori was baffled. "But how can that be? If –"

"If anything, Shelley is a pantheist, since he believes that the entire universe is God, and that this limited finite world is just an aspect of one eternal Being who *is* infinite, and the human mind is merely a part of the infinite mind of God."

Polidori was even more perplexed, frowning prodigiously. "Do you agree with that?"

"I really don't know, but Wordsworth does; and of all the modern poets, the one Shelley reveres most is Wordsworth."

"Not you?"

"No. Wordsworth. Both men believe that the power of a universal God can be seen every moment of every day in the animation and essence of Nature – *sacred* Nature – from the movement of the sky to the beauty of a growing flower. And that's why Shelley makes no difference between humans, animals, or even plants. He believes every single flower is divinely touched by God and has its own sort of soul. To Shelley, every living thing is God."

"Even animals?" Polidori restrained the urge to laugh at such nonsense.

"Yes, even animals." Byron leaned his forearms on the balustrade and gazed around him. "And every bird, every tree, and every mountain, river and lake."

Polidori sighed, somewhat relieved; for now he knew that Mr Percy Bysshe Shelley was not so very clever after all.

~~~

A few days later Polidori came up with an idea, a brilliant idea, which would not only serve to make him a closer member of this poetical group of friends, but also help him to move a few steps further along the path to his own future literary fame.

After all, here he was, living in the same house as the man reputed to be the greatest poet of the age, in a pretty villa with servants to tend to their every need; and, as a doctor, his patient was extremely healthy, not needing his ministrations in any way – so the conditions, the atmosphere, and the literary influence on the writing of his new composition would be perfect.

He would compose, in verse, a moving tragedy, and he would become a great writer.

After all, if a crackpot like Percy Bysshe Shelley could write poetry, then why not he?
~~~

Chapter Ten

~~~

Mary considered her new residence at Montalègre, *Maison Chapuis,* to be a delightful home – "Our little cottage" she playfully called the fair-sized two-storey house, for that's how much smaller it seemed in comparison to the four-storey Villa Diodati with all its spacious rooms.

It was all so different now to life at the crowded hotel. Their house was surrounded by trees; and the solitude and seclusion of their surroundings delighted them.

The Villa Diodati did not enjoy such seclusion, placed as it was, higher on the hillside. Stone pillars carved in the seventeenth century ran around three sides of the villa, supporting the long balcony on the first floor above. Mary loved her times on that balcony with all its magnificent views. From the front balcony, facing the lake, one saw the huge range of the Swiss Jura mountains, and from one of the side-balconies, she could see, on a far hill, the Cathedral, around which Geneva had been built.

She also now had more freedom to venture out and explore the landscape, due to Shelley hiring a local Swiss girl from the hotel as a nursemaid for baby William. The girl's name was Elise Duvillard and she was agreeable to joining them; but only if they promised not to *scold* her with their tongues, as all the other haughty English ladies did; something that was very unusual to the Swiss.

"We do not *scold* anyone," Mary had assured her, and so Elise, who adored all babies, was happy to leave the hotel and take up her new position at Maison Chapuis.

Most afternoons, after lunch, the group of three ventured up through the vineyard to see Lord Byron; and he always looked happy to see them; even Claire occasionally received a few smiles from him now. She
~~~

was still acting *demure,* and still intent on becoming his mistress, all she needed was to keep a firm grip on her patience.

Each day passed swiftly. The hot afternoons were spent on Diodati's shaded balcony, talking or reading books.

One afternoon, while all were quietly reading, Shelley was reading Rousseau, inwardly marvelling at Rousseau's honesty when describing the emotions of a man hopelessly in love –

> *'As I walked I dreamed of her I was about to see, of the affectionate welcome she would give me, and of the kiss, that fatal kiss, even before I received it. It so fired my blood that my head was dizzy, my eyes were dazzled and blind, and my trembling knees could no longer support me. I had to stop and sit down, my whole bodily mechanism was in utter disorder; I was on the point of fainting.*

He moved the book halfway across the balcony table to point out the paragraph to Byron. "Have you ever come across a writer so wonderfully emotive in his descriptions as Rousseau?"

Byron looked up from his own book, read the paragraph, and admitted that Rousseau seemed to possess a passion beyond the scope of most men.

A short time later, Byron removed a book from his collection and brought it out to Shelley. "As you are such an admirer of Rousseau, have you read this?"

Shelley took the book and read the title: *Julie, au la Novelle Héloïse.*

"It's a novel," Byron said. "A love story."

Shelley stared. "A love story – from Rousseau?"

"You know Rousseau was born here in Geneva," said Byron, "and the story of *Julie* is set right here on the banks of Lake Leman, so what better place for you to read it?"

Shelley grabbed the book as if it was gold, quickly moving off on his own to a side balcony where he sat down and began devouring every new word from Rousseau: *Julie,* the heroine, falls in love with her tutor, St Preux. The two young lovers want to marry, but Julie's father refuses to even consider the suggestion of Julie marrying her tutor, so beneath her own status and social standing. And besides, he had already promised Julie to one of his old friends.

The love story was not unique, no more than Romeo and Juliet; yet it was the divine beauty of Rousseau's imaginative visions and the genius of his descriptions that stopped the breath and left the reader in a state of self-eclipse, seeing only the two people in the story and witnessing their love and devouring emotions.

Some time later, when he had finished reading, Shelley came back to Byron, declaring it to be the most moving love story he had ever read.

"Such a wonderful novel!" Shelley was glowing. "May I hold on to it for a while, to read it again, more slowly?"

Byron shrugged. "In my opinion, there is nothing so boring as a twice-read novel – *except* when it is a classic written by Rousseau."

"A classic?" Shelley was perplexed. "Why then have *I* never come across it?"

"*La 'Novelle Héloïse* has been banned and unavailable in English since 1803, as are all books by Rousseau. Our monarchy and government do not want the English people to be influenced by French ideas."

"So how did you get hold of this English edition?"

"It belonged to my mother. She loved reading novels. I found it amongst her collection after her death."

"So this is a rare copy?"

"A treasure."

Shelley smiled. "I will take very good care of it."

Sitting silently and listening, Claire was white-faced in her gloom. Byron had not once spoken to her, nor even looked in her direction. What could she do about it? A remedy was needed

The following afternoon Claire arrived at Diodati looking smug, having devised a solution that would ensure that she, and she alone, would receive all the attention by bringing along a German book by Goethe, and offering to read it to the group in English.

Byron was surprised. "You can read German?"

Claire nodded. "And speak it – fluently."

All settled back in their chairs as Claire begin to translate Goethe's word into English – fluently – a language she had chosen to study while in school.

Mary sighed, half-listening, while her thoughts drifted back to the days of Claire at school, and Claire's awful mother. Mrs Clairmont had always favoured her own child above all others, sending Claire to an expensive London school while claiming there was not enough money to send Mary also; insisting she be schooled at home by Godwin himself, a father who had been too cowardly to fight for the equal rights of *his* daughter.

During those earlier disappointed days, Mary recalled, she had often wondered how different it might have been if her own mother had been alive ... her own mother, Mary Wollstonecraft ... who had written the book on the necessity of equality in her *Vindication of the Rights of Women.*

But that was all in the sad past, and not to be thought of now in these happy days in Geneva.

Mary paused in her thoughts, realising that she owed gratitude for a good deal of her present happiness to Lord B. His very presence had removed all Claire's former interfering influence over Shelley.

Claire gave little of her attention to Shelley now. There was only one poet in Claire's sight and she was determined to get him for herself, even if it meant using underhand Byzantine methods, or simply by good old fair means or foul.

Nothing was beyond Claire in her passion for Lord Byron.

Chapter Eleven

~~~

And the friendship continued. Byron genuinely enjoyed the company of the small group. It was impossible not to like Shelley, even though he could be indignantly highly-strung at times, a perfectionist who envisioned wonderful possibilities and improvements for the human race, if *only* the human race would agree and strive for those possibilities also. An end to poverty. An end to slave-labour and the unfair distribution of wealth. An end to unelected politicians. An end to the tyranny of bishops and church leaders preaching to the people that it was "God's Will" for them to be poor. An end to the consumption of *sugar!*

More than once he had worked himself up into such a state of fury and flushed cheeks that he almost fainted and had to sit down; always resuming his calm with apologies for his passion.

And day-by-day Byron was also growing fonder of Mary. She was petite and fair, fair indeed, and she had a sensible and calm balance in her manner that he liked.

And he especially liked her name ... "*I have a passion for the name Mary*" ... which was just as true now as when he had written those words in the past ... because it reminded him of his one and only true love ... Mary Ann Chaworth ... Love's lost dream indeed.

He shrugged the memory away, and brought his thoughts back to the Shelley clan ... At least now, he had noticed, to his relief, even the persistent Claire had settled down and had stopped harassing him with letters.

One afternoon the Shelley group arrived with the news that they had decided to make the long walk into Geneva.

Byron apologised and declined to join them, explaining that on such a *long* walk, his limp would surely slow them down.
~~~

"We will bring you back our honest opinion of the place," Mary told him, not knowing that he had already been into the town of Geneva and had his own opinion of it.

Polidori went with them, for he too was eager to explore Geneva; and once they had all gone, Byron sat at the table on the balcony in the peaceful silence of the afternoon, and continued writing new verses for the third canto of *Child Harold's Pilgrimage,* based on his own observations of the world as he saw it.

All heaven and earth are still – though not in sleep,

But breathless, as we grow when feeling most;

And silent, as we stand in thoughts too deep –

When the group later returned, Mary was exhausted and full of complaints about Geneva.

"The town ...? Well, the town has *nothing* that can repay you for the trouble of walking over its rough stones, or tripping down so many narrow streets with high houses on both sides. And there are *no* public buildings of any beauty to attract your eye. No, nor any architecture at all worth talking about."

"It was not all bad," Shelley said laughingly. "At least we had the pleasure of seeing Rousseau's statue in the town square."

"We also bought more books," said Claire.

Byron stared at Claire who was taking a number of books out of a bag. "More books?"

"As I said," Claire quipped.

She then told Byron about their visit to Manget's bookshop in the Rue de la Cité where they had been able to buy English magazines and English translations of French and Italian books. "These should keep us occupied for a while."

"But this particular book I bought especially for *me,"* said Shelley gleefully, showing Byron an English edition of Rousseau's *Julie, au la Novelle Hélöise.* "And now I will be able to return your mother's book to you safely and undamaged."

"I'm relieved to hear that," Byron grinned.

Later, after they had dined, the group of five strolled down over Diodati's sloping green lawn that led to the lake, relaxed and content in their own private world – unaware that they were being spied upon.

~~~

Monsieur Dejean had been extremely discommoded when Lord Byron had left his hotel, accusing the staff of stealing from him. His lordship's departure had also removed the lure of the hotel to more new guests – the lure of a famous aristocrat residing within was always good – but when that guest was the famous Lord Byron, the lure was powerful.

And then, when the group of atheists had left the hotel also, the other English guests were left with nothing scandalous to gossip about.

And so, instead, they occupied themselves with daily complaints to Monsieur Dejean about his food, his beds, his servants; the flying insects in the garden; the lizards on the south wall of the courtyard; the narrow paths up to the mountains; and "*just too much sunshine*" for their delicate English skins.

If only Lord Byron and his party of young friends had stayed to mesmerise and fascinate the English guests into more weeks of condemning rumours, then all would have remained happy and satisfied. Now the hotel had become very quiet and humdrum, the guests all bored.

Monsieur Dejean consoled his agitation by continuing to carry out long and harsh inquiries amongst his staff, demanding to know which of them had transgressed the hotel's rules and entered Lord Byron's rooms for any reason other than service?

The line of blank faces gave him no answer. All looked innocent, so he knew all were guilty. As soon as the summer was over he would dismiss every one of
~~~

them. They had disgraced the Hotel d'Angleterre.

Madame Dejean had felt as disconsolate as her husband, but now she had found a solution. A solution that had kept her engrossed for hours until her husband found her in one of the empty attic rooms – the room that had previously been occupied by Monsieur Shelley and his imitation wife.

Madame Dejean was peering through a telescope, glancing round when her husband entered. "Jacques, come and see –" she said excitedly.

"See what," he asked ill-humouredly "some new mountains have arrived?"

"No, no ... if you look, Jacques, you will see our 'Otel d'Angleterre is diagonally across from the Villa Diodati where Milord Byron now lives."

She put the telescope into his hands and pointed it for him. "Look, and see ... the big house on the hill."

Dejean was amazed as he peered at the Villa. He usually only used the telescope to scour the mountain paths when some of the guests were late arriving back for dinner. It had never occurred to him to turn it onto the hills, for what was there but the empty Diodati house, and that had been standing there for over two centuries, so why should he look at it again?

"I can see only the house, nothing else. This telescope is not strong enough ... are you sure Milord Byron is living there?"

Madame nodded. "I was told so today by one of the women working in the vineyard. She sees him sometimes alone on the balcony, and many other times the atheists are with him."

Monsieur Dejean lowered the telescope and stared at his wife. "The atheists? They are all living there with him?"

Madame nodded. "I think so. All living together, two males, two females ..." she winked one eye.

Jacques was shocked; but his business mind was working rapidly, for now he saw a way not only to entertain his guests, but also a way to financially profit from it.

~~~

The evenings were their favourite time of the day. As soon as dinner was over, whether they dined at Diodati or Maison Chapuis, every evening at about seven o'clock they hired a boat and cruised on the glassy surface of the lake.

For such a normally serious person, Mary – sitting back on the cushions, and talking about every subject under the sky – was surprised by the happy change in herself.

It was during these water excursions that Byron told the group all about his adventures in Albania, and Ali Pasha, the Moslem ruling chief of that province.

Unlike the sombre way he had described Albania in his first book of *Childe Harold's Pilgrimage*, some of the stories he told them now were often very funny, inspiring Mary into extraordinary bursts of hilarity.

Tonight though, all were very quiet in talk and mood, due to their long and exhausting walk into Geneva.

Shelley asked Claire to sing them a song, and she did so, her singing voice soft and beautiful.

Lying back on his cushion, Byron turned away from her, gazing down into the depths of the clear lake as he listened to her song, his arm draped over the side of the boat and his hand moving in the water.

Shelley had always admired Claire's singing voice, and asked her to sing another song; which she did, slow and sweet; rendering Shelley into a peaceful trance as he stared above at the twilight, now beginning to darken the sky.

Byron too, uttered not a word, his back still turned to them, until Mary asked him, "Byron, what are you doing?"

"Lake Leman is wooing me with her crystal face," he replied.

Polidori, who was rowing, leaned on his oars to tell them about his new tragedy which he had written in two
~~~

nights, and then changed his mind, deciding, "No, not yet, I will surprise them." He sat motionless for a time, relishing the prospect of their surprise.

In the long silence, and still gazing into the lake, Byron closed his eyes and allowed his senses to draw in all the sounds and smells around him ...

There breathes a living fragrance from the shore

Of flowers yet fresh with childhood; on the ear

Drops the light drip of the suspended oar.

At intervals, some bird from out the brakes

Starts into voice a moment, then is still.

There –

Polidori interrupted, saying, "My lord, pray now tell us some more about your time in Albania."

"No ..." Byron took his hand out of the water and sat up. "But I *will* sing you an Albanian song if you wish?"

"Oh, do," Claire clapped her hands together. "A love song?"

"No, please not another love song," Polidori begged.

But Byron merely smiled, saying: "Now prepare yourselves to feel emotional, because this is a song the Albanians love."

Mary leaned forward, ready to listen intently; almost jumping in her seat with fright when Byron began to sing a strange wild howling song, while laughing all the time at their shocked disappointment.

"What kind of a song is that?" said Claire. "It's certainly not a love song."

"It is if you love war," Byron grinned. "It's an Albanian war song."

Often referring to Byron amongst themselves as "LB" it was then Shelley had the idea of joining the name of Albania to the contraction of LB's name and calling him "Albè".

"Now we can talk about you in bookshops and

anywhere else in public without whispering, and no one will know that we are talking about *you*."

Byron shrugged. "Do you as you wish. But now allow me to compensate for your disappointment by singing you another war song."

"No!" Claire declared. "No, we will not allow it!"

Byron was still grinning. "This one has proper words, and it was written by one of my own friends, Thomas Moore."

"So, an *Irish* war song?" Shelley said.

"No, in fact, it's a translation of the Tyrolese Song of Liberty, so this is the very place to sing it," Byron said, and began to softly sing –

"If a glorious death won by bravery,
Is sweeter than breath sighed in slavery,
Round the flag of freedom rally,
Cheerily, oh! Cheerily, oh!
Cheerily, cheerily, cheerily, cheerily oh!

Where the song of freedom soundeth,
Where merrily every bosom boundeth,
The warriors arms shed more splendour,
The maidens charms are more tender,
Merrily, oh! Merrily, oh!
Merrily, merrily, merrily, merrily, oh!"

They all quickly picked up the air and began to clap and sing along with the chorus while Byron continued to sing the verses.

"Cheerily then, from hill and valley
Like your native mountains, Sally,

Cheerily, oh! Cheerily, oh!

The twilight had passed, and an increasing moon was beginning to shine brighter and brighter on the surface of the lake.

They did not return to land until ten o'clock, when, as they approached the shore the delightful scent of flowers and new mown grass; the chirp of grasshoppers, and the song of the evening birds greeted them.

And there, as always, eagerly waiting to greet them was Byron's dog, Leander. From the moment Byron stepped into the boat his dog would sit patiently on the shore of the lake waiting for his return, and then up on his legs and barking excitedly as soon as he saw him again.

"We will take supper at Diodati," Byron said, and led the way up the lawn, singing to himself, "Cheerily, oh, cheerily, oh."

They always ended their evenings at Diodati, where Claire had taken it upon herself to sit down and write out in a neat hand, the fair copy of whatever Byron had written that day for Canto Three of *Childe Harold's Pilgrimage;* while Byron, Shelley and Polidori sat around the fireplace in conversation.

Although, poor Polidori remained silent as usual, Mary noticed, and seemed distant and alien to the conversation, as if the poets did not speak the same language as he. And tonight, as usual, he soon stood up and retired early to bed.

Mary glanced at Claire, who appeared to be happily engrossed in her copying of Byron's poetry, as if determined that he would admire every stroke of her fine handwriting.

Mary smiled, and decided to sit at the table opposite Claire and write also; eager to set down her feelings of these golden days of love with Shelley, and friendship with Albè."

I feel as happy as a new-fledged bird, and hardly

care what twig I fly to, so that I may enjoy my new-found wings. A more experienced bird may be more difficult in its choice of bower; but in my present temper of mind, the budding flowers, the lake, and the happy people about me that live and enjoy these pleasures, are quite enough to afford me exquisite delight.

Chapter Twelve

~~~

The following morning, rushing out to his calèche to journey to Geneva, Monsieur Dejean's path was blocked by two middle-aged ladies waving their fans. "Any news yet of Lord Byron? We need to know where we have to go in order to *see* him."

"Perhaps tomorrow, or perhaps the next day I will be able to tell you something," said Dejean, smiling.

"We *could* have stayed at a hotel in the town, you know? And we would have done so, had we not been told that Lord Byron was residing here."

"Mesdames, pray be patient," Dejean begged, "and very soon you will see Milord Byron."

"Well, they say he is a dandy, just like Beau Brummell, and that he dresses like a prince – but how will we be able to tell that with any certainty to our friends back in England, unless we see him with our own eyes?"

"Ah yes, your own eyes, very wise," murmured Dejean, and quickly made his escape.

Some hours later Dejean returned in his calèche and carried two large boxes into his office at the hotel.

Madame Dejean had been anxiously waiting for him. She quickly followed him into the office. "You have them, Jacques? And are they good ones?"

"*Oui,* very good, very strong. Fifteen napoleons for each, so we will charge the English guests twenty napoleons for each. They do not understand our money, so they will pay."

"*Très bien!"* Madame Dejean smiled her satisfaction.

~~~

They had left Diodati very late. and so had slept soundly into the late morning. Shelley had taken the baby downstairs to hand into the care of Elise, while Mary delayed longer in bed, gazing towards the open window and listening to the songs of the vine-dressers in the vineyard. They were all women, and most had harmonious voices. The themes of their ballads were always the same ... songs of shepherds, love, flocks, and the sons of kings who fall in love with beautiful shepherdesses.

Their tunes rarely varied, but it was sweet to hear them in the morning while enjoying the gentle breeze from the lake drifting through the open window.

In the bedroom next door, Claire was not feeling so content. She had stopped harassing Byron with letters, preferring to use "looks" instead; constantly giving him looks with a significant message in her eyes, but he was failing to notice. Her manner of *demureness* was not working, so now what should she do?

One thing she had learned, to her annoyance, was that it was impossible to find him alone. Twice she had slipped out and gone up to Diodati on her own with some random excuse for calling, but always Dr Polidori was there with him, standing around like a bodyguard.

Still, faint heart, and all that, never got anyone anywhere.

She gave herself a quick look in the mirror on the dressing-table, tussled her black hair into its usual exotic gypsy style, and then went downstairs, passing through the kitchen to tell Shelley and Elise of her need to take a slow walk through the vineyard ... "To clear my head."

She moved quickly up through the vineyard, reaching Diodati just as she saw Byron step out onto the balcony to stand at the balustrade and gaze around at the scenery. He paused, and saw her approaching. She waved, and he waved back, and then he turned and walked back indoors.

Her heartbeats quickened as she sped into the villa and up the flight of stairs to the main salon ... her steps slowing in disappointment when she saw Polidori standing nearby as usual. And was it her imagination, or did Polidori look amused?

"Miss Clairmont, good morning," Byron said curiously. "Are the others not coming today?"

"Yes ... later, " Claire stammered. "I think I made an error in the fair copy I wrote last night ... in Childe Harold? Did you check it?"

"No, but I shall do so now," Byron replied, walking to the table where her copy still lay.

"I wanted to make sure, before I forgot," Claire said, joining him and standing by his side as he leaned over the page and began to read each line carefully.

Claire shot a pointed look at Polidori, hoping he would be courteous enough to leave them alone; but the doctor self-importantly remained where he was, as if he owned the villa.

Furiously frustrated, Claire slyly lifted a sheet of paper and a pencil and quickly wrote a message on it, which she placed on top of the fair copy, under Byron's eyes.

Looking down at her pencilled scrawl, his expression did not change as his eyes dwelt on the words ... *Can't you send Polidori away with instructions to write a Dictionary or something?*

More footsteps entered the room and this time it was Fletcher, holding up a wet white tablecloth.

"Is it all right, my lord, if I hang this tablecloth out on one of the side-balconies? I know you don't want laundry put out to dry on the lawn, but on the balcony this will be dry in no time, and we need it for luncheon in the dining room."

Byron frowned. "What are you doing washing tablecloths? Should not one of the domestics be doing that?"

"Aye, my lord, and they do, but they are too shy to ask you about hanging washing on the balcony, so they asked me to ask you for them."

Byron shrugged in his usual way. "Do as you wish, as long as laundry is never put out on the *front* balcony where I like to sit and write or just view the lake."

"Oh no, my lord, it would be death by firing squad if they ever did that, and I've told them so." Fletcher grinned as he turned to leave.

"Oh, and Fletcher ... did you attend to that other matter I spoke to you about this morning?"

Fletcher looked puzzled. "What other matter?"

"Have you forgotten already?"

Fletcher puckered his eyebrows. "I think I must have forgotten ... what was it again?"

Claire knew her chance had gone, and begged to be excused. "Mary will be wondering where I am."

When she had swiftly left the room, Fletcher's eyebrows were still puckered. "It's no good, my lord, I can't remember, so you'll have to tell me again."

Byron exchanged a quick smile with Polidori. "Never mind, Fletcher, because now you have made *me* forget it too."

"I'm sorry, my lord."

"You're forgiven. So take your tablecloth and off you go."

Polidori, who had been quickly instructed by Byron to make himself present before Claire had mounted the stairs, watched Fletcher head out to the balcony, and then cocked a questioning look at his lordship.

"Was there an error in the fair copy?"

"No." Byron picked up the sheet of paper with Claire's words about Polidori and slipped it inside the manuscript. "No error."

PART FOUR

~~~

Nothing in the world is single;
All things by a law divine
In one spirit meet and mingle.
Why not I with thine? –

And the sunlight clasps the earth
And the moonbeams kiss the sea:
What is all this sweet work worth
If thou kiss not me?

'Love's Philosophy' – Shelley
~~~

Chapter Thirteen

~~~

Claire did not return to the house at Montalègre, nor would she, not until her tears had dried.

Polidori's smug and mocking smile had wounded her dignity, and Byron had ignored her request to send him away. Then he had occupied himself speaking to Fletcher as if she was not there, causing a deep hurt to come into her heart as she sensed his rejection. She had gone there solely to satisfy her increasing need to communicate with Byron alone, instead of always being in a group, when he often did not speak to her at all.

They had met in London, and since then she had sent him many personal letters, so why was he keeping up this pretence of being some indifferent stranger who did not know her at all?

His breeding and education as a gentleman forced him to be polite to her, always very polite, but that was all. Yet since their evening excursions on the lake, he had occasionally given her a smile now and then, and every time she had accepted his smile as a gift, as a promise of something more.

He was even more beautiful here in Switzerland than he was in London; probably because he was more relaxed in his manner; and probably because she was seeing him more, every day, for many hours; especially in the evenings. It was so hard to sit in a boat gazing longingly at your beloved across an invisible barrier of inaccessibility. To feel alone, and excluded, and yet feel happy just to be a part of it all, was very confusing.

While the others talked, she had been content to be a silent and lone watcher. She had seen the way the changing moods of his mind reflected in his eyes, and she had wanted to move closer. She wanted to know what he thought and felt, and she wanted him to be as besotted and as devoted to her as Shelley was to Mary.
~~~

Resentment and self-pity flooded through her as she began to walk back to Montalègre and the company of Shelley and Mary, adding to her discontent. Her misery would not helped or relieved by all the love and happiness she was forced to witness in that household with those two.

Shelley and Mary ... sweet and blonde gentle Mary whom Shelley had pined over for months; until sweet and blonde gentle Mary had confessed that she loved him too.

And Claire had still not forgiven her stepsister for that timid little confession; not forgiven her at all.

~~~

Byron was relieved when Claire did not return to the Villa Diodati with Shelley and Mary later that afternoon. They arrived much later than usual; and they had brought their child with them.

Claire, they explained, had been so ill-tempered with everyone, especially Elise, they had given Elise the afternoon off and brought baby William with them.

"Claire does sometimes suffer from terrible headaches," Shelley said. "Although an afternoon sleep usually cures her."

Byron did not seem to be listening; his eyes on the child. His expression was so strange, so sad, it reminded Shelley of Byron's sorrow about his own child.

Shelley waited for an opportune moment to whisper a few words to Mary about Byron's baby daughter. Mary's eyes widened as she listened, and then she nodded to show that she understood, looking down tenderly at her own child, before raising her head and making a sudden request to Dr Polidori.

"I wonder, Poli, if you would agree to help me with my understanding of Italian? Just the basics, of course, but I do get terribly confused."

Mary was the only one of the three whom Polidori actually liked, and he readily agreed. "My word," he exclaimed, smirking. "It seems that I am to be of some
~~~

use to everyone today."

Mary rose to her feet, holding William. "Shall we sit out on the lawn?"

"If you wish."

"When they had gone Byron and Shelley walked out to the balcony and stood by the balustrade.

Byron was gazing around at the lake. "I had a thought," he said, "of taking a boat to go on a tour of Lake Leman and see all the places described by Rousseau in his novel."

"A rowing boat?"

"And row all the way to Lausanne?" Byron laughed. "No, a rowing boat with sails, properly rigged and keeled, with a boatman to master it."

"We could go together." Shelley's excitement was increasing by the second. "We could see all of it – all the places immortalised by Rousseau."

Byron paused, staring in the direction of Sécheron. "Those small flashes of light ... are they sunbeams?"

"What?" Shelley looked in the same direction as Byron, seeing the intermittent flashes of sunlight coming from the Sécheron side of the lake.

And as they kept looking, their vision sharpened and it dawned – with disgusted disbelief – what was actually causing the continual flashes of sun.

"Binoculars!" Shelley gasped. "We are being watched by people holding binoculars!"

"Two ... three ... four ... God knows how many..." Byron could not believe it.

Byron returned indoor, furious. "Now my mind is certain. I *will* take a boat and sail off into the scenery of Rousseau's novel. Will you come?"

Shelley was smiling. "Only if I can share the cost of the boat."

Byron nodded, knowing that Shelley never took, unless he could give back or share.

Mary and Polidori returned and were told about the binoculars. Neither could believe it, and went out to the balcony to see for themselves.

"Oh, my goodness ..." said Mary, and rushed back inside. "Sunlight moving on glass like sunbeams ... all along the hotel side of Sécheron."

Polidori thought it hilarious. His vanity kept taking him back and forth onto the balcony so anyone watching him could get a good view. After all, he had to prepare for fame himself.

"I have written a tragedy," he announced upon his return to the salon. "My lord, if I bring the manuscript down here after dinner, will you do me the honour of reading it aloud for us?"

Byron stared. "A tragedy?"

"Yes. It's tremendously sad."

"Oh, that is all I need in my life right now," Byron declared. "Another tragedy."

"Only to read," Polidori soothed, "not to suffer."

~~~

Claire did not arrive at Diodati until dinner was over, and was not at all happy to learn that their excursion on the lake would be delayed this evening, due to Polidori's new tragedy.

"His tragedy? Something life-threatening?" she said hopefully. "Although he looks healthy enough to me."

"A tragedy in verse," Shelley explained. "Albè is now going to read it to us. Be fair in any criticism, Claire, because it is Poli's first venture into serious verse."

Claire shrugged, wishing Poli would venture back to England and never return.

"It is a play," Polidori corrected Shelley. "A play in three acts."

Once everyone was seated comfortably, Byron stood by the fireplace with the manuscript in his hands. It took his memory back to his time as a director on the Drury Lane Theatre committee, when his role was to read through all the scripts sent in by playwrights, hoping to find one that was worth producing.

Now he was about to read a play entitled *Cajetan* by John William Polidori, who had insisted that he read it
~~~

aloud.

"I have never read my own verses aloud to anyone," he said to Polidori. " Do you think this is wise?"

"They say you should always read your work aloud in order to hear any inconsonant notes in the flow," Polidori contended. "Yet it is difficult to hear oneself objectively, don't you think?"

"I don't know, as I have never tried," Byron replied, and opened the first page and began to read the words of the characters.

It did not take him long to realise that the play had little merit and was quite nonsensical in places; but he continued to read it as seriously as if it was *Hamlet* he was vocalising, even when Claire put a hand to her mouth to stifle her laughter, and Shelley lowered his head with embarrassment at the awfulness of the play.

Only Mary kept a straight face, feeling such sympathy for poor Polidori who had set his heart upon shining as an author. She also felt pity for Byron who was struggling to concentrate while ignoring Claire's muffled laughter as he read on – "*'Tis thus the goitered idiot of the Alps ...*"

He paused, and looked curiously at Polidori. "Or should that be *gartered* idiot?"

Claire's laughter erupted, and now even Shelley was smiling.

"So you all think it is so bad!" Polidori sprang to his feet and rushed out of the salon, up to his own room where he was determined to commit suicide.

Frantically opening his medical bag, he took out a bottle of prussic acid and poured some into a glass. If he could not be a literary genius and famous, he would not live at all!

First, though, he would leave behind a testimonial to let the world know how badly he had been treated by these literary people. How they had tried to stifle and deny his talent – and he would not do it in pencil which could be erased – he would do it *ink!*

Opening his journal and lifting his pen he wrote

quickly – *Shelley etc., came in the evening; talked of my play, which all agreed was worth nothing.*

He threw down the pen, lifted the glass of prussic acid to his mouth, pausing to mutter a final prayer, when a knock on the door was followed by Byron entering the room. "Don't take it so hard, Poli. It's not so bad, and I have read much worse."

Polidori lowered the glass and shoved it to one side, hoping his lordship would not notice the content.

"Have you? Much worse?"

"Oh yes. When I was at Drury Lane we were often offered some very poor manuscripts. Yours has some fine points, and yes, some flaws too, but perhaps you wrote it all too quickly."

Polidori stared furiously. "How can you say that, *you*, who always writes so *rapidly."*

"Because poetry is a distinct faculty – it won't come when called – you may as well whistle for a wind. I have thought over most of my subjects for years before writing a line."

"I don't believe you," Polidori said.

"If you want to know all about rejection and criticism then take a lesson from me. My own first book of poetry was lacerated by the critics."

"Was it?" Polidori was very surprised. "What did they say?"

"The Edinburgh Review said all sorts of terrible things, too cruel to repeat. The only good thing they said about my book was that if it was presented as a school essay, it *might* pass."

"And how old were you then?"

"Nineteen."

"And they deemed it the work of a schoolboy?"

"Which taught me never to pay any attention to critics. No man is ever written off, except by himself."

Polidori smiled. "And then later you showed them, that you could do it – write fine poetry."

"No, Poli, I showed myself."

Polidori was beginning to feel a lot better. "I know I

am *too* sensitive ... yes, much too sensitive. In future I must learn to be more gallant about these things."

~~~

The next morning Polidori and Byron were standing on one of the side balconies of the house – the side that could not be seen from the Sécheron side of the lake – discussing their coming boat trip, when Byron noticed Mary making her way up the path to Diodati, carrying a large bag.

He said quietly: "Now you, Poli, who wish to be gallant, ought to jump down from this small height and offer her your arm."

Polidori nonchalantly agreed, climbing onto the balustrade like a dashing cavalier – jumped down – letting out a yelp of pain as his foot buckled under him on landing.

Moments later Mary was at his side trying to help him up until Byron and Fletcher arrived on the scene and carried him back into the house, laying him down on the sofa.

Fletcher fetched some pillows which Byron placed under Polidori's foot. Once again the doctor was being cared for by the patient.

Fletcher rolled his eyes with exasperation. "What now?" he asked his lordship in a low voice. "What caused the collapse this time? Fear of heights again or what? You know he can't stand heights."

"How was I to know he also can't jump!"

"I will need bandages," Polidori called from the sofa. "And you will have to tie them very tight. Now you, Fletcher, you go to my room and bring the bandages from my bag. And, my lord, I doubt I will be able to undergo a long boat trip with you now. You will have to go without me."

"A blessing, at last," Byron whispered to Fletcher. "Perhaps there is a God after all."
~~~

Chapter Fourteen

~~~

The brilliant blue sky seemed to vanish in a flash, replaced by torrential rain; confining the group to the house and preventing their usual evening excursion on the lake.

They all stood by one of the long windows of the Diodati salon, watching the most terrific thunderstorm they had ever seen. Lightning flashed across the heavens and darted in jagged shapes over the piny mountainous heights of the Jura.

The lake was vividly lit up and for a long moment all the world around them was illuminated; followed by a sudden pitchy blackness as thunder rolled in frightening bursts above the house.

"This," said Mary, "reminds me of all those Gothic horror novels Mrs Radcliffe writes. Thunder and lightning above and darkness without."

"And we are now trapped within," Byron said, "So we may as well make the most of it and try to enjoy ourselves in some other way."

Mr Berger had lit a glowing fire in the large fireplace to cheer up the rainy night, and Fletcher had lit all the candles around the room.

"Every one of my five sisters has always loved those Gothic novels," Shelley said. "It's strange, isn't it, how females love to be frightened out of their wits reading horror and ghost stories?"

"Not I," said Claire. "No horror or ghost story could frighten me."

Mary glanced at Claire, who, throughout her childhood could be reduced to hysterics by the slightest frightening thing."

"How about this one?" Byron asked, taking down a book from one of the bookshelves ... a translation of German ghost stories entitled *Phantasmagoriana*.
~~~

Most of the stories they already knew, but dipping into *Phantasmagoriana* served to darken the atmosphere of the room. And in this strange light, with the storm still raging, Shelley confessed that in the past, not only had he secretly read all of his sisters' novels by Mrs Radcliffe, he had written and published two Gothic novels himself in 1810 and 1811. The first, "*Zastrozzi*", in which he had expounded his ideas on atheism, was damned and banned. The second, "*The Rosicrucian*" had dropped from the printing press quite dead, with no bookshop orders.

"No one wanted to read a book written by an atheist," he said. "I was branded as Satanic and a disciple of the Devil."

But yet – a ray of hope in all the darkness – his third book, which he and his sister Elizabeth had written together, *Original Poetry by Victor and Cazir* had been very well received.

"Probably because the critics had no idea that *I* was Victor," said Shelley, smiling.

Mary agreed. "Percy has written several pieces under his *nom de plume* of Victor; because he knows his poetry will be victorious in the end."

"His poetry should be victorious *now*," Byron said, having read a lot more of Shelley's work since his arrival in Switzerland, and judged him a fine poet.

Yet he could see that Shelley viewed himself as a literary failure, and endeavoured to change the subject. Another flash of lightning lit up the windows in a blue light, followed by more growling thunder.

"May I suggest," Byron said, "that we use all this thunder and black rain as the perfect atmosphere for each of us to invent our own ghost or horror story?"

"Us?" asked Polidori. "Each of us? Does that mean all of us?"

"Poli," Byron responded impatiently, "I know you speak bad Italian, and even worse Latin, but I did suspect that you had a good comprehension of English, or do you?"

"Of course, my comprehension of everything is perfect, but pray clarify – do you mean that each of us must conceive and then write his own ghost story?"

Shelley was all for it. "It's an excellent idea, although I'm not very comfortable writing prose, but I'm willing to give it a go."

"We could have a story contest?" Polidori's challenge was aimed directly at Shelley. "And he who writes the most chilling story is crowned the winner."

"He?" quipped Claire indignantly. "*He?* Are you forgetting there are two females in this group? Or are we invisible to you, Dr Pollydolly?"

Mary cut through their bickering with an embarrassed admission. "I would not have a clue what to write about. Shelley ardently believes in ghosts and apparitions, but I'm not sure that *I* believe in ghosts."

"And yet so many people do believe," Byron said, "and who is to say they or Shelley are wrong? Certainly not I, because I lived with a very polite ghost in my Nottinghamshire home at Newstead Abbey. The ghost of a monk. He caused me no fear or anxiety, nor I him. I wandered around Newstead by day, and he wandered around at night."

"A ghost?" Claire said "*A ghost?*"

Byron nodded. "What else? – since he had obviously been dead since the sixteenth century, when King Henry the Eighth renounced Catholicism and ordered the dissolution of all monasteries, which Newstead Abbey then was – a monastery – before the Byrons later turned it into a home."

Byron sipped his brandy, blithely ignoring their sceptical expressions. "My belief," he said, "is that the monk was the *Friar* of the monastery, the Father of the place, and even after death he couldn't bear to leave beautiful Newstead behind; so he either remains there, or he keeps coming back."

Shelley was seriously intrigued. "How old were you when you first saw the ghost?"

"I was ten."

"And at ten, "Mary asked, "did you know the history of the Abbey?"

"It was the first thing I was told by Mr Hanson. That it had once been a monastery, full of holy monks."

"And so, at the age of ten, knowing the history of the place," Mary concluded, "you doubtlessly *imagined* the ghost of the monk."

"No, I saw him, clear as day – but only at night."

"An optical illusion,!" said Polidori.

"Tell that to William Shakespeare," Byron said "*'There are more things in heaven and earth, Horatio, than are dreamnt of in your philosophy'.*"

Polidori rolled his eyes. "Hamlet! – who would believe a word *he* said. He also saw a ghost, but it was just a play. Shakespeare made it all up."

"Or perhaps," said Byron, "Shakespeare was pointing out – in his play – that our human knowledge is limited; and if our existing philosophy is based on science, then we need to do more to speed up the progress of science and find out the true secrets of this world."

"Yes, yes, the secrets of this world ... and other worlds," said Shelley eagerly.

Byron could not help smiling. For a man who did not believe in religion, Shelley continued to have an insatiable yearning to try and see into what he called "the invisible world all around us."

Except for Polidori, who remained sullenly silent, it was a subject they discussed for a long time, until almost midnight, when Shelley and Mary took the opportunity of a break in the storm to try and dash back through the vineyard to their own house; joined reluctantly by Claire.

"Tomorrow, if you wish to return and the weather has not cleared, you are welcome to bring the baby and his nursemaid with you," Byron said. "Why get drenched in the rain running to and fro, when there are so many spare bedrooms here?"

Mary thought it a wonderful suggestion. The Villa Diodati, with all of its beautiful French furniture, was such a large and lovely house in comparison to Maison Chapuis, and to have her baby close by, while enjoying the company and conversations of friends, would help her to relax more and worry less.

"And you will think of a story to write for our contest?" Polidori reminded them.

"We will," said Shelley, and then took Mary's hand to lead her in the dash, but within minutes the storm came back with even greater intensity, and Byron feared for their safety.

"Why so?" asked Polidori. "The journey is short and they are young and strong, and if they slip they will get up again and run on."

"Unlike you then, Poli – when *you* slipped and fell?"

Polidori did not trouble to answer; his mind now more intent on his burning resentment about the group having been invited to stay at Diodati, which would place them on an equal level with himself. Not visitors to the villa, nor merely neighbours, but *residents* of the house. And why his lordship liked Shelley was something he could not understand.

"It is strange to me, my lord, why you like Mr Shelley. He is the keeper of two women, and not one is his wife, and yet they have a child. He had a bad reputation in the hotel, so I would think, my lord, that he would not be considered a fit companion for a man of your noble rank."

Byron looked at Polidori, sick of his eternal nonsense, shallowness, and ridiculous vanity. "I like him, Poli, because Shelley is a true intellectual – which makes him a very *fitting* companion for me. It is a blessed relief for me to find a man of his fine intellect here in this wilderness."

"But, my lord, his morals –"

"Are no better or worse than *mine!*" Byron snapped, and walked off towards his bedroom, which was on the same floor as the salon.

Grieved and aggrieved, Polidori slowly climbed the stairs to his own room, directly above his employer's bedroom, wondering jealously if there was a way he could kill Shelley without anyone finding out? A few drops of poison in one of his precious vegetable dinners perhaps?

Entering his bedroom, the first thing Polidori saw on his bedside-table was the large black crucifix which his mother had given to him upon his departure from England – and just the sight of that holy object brought him back to his rational senses.

"God forgive me," he said, picking up the crucifix, "I truly meant no harm ... but when the Cambridge man keeps defending the Oxford man, it makes my blood boil."

He piously kissed the feet of the Saviour on the Cross, and it soothed him, slowly bringing another thought into his mind ... "Or perhaps it was just this infernal heat that was making my blood boil, as well as the constant noise of this unsettling storm.

~~~

In his own bedroom, standing by the window and looking out towards the mountains, Byron had forgotten his irritation with Polidori, so transfixed was his eyes and mind upon the power of the storm. Nature was such a mystery. He knew what caused the lightning – the summer heat – but what caused the roaring thunder which was coming now from the range of the Alps behind the house, as if roaring towards the Jura mountains at the front

His eyes moved over the black sky. Today the sky had been so peaceful and calm and so vividly blue ... but now look at it ...

The sky is changed! – and such a change; Oh, night!

And storm and darkness, you are wondrous strong,

Yet lovely in your strength, as is the light

Of dark eye in woman! Far along
~~~

From peak to peak, the rattling crags among
Leaps the thunder! Not from one lone cloud,
But every mountain now hath found a tongue.

Chapter Fifteen

~~~

The new day was a strange one, with almost perpetual rain, but when the sun burst forth for a short time, it was with a splendour and heat unknown in England.

The Shelley clan had all arrived at Diodati during one of the sun breaks, with baby William and his nursemaid Elise included.

Time passed swiftly, for all had settled down separately in various rooms of the house to write their story for the competition.

"Remember, it must be a ghost or horror story," Polidori reminded them, darting a disdainful glance at Claire. "No romance."

During the short heats of the afternoon, they moved out to the balcony and sipped tea, conferring with each other on their progress; but Mary was still bereft of an idea for her story.

They saw very little of Byron that afternoon, not even for tea. "He must be working hard on his story," Polidori remarked airily. "I have finished mine."

Mary stared at him with disbelief. "You have finished it already?"

"Yes," Polidori smiled, "because I wrote it last night. The noise of the storm prevented sleep, so I got up and wrote my story instead."

"Is it a very *short* story?" Claire asked.

"No, not short, but not too long. This morning Fletcher told me how Lord Byron was still writing at his desk at dawn, and now he is in his room writing again, so his story must be *very* long."

Byron had not even started his story. He had spent most of the night writing stanzas for the third canto of *Childe Harold;* and now he was writing a letter to his dearest and best friend, John Hobhouse, who had been his companion during their travels through Albania and
~~~

Greece. Now, though, in his letters, Hobhouse was insisting on being told "every detail" of Byron's journey through Europe. He had been endeavouring to comply with Hobby's didactic command, in the hope he would become so bored when reading the letter, he would not beg for all such small details again.

> *At Ghent we stared at pictures; churches, and climbed up a steeple, 450 steps in altitude.*

Byron paused, remembering that was the *first* time Polidori had suffered one of his many vertigo dizzy spells.

> *At Antwerp we pictured – churched – and steepled again, but the principal street and bason pleased me most – poor dear Bonaparte !!!*
>
> *As for Rubens, and his superb "tableux", he seems to me (who by the way know nothing of the matter) to be the most glaring – flaring – staring – harlotry impostor that ever passed a trick upon the senses of mankind, – it is not nature – it is not art. I never saw such an assemblage of florid nightmares; his portraits seemed clothed in pulpit cushions.*

Across the far side of the lake at Sécheron, the proprietor of the Hotel d'Angleterre was also concerned with cushions – the spare cushions needed to place on the wooden window-bench of the attic room at the top of the building where his telescope was housed.

After all, one could not expect the English ladies to suffer from hurt legs while they kneeled and stared through his telescope.

Their obsessed inquisitiveness about Lord Byron

fascinated as well as pleased Dejean, for in this weather of storms and soaking-wet grass, none could venture out to use their binoculars; and so all were all happy to pay a small fee to use his telescope instead.

The zoom on the telescope was now fixed so that they could see the Diodati balcony very clearly – and at night, in the darkness, when the Diodati salon windows were aglow with lights; sometimes it was possible to see directly into the room.

Usually it was the men who liked to take a peek at night. To see what? Never had a young man fascinated so many – it was like they were being given the chance of seeing Napoleon himself – such was the draw of those who were unknown – to men who were gigantically famous.

Dejean stood guard as each lady took up position at the telescope; for all were timed to a viewing of ten minutes exactly, not a second more. He had a paper in his hand containing a waiting-list, and when one lady's time was almost up, a maid was sent down to bring up the next one.

"There are two young women sitting on the balcony, drinking tea by the looks of it," said the lady at the telescope, "one fair, one dark."

"You are new to this hotel, so you do not know," Dejean said. "They are the atheist sisters."

"Atheists? – Lord preserve us!"

"*Il vous préservera,*" Dejean said obsequiously. "In *this* hotel, He will preserve you."

"Oh, and now there's a man on the balcony ... tall and slender with long fair hair. That cannot be Lord Byron. He is reputed to have black hair."

"That man is the chief atheist, Mr Shelley. The two sisters are his disciples."

"Lord protect us!"

The lady's time was up. Dejean moved forward a few steps to politely inform her of such, when she let out a piercing excited shriek – "Ohhh! Dear Lord! Oh my goodness! – there are white *petticoats* hanging to dry on the side balcony! Those young women must be *living* there with Lord Byron and that other man!"

Dejean nodded. "And none are truly married. It is all a deceit. Those sisters have no morals."

"Oh, such wickedness!"

She was still there when the next lady entered – still in the room having palpitations caused by what she had seen – and then rushing to grab the new lady's arm to pull her over to the telescope for her to peer through it.

"Look, my dear, do you see ... women's white *petticoats* hanging from a line on the side balcony? Now how do you think Lady Byron will feel, when she hears about *that?"*

The companion drew her face away from the telescope and appeared to be quite shaken. "She will be shocked."

"Oh, yes, poor Lady Byron will be very shocked indeed, and *hurt* too, I daresay; because everyone and anyone who knows her in London say that she now regrets the separation, and is desperately hoping Lord Byron will come back to her."

All the fuss and gossip about the petticoats now buzzing around the main salon of the hotel, caused Madame Dejean to lug herself up to the attic room to see it for herself; her thoughts and attitude indignant in the extreme.

Who did those young English people think they were to flaunt their bad behaviour in such a way – and to do so in *Geneva?* This was not sinful London where even the reigning prince flaunted his promiscuity without any shame.

Dejean was wiping down the telescope when she rushed into the room and brushed him aside. "Is it true? Let me see?"

He was reluctant. "You are too busy for such amusements, *ma chere*. You must return to our guests. Gossip and chattering always makes them very thirsty and in need of more wine; and *we* must always think of the profits."

"Let me see," she said, brushing him aside and peering avidly through the telescope; and then slowly pulling back with a frown on her face. "Did you know this, Jacques?"

Jacques merely shrugged.

Unlike the other ladies, Madame Dejean now took out a pair of spectacles from her apron pocket and put them on, before peering through the telescope again.

Finally, she nodded: yes, now she was sure.

"Tablecloths!" she said. "Those English ladies must never have done any laundry in their lives! They are white, yes, but those are tablecloths hanging on the line, *not* petticoats.

Jacques put a finger to his lips, urging her to be silent.

"But *why?* It is a lie, Jacques, a lie."

"Not from me. I have said nothing. I have stood by in silence and let them see and speak as they wished."

"We must tell them," said Madame, turning to leave. "It is a sin to support a lie."

Dejean caught her by the shoulders, halting her in her steps. "*Non, non, ma chere, non, non ...*" His face moved into an expression of saintly compassion. "Why spoil it for our guests, when all the talk is giving them so much pleasure? What else have they to enjoy, when this year our Swiss weather is so bad? Do you wish them to go home saying their stay at the Angleterre was *dull?*"

Madame meditated, and then sighed, and nodded her agreement. When it came to success in business, Jacques always knew best.

Chapter Sixteen

~ ~ ~

Across the lake from Sécheron, unaware of all the gossip in the Hotel d'Angleterre, Byron was still writing his letter of details to Hobhouse.

> *Throughout our journey, Dr Polidori treated only two patients. One was a blacksmith – I daresay he is dead now – and the other was himself.*

And then remembering to give Hobby some information about his latest dwelling place.

> *I have taken a very pretty villa in a vineyard, with the Alps behind and Mount Jura and the lake before. When you come out, don't go to an inn, not even in Sécheron; but come on to headquarters where I will have rooms ready for you and Scrope. Bring with you a new Sword-cane for me, procured by John Jackson – he alone knows the sort I like (my last one tumbled into this lake) – also some of Waite's tooth powder and toothbrushes, and – I forget the other things – so Adieu.*
>
> *Yours ever most truly, B.*
>
> *P.S. – If you hear anything of my child let me know.*

Later that evening, after dinner, familiar sounds outside drew them all over to the windows of the salon where they watched another storm approach from the opposite side of the lake, dark with the shadows of overhanging black rain clouds.

"Again, a perfect night for our horror stories," Byron grinned. "I am prepared to be chilled to the bone."

As soon as they were all seated around the fire, Shelley said, "I considered my story so poor, I eventually tore it up. I will try again tomorrow."

Mary shook her head. "And I have failed to come up with even the faintest idea."

Byron looked questioningly at Claire, who blushed and fussed. "Mine is ... not ready. And yours?"

"Started, but not finished" Byron said. "What a poor literary bunch we are. How about you, Poli?"

"Mine is finished." Polidori looked around at the group. "Shall I read it to you?"

All agreed that he should read it.

"But relax and remain in your chair," Byron added. "No need for you to stand as if performing for an audition."

All listened silently as Polidori began to read his story, about an ugly skull-headed lady who had a habit of wandering around a hotel at night to peep through the keyholes of the doors of other people's rooms, hoping to see terrible things.

Everyone else in the hotel knew she did this, and told others of her wanderings at night, peeping here and peeping there. And then one night – one *fatal* night – the skull-headed lady *does* see something rather obscene, and gasps in delight; but she is heard, and is killed when a thin knitting-needle is pushed through the keyhole into her eye and through her brain.

No one said a word. The silence seemed to go on forever, until Byron decided that poor Polidori's literary efforts had been mocked too much already – clapping his hands in applause and praise. "Excellent!"

"It was utter rubbish!" Claire declared.

"His lordship liked it," Polidori retorted. "So now you are jealous!"

Polidori turned to Mary. "Did you like it, Mary?"

Mary, unwilling to hurt him, struggled for an answer, while Shelley – terrified that Polidori would ask him for his opinion – quickly suggested to Byron that although *his* story was incomplete, would he not read to them what he had written so far?

"Why did the silly peeping woman have a 'skull head'?" Claire asked Polidori.

"Because she was old and withered – as *you* will be one day," Polidori responded.

Byron decided to read his unfinished story – and went to his bedroom to fetch it – anything to stop the bickering between Polidori and Claire.

He returned to the salon with his manuscript, only to hear Polidori telling yet another of his horror stories, about a man who woke up one night to see the ghost of an old man in a white apron standing by his bed. Shocked, he could only lay there staring, as frozen as a corpse, while the ghost produced a razor, and then gently shaved all the hair off his head, leaving him as bald as the moon.

"Ah," Byron said. "When alive, the ghost had been a barber?"

"Utter rubbish!" Claire declared again. "Just more of Dr Pollydolly's nonsense! The man lost all his hair in one night, as some men do, and in the morning he blamed the loss on a barbering ghost."

Shelley cut in politely: "Byron, pray entertain us with something more believable."

"Oh, I could not do that," Byron replied, sitting down. "Because some might say that the story I have written is truly *un*believable."

From outside the gathering storm made its presence known. More flashes of lightning were followed by thunder coming again in bursts over their heads.

"Call it superstition," Byron said, by way of explanation, "but there is a belief in the East which is common among the Turks and Arabs, although not believed in Greece until after the arrival of Christianity. A superstition about certain members of the dead rising from their graves, and feeding upon the blood of the young and healthy by draining them dry. In the last century it was a belief that spread through Hungary, Poland and Austria, and then Greece. The 'undead' they were called."

"The undead?" Mary said. "How can that be? When a human is dead, they are dead."

"You would think so," Byron agreed. "I gave it no credence, not until I came across an article in an old London Journal, dating back to as far as 1732, stating that an Englishman, in Cassovia, on the borders of Turkish Serbia, had been tormented by one of these demons – or *vampyres,* as they are called – but managed to escape back to England as fast as a ship could take him."

Shelley grinned. "Thankfully, we are by no means so credulous. And surely *you* don't give vampyres any credibility, Byron?"

"No, but it was firmly believed in Greece to be a sort of punishment after death for some heinous crime committed while the person was alive. That is why I wrote about it in *The Corsair* when all the various influences of Greece were still with me." Byron quoted from his Eastern tale –

But first on earth, as vampyre sent,

Thy corpse shall from its tomb be rent;

Then ghastly haunt the native place

And suck the blood of all thy race.

Claire was visibly shivering at the very thought, but Mary was intrigued. "Albè, pray read your story now?"

"Even though it has no ending yet?"

"Even though."

"Very well."

Holding the incomplete manuscript, Byron sat back and began to read aloud his story about a young man, the narrator of the story, who travels to Greece in the company of a rather mysterious, yet fascinating nobleman, named Augustus Darvell.

"He was a few years older than I. My friendship with him was recent, although we had attended the same schools and university, but being older his passage through them had preceded me, and by the time I left university he was already a man of the world, while I was still a novice.

"I was very young, and having spent some time thinking about the possibility of travelling to lands unknown to the travellers, I was told that Darvell had travelled extensively, many times, and was preparing to travel again.

"I made a visit and called on him, to seek his advice on foreign places, and also to ask him about the journey he intended to carry out, hoping he would allow me to travel with him.

"He was not enthusiastic, appearing to be very reluctant to agree, and so the prospect of my joining him seemed unlikely. But while he considered the suggestion, the expressions on his face varied so rapidly, it was impossible to know what he was thinking.

"His response, when it came, gave me all the pleasure of a surprise, because he agreed that I could travel with him, saying to me, 'You are young and strong, so you may be of some help to me.'

"And thereafter, all the necessary packing and preparations were made, and we began our journey.

"Darvell was a man of significant fortune and aristocratic family. Advantages that he neither devalued nor over-estimated. Some strange circumstances in his personal history had made him an object of interest, which did not affect either his reserved manners or the occasional glimpses of torment that sometimes brought him close to alienation. His friendship to most people, including myself, seemed unattainable.

"As we travelled it became very apparent that an incurable anguish tormented him; but I could never discover whether it was due to ambition, love, remorse or grief, or one or all of these things; or if it was simply due to a morbid temperament. He did tell me some details of his life, although there were many contradictions in his story, which perplexed me.

"After travelling through several countries, we turned our attention to the East, in accordance to our original destination. And it was on our journey through these regions that an incident occurred, which gives the cause for my account of him."

All the Shelley group were still and silent as they listened, as was Polidori, all intrigued, due to the hints that something very peculiar was going on.

Mary, especially, was rapt, because one of the things she had always loved about Byron was his voice, and now, being a rather good amateur actor, he read in the differing voices of the young narrator of the story, and Augustus Darvell.

"As we journeyed on, the complexion of Darvell's face began to pale and decline, without any manifest illness. His habits were moderate. He did not complain nor ever admit to fatigue. Nevertheless, every day he weakened more, and at last he was altered in such a remarkable way that my concern increased.

"On our arrival in Izmir, we set out to go on an excursion to the ruins of Ephesus, from which I tried to dissuade him because of his indisposition, but in vain. There seemed to be an increasing anxiety in his mind and his manner, and a frantic determination to go on with a journey that I had considered to be a mere voyage of pleasure, but now seemed wholly inadequate for a delicate person; but Darvell would not heed any of my objections.

"We had made our way halfway to the remains of Ephesus, leaving behind the most fertile contours of Smyrna, and we entered into that inhospitable and uninhabited region through the marshes and gorges that lead to the few remaining shattered columns of Diana – the homeless walls of expelled Christendom, and the desolation of abandoned mosques.

"It was there that a sudden and dizzying illness of my comrade forced us to stop at a Turkish cemetery, whose tombstones crowned with turbans were the only clue that human life had once dwelt in that wilderness.

"The only caravan of camels that we had seen had passed us some hours ago. You could not see any vestige of a village or a hut at all, and this 'city of the dead' seemed to be the only refuge for my unfortunate companion to rest.

"I looked around for where we could rest more comfortably out of the sun, but unlike the usual aspect of the Eastern cemeteries, the cypress trees of this one were scarce, scattered over the whole surface. Most of the tombs were crumbling and had worn down over the years.

"Against one of the lowest trees Darvell leaned with great difficulty. He asked for water. I doubted we could find any, although I set out to try and fetch some, but he called me back, wanting me to stay with him.

"And then, turning to Sulieman, our guide, who sat smoking with great tranquillity, Darvell said: '*Sulieman, verbenu su'* – that is, *he* must bring some water. And then Darvell went on to describe in exact detail to Sulieman the place where he could find it. It was a small camel oasis, a few hundred yards to the right.

"The guide obeyed.

"I said to Darvell: 'How did you know this?'

'I have been here before.'

"You've already been here! How could you not mention it to me? And what did you do in such a place where no one could stay another moment without seeking help?

"He did not reply to my question. Meanwhile Sulieman had returned with the water and it seemed that by alleviating his thirst, Darvell revived for a moment.

"I told him that I hoped that we could go on, or at least return, and urged him to try.

"He was silent. He seemed to be putting his thoughts in order, before he struggled to speak. 'This is the end of my journey," he said, "and the end of my life. I came here to die. But I have a supplication to make, an order to give, for such will be my last words. Will you fulfil it?'

"'Of course, but I have the better intention of helping you to some place where you will recover.'

'I have no hopes, no desires but this one – hide my death from every human being.'

"'I hope that occasion will not come. You will recover.'

'No, no, I cannot explain – but if you will conceal all you know of me – and keep my reputation free from stain – and my death must be kept unknown to all in England – that you must *promise* me you will do.'

"But why?"

'Silence, it must be so: promise it. Promise it.'

"Yes."

'Swear to it.'

"There is no reason for me to swear. I will comply with your request."

'I cannot help it. You must *swear* to it – *swear* by all that your soul reveres – *swear* that you will not impart your knowledge of my death to any living being, whatever may happen. *Swear* a solemn oath upon your own soul.'

"I decided his illness and the sun had made him a little mad in his mind, so I said the oath, and that seemed to relieve him.

"He removed a seal ring from his finger, which had some Arabic characters etched on it, and he gave it to me.

'On the ninth day of the month,' he said, 'at noon – the month you can choose but the day must be that – you must throw this ring at the water fountains that feed the bay of Eleusis. The next day, at the same time, at noon, you must go to the ruins at the temple of Ceres and wait for an hour.'

"For what?"

'You'll see.'

"You say on the ninth day of the month?"

'The ninth.'

"When I made the observation that the present day was the ninth day of the month, his face changed, and he paused speaking, retreating into a silence.

"While he was sitting there, visibly weakening, a stork with a snake in its beak rested on a grave near us; and without devouring his prey he seemed to stare at us.

"I don't know what prompted me to frighten it, but the attempt was futile. He made some circles in the air and returned exactly to the same place.

"Darvell pointed at the bird and smiled. I don't know if the words were for himself, or for me, or the bird; but the words were only: 'It's all right.'

"What is all right?' I asked. 'What does it mean?'

'It does not matter. You must bury me here tonight, and at the exact place where that bird is standing. You know the rest of my mandates.'

"Then he gave me some instructions on how I might hide his death better. When he finished, he said, 'Do you see that bird?'

"Of course."

'And the snake that shudders in its beak?'

"'No doubt there is nothing strange about it; it is natural prey. But it is strange that he does not devour it.'

"He laughed in a strange way, and said languidly, 'He does not devour it, because he knows now is not the time.'

"As he spoke the stork took off. I followed it with my eyes for a moment. Not for more than ten seconds. But when I looked at Darvell again, I saw in his face that he had died.

"I was struck by the sudden and unmistakable certainty. Within a few minutes his face had almost turned black. I could have attributed this change so quickly to the action of some poison, had I not been aware that he had no opportunity to take it without my seeing it.

"The day was reaching its end, the body decomposing quickly. There was nothing left to do but fulfil his request.

"With the help of Sulieman's yatagán, and my own sabre, we excavated a shallow grave in the place where Darvell had indicated, and the earth yielded its soil easily, for it was clear that the grave had been occupied in the past by some other occupant.

"We dug as deep as time permitted; and then, throwing the dry ground over the dead man, we cut a few blocks of the greener grass that grew in the less worn earth that surrounded us, and we put it on his grave.

"Whether due to my astonishment or fatigue, I could not shed a tear for him."

Byron paused, closing the manuscript. "And that is all I have written so far – the beginning of the story."

All were staring at him.

"The *beginning* ...?" exclaimed Shelley. "How can that be? Darvell died!"

"Did he?" Byron had a mischievous smile on his face. "Or was he one of the 'undead'? Was that his secret? Is that why he wanted the fact of his death to remain unknown to all in England?"

"Oh, do tell us, Albè," Mary pleaded. "Tell us what happened next?"

"Yes you must," Shelley insisted. "You can't leave us wondering and guessing for days until you finish writing it."

"Well, now that I have read it aloud, I am not happy with it," Byron replied vaguely. "Perhaps I won't finish it. And as that is very probable, I may as well reveal to you now what I had planned for the second part of the story."

"The young man?" Claire was eager to know. "On the ninth day did he go to the fountains of the ruins and throw in the ring; and did he wait there for an hour?"

"I would say not," Byron replied. "I don't see why he would hang around in that awful place to do so. He was a down-to-earth, practical young man, not a mysterious enigma like Darvell. And Darvell was dead and buried, so why should he pay heed to such a bizarre request?"

Claire pouted. "I merely asked."

The clout of the storm and its echoing thunder was now directly above – and yet inside the salon none paid any heed to the storm's fury as Byron explained to them how the young man – "We shall call him Aubrey" – after travelling alone for some months, had returned home to a London winter and all the festivities and parties of Christmas time.

"He had more or less forgotten Augustus Darvell, putting that strange experience behind him, eager to get on with his life and make some good of the new maturity he had derived from his long travels abroad.

"Aubrey escorted his sister to her first Christmas ball; an innocent and pretty girl of almost eighteen, who caught the attention of most of the young men, but she had eyes for only one handsome man ... Augustus Darvell."

"What?"

"Aubrey was stunned beyond belief, staring at the man he had buried in Greece, now dancing with his sister. He rushed onto the dance floor to interrupt them, staring at Darvell, who merely smiled and whispered in his ear: *'Remember your oath?'*

"Bedamned to my oath!

"'Indeed,' Darvell replied softly. 'Damnation will certainly come to you if you break it. Damnation in blood'."

Byron had thought this reappearance of Darvell would have been expected by the group; but all were shocked, which made him laugh: "Of course he was a *vampyre!* Was it not obvious from the end of the first part?"

On the contrary, Mary was quite shaken. "Darvell had come back to life, as normal as before?"

The thick black rain clouds of the storm were now pouring their heavy rage down upon the house as all listened to how poor Aubrey went around desperately endeavouring to persuade everyone – including his sister – that Darvell was unnatural, one of the supernatural, one of the 'undead' – *a vampyre* – but none would believe him, no, not one; not even his sister, who married Darvell.

"So ..." Shelley was puzzled, "did Aubrey imagine it all? The death and burial in the grave ... everything?"

Byron shrugged. "Everyone must have thought so, because poor Aubrey ended up confined in a lunatic asylum."

"And his sister?" Mary asked.

"Oh well, she, poor thing, a short time after her marriage to Darvell, was found in her bedroom, dead from a burst blood vessel in her neck."

~~~

Inside the Hotel d'Angleterre, confused and ill-informed letters were hastily being written to England, full of shock and scandal about the dreadful orgies that were being carried on at the Villa Diodati where Lord Byron was living with a woman who called herself Mrs Shelley. Her pretend husband, the notorious atheist, Percy Shelley, was living with his wife's sister – and all in Lord Byron's house, which was now an outrageous den of *promiscuity* and *incest*.

In her own apartment, Madame Dejean was sighing and shaking her head. She was as keen as her husband to keep the guests happy and to make as much profit from them as possible during the summer. Few visitors came to Geneva during the harsh cold of winter, when the hotel's profits were very lean.

And Jacques was a businessman, so who could blame him for selling binoculars and peeps through his telescope to the guests? He always had the worry and cost of the coming winter to consider, so the hay must be reaped while the sun was still warm.

Yet, she was troubled, for at heart she knew herself to be a kind and decent person with a good Calvinist
~~~

Christian soul, and all this devilish curiosity and blackening of the young lord's name and conduct was going too far.

She would have to speak to Jacques about it. Perhaps it was time to shut down the telescope and say it was broken?

In the meantime she decided to write a letter herself, to her sister in Lausanne, relieving her own conscience by telling her sister how truly awful some of the English ladies were – demons in skirts – jealous and mean and gloating, and always looking for scandal. And now, to occupy themselves during the storms, they were writing letters to England full of lies and false tales about the famous Lord Byron.

"*Oh, l'anglaise*!" she wrote, "*Certaines de ces anciennes femmes anglaises me terrifient.*"

And some of those older English ladies truly did terrify her; which is why she behaved as timidly as she did when she went out to the lobby to place her letter in the hotel's post box; and came face to face with one of those grand dames who was posting her own letter to someone in England.

"Oh, good evening, Madame Dejean," she said gravely. "We have some more news. Henry has just come down from the telescope, and he tells me that the windows of the Villa Diodati are all lit up brightly again, as they were last night until all hours."

"All hours?"

"Oh, yes. Henry could not sleep due to the noise of the storm. And so, in the darkness, from our window, he said he could clearly see the candles still glowing in the windows of Diodati at past three o'clock. So one *does* wonder what kind of jinks and mischief were still going on in that scandalous house so late into the night?"

"Scandalous," Madame agreed timidly. "Those young people, all living together ... with no fear of God in them

... *Oh le plus scandaleux!*"

~~~

In the salon at Diodati, the group sitting around the fire were still quietly discussing the details of Byron's story. "If you finished and published it, what title would you give it?" Shelley asked.

"I won't finish it," Byron said decisively. "I prefer whatever I publish to be in classic poetry, not mediocre prose. This story was just a piece of nonsense I made up to fulfil my part in the competition."

Polidori had been listening avidly. "Did you not give the story a title when you began it?"

"I thought of calling it *'The Vampyre'* but decided that title would provide too many clues and give the ending away." Byron lifted his manuscript. "So I have written here ... *The Burial: A Fragment."*

"It's not as bad as 'The Vampyre'," said Shelley. "That's a horrid title."

Byron looked at him with some surprise. "Are vampyres not horrid?"

"No, because they are not real. To me, 'vampyre' is a *political* word, and the only word fit to describe politicians. *They* are the ones who feed on the poor man's labour and the unshared harvests of the country's wealth. *They* are the ones who suck the blood and nerve and guts of the working people and drain them dry, until the people have no self-determination left, but only the will to obey their political masters, who are the real vampyres – the *real* bloodsuckers."

Now that the topic had turned to politics and Shelley was in full flow, Polidori complained of a headache. "I must go to bed," he said. "Only sleep will cure me."

He quickly left the room and rushed towards the stairs, unwilling to be distracted by any other topic but that of Augustus Darvell.
~~~

Once inside his bedroom, he tore out a number of blank pages from his journal, and then tossed the journal aside; finally sitting down at his desk with the blank pages and a pencil, and began to quickly write down every word he could remember of Byron's story about a vampyre.

Chapter Seventeen

~~~

That night, after all had gone to bed and sleep, Mary awoke with a start. She often dreamed of her beloved first child, but never more vividly than tonight.

This time, her darling baby girl had come back to life, but in the dream she was no longer a baby, but an adorable little toddler of two years old with blue sparkling eyes and a delicious little laugh ... what Ianthe *could* have been now, if only she had lived.

Turning her face into the pillow with an aching sadness, she knew that it was Albè's story about a dead person returning to life that had caused her dream; for even as she had sat there in the salon, listening to him, her mind had drifted back to that night when her daughter had died, and how she had desperately kept rubbing her little arms and legs to try and make Ianthe's blood flow again, and bring her beloved baby back to her.

As always after one of these dreams, she knew she would not sleep for some time, but did she want to lay here in the darkness with her unsettling thoughts?

Slowly slipping her body out from under the bedclothes, unwilling to wake Shelley, she picked up the unlit candle in its holder and carried it to the door; and then outside to the landing where she relit it from one of the burning candles in a sconce on the wall.

A strange and unexpected smell reached her nostrils as she walked along the landing ... a flowery smell ... becoming more intense as she passed the door of Polidori's room. It was a familiar smell, she now realised, for she had occasionally smelt a trace of the same flowery substance on Polidori's clothes ... Perhaps he was a man who liked to wear scent? He was certainly vain enough.

Descending to the first floor and the salon, the first
~~~

place her eyes looked was down the adjoining hall towards Byron's bedroom; relieved to see no light under his door and no sign of his dog.

She had once heard Fletcher saying that he always knew when his lordship was still up and writing at his desk, because his hound would always be stretched on the mat outside his door keeping guard and even Fletcher away; but as soon as his lordship had finished and was ready to retire, the dog was brought inside the room to sleep by the bed.

All was silent, and Mary was glad. She needed to be completely alone, to sit and think, for something was frizzing at the back of her mind and yet she could not grasp what it was.

The red embers of the salon fire were still sending out warmth. She sank down into one of the armchairs and sat staring at the embers, forcing herself to forget the futile dream of an adorable two-year old Ianthe, and think of something else.

Perhaps she was being influence by the room itself, the room where Albè had told his story of Augustus Darvell; because all she could think of now was the chilling terror that any person would feel upon discovering that a man they had journeyed and talked with so freely, was not a real man at all, not fully human.

Was it possible? – to restore a dead person to life? To make the heart pump again and the blood to flow? To bring a mind back from the nullity and void of the abyss to full consciousness again?

Unlike Byron, she did not believe in ghosts. She believed in scientific evidence, and as yet there was none to support ghosts.

All her beliefs were rooted in science; all the joy of her soul was inspired by the sublime organic beauty of Nature; and if there truly was a creator of the entire universe and human life, then God would have to be acknowledged as the greatest scientist of all.

She sat for a long time, her eyes on the fire, her face

pale as a series of new and strange thoughts began to flow through her mind. "Am I mad?" she asked herself. "Yes, possibly ... if these bizarre and outlandish thoughts in my mind are to be the evidence."

Nevertheless, she left the comfort of her armchair, picked up her candle and fled back up the stairs to her room, where she set her candlestick down on the small desk, and then rummaged through her overnight bag for her notebook and a pencil. Finally she seated herself down at the desk and she began to write.

She had awakened Shelley who opened his eyes and looked at her blearily in the candlelight. "Mary ... what are you doing?"

Mary smiled, but did not look up from her notebook as she replied: "I am writing my story for the contest."

Shelley shrugged. "Oh, my love, why bother? Byron has already won it."

Moments later he was sleeping again, and Mary kept on writing.

~~~

The morning came in soft and golden with sunshine. The storm had passed and the rain had stopped, although the grass underfoot was still quite sodden.

In the bedroom which Byron had designated as a nursery for baby William and his nurse, Mary listened as the Swiss girl voiced her confusion about the weather.

"It is not usual in Geneva," said Elise. "The summer storms, yes, they come and go, but for no longer than a few hours, then they are gone. But now –" Elise shuddered – "last night I was certain the end of the world was coming, so angry have been the storms."

"And now all is calm and bright again," Mary assured her. "So it was just a freak of unusual bad weather, and not the ending of the world."

Byron did not join them during their first breakfast at Diodati, and they wondered why – until Fletcher entered the salon with yet another bundle of his wet
~~~

white tablecloths to hang on the side balcony to dry.

"Oh, no, his lordship never shows for breakfast," Fletcher explained, "but Dr Dori could have told you that."

Polidori glanced up, his eyes slightly bloodshot and his manner slow and sour.

"Am I my master's keeper, pray? I am here as a doctor, not the *maître d'* of the Diodati Hotel who must keep all the guests so fully informed."

Claire tutted condescendingly. "I believe you must have drank too much brandy last night, Pollydolly. In fact, I believe you probably drink too much every night, because you are always such a grunting pig in the mornings."

"As you asked," Fletcher cut in, looking directly at Mary, "his lordship takes only a cup of tea in his room and some salt crackers before spending hours washing or bathing himself prior to dressing and facing the day."

"Hours washing and bathing?" Claire asked. "Why so long?"

"His lordship is very particular about cleanliness, and always has been," said Fletcher." I believe it was something he learned during his schooldays at Harrow, never to put clean clothes on an unclean body."

Shelley groaned. "It was the same at Eton. Every morning we boys had to stand in the washroom, even in freezing winter, and scrub our naked bodies clean from head to foot. I thought it one of the cruellest things about Eton, especially when so many of us in the winter kept suffering from bouts of severe influenza."

Polidori's head shot up. "Oh, so I was right about you having suffered from consumption?"

"No you were not!" Shelley indignantly put down his fork. "Influenza is different to consumption, and you being a doctor should know that."

"Of course," added Fletcher, endeavouring to lighten the fractious mood again, "Mr Beau Brummell, the greatest dandy of them all, was also very particular about cleanliness. He was a good friend of Lord Byron back in England, and both of them shared an out-and-out disapproval of any man who wore scent."

Mary could not help shooting a look at Polidori, surprised to see that he was nodding agreement. "Any male," Polidori declared, "who wears artificial scent is surely doing so in order to mask some unpleasant odour. Why else?"

"What about women?" Claire said. "I love to wear scent, whenever I can get some, but it doesn't mean I am unclean."

"Scent is different on women," Shelley smiled. "Scent is feminine, and men love the fragrance of scent on a woman."

Fletcher left them to it, taking his tablecloths out to the side balcony and pegging them on the line to dry, frowning prodigiously as he did so. Dr Dori was a sly adder in his opinion, and a liar too, for even the domestics who did all the laundry had spoken of the flowery scent they regularly sniffed on his shirts, and sometimes even his bedsheets.

~~~

Later that afternoon, while all the friends were relaxing on the balcony, Polidori was more his usual self again, vain and foppish, eager to please or take offence, and plaguing Byron with questions about Greece.

"Did you, personally, visit the ruins of Ephesus?"

"Yes, I went there in the company of my Cambridge friend, John Hobhouse." Byron grinned. "But I can assure you, Hobhouse is *not* a vampyre."

"I thought you must have gone there, because you described that wilderness so clearly."

Byron shrugged. "Everything I write is based on places and events that I have seen with my own eyes. My capacity for creating something solely from pure imagination is not good."

Shelley was surprised. "Yet most poets are motivated solely by the force of their imagination."

"So how," asked Polidori, "were you able to describe
~~~

the death of Augustus Darvell if you had not seen it? The blackening of his face on death and all that?"

"From all the tales and superstitions told to me by the Greeks and Albanians."

Claire smiled. "The Albanians again! I don't believe anyone in the world had ever heard of Albania until you wrote about it."

"The Albanians," said Byron, "like most people in very poor countries, nurse a whole household of superstitions. They imagine that bad men, after death, become *voorthoolakases* – meaning vampyres – and believe they often pay visits to their past foes, in the same way that in England they say 'ghosts walk abroad.' Their visiting hour is always at midnight, at which time some member of the family must keep a wakeful vigil all the livelong night, beside a good and cheerful fire."

"So sad," said Mary, "and so ridiculous."

"Not the Greeks," Byron went on, "but the Albanians also believe they are pestered by another species of malignant creatures; men and women whose acquaintance is usually followed by misfortune, whose eyes glimpse evil, and by whose touch the most prosperous affairs are blasted. They work their malicious sorceries in the dark, collect herbs that harm, and use them to strike their enemies with palsy, and their cattle with distemper. The females are called *maissa,* and the males *maissi* – what we call witches and warlocks."

Byron glanced up as Fletcher placed a tray of glasses and a jug of water and cordial on the table. "Fletcher can tell you. He was there with me, and saw and heard it all."

"Did you?" Polidori stared at Fletcher. "Did *you* go to the ruins of Ephesus? Did you see the dying man who was a vampyre?"

"A what?" Fletcher stared at Polidori as if thinking him cracked. "I saw no dying man at Ephesus, that awful place full of big broken stones underfoot that ripped my shoe. Isn't that true, my lord?"

Byron nodded. "Ripped the sole of his shoe right off, leaving poor Fletcher limping along even worse than myself."

"The only people I saw in that place," Fletcher said, "was his lordship and Mr Hobhouse and our entourage of guides and guards. None of us liked it, and we got out of there quick – but not quick enough for me or my destroyed shoe!"

Byron was quietly laughing. "You know, I do believe that Poli believes the vampyre story is true; that it actually happened."

Polidori's face reddened. "No, I don't believe it; no, not at all."

"Then why do you keep repeating the same questions over and over like a cuckoo?"

"I am interested, because, as a medical man, I find the superstitions of those ignorant and vulgar people very amusing."

"I daresay they might find you rather ignorant and vulgar too, Poli – but yes, *some* of their superstitions are amusing, especially their belief in second-hearing."

"What? Do you mean the belief in second-*sight*, like in Scotland?

"No, I meant precisely what I said, second-*hearing*. For instance, on our journey to Cape Colonna, we were passing through the country that leads from Keratéa to Colonna when I observed Dervish Tahiri, one of the Albanian servants, riding rather out of our path and continually pausing to lean his head upon his hand. I thought he must be in some kind of pain, a bad toothache perhaps, and rode up to him to inquire.

"'We are in peril,' he said.

"What peril? We are not now in Albania, nor in the passes to Missolonghi or Lepanto, and there are plenty of us well-armed."

'That is true, Affendi, but the shot is ringing in my ears.'

"What shot! Not a tophaike has been fired this morning.

'Even so, I hear it, Affendi – *bom – bom* – as plainly as I hear your voice.'

"Nonsense.

'As you please, Affendi; but if it is written, so it will be.'

"I left this sharp-eared prophet of doom, and rode up to his Christian compatriot, Vassilly, whose ears, though not at all prophetic, did not like this intelligence coming from Dervish and he was immediately uneasy. He told me that many Albanians claim to hear things before they happen, and always regard them as a warning to be prepared.

"Nevertheless, we all arrived safely at Colonna, remained some hours, and returned leisurely, with most of the Christians making light fun of Dervish, who had disappeared, until I observed him moving stealthily about amongst the stone columns.

"I thought he had become a little deranged and laughingly asked him if he had become a *palaocastro* man.

'No', said he, 'but these pillars will be useful when we make our stand.'

"Against what?"

'The thieving banditti who plan to rob and kill us.'

"Again I assured him that we were all well-armed enough to fight any banditti; and, in any event, it was impossible to hear something before it actually happened. But Dervish, convinced of his own faculty of fore-hearing, was not appeased.

"Upon our return to Athens, we heard directly from Leoné – a prisoner who was set free some days after – of the intended attack on us, and their capture which was the cause of the attack not taking place. I was at some pains to question the man, and he described the dresses, arms, and marks on the horses of our party so accurately, that we could not doubt his having been in villainous company, and us in a bad neighbourhood.

"Dervish was then acknowledged by all as a great soothsayer, and I dare say he is now hearing more musketry than ever will be fired."

Shelley was fascinated, and only now clearly understood how such incidents, in the midst of the most romantic scenery in the world, accompanied by wild Greeks and Albanians, were the makings of poetry and undoubtedly contributed to Byron's genius. His mind and memory must now be filled with stores of authentic imagery to provide the backgrounds and characters which he described in his poetry with such truth.

Polidori's mind was still fixed on one track. "But pray clarify, my lord? In your story you say that Augustus Darvell was an aristocrat, a noble, like yourself?"

Byron rolled his eyes impatiently and Mary instantly came to his rescue. "Enough, Poli, why fix your mind on that silly story when I have so many interesting questions I wish to ask you."

"To ask me?" Polidori appeared astounded. "What can you need to ask of me – a mere doctor who has not travelled to anywhere but Switzerland?"

"Even so, you are a medical man, so you must be interested in the advance of medical science. May I ask if you have heard of Galvanism?"

"Reanimating dead people? Yes, of course. In Scotland, where I studied, in the hospital, I often went down to the morgue where they did experiments on the cadavers."

"What kind of experiments?"

"Well, on one occasion, I saw them put moisture on the body of a newly dead man, on the area of his heart, and then they placed two wires over his heart before charging the wires with electricity from a battery to see if the energy would jolt his heart back to life and get the blood flowing. His hand moved, just for a second, but that was all."

Shelley, who had always been fascinated with scientific experiments, said, "I know they are experimenting a lot with electricity, but I don't see how much can be achieved from small batteries. The charge is not great enough. I recently read of scientists doing the same thing with a man notorious for his criminality, which they tried to remove by applying the wires to his brain. It was not successful, so fortunately he is still incarcerated."

Claire was perplexed. "But why are they doing it? Surely it is pointless?"

"Blame the *Humane Society* in London," Polidori advised. "There are so many suicides in England now, especially by young people, they are desperate to find a way of restoring them back to life as quickly as possible."

"I would blame the fat Prince Regent and his political cohorts," replied Shelley. "If they showed more consideration for the poor, and gave them some hope of a better life, so many suicides would not be happening."

Polidori sighed. "Most of the suicides are caused by drowning."

"That is because most people can't swim," Byron said. "Everyone should learn how to swim. After all, when we travel abroad, we do so by ships on the sea. And even in England, those who do not have carriages or horses, and can't afford the stagecoach, usually travel on boats up and down the canals."

Polidori agreed. "And that is why the Humane Society are teaching people how to try and resuscitate any drowned person dragged from the water. They are even offering payment to anyone who does so, and saves a life. Some fishermen now spend their nights cruising up and down the Thames in the hope of making money –"

"Stop!" Mary said in an agonised voice. "Pray stop, *stop!*"

She quickly stood and ran from the balcony into the house, leaving them all incredulous at the sudden and disturbing change in her.

~~~

Mary had fled from the house, away from the vineyard and up to a small wood, walking slowly now along the dark paths through the pines and endeavouring to
~~~

stabilise her breath. What had happened to her? She had been so content on the balcony – so what flight of fantasy had brought the ash clouds down upon her mind so suddenly?

Not suddenly, and no flight of fantasy, she realised ... but memories ... Last night the memory of her little dead daughter; and today the memory of poor dead mother. A woman she had never known, and yet a woman she now knew very well.

Perhaps if Polidori had not mentioned the *Humane Society,* her mother would not have entered her mind at all; but he did mention it, more than once, so how could she *not* remember?

Her mother, Mary Wollstonecraft, an intellectual and a writer who had already published *'A Vindication On The Rights Of Women,* had consistently kept a personal diary, a very honest diary, confessing to her periods of severe depression, and detailing all the experiences of her unhappy young life with Gilbert Imlay, an American speculator, her lover, before she had later married William Godwin.

A marriage, and her own existence, that might never have taken place, but for the activities of the *Humane Society.*

A gambler, a womaniser, a man who drained away her small income, Mary Wollstonecraft's life with Gilbert Imlay had become utter misery, especially as she could not stop loving him, until finally finding herself crushed and devastated beyond belief when he had brazenly brought his mistress home to live in the same house with them. Cruel – because only a few days earlier, Mary had given birth to Gimlay's daughter, Fanny.

The insult, the degradation of herself, was too much to bear. Such a life was not worth living. So Mary Wollstonecraft decided to end it, quickly, the only way she knew how. She did not have any drugs. She did not posses any money to buy drugs in order to end her life. So there was only one way.

"My thoughts darted from earth to Heaven, and I asked myself why I was chained to this life and its misery?"

It was night when she had walked from their home to the Strand in the rain. She hired a boatman to take her to Putney Bridge. As they sailed upriver the weather worsened and the rain poured down.

The landing platform at Putney was deserted. She paid the boatman and climbed out, standing to watch his boat vanish in the darkness. For a long time afterwards she walked back and forth on the bridge, her clothes drenched from the rain, which pleased her. Wet clothes would help her to sink more quickly.

Finally she climbed onto the railing of the bridge and plunged down into the River Thames. Under water, keeping her head down and fighting the urge to breathe, she finally drifted into merciful unconsciousness and her body began to float downriver.

Her horror and rage, when she found herself rescued and resuscitated by two fishermen who had been cruising the river on the look-out for suicides and a lucrative fee from the *Humane Society*. They had spotted her and chased after her floating body, dragged her on board, and managed to resuscitate her; finally dropping her off at the tavern, the Duke's Head – the place designated by the Humane Society for the leaving of all the revived – where the fishermen had claimed and were paid their reward.

Frozen and dripping wet, she was left sitting in a back room shivering – "I was *inhumanely* brought back to life and misery," she wrote in her diary.

And no thanks did she give to the doctor who finally came to her without much hurry: suicides in London were two an hour these days. Once he had declared her lungs clear of water, she had no alternative but to make her way back home. Gilbert and his mistress had read her suicide note and done a quick flit, taking all their clothes with them, Due, no doubt, to the rogue, Gilbert Imlay, fearing any visits or questions from the police.

Even more devastated, Mary Wollstonecraft found herself left completely alone with an infant to care for, in a tumultuous world of the French Revolution and an England at war with France.

Sitting under a tree and weeping, Mary wished that her mother had not written down every horrible detail of that event so clearly. She had stopped reading the diary years ago, but today Polidori had brought that event flooding back to her.

Mary picked herself up and slowly made her way back to Maison Chapuis, too embarrassed to return to Diodati where her behaviour must have seemed so inexplicable to the others. *She* had asked the questions, and then *she* had fled from the answers.

On reaching Maison Chapuis, she had been sitting in the kitchen for only a few minutes when Shelley entered. "What happened to you? This is the second time I have been here searching for you. Where did you go? And why?"

Mary quietly told him where and why; but then Shelley had also read Mary Wollstonecraft's diary, so she did not have to explain much, before he pulled her up on her feet and hugged her.

"And the saddest thing of all," Mary said, "is the knowledge that when my mother married my father and was at last happy to live, she died giving birth to *me*."

~~~

Byron asked no questions when Mary returned later
~~~

that evening to Diodati, holding onto the arm of Shelley. She looked drained and pale and he could not fathom what had caused her distress, but he was still a little surprised by it all.

He liked Mary, liked her quiet and modest ways, as well as her acute intellect in serious conversation. He had never flirted with her, nor she with him. He could relax with Mary, as with a friend, and she did not sit silently for hours staring at him across the room, as Claire did.

"Are you sure you want to go out on the lake this evening?" Shelley asked Mary. "Are you sure?"

Mary nodded, for she had long ago learned to conquer her fear of the water's depths; and knowing how much Shelley loved boating, she had slowly began to feel that peace which he always felt when drifting serenely on the lake's calm surface.

Polidori was tired of the lake, and bored with always feeling like an intruder, an outsider, in this group of four. Also, he desperately needed to find a doctor. He pulled a piece of paper from his pocket and stared at the address on it.

"My lord, may I be excused from the lake excursion tonight? Someone in England gave me this recommendation to a doctor in Geneva ... a Dr Odier, who will hopefully be able to introduce me to a good apothecary who will view my medical credentials and fulfil my prescriptions."

"As long as I am healthy you have always been free to do whatever you wish, Poli, you know that."

Polidori smiled. "Thank you. May I use your calèche to go into Geneva?"

"Certainly."

"Do you wish me to acquire for you some more vials of laudanum?"

"No, I still have some left. I have been sleeping quite well of late – when I do eventually get to bed."

Shelley was curiously viewing the expanse of the lake. "There's a boatman," he said. "Shall I hail him, or would you prefer to row?"

"No, let us cruise this evening," Byron agreed.

Polidori went off to sort out the calèche and horses while the four strolled down to the lake.

Claire was smiling to herself, delighted that tonight there would be only the four of them out on the water, without the annoying Pollydolly always getting in the way.

While waiting on the shore for the boat to come alongside, Byron's dog was jumping up and down and barking his usual protests at being left behind.

Byron, laughing at the dog's antics, relented. "Oh, very well, you may come and take Poli's place in the boat tonight – but only if you stop that infernal yelping."

Claire was stunned with dismay, keeping her head lowered as Byron took her arm to assist her into the boat, before lifting up his dog and bringing him along also.

Claire silently fumed at this unexpected rival. At least Polidori greatly irritated Byron most of the time; but look at him now, fussing over his beloved dog – it was very wrong the way some people gave more love to animals than they did to humans – *cruelly* wrong.

Very little conversation took place during the excursion, probably due to the presence of the boatman, and moreso because Mary showed no willingness to talk tonight. She was lying down with her head on Shelley's knee, her eyes closed, and Shelley gently stroking her hair.

Mary now felt a great peace, leaving all her darker memories behind her; feeling only the soft breeze on her face and the gentle motion of the boat, and the love of her beloved Shelley.

Byron's dog, who had spent some time standing up on his hind legs with his front paws resting on the edge of the boat, his head erect as he stared around at everything in sight, occasionally barking up at the birds; was now sitting quietly at Byron's feet, while Byron appeared lost in his own contemplation of the far banks around the lake.

Claire sat alone, feeling miserable. She had left England and travelled to Geneva for the sole purpose of achieving only one thing, and that was to make Byron love her. And still she hoped for it, longed for it, and was even prepared to beg for it, if only he would give her the chance and stop avoiding every opportunity of being alone with her.

Chapter Eighteen

~~~

The mists came down suddenly upon the pine forests. The weather continued unreliable; sometimes heavy rain, sometimes hot sun. Even the vine-dressers in the vineyard said it was the strangest summer weather they had ever known.

Shelley and Byron's planned boat tour to see all the places described in Rousseau's *Novelle Héloïse,* had to be postponed until better weather.

"Every cloud has a silver lining," Byron remarked good-humouredly. "At least the mists and rain protect us from the spying of all the binoculars."

He had no knowledge of the telescope which did all its spying at night.

So they sat around in the salon, or on the balcony, and read books or talked – the sort of talk that would not have offended any matron or preacher. They read poetry and wrote it; while Mary worked on her story, and Claire silently gloomed at Shelley and Byron's engrossment in the works of Wordsworth.

Polidori was tired of it all: too often the intellectual conversation of the brother poets was high above his head, and did nothing to soothe his restless temperament. So every day, come rain or shine, as soon as luncheon was over, he begged all pardons and made his excuses before taking the calèche into Geneva to visit his new friend, Dr Odier; always looking slightly drunk when he returned, and on two occasions not returning until the following day.

He shrugged off Byron's inquiry. "I lost track of the time. The gates shut at ten o'clock and not even bribery will make the guards open them again."

"So where did you stay? At Dr Odier's?"
~~~

"No ... well, no, I could not go back and awaken his household. That would be extremely rude. So I stayed in a hotel."

Byron did not care where Polidori went or stayed. "But I would ask you to remember, Poli, that Fletcher occasionally needs the calèche in the mornings to go into Geneva and bring back our provisions. You would be the first to complain if there was no food to eat."

Polidori apologised for his lack of consideration; but then, again, did not return that night.

Byron was grinning. "I think Polidori must have found himself a lady-love in the household of Dr Odier. One of the daughters, perhaps?"

They jokingly discussed it during a walk through the woods in the afternoon. Mary hoped that "Poor Poli" *had* met a young lady in Geneva; but Claire was convinced that no female would have the slightest interest in him. "He's too full of himself, and any female would see it immediately."

In the following days Byron was forced to give Fletcher the task of reprimanding Polidori about his continual use of the calèche; due to his own time being taken up by unexpected visitors calling at Diodati to meet him, pay their respects, and hopefully form an acquaintance.

The first was Monsieur Mark-Auguste Pictet, a Genovese delegate to the Congress of Vienna, who bowed low and confessed it to be "a true honour" to finally meet Lord Byron in person.

"Every word of your poetry I know and admire. Thank you for coming to stay in Geneva. Many of my associates also wish to meet you, so I hope you will be kind enough, milord, to join us one evening for dinner?"

Byron was politeness itself, accepting Monsieur Pictet's card; as he also did with other distinguished Genèvese who were now beginning to call at Diodati to introduce themselves – all nice, fine gentlemen – but no matter how many cards he accepted, or invitations he received, Byron had no intention of returning the visit or dining with any of them.

An honoured guest? – No, an object of curiosity, leaving behind a story to tell, an opinion to elaborate, or even a *book* to write.

He had once spent no more than a few minutes talking to a man, a stranger, in the foyer of the Sadler's Well Theatre in London. A few months later that same man published a book entitled, *My Personal Conversations with Lord Byron.*

Those ridiculous days were behind him, and now he was very careful to whom he spoke to about anything at all.

Emotionally, he knew he was still in stormy waters; but real help had been rendered to him during this deep and isolating crisis in his life by the friendship of Shelley and Mary Godwin, who were not only giving him constant moral support, but had unexpectedly brought him back once more to cheerfulness ... and for that, for their presence here in Geneva, he realised, he owed some gratitude to Claire.

~~~

In the town of Geneva, Dr Polidori took his leave of Dr Odier at the same time he always did, at seven, having taken tea with the family and talking of many things, including his noble patient, Lord Byron, who demanded so much of his time.

The Odiers thought Dr Polidori a wonderful young gentleman, so caring and considerate, and never staying a moment longer in Geneva than his employer would allow.

At the door of his house, Dr Odier said with some insistence to Polidori: "One evening you must acquire his lordship's permission for you to stay with us longer, until some half an hour before the gates close, for we still have so much to discuss."

Dr Odier – whom Polidori considered to be "a good old, toothless, chatty, easy-believing man" – was an
~~~

expert in *somnambulism,* and had been elated to meet another specialist on the subject, and never tired of discussing more ways to ameliorate the condition of sleepwalking.

"We will talk more tomorrow," Polidori assured him.

"Good, good ..." Dr Odier frowned. "And yet, despite all your efforts, you say Lord Byron still sleepwalks?"

Polidori sighed. "He is improving, yes, but I must keep watch and guard every night. That is why I usually feel so tired, due to such little sleep. You will now, my good sir, allow me to return to him."

"Of course, Dr Polidori, of course. Until tomorrow then."

Polidori was relieved when the door closed behind him and he was able to hurry away down the street, eager to make another visit to the *Apothicaire* before his pharmacy closed at eight.

"*Bonsoir docteur."* The apothicaire greeted him with some surprise – and was even more surprised when he viewed Dr Polidori's prescription.

"More opium for Milord Byron?"

Polidori nodded. "He suffers much."

"And all from the lameness in his foot?"

"Sadly, a curse he is forced to live with – but he also suffers severely from aches in his head." Polidori sighed. "I am beginning to suspect he is a little ..." He twirled his fingers up towards his head and pointed to his brain.

"*Ah,"* said the apothicaire, understanding, "*un per fou?"*

Polidori grinned. "I am, of course, jesting. He is as sane as you or I."

The apothicaire did not think it so funny a jest. In Geneva, one did not speak of distinguished men in such a disrespectful way. But then, the English were not so polite as the Genèvese.

He turned away and began to pour some opium pellets from a bottle into a cone of paper, until Polidori interrupted him in a slightly edgy tone.

"Some pellets to chew, yes – but his lordship

occasionally likes his opium raw, to smoke in his pipe with some water and lemon juice. He says it provides a better effect for soothing his nerves. The last piece you provided helped him to sleep."

"The poor man ... he sounds tortured by many things," muttered the apothicaire, unwrapping a sticky ball of raw opium and slicing off a piece.

"As this reaches the brain very fast, raw opium, you must ensure he is in a relaxed position when he smokes it."

"Of course."

"It is better to use pills or pellets."

"I have told him so, but he prefers to smoke it."

Polidori quickly placed the two items in his medical bag and paid the apothicaire. "Lord Byron, you know ... his reputation ... pray assure me you will keep this matter confidential?"

"Bien sûr," agreed the apothicaire, still feeling rather puzzled when Dr Polidori had left his premises.

Something about that young man was not right, not good. Perhaps it was due to him being very young, and new to the medical profession? How long had he been a doctor? Not long enough to know that one did not need a medical prescription to acquire opium.

He walked to the door and stood to look down the narrow street, but the Englishman was gone from sight. Why so furtive? Why the plea for secrecy? Opium preparations were sold in towns and on market stalls everywhere throughout the Continent. Was it not the same in England?

Here in Geneva, and in France and everywhere else, gentlemen often drank opium pills or ate pellets when they suffered neuralgic pain or severe headaches. It was a common medicine for many ailments, and the favourite remedy of choice for women. They used it to stop coughs, hiccups, vomiting, female troubles; and they even gave a tincture of opium to their babies when they were teething and whining from the pain of first teeth. That was why so many called it – *"L'Amie de la mère"* – A mother's friend.

He turned back indoors and looked around at all the items containing opium which he sold regularly in his shop; liquorice with opium; plasters of opium; liniment with opium; suppositories; the list went on and on.

He scratched his head, trying to make sense of it. Could it be true that the British Empire, the biggest importer of opium from China into Europe, did not allow it to be sold freely in England?

No, over time, he had met too many English men and ladies in Geneva who had brought their own opium remedies with them from England.

He glanced down at the prescription still lying on the counter, signed by Dr J. W. Polidori, requesting two dozen pellets and eight ounces of *Papaver somniferum*.

Well, the young doctor knew the Latin name for raw opium well enough, but how anyone could happily smoke it was beyond the apothicaire's understanding, so sickly was its flowery smell.

A ten-minute brisk walk took John Polidori into Geneva's 'Red Light' district, knocking on the door of a house in the Rue Basse.

The Madame of the house smiled when she saw him again, for he was becoming a regular in the evenings now.

"The same?" she asked him. "Or do you wish to choose another?"

"The same," said Polidori, for of all the grisettes he had seen in the house, he liked her best. She was pretty and she was clean, and she was also as ignorant as a dumb animal. Even in French she did not know what month followed June or what day followed Wednesday. Such a refreshing relief from all the intellectualism at Diodati.

"From the sublime to the ridiculous," he laughingly said to her later that night, and although she did not understand, she laughed with him, happy to be allowed to share the bliss of his opium pipe until the room was hazed with the sweet scent of flowery smoke.

Chapter Nineteen

~~~

The Shelley group had left Diodati early and gone back to Maison Chapuis, due to baby William being sick from teething or colic and crying non-stop.

Byron was glad when they had gone: the constant crying of their baby had made him think and wonder about the health and development of his own baby.

Left alone, save for Fletcher, whom he had now sent to bed, he wandered down to the lake's shore, accompanied by his dog.

Together they walked aimlessly for hours while he thought about his child. What was he to do about the situation? What *could* he do? He had no desire to return to his wife, but that appeared to be the only way he could have a life that included his daughter, at least during her early years.

There were times, like tonight, when he regretted coming to Switzerland. He had done so solely to calm down the noise of the newspapers and all the brouhaha and scandal of the separation – which was not all *that* scandalous in these days of increasing divorce cases – yet anything that concerned him sent the press into a frenzied hullabaloo of reports; pages upon pages of the stuff, day after day, and most of it based on unsubstantiated false reports from some person or another who was so certain of their "facts", they wished to remain *anonymous*.

It was a hard and shocking lesson that he had now learned –

He who ascends to the mountain tops, shall find

The loftiest peaks most wrapt in clouds and snow;

He who surpasses or subdues mankind,

Must look down on the hate of those below.
~~~

So many of his own countrymen were now in a bad humour with him. He had been guilty of the offence, which, of all offences, had to be punished the most severely – he had been over-praised; he had excited too much admiration, risen too high in fame. They had praised him up, and now they were pulling him down.

On the advice of his friends, he had agreed to make a peaceful retreat and go abroad for a time, but only for a time, and not for too long. He had no intention of abandoning his little girl to the sole care of Annabella and her peculiar family.

Leander barked, and then suddenly darted away, up towards the vineyard, racing as fast as if he was chasing a rat or a cat or some other creature in the undergrowth.

Hopefully it was not a cat. All the cats around here were fairly docile and gentle and deserved to be left in peace.

He sat down on a boulder and gazed up at the glowing light of the moon, so luminous, hanging as if motionless above the mountains.

"*The moon, my faithful mistress of the night, always there, wherever I may go in this universe.*"

All around him the land was empty and silent. His gaze moved across the lake in the direction of the Hotel d'Angleterre in the distance, but all he could see was some far-off dull lights in two of the windows; the rest of its structure was invisible in the darkness.

Yet strangely and intuitively, he felt he was not alone, and sat alert for some moments, finally shrugging off the feeling in the darkness. Night brought some weird thoughts to the mind.

There seems a floating whisper on the hill,

But that is fancy...

Leander came back to him, tongue hanging, breath panting, and tail wagging. Wherever he had gone and for what reason, he had enjoyed the race.

He patted the dog lovingly, knowing that without his

company he would have felt lonely tonight, very lonely.

Tired out, Leander lay down on his belly, stretched out his front paws, and then fixed his eyes on him, asking a question.

"Just a while longer," he replied. "That house feels as empty as Newstead tonight."

Leander snuffled in sympathy, and then dropped his face on his front paws, keeping one eye open, steadfastly watching him.

The moon was also watching him, and he stared back, wondering why, even in the beauty of this place, he could not feel happy.

Never more than tonight did he sorely miss his friends in England ... Hobhouse, Scrope Davies, Tom Moore ... missed all their wit and laughter. No one could make him laugh more than Scrope Davies; although Moore, with his Irish wit, often came a close second.

Here in Switzerland he often laughed because it was better than crying; and long gone now seemed the days when he had laughed because he had found so many things funny, and because he enjoyed laughing.

He liked Shelley. He had warmed to Shelley quickly, and now he respected him – but Shelley's mind was too serious – a young *Shiloh* who wanted to save the world from all its torments and start the fight for a better life for all.

A *non-violent* revolution by all the poor people of England against their political tyrants is what Shelley dreamed of. And Shelley believed that revolution would soon come; and so did he. The brutally oppressed people of a nation could only be beaten down for so long, before they rose up en masse and fought back, as the American and French Revolutions had proved.

And yet Shelley's true nature was good and kind. In ways he was an innocent, believing that man could be his own god and be noble and brave and heroic on behalf of the people. No wonder he loved Rousseau and Goethe.

"Perhaps I am an innocent too,' he said aloud, but

absent, "for who else but a fool would choose to spend his hours of darkness staring up at the moon?'

Hearing his voice, the dog's ear pricked, and now he was up on his four feet, nuzzling into him with whimpers.

He kissed the faithful golden head and rubbed the dog's ears. "Oh, very well," he agreed. "If it's to sleep you want, we shall go back now."

As he stood, he looked once more towards the Hotel Angleterre and wondered in amazement about their insane curiosity – just as he had once wondered about all the hullabaloo and outrage he had caused in England amongst people who only knew his name and fame; and then the fury of his friends when he refused to answer the newspapers or defend himself. Why would he have been stupid enough to give them that satisfaction? Whether it be adoring supporters, or a hissing crowd, his attitude throughout had always been the same ... *A wave to those who love, a smile to those who hate.*

The dog barked, and they ambled together back up to the house where Byron saw that the calèche had not returned and Polidori's window was still in darkness. Either he had stayed at an hotel again, or he had remained with the Odiers.

Who cared? Although – if Polidori had been here this evening he might have been able to give some doctoring and help to Mary's sick baby.

The door locked, he made his way in the dim light of the wall candles up to the salon and into his bedroom where the last embers of a fire were still burning in the grate.

He lifted a taper and was about to light a candle from the fire when he heard a quick intake of someone's breath and swiftly turned ... his eyes widening as he stared at Claire, lying in his bed, her back against the pillows.

Her black hair was long and loose and he saw the light in her dark eyes as she put her hands up to her shoulders and slipped the open gown down over her arms, baring her neck and breast.

He could not stop staring at her, at the silent, trembling, naked girl in his bed ... and then he turned and walked to the door and opened it.

Claire let out a cry, about to burst into agonised sobs, until she saw that he was beckoning to his dog, sending him out of the room to sleep on his mat outside the door.

PART FIVE

"And, indeed, to witness this noble and gifted young man, but a few days back the idol of the nation, and from whom a word – a glance even – was deemed the greatest distinction – and whom all classes of men and women had combined in adulation of him – and then to see him thus assailed with the savage execrations of all those vile beings who exult in the fall of everything that is great, was indeed a spectacle of dark malice and satisfied envy.

There are no fits of caprice so hasty or so violent as those of society. He was branded by every newspaper in London as an unprincipled and unparalleled reprobate. The public, without waiting to think or even to inquire after the truth, instantly selected as genuine the most false and the most flagrant of the fifty libellous stories that were circulated against him."

Benjamin Disraeli
(Later to become Prime Minister of Great Britain)

Chapter Twenty

~~~

In Geneva, they came out of the most affluent houses and they came out in force; all eager to attend the house-party at the *Château de Coppet*, hosted by the celebrated French novelist, Germaine de Staël.

It was not Madame de Staël they were coming out to curiously meet, but her *special guest* – Lord Byron.

Few could believe that Lord Byron had truly accepted her invitation, when he had previously ignored all invitations from others.

Perhaps he would not arrive, and Madame de Staël would shrug and say it was not her fault – as Lady Dalrymple-Hamilton had done only a week ago.

In her bedroom above Coppet's Great Salon, Germaine de Staël stood before a long mirror inspecting her appearance. She was clad in a loose flowing gown of red silk. Her dark curly hair was swept up inside a magnificent red turban, decorated at the front with a large diamond brooch.

Her maid stood by her side, smiling at her like an adoring child. "*Madame, tu as l'air si magnifique!*"

Germaine shrugged dismissively. "I am now fifty years old, so how can I look magnificent?" She put her hands to her head. "This turban – it is not the fashion here in Geneva."

"No, Madame, but when the guests see you tonight, there will soon be turbans worn on the heads of every lady in Switzerland."

Germaine glanced at her maid, and laughed. "Your flattery is not even good, it is deplorable."

"*Oui*, Madame."

"Tonight I am wearing this beautiful turban in tribute to my dear *Byronn*. You know it was he who started the fashion all over England with his tales of Greece and Turkey? *Oui*. Soon after his first book about his travels
~~~

in Greece and Turkey was published, all the enraptured ladies of London's *beau monde* began to dress in the Turkish style with turbans on their heads. They still do. It is a very stylish cover when one's hair won't shape."

Enraptured? The maid could not hide her puzzlement, wondering why that should be so ... all the men who came to see Madame at the château were poets also, and all were *old* men, some as old as fifty or more, and ugly.

"*Enraptured,* Madame? *Pourquoi?"*

"Because his poetry comes from genius, and because he is young, and beautiful, and like no other!"

"Ah!" exclaimed the maid, smiling. "*Un bel homme!"*

Madame nodded. "I cannot tell you in words. You have to *know* him."

Germaine eventually descended to the Salon and moved amongst her guests, her manner warm and gracious, but inwardly she was enraged. Her secretary had sent out precisely sixty invitations, but almost a hundred guests had now arrived; and most of the uninvited interlopers were English, tagging onto the arms or tails of those who *had* been officially invited.

All the Genèvese guests, she knew well, for she had lived part of her life in Geneva, and Coppet was her late father's chateau. In the past, many great men had come to this house in the Alps. As a girl she had met Voltaire, and in this library she had written her biography on Rousseau.

She looked around at the English strangers, the ones who had *not* been invited, and her emotions changed from rage to an increasing terror that one glance at these chattering English would make Lord Byron turn about and leave again.

The Byron she had known in London had often been delightfully warm and friendly; a young man full of fun with exquisite humour – but he could also be icily cold and abrupt, even with her. So what would he think when he saw all these strange English people? Would he think his dear friend Germaine had fooled him?

Inside the boat sailing the few miles up the lake to Coppet, John Polidori was dressed in his best and excited at the prospect of meeting new people. He had been forced to preen himself in a hurry, because it was only an hour ago that his lordship had finally made his decision and had stopped changing his mind back and forth from go to no.

"But pray explain to me, my lord, why you have agreed to this woman's invitation, and not accepted any other?"

"Madame de Staël and I were social friends in London. She and I met frequently in society." Byron paused, remembering... "She often irritated me beyond words when we sat next to each other at dinner parties, because she talked to me non-stop, and usually directly into my ear. And whenever I managed to sit *opposite* her at a table, she always accused me of listening to her with my eyes half-shut."

"You do sometimes do that – sit listening to people with your eyes half shut."

"No, if my eyes are half-shut it is usually because I am *not* listening."

"So why then, have you accepted her invitation now?"

"Because now I have learned from Hobhouse that she has been fighting many valiant battles on my behalf in London. It seems she has been a true friend to me, even in my absence."

"And she is a writer too?"

"Oh yes, one of the greats. She was also once a great revolutionary who participated in writing the French Constitution in her own Paris salon in 1791."

Byron looked searchingly around to try and ascertain how far they had travelled and how near they were to Coppet.

"But if she speaks to you, Poli, pray hesitate before you answer her, because it is not a reply she seeks when she speaks, merely an audience. In London she held me once for two hours in a salon in order to lecture me."

Polidori frowned.

"And whatever you do, don't get on your high horse with her. She is a woman who has told the Prince Regent precisely where he is going wrong in his rule of England, and she has also known and argued fiercely with Napoleon – so in comparison to them, we are nothing."

Polidori was still frowning. "You speak as if you do not like her, so why go?"

Byron smiled. "In my own way I adore her, especially as she is a superb writer and I am a fan – but I am not a hypocrite, and she, like us all, has her little faults."

They disembarked at the small landing port of Ghenthoud; hired two of the horses at the stables there; and then set off to finish their journey on horseback.

~~~

In a corner of Coppet's large salon, Mrs Elizabeth Hervey, a minor novelist, was speaking to her English female companions with firm instructions: "Now, you know what we agreed. If he does come tonight, then as soon as he enters the salon, we all cut him dead by immediately turning our backs and walking into another room."

Some of the young ladies whimpered their protests:

"Would that not be rather rude?"

"And we would like the chance to at least *see* what he really looks like."

"Goodness, no!" Mrs Hervey declared. "I have never in my life clapped eyes on him, but I am told he is a man with a swooning kind of appearance. And whatever you do, if he somehow manages to get close to you, do *not* look into his eyes, do *not*. They say any female who meets his eyes is forever lost to the temptations of sin."

"Oh mercy me!" gasped one young lady.

Across the salon, Germaine de Staël was not in good humour. "He is very late," she said to her daughter, Albertine. He will not come. And I promised the Abbé di
~~~

Brême that tonight he would meet him."

The Château de Coppet was a huge light-stone building surrounding a wide courtyard on three sides. A long cobbled drive led up to the courtyard and someone standing by one of the salon's long windows saw the two horsemen approach.

"He has come! He is here!"

A huge rushing sound engulfed the salon as many of the guests hurried to the windows to peer out.

Germaine de Staël walked with dignified grace to the open front door where she smiled in warm relief at the sight of her beloved Byron sitting on his horse, wearing a long dark-blue cloak over clothes which she knew would be in the very best taste. He was not only an aristocrat in title, he was also an aristocrat in nature.

As soon as he dismounted she walked towards him with arms wide. "*Mon Byronn, mon cher,* welcome to my Suisse home!"

Byron smiled as she warmly embraced him, feeling a sudden nostalgia and homesickness as her voice, her accent, reminded him of times past in London.

"Oh, *mon Byronn,* I am so 'appy now we meet once more. To me der is no oder like you. Why do you not come before?"

"Because you invited me on a Friday, and I never go anywhere on a Friday for fear of bad luck."

"Why?"

"Friday is the Mohammedan Sabbath, and I religiously uphold it."

Her brows puckered. "My last invitation was for a Saturday."

"And Saturday is the Jewish Sabbath, which I also religiously uphold."

"Oh, you and your silly excuses!" She laughed and slapped his arm. "Now come, I have many good Genèvese people I wish you to meet."

At the Salon door "Milord Byron" was announced by a butler, and Polidori waited imperiously for his own name to be announced ... but no ... once again he found himself to be like a star in the halo of the moon – *invisible.*

The first person to rush forward to be introduced to his lordship was Mrs Elizabeth Hervey, offering him her hand and staring into his face.

Byron smiled, took her hand and bowed, and she swooned into a dead faint, falling back on others and having to be revived with waving fans and smelling salts wafting under her nose.

Madame de Staël's daughter, Albertine, was outraged by Mrs Hervey's behaviour:, declaring: "This is *too much* – at *sixty-five* years of age!"

Charles Hentsch was also furious, murmuring to Madame de Staël – "It is shameful the way some of the English visitors in Geneva pester him and try to make his life and abode here uncomfortable. That I hate of all things – why can they not leave him alone?"

"Madame! *Madame!"* The furious voice of Albertine appeared to bring the woman back to her senses, struggling to her feet with numerous weak apologies. "I'm sorry, oh my goodness, dear me, some kind of disorder came over me ..."

Her friends gave her all their concerned assistance, walking her slowly out to the air of the garden where she inhaled deep breaths for some moments, before saying: "There, did I not tell you young gels what happens if you go anywhere near that "Man of Sin'."

Inside the salon Byron was still looking rather incredulous, wondering what he had done to provoke such a reaction.

"That *ridiculous* woman – you must keep your distance from her," Germaine de Staël quietly warned him. "She is a scandal-monger from the Hotel d'Angleterre and a close friend of your mother-in-law."

Byron stared. "So why did you invite her when you knew you had also invited me?"

"I did *not* invite her. She came on the arm of another guest. I had set my face against any English coming here tonight, apart from an invited few. But you know the

English always beg leave to bring somebody else along, and so they got in by introducing themselves to my guests and then elbowing their way in."

"I have no wish to be stared at, so you will excuse me if I leave."

"No, I will not allow it. I will now instruct them to take that woman and her vapours back to the hotel, and I will make it known that I want all the residents of d'Anglettere to leave with her. Such preposterous pantomimes in my salon are not to be tolerated."

She patted his arm cajolingly. "But first, you must take some wine, and then I will escort you to the library and introduce you to the Abbé di Brême. He has come all the way from Milan to Geneva only for the hope of meeting you."

Byron sighed, annoyed, wondering if he should or could make a quick and peaceful retreat. As for the Abbé di Brême, he was quite sure that the man had come to Geneva solely for the purpose of getting away from the stifling summer heat in Milan, and for no other reason.

~~~

Monsieur Dejean was greatly surprised by the very early return of those guests who had gone up to the party at Coppet –"*Pourquoi?"*

"Why?" said Mrs Hervey indignantly. "Why, I have never met a *ruder* woman in my life as that Madam!"

"Madame de Staël? *Non!* She is a great celebrity here in Geneva, and in all Europe."

"I don't care what she is – the woman is *demmed* rude!"

The others joined in, all complaining about Madame de Staël and the "*simply horrid*" way she had ordered them all out of her house without any respect or finesse.

"*Aller! Aller!"* said one of the young gels, imitating Madame de Staël furiously waving her hand as she ordered them to go, "*Aller! Aller!"*

"How absolutely frightful," said one of the dowagers with disgust. "But then, you know, the French have
~~~

already proved themselves uncivilized with their dastardly guillotines and killing their king. And then all that nonsensical *'Vive l'Empereur'!"*

She croaked a hollow laugh. "And now their great Emperor Napoleon is imprisoned on the rocks of St. Helena in the middle of the South Atlantic Ocean where he can cause no more trouble. Too good for him, I say. He should have been shot!"

Mrs Hervey left the others to pass on all the gossip while she conserved her energy for the important task ahead. She urgently needed to go to her room and write a letter full of news to her dear friend, Lady Milbanke-Noel, the former mother-in-law of Lord Byron; and she wanted to do so before anyone else told Lady Noel a different story.

> *... the sight of him quite disordered me, and he pretended tender concern at my collapse. I could not prevent him seizing my hands, but I behaved to him the whole time with a marked coldness, despite all the pains he took to conciliate me, and my coldness to him was noticed by everybody.*

~~~

Now that the troublemakers from the Hotel d'Angleterre had gone and everyone had relaxed, most of Madame de Staël's guests were enchanted by Lord Byron, as she knew they would be. Byron was not of the norm; he was witty and glamorous, and because of his major status in Europe he was a prize for any hostess to have sitting at her table.

And also, they too, her guests, were some of the most renowned figures of intellectual Europe. Charles Victor de Bonstetten, Swiss literary veteran; August Wilhelm von Schlegel; oh, so many good people – but Byron's favourite of them all, she could see, were Charles
~~~

Hentsch, the banker, and the Abbé di Brême – who was no longer an Abbé but a charming man of thirty-six who had once been Napoleon's almoner, but had given up religion for literature, and was now a respected Italian writer of poetry under his own name of Ludovico di Brême.

In Italian literary circles the name of Byron was often spoken, a name to be admired and conjured with; and now di Brême was thrilled to meet the man in person.

They hit it off immediately, both having a similar sense of humour; the subject of their conversation being their hostess, Madame de Staël, whom di Brême did not know very well.

"She is an exquisite writer, a philosophical genius in many ways, and an extraordinary, eccentric woman," Byron explained, "but she can be very *exacting* in her reprimands if she does not understand what you do, or why you do it."

"And that is my predicament," said di Brême. "She continues to say that she does not understand my sentiments or philosophy."

"Then you must give her the same answer as Goethe did." Byron smiled. "When she complained to him that she could not understand him or his German philosophy, Goethe merely sighed kindly and suggested to her, 'Perhaps, if you spoke German ...?"

Di Brême's laughter caught the attention of Dr Polidori, who was also enjoying himself, and feeling more at home here with these superior people than he had ever done with the Shelleys or the grisettes of the Rue Basse. Yes, *these* were the type of upper-class people he would mix with in his own right and his own fame one day, when his name *would* be announced upon arrival.

He turned his attention and conversation back to Dr Pellegrino Rossi, an Italian who had already invited him to attend a Ball in Geneva the following week. Although both were doctors, their conversation at first had been somewhat confusing, until Polidori discovered that Rossi was a Doctor of Law, not medicine.

At supper, Polidori's pleasure in the evening was greatly increased when Lord Byron asked Madame de Staël if she had heard of "the poet, Percy Bysshe Shelley?"

"He is a poet?" she asked, somewhat bewildered, for she knew all the poets worth knowing. "No, I have never heard of him ... not even in England."

Polidori's delight began to slowly drain away when the subject turned to "plays" that they had recently seen or read, for all were great admirers of the theatre.

Ludovico de Brême spoke amusingly of one awful play he had recently seen in Milan, causing much laughter; and then Lord Byron spoke of a play that he had read, which was even worse.

"A tragedy," Byron said, and Polidori slid lower in his seat, fearing it was his own play which all in Diodati had thought so bad.

"It had the grand title of *Manilus*, and it was sent to me when I was on the committee of the Drury Lane Theatre, by an Irish schoolmaster who believed his true forte was that of a great dramatist, and, in consequence, he was of the certain opinion that we would be very pleased to produce his '*classic*' play on the London stage.

"Well, I read through page after page of his hero declaiming most heroically on his country's wrongs; and then, after bringing his hero to the very edge of the Tarpeian rock, makes him exclaim, 'Oh, Jasus! where am I going to?'"

An evening that had begun so disastrously by the antics of Mrs Hervey, developed on into a night of pleasure for all; much to the delight of Germaine de Staël. She had always loved Byron's droll wit, and was so disappointed when the time came for him to leave.

She begged him: "Many of my guests are lodging here overnight, so will you not stay also?"

"No, because I have a boatman waiting for us in his boat at Ghenthoud. Would you have me leave the poor man waiting there all night?"

One of the guests, Charles de Bonstetten, the seventy-year-old Swiss literary veteran, was so fascinated by Byron he could not bear to see him go, and insisted upon riding with him and Polidori down to the landing port at Ghenthoud.

Byron was surprised. "Are you not lodging here at Coppet?"

"Yes, but the château and my bedroom will still be here when I get back. It will not have vanished into the mist like in a fairytale."

Byron smiled at the old man and agreed he could come along, and the two of them talked and laughed all through the short ride down to the boat, while Polidori remained silent.

De Bonstetten was still smiling as he watched the boat row off into the darkness of the lake; and then rode back slowly to Coppet, where he waved his goodnights to the remaining guests and went straight up to his room to sit and write a letter to his literary friend, Friedrich von Matthisson.

> *Lord Byron inquires eagerly about you. I had to tell him how and where you live; your poetry dazzles him; he compares it with that of Bürger and Salis. We rode in the moonlight from Coppet to Ghenthoud whence the two men took a boat to their villa. I spent a whole evening with all these imaginative people at Coppet and M. de Staël and her beautiful daughter the Duchess of Broglie. Gaiety and wit flew all around. I cannot compare Byron with any other creature. His voice is music; his features those of an angel; but it is only a half-honest little demon that lightens through his*

sarcasm.

Entering Diodati, and tired now, Byron gave Polidori a vague wave and headed straight to his bedroom, eager for sleep ... only to find Claire once more lying naked in his bed.

Chapter Twenty-One

~~~

The following day Byron spoke quietly to Shelley about the difficulty of his situation with Claire.

Shelley, who was not only fond, but protective of Claire, showed no sympathy.

"Then why did you sleep with her? You could have sent her back to Maison Chapuis."

"Could I? You know what Claire is like? Did you not tell me that it was she who persuaded you to come to Geneva when your determined plan was to go to Italy?"

"Yes, but surely you could have found a way –"

"A man is a man, and if a girl of eighteen continually comes prancing to you naked at all hours of the night, there is but *one* way. Would you have acted differently in the same circumstances?"

Shelley shrugged. "I really have no wish to be involved in this, but I suppose you know that Claire is in love with you?"

"No, she is not." Byron was certain. "She sought me out in the first place solely because I was famous, which appealed to her vanity, and now she is merely amusing herself with me."

Shelley, reluctant to quarrel with Byron about Claire or anything else, changed the subject to their boating excursion around Rousseau's Lake Leman.

"Do you still want to go?"

"Of course I do." Byron looked up at the clear blue sky. "And the weather is clear and fine enough now. So when will we go?"

Shelley smiled. "I have already located a suitable boat, and an experienced boatman. He says that whenever we are ready to go, so he is he."

"Then let us go as soon as possible," Byron urged; eager to have time away from Diodati, if only to get Claire out of his hair and his bed.
~~~

"The day after tomorrow," Shelley said. "Would that be too soon?"

"Not soon enough," Byron replied, turning into the salon where his smile lighted on Mary, asking her the same question he asked her every day. "Have you thought of a ghost story yet?"

Usually Mary shook her head in the negative, but today she said, "Yes."

"Yes?"

"But it is not a ghost story."

Byron sighed. "Oh pray assure me that you have not written a *romance*. Our competition was for a ghost or horror story."

"And my story *is* full of horror ... of a kind," Mary told him. "I have written an untidy first draft, a sketch, which even Shelley has not yet seen."

Shelley was astounded. "Is that what you have been doing? I thought you were writing endless notes for your travel journal."

"No," Mary said, showing she possessed a secretive side to her nature, "I wanted to be sure I *had* a story to tell, before I spoke about it."

Byron was intrigued. "Tonight, Mary, that which you have written so far, will you read it to us tonight?"

Colouring like a rose, Mary hesitated, and then nervously agreed. Her story was based on the experiments of Erasmus Darwin and all the trials and experiments of Galvanism, and now she feared the group would judge it to be absurd.

"Although, when I do read it to you," she said, "pray do not judge it too harshly. It is still quite embryonic in its form."

The sun had set, the shadows of evening dimming the salon. The wood burning in the fire-grate was the wood of an old apple tree that had recently been cut down, and yet a faint smell of fresh apples hung in the air, like the clean smell of summer.

Only Polidori was missing from the group, having

taken off on his horse for his promised appointment to visit Dr Odier again.

Seated here and there around the fire, all were prepared and attentive as Mary nervously began, in a quickly-steadying voice, to read aloud her story:

> *"My name is Victor Frankenstein. I am by birth a Genèvese, and my family is one of the most distinguished of that republic. Natural philosophy is the genius that has regulated my fate; I desire therefore, in this narration, to state those facts which led to my predilection for that science."*

It was not what Byron had expected, not from this sweet and often-timid girl ... a story about a young Swiss scientist who is obsessed with the idea of creating a living human by cobbling together inanimate parts of a dead body and bringing it to life in one perfect living creation.

> *"It was on a dreary night in November, that I beheld the accomplishment of my toils. With an anxiety that almost amounted to agony, I collected the instruments of life around me, that I might infuse a spark of being into the lifeless thing that lay at my feet. It was already one in the morning; the rain pattered dismally against the panes, and my candle was almost burnt out, when, by the glimmer of the half-extinguished light, I saw the dull yellow eye of the creature open; it breathed hard, and a convulsive motion agitated its limbs ..."*

A long time later, when the story of Victor Frankenstein and his newly-created human had come to its unfinished end, the dark logs in the fire were coated in white ashes.

A long amazed silence.

Byron stood and put more wood on the flames and then stoked the embers, so that the fire leapt to life again. And then, still stunned by her unexpected talent, he turned to Mary.

"Unfinished or not, your Frankenstein is already the winner of our story contest. But who or what inspired you to even *think* of such a story?"

"Shelley," Mary replied, glancing at her shocked lover. "In the past Shelley has used the pen name of Victor, and in the past Shelley has got himself into serious trouble as a result of his scientific experiments, not only at Eton, but also at Oxford."

Shelley half laughed. "Although I was never so mad as to try and invent a living creature."

"A monster!" Clare exclaimed. "What a horror it would be to *really* have those eyes staring at you."

Byron disagreed. "I feel rather sorry for the poor creature. Imagine awakening at birth as a grown man, and yet knowing nothing about life, or how to live it. Not even how to walk or talk." He looked to Mary. "Does he eventually learn how to walk and talk?"

Mary nodded. "But the creature *is* a type of monster, Byron, a freak of science."

A loud banging on the front door brought the conversation to a halt. All instantly became alert; certain it must be something ominous for someone to come banging at this time of night.

They heard Fletcher making his way to the door, and moments later Fletcher led a uniformed police officer into the salon.

The police officer bowed. "Milord, pray excuse the late hour. I come in matter relating to a man who claims to be your physician, a Doctor Polidori."

"Yes, what about him?"

"He has been arrested and will be detained inside the walls of Geneva until the morning."

"Arrested? Good God, for doing what?"

Shelley stood and moved to stand beside Byron, both listening in disbelief as the officer informed them that Dr Polidori had most violently attacked an apothicaire of the town with his fists, and had not only injured the man, but had also broken his spectacles."

Byron could hardly believe it. "Polidori did that?"

The officer nodded. "He insisted that as he is employed in your noble service, he should be allowed to pass through the gates and leave, but we do not allow such behaviour in Geneva. He will have to attend his trial at court in the morning."

"So where is he now? In a cell?"

"No. He was detained for some time, but as the gates are locked we have allowed him to reside overnight at the Balance Hotel, where he stated he was known by the proprietor. The proprietor of the hotel confirmed that Dr Polidori has stayed there overnight on three previous occasions, and on each of those times, the doctor instructed that the bills for his stay to be sent to the Villa Diodati, the residence of Lord Byron."

Byron's fury was evident, although he maintained his politeness to the officer, apologising sincerely for the bad behaviour of his employee to one of the good citizens of Geneva.

The officer declined the offer of refreshment, thanked his lordship, gave another bow, and left the house.

As soon as he had gone, Byron turned to stare at Mary. "You were talking about Dr Frankenstein's creature being a freak of science? Well now we know there is *another* freak of science – his twin – lying off in his bed in the Balance Hotel and probably not caring a damn about dragging my name through another trench of mud in Geneva."

~~~
~~~

The next morning, Fletcher was despatched into Geneva with a sum of money to assist Polidori in case he did not possess enough to secure his freedom.

"It will result in a fine, and nothing more," Byron said. "I'm sure of it."

"Could we not just leave him in jail?" Fletcher asked. "Mr Berger is praying so, for Dr Dori to be ordered to spend more time in jail, at least for a few more days."

Byron looked curiously at Fletcher. "Why do you and Berger and the servants all dislike him so much?"

"Same reason you do, my lord." Fletcher shrugged. "Of course, he behaves himself with you, but whenever you go down to Mr Shelley's house, and Dr Dori is here on his own with us, well – you would think he was the Prince Regent they way he carries on – ordering us all about, telling us what to do and not do, and reminding us that *we* are the *servants,* while he struts around all haughty and proud."

"I'm tired of all his damned *tracasseries,"* Byron said, "but as his employer it is my duty to do what I can to extricate him from this situation. So off you go, or his trial will be over and done."

In the Geneva courthouse, Polidori's trial had just began when Fletcher entered and slipped into a seat at the back of the room.

"*My God, he looks a sad sight*," thought Fletcher, staring at Polidori whose eyes were badly bloodshot, and his haggard face as pale as a sheet.

One of the judges asked to know why he had made such a violent attack on the apothicaire?

Dr Dori said the apothicaire had sold him some bad magnesia.

"Bad magnesia? *Milk* of magnesia?"

"I found it bad by the experiment of sulphuric acid which coloured it a red rose colour."

"Why did you experiment with the magnesia?"

"Our servants had complained about it."

Fletcher gaped – not having a clue what Dr Dori was talking about. No one had complained about magnesia, bad or otherwise."

"And is that the only reason why you violently struck Monsieur Castan? Bad magnesia?"

"No. He must have said something extremely insulting to me to provoke my reaction. I can't remember what it was. I was on an urgent errand for Lord Byron."

"Lord Byron?"

"Yes. I am his personal physician."

The judges looked at one another and murmured quietly; and from then on Dr Dori got off lightly.

Returning to Villa Diodati, no one else was around when Polidori and Fletcher entered the house.

Polidori went directly up to his room, flopped down on his bed, and then got up again to write in his journal about the apothicaire, Monsieur Castan, who, due to his injuries, was unable to appear in court.

> *Brought me to trial before five judges. He sent an advocate to plead. I pleaded for myself; and laughed at his advocate. Judges made me pay 12 florins for the broken spectacles and court cost.*

Later that afternoon, Polidori wrote in his journal again. Having gone downstairs, he had –

> *Found Lord Byron and Shelley returned. Had a long explanation with Lord Byron and Shelley about my conduct. Threatened to shoot Shelley –*

A knock on the door was followed by Byron entering the room.

Polidori remained sitting at his desk, pen still in hand, his head lowered.

"Shelley has gone. Be glad that he holds no malice against you," Byron said. "However, I think the time has come for you and I to discuss your future."

Polidori's head shot round, certain he was about to be dismissed. "Discuss my future ...?"

"It would be a sensible thing to do, in light of the circumstances."

"I know ..." Polidori said quietly, "I *know* I am too hot-headed with a quick temper. My father always said so."

"And your father, no doubt, also paid highly for your medical studies. So how are you going to repay him? By becoming a rowdy quack or a good doctor?"

"I *am* a good doctor," insisted Polidori.

"Then you must learn, and quickly, that a good doctor always needs to command respect from the people of his community, if they are ever to allow him to enter their homes. Why I allow you to remain in mine is still a mystery to me."

Sullen, Polidori looked at his employer from under heavy dark eyebrows. "You intend to dismiss me?"

"That is up to you. If you will assure me there will be no more violent attacks on apothicaires or anyone else; no more threats to shoot Shelley; no more squabbles with Claire Clairmont; and no more aggravation or disrespect to Fletcher or Berger, then we can put all this behind us, and never speak of it again."

Polidori was so relieved he stuttered, "You d-do not prefer me to leave?"

"No," Byron replied, walking to the door. "I prefer to put it down to the impetuous folly of youth. I, too, made many mistakes when I was twenty."

Later that day Byron said to Shelley: "And it is *because* he is only twenty that I can't dismiss him here, in the middle of Switzerland, and send him home to his father in disgrace. I did not realise he was so young when I first employed him."

It was a situation that Shelley, too, had often puzzled on. "It is rare for any man to get his medical degree at such a young age. He must have been only nineteen when he got it."

"On *somnambulism."* Byron sighed. "Perhaps he was the only one taking that subject and they gave him his degree to get rid of him."

"It can't have been due to him being extremely clever, because at times he shows himself to be a strange idiot. Do you not find him strange?"

"I do." Byron nodded. "When he's not suffering dizzy faints or falling over or spraying himself with a whore-like scent, I veer between feeling sorry for him one day, and wanting to throttle him the next."

They were walking along the small harbour at Montalègre to inspect the boat which Shelley had secured for their tour of Lake Leman the following day.

Shelley said: "My friend, Thomas Love Peacock, once told me that most medical students who want to learn their profession, go to London; but those who just want to get a degree, go to Edinburgh."

"And no doubt this Peacock is an Englishman who thinks the Scots and all their institutions to be inferior?" Byron scoffed. "Where is he from?"

"Dorset, originally, but now a Londoner."

"Thomas *Love* Peacock?" Byron smiled. "Upon his birth did his mother love him at first sight?"

"No, that was her own surname, Love, before she married, and she determined that he would carry her name also."

They had reached the boat. Byron silently inspected it while Shelley made all the arrangements with the boatman, Maurice.

"You have secured a suitable crew?" Shelley asked.

Maurice nodded emphatically, staring at Byron, "A good crew, milord."

And so it went on; Shelley asking all the questions, and Maurice giving all the answers to Lord Byron who ignored him, more interested in stepping into the boat and inspecting it.

Maurice tried harder. "They say you are a true admirer of Bonaparte, milord? I too, I too ... It was Napoleon that caused me to get all my children – *tous mes garçons!"*

From the boat, Byron turned his head, and after a vacant stare at the boatman, he said to Shelley, "Do you have any idea what he is talking about?"

Shelley questioned Maurice in French and received a long babble in reply.

"All his five children are boys," Shelley relayed. "He said he prayed and ordered it, because Napoleon was calling on all men of French blood to give their sons to his army, and so he was breeding and rearing his own sons to go and serve Napoleon."

Byron stepped out of the boat, looking curiously at Maurice, before turning away and speaking quietly into Shelley's ear. "And you expect me to spend a week on a boat with this fool?"

Shelley laughed, and nodded to Maurice. "Very good, *très bon,* his lordship is satisfied and eager to set off on our tour of the Lake tomorrow."

~~~

John Polidori, early that evening, left Diodati to go into Geneva. An invitation to a party had arrived from Pellegrino Rossi, whom Polidori had met at Madame de Staël's chateau at Coppet. He had liked Rossi, a shrewd, quick, and manly-minded fellow.

Rossi's invitation, of course, was addressed to Lord Byron; but as Lord Byron did not wish to go, Polidori decided to deputise in his place and go alone. No more Rue Basse or *grisettes* for him; no, not now that he was socially moving up into the world of important people.

All was silent when he returned to Diodati after darkness. He went directly up to his room, crestfallen and sullen. The evening had not turned out as he had hoped; an utter flop.

Before going to bed he made his usual entry in his journal, complaining miserably:

Went to Rossi's – tired his patience and he
~~~

avoided me. Left and went to a soiree at Dr Odier's who stood and talked to me about somnambulism. Was at last seated, and conversed with some Genovoises – so-so: – all too fine. Quantities of English people there, speaking amongst themselves, arms by their sides, mouths open and eyes glowing; might as well have made a tour of the Isle of Dogs.

He threw down his pen and stood up. It had been a terrible night, from start to end. He yawned his way over to the box where he kept his secrets, unlocked it, and took out an opium pellet to chew on.

Into bed and dreamland, his eyes glazed, thinking more kindly now about Pellegrino Rossi ... God help him, poor soul, for like those English ladies, he too was an ugly dog.

PART SIX

Pacing, two brother Pilgrims, or alone
Each with his humour, could they fail to abound
In dreams and fictions pensively composed.

William Wordsworth

Chapter Twenty-Two

~~~

"The world is too much with us," Wordsworth had written; and then had turned his back on the troubling world for the tranquil peace of England's Lakes.

And now, in the same way, the two poets, accompanied by Byron's Swiss servant, Berger, sailed with the wind over the deserted vastness of Lake Leman, hoping to travel back in time and explore the world of Jean-Jacques Rousseau, and the scenery of his greatest novel, *Julie, ou La Novelle Héloïse.*

Cruising along, Maurice watched the young poets with curious fascination. Each held a notebook and pencil in his hands and occasionally scribbled down many words. It seemed to be their habit, whenever they saw a view they wanted to capture, of writing about it on the spot.

At other times, when there was no wind to carry them along, the crew rowed the oars while Monsieur Shelley read aloud passages from Rousseau's book to Lord Byron, who listened silently while gazing meditatively at the world around him.

By the time they had reached the small Savoy port of Evian, on the second eve of their journey, Byron finally realised what it was about the trip that was giving him so much relaxation, so much peace.

"Thank God Polidori is not here," he said to Shelley. "By now he would have fainted five times, threatened to throw you or himself overboard, complained about having no meat and only fish to eat, and given me an unending headache."

The mountains of Savoy, their summits bright with snow, descended in broken slopes to the lake; but below groves of walnut, chestnut, and oak trees opened down onto lawny fields, confirming the lower warmer climate.

"*Besolets!"* said Maurice, pointing.
~~~

They looked to where Maurice was pointing; and saw thousands of beautiful water birds, like seagulls, but smaller, with a purple colour on their backs, playing in the shallows where the waters mingled with the lake.

"Those must be the birds that Rousseau said were not good to eat, not edible," Shelley said. "Birds of Passage."

"Like us then," Byron said. "Two birds of passage journeying through Rousseau's world."

The village was small, the inn was good, although Shelley was amused by the simplicity of it all when he was shown into his room. He walked back down the small landing to see if Byron had been given a better room than he – but no, Byron's room was the same – almost bare of furniture, with just a mattress on the floor, with bedclothes, to serve as a bed.

Byron was laughing. "The last time I slept in beds like these, a mattress on the floor, was five years ago, in Greece."

"Will we sail on?"

"Oh, heigho," Byron shrugged, "it will be part of the adventure. And perhaps Julie's lover, St Preux, slept on mattresses on floors like these? Perhaps Rousseau did?"

At dinner, neither man liked the look of the food in the inn – animal meat covered in a sauce.

Instead they chose to dine outdoors on bread and honey, sitting on a wall in the glow of the evening, down by the lake. The honey was the best they had ever tasted, containing the very essence of the mountain flowers, and as fragrant.

They stayed there for some hours, talking idly, during which time Byron learned more about Shelley's life before Switzerland.

Shelley spoke of his wife, Harriet; how they had both been in their teens and had married too young. She was pretty and sweet and intelligent, but the space of time living together had proved their natures to be mostly incompatible, leading to many disagreements and much discontent. In the three years that followed, two children had been born; yet Harriet had shown no real interest in them. Then there was the subject of money.

Shelley's friends, Peacock and Hogg, had become convinced that Harriet's family had urged her to marry Shelley because he would one day inherit richly from his father.

Byron sighed: when it came to marriage these days, wasn't it always about money and riches? In the case of his own wife and her family, it seemed so; and now, after only one year of marriage, they had managed, through their lawyers, to get half of everything he owned, including half the ownership of his beloved Newstead Abbey, which had been owned by the Byrons since the reign of Henry the Eighth. Now it was half-owned by the Milbanke-Noels, and once it sold, as they determined it would be, they would collect half the proceeds.

"Of course that was not true," Shelley added, "no matter what Peacock or Hogg said, because Harriet's father was rich enough himself."

Shelley then told Byron about his own grandfather, Sir Bysshe Shelley, an American from Newark, in New Jersey.

"He was an English-American, from a rich English family, and his only dream was to return to England one day, which he did, and where he hired an architect to build Goring Castle. He was also made a Baronet by King George.

"Goring Castle in Sussex?" Byron was surprised "Is that your ancestral home?"

"I doubt I will ever live there. I prefer the house in Fielding Place where I grew up. And Mary has no wish to live at Goring in the future. I always hated the place. Too big. Too impersonal. A normal house with Mary will be home enough for me."

Byron was puzzled. "Your two children?"

"I probably would have stayed with Harriet, if only for the children – if her hateful sister Eliza Westbrook had not moved in with us. She was much older than Harriet –aged thirty – so older than both of us, and you could never meet a more domineering woman than Eliza Westbrook. She ruled Harriet, and Harriet obeyed her every command, always ignoring my interference. Eventually the time came when I was rarely to be found in my own home. In the end I left for good. I had met and fallen in love with Mary Godwin. The marriage was over."

"And Harriet? How did she take it?"

"Badly. And now I am held up in disgrace by everyone we know as the man who deserted his wife and children to go off with another woman. No one we know will speak to us, or have anything to do with us, but then nobody warned me beforehand that when I married Harriet I would also be marrying her sister, Eliza Westbrook."

After a silence Shelley quietly continued, "My father continually writes to me insisting I return to Harriet – and unless I do, and until the day I do – he is punishing me by cutting my hereditary annual allowance down from seven thousand pounds a year, to one thousand a year."

Which was still a great deal of money. Yet as the conversation moved on to Shelley's long-time friends, Byron could not help concluding that those friends seemed not only to have lived off Shelley, but had continually drawn upon him as their banker. Including Mary's father, William Godwin – who, upon hearing that Shelley was leaving England for Switzerland with Mary, had only been prepared to allow it, if Shelley gave him the sum of two thousand pounds in order for Godwin to pay off his debts."

Byron stared. "And did you give it?"

"Yes, but pray don't tell Mary."

Shelley smiled sardonically. "So now you know why I chose the cheapest rooms at Dejean's hotel, up on the top floor."

Byron gazed out on the lake, thoughtful. "I thought I had my troubles," he said, "but your situation is as bad. How do you cope?"

"How do you mean?"

"How do you sleep at night?"

"Oh, easily," Shelley reached into his pocket and took out a small vial of laudanum. "I live on this."

Byron laughed. "I hope you *don't* live on it, not in truth. I take laudanum too, but only occasionally, and only at night."

"Well now ..." Shelley held the small glass vial up to the light, "what is there in this tiny thing to be feared – less than a spoonful in all. Only ten-per-cent of it is opium, a mere *tincture* of opium at that, and the rest is a mixture of water and wine. Is your compound the same?"

"Exactly the same. Ten-per-cent of what Fletcher calls *'hopeum'* mixed in water and wine."

After a silence Shelley said, "No wonder we need it occasionally. The social standards of life in England are detestable. And as for our refined young women – I hate all that sickly sensibility. And all of it for the sole purpose of gaining a husband."

Byron suddenly moved off the wall and down to the shore of the lake where his dog was causing a rumpus, barking and chasing those last few birds that had not yet retired for the night.

Shelley opened his small vial of laudanum and lazily drank it, placing the empty vial in his pocket and slipping down off the wall.

He called out a "good night" to Byron who looked back at him, laughing, "He doesn't know those besolet birds are not *edible*."

"Would he still chase them if he knew?"

"Of course he would. He is playing, that's all."

Shelley gazed up at the darkening sky but saw no stars, only the pale orb of a full moon drifting slowly and silently through the clouds over Evian.

In his tremendous love for all Nature he found himself feeling pity for the poor old moon, so pale and dreary tonight.

Art thou pale for weariness
Of climbing Heaven and gazing on the earth,
Wandering companionless
Among the stars that have a different birth,
And ever moving, like a joyless eye
That finds no object worth its constancy?

Chapter Twenty-Three

~~~

The next day they reached Meillerie, Rousseau's '*Arcadia*' where Julie and her lover St Preux had walked hand in hand, and carved their names on a stone boulder.

"*In the midst of these woods,*" Shelley jotted in his notebook on the spot, "*are dells, adorned with a thousand of the rarest flowers and odorous with thyme.*"

As they walked back down towards the lake, Byron's eyes moved up to the vast and beautiful panorama of snow-capped mountains standing serenely in all their glory. He pointed up, and Shelley looked up too, in absolute awe of the natural splendours of this earth.

Seeing the reverence on Shelley's face, Byron could not resist the chance to tease him, waving his hand up to the mountains and asking if such splendours would not inspire any man to a belief in the existence of a God.

"Who *would* be, who *could* be, an atheist in this valley of wonders?"

Shelley was not amused, insisting the vastness of the universe owed more to natural physics than a man up in the sky.

"I merely quote Coleridge. That is what *he* wrote when he stood before these mountains."

Shelley realised that Byron was ribbing him. "If you admire Coleridge so much, why are you laughing?"

"Because laughing is good for the soul," Byron replied as they walked on. "Although my former wife would not agree with me. There were times when she would put me in mind of a Methodist preacher I once saw, who, while giving a pious sermon, saw a big grin on the face of one of his congregation and thundered, "*No hopes for them as laughs.*"
~~~

Down on the shore, Maurice and Mr Berger stopped smoking their pipes and jumped alert when the two poets returned to the boat, ready to sail on.

Mr Berger, who knew Switzerland and the lakes as well as Maurice, gazed uneasily up at the sky and expressed his doubts about the weather.

Maurice shrugged dismissively. This was a bad summer, he argued, when sunshine came and went, so all must sail with the wind.

The lake was calm as they sailed; the poets gazing across to the banks whose beauty increased with the turn of every peninsula.

Every so often, proud of his superior knowledge of the weather, Maurice enjoyed irritating Mr Berger with a succession of smug grins; until he slowly began to realise that he had been congratulating himself too soon.

The wind was increasing in strength; blowing in fierce blasts, speeding them on too roughly for comfort in their cabin-less open boat.

The currents beneath the boat became stronger and stronger as the sudden storm turned as violent as an Atlantic hurricane, rocking and tossing the boat as if trying to overturn it.

The previously calm surface of the lake had now risen up in furious turbulence, quickly producing waves of a frightening height, covering the whole surface of the water in a chaos of white foam.

Shelley's face had turned pale, realising they were in a life-threatening situation, and he could not swim.

Byron looked up at the mainsails and saw that the second boatman was stupidly persisting in holding the sail while the boat was in danger of being driven underwater.

"You damned idiot – let it go!" Byron shouted.

The boatman let the sail go, but for long moments the boat refused to obey the helm; and now the rudder was so damaged it rendered the management of the boat very difficult.

Maurice was now shouting curses at his second boatman.

One huge wave fell into the boat, and then another; leaving the two poets in no doubt that the boat would soon be swamped under water, and sink.

Despite his gift for wild poetry, one of Byron's traits was his matter-of-factness, his refusal to let go of the bleak reality of life; and now he looked towards the nearest shore, some quarter of a mile away, but it was rocky. And the probability was that even if the boat could make it to the shore, these high winds would smash it against the rocks.

An excellent swimmer, Byron hurriedly stripped off his coat, and told Shelley: "Once we are in the water I will be able to take us to the land safely – as long as you *don't* struggle."

Shelley remained silent, staring at the violence of the waves and foam all around the boat,

"No," he said. "It will be harder for you to swim through this to safety if you have me to haul. You will have enough to do to save yourself and your dog."

Byron argued – "My dog is a fierce swimmer and a skilled lifesaver. I train all my dogs to rescue any man who might be drowning."

Shelley, positively refusing any offer of help, stubbornly sat down upon a locker and grasped the rings at either end, insisting that if he was to sink, he would do so "without a struggle"

"I can swim strong enough for both of us!" Byron insisted.

Moments later he was relieved of the necessity when the boat obeyed the helm, and Maurice was back in control.

Although still in imminent peril from the immensity of the waves, Maurice used all his skill in steering the boat towards the shore of the small fishing port of St Gingolph – where all the villagers had been standing and watching in horror, certain that the boat would go down – and now were cheering and raising their hands to Heaven in thanks for the safety of all.

Their faces full of wonder, they rushed forward to congratulate Maurice, and then each man in turn as he stepped ashore. "A miracle!" they insisted. "Praise be to God!"

They then pointed up to an immense chestnut tree which had been brought down by the storm.

Byron was still somewhat amazed by Shelley's cool and calm conduct in the face of such danger. "And you are the man who once told me you were a coward?"

Shelley smiled shakily. "Perhaps I was never truly tested before."

All were drenched to the skin. The villagers welcomed them warmly and led them to the small local inn where they could dry off and dine and stay overnight while their boat was being repaired.

Later that evening Byron wrote in his journal about Shelley's actions, concluding – "*He don't lack courage.*"

Shelley, too, recorded the event of his precarious dilemma in the boat:

> *"I felt in this near prospect of death, a mixture of sensations, amongst which terror entered. My feelings would have been less painful had I been alone; but I knew that my companion would have attempted to save me, and I was overwrought with humiliation, when I thought that his life might have been risked to preserve mine."*

Chapter Twenty-Four

~~~

After dinner; and after surviving such a close risk of death; Shelley decided to draft his will, intending to despatch it from the next port to his lawyers in London to have it legally drawn up.

He chose Byron as one of the executors, and Thomas Love Peacock as the other. He left all of the estate which he expected to inherit to Mary; with the exception of a bequest of £6000 made to his wife Harriet, and £5000 to each of his two children by her.

The part of the will which surprised Byron the most, was the bequest to Jane Mary (Claire) Clairmont.

To Claire, Shelley had left the sum of £6000, the same amount he had left to his wife, and more than he had left to each of his children. But even more puzzling was a further £6000 he had left to Claire – "*to be laid out in an annuity for her own life, or that of any person she may name, if she pleases to name any other*" making a total of £12,000 left to Claire.

In response to the somewhat curious expression on Byron's face, Shelley shrugged ... "I promised Claire that come what may, I would always look after her."

"Did she ask you to give her that promise?"

"Yes."

Byron was silent.

"Of course it is all academic," Shelley went on. "We Shelleys have a history of long lives, and my father would have to die first, before I inherit, which he probably won't do until his nineties. ... But if *I* had died today, William Godwin might be prepared to protect Mary, who *is* his legitimate daughter – but Claire is merely an illegitimate child that Mrs Clairmont brought along with her."

The name "Clairmont" was still an detestable name to Byron, because it reminded him so much of his
~~~

wife's governess who had also been brought into their marriage to live with them – Mrs Clermont – a hateful old hag; and she too had conspired with Annabella at every opportunity.

"And then," said Shelley, "there is Fanny."

"Fanny?"

Shelley nodded. "Poor Fanny, I wish we could have brought her with us, but Mary and Claire said no, that it would cause too many complications; although I don't see why."

Byron was becoming confused. He knew Shelley was not adverse to communal living, as he had proved by allowing Claire to tag along and live with himself and Mary, but now *who* was this Fanny?

"Fanny Imlay," Shelley said. "Mary's older half-sister."

"She has another half-sister?"

"No. Claire is her *step*sister – no blood connection at all; but Fanny is her *half*-sister, the first child of Mary's mother, Mary Wollstonecraft, by her lover Gilbert Imlay.

"So, Mary Wollstonecraft already had a child before she married William Godwin?"

"Yes, and then she died giving birth to *my* Mary. Godwin then married Mrs Clairmont who came along with her own daughter. So, three girls, of which Fanny Imlay is the oldest.

Byron's mind was getting boggled by it all. "Now I know why William Godwin was strapped for cash and why he wrote to me last year requesting a donation to help him complete his latest book."

Shelley nodded, remembering how Godwin had bragged to others about *"Lord Byron's generous donation to his work."* And the bragging had worked, inspiring others to also donate to what must be a very important book coming down the line from Godwin.

"What is the book?" Byron asked. "Politics or philosophy? I can't recall."

"Nor can Godwin. He still hasn't started it." Shelley

shrugged. "All I know for sure is that any writing talent which Mary might possess, she inherited from her mother, Mary Wollstonecraft, and not from Godwin."

"Or maybe," said Byron tiredly, standing up to go to his bed, "any talent Mary might possess springs from her own spirit, her own creativity, and has nothing to do with either of them."

Chapter Twenty-Five

~~~

In her sitting-room at Maison Chapuis, Mary was writing:

> *I remained motionless. The thunder ceased; but the rain still continued and the scene was enveloped in an impenetrable darkness. I revolved in my mind the events which I had until now sought to forget; the whole train towards my creation. Two years had now elapsed since the night on which he first received life; and was this his first crime? Alas! I had loosed into the world a depraved wretch, whose delight was in carnage and misery; had he not murdered my brother?*

Encouraged by both Shelley and Byron to turn her short sketch of Victor Frankenstein's story into a full novel, this Mary was attempting to do.

In turn Mary had begged Byron to finish his vampyre story, and he had shrugged his head one way, and then another, not sure. But then he had smiled and relented and agreed to complete his story of the vampyre, telling her: "You and I will publish ours together."

Oh, how her face had glowed at that! How her heart had throbbed with amazed delight. For someone like her, unknown to the world, to be partnered and published in the same volume as Lord Byron, was the stuff of dreams.

How proud her father would be. And perhaps then, his insulting disregard and disowning of her would end.
~~~

Spurred on by such a dream, she spent all her free hours writing on and on, begging for no distractions.

Not that she was ever distracted much by Claire, who had been left severely bad-tempered by the two men going off without her. In the past, had not Shelley always agreed that she could join himself and Mary wherever they went? Why could Byron not be as agreeable?

Mary rarely answered, for what could she say? Her own relief, her own joy, was now that Claire was so obsessed with Byron, she no longer spent every minute seeking Shelley's attention.

In earlier days, in her private journal, Mary had often sarcastically referred to her stepsister as "Shelley's friend", for Claire had once been a fierce rival in the battle for Shelley's love, wanting him for herself, and not caring how much she hurt Mary in the process.

Mary looked back on that time as a time of continued awfulness ... so much discontent, such violent scenes, such a turmoil of passion and hatred ... until a time when she was unable to even utter her stepsister's name.

Peace had eventually been restored when Claire had been sent away by Shelley to relatives in the country for a while, and not returning until Mary was heavily pregnant with Shelley's first child. Then Claire had seemed more peaceful in her manner, more helpful, and more resigned to the fact that it was Mary who had won Shelley's love.

Dear Shelley ... he was more fragile than anyone knew, and Mary was certain that he would not be able to survive this life without her. He had told her so, and she knew it to be true.

And since Claire's liaison with Lord Byron, which she kept boasting was "*perfect, so perfect,*" now whenever Mary mentioned Claire in her journal – Claire, with all her new and grand airs – she usually referred to her simply as "the lady".

Claire now spent whole afternoons walking up and

down the paths of the woods in a world of her own. Feeling unloved and neglected by Byron, she had no interest in anyone else. Her responses to everyone were always cold and repelling – especially to poor Polidori who often popped down to Maison Chapuis to join them for tea.

Mary wondered again, and not for the first time, why she, of all the group, did not find Dr Polidori irritating? Instead she felt immense pity for him, because there was always something of the child about him – a rascally and delinquent child, to be sure – but still a child in so many of his juvenile ways.

~~~

John Polidori had never felt more like a *man;* because now, for the first time in his life, he was in love; truly and ridiculously *in love.* "How did it happen?" he wondered. "And so suddenly."

It had happened on the same day that his lordship and his leech Shelley had sailed off on their own without him. Even his lordship's *dog* could not be left behind and was taken along in the boat – but not he, not John Polidori.

True, he had not wanted to go, and had been ready to use his sore ankle as an excuse not to go. What did he care for Rousseau – that revolutionary troublemaker? Still, to not even be *invited* to go, was such an insult.

So certain was he that his lordship was punishing him for getting arrested in Geneva, he had been feeling wretched and disconsolate, walking aimlessly hither and dither through the vineyard, when he had met Mary on her way up to Diodati. She had left some of her child's things at the villa, and was going up to collect them.

She had looked with kindness into his face, and, had asked in a concerned and soothing voice, if he was feeling ill?

It was then that he had seen the inner beauty of Mary, and why Shelley had been willing to abandon all for her – not that *he,* a married man – was worthy of
~~~

such a kind and beautiful angel.

He had helped her to find the things she wanted at Diodati, had walked her back to Maison Chapuis, where she had invited him to join her in drinking some tea (*green tea,* but never mind) and by the time he had left her, with a promise to go down again to Maison Chapuis for tea the next day, he knew he was hopelessly in love with her.

Perhaps he had been in love with Mary from the beginning, and had not realised it? Perhaps that was why he detested Shelley?

No, anyone would detest that lean and lanky Shelley with his fair boyish looks and long hair and his ever-serious big blue eyes. Not to mention his dizzying intellectual talk about humanity and principles and the need for all classes of people to be more equal.

There was only one person Polidori disliked more than Shelley, and she was Claire Clairmont. Such an ill-mannered girl. So different to Mary. And how joyous it was when day after day she did not appear to take tea with himself and Mary. How delighted he felt at her absence. And as Elise always took the child up for his nap at that time, he was able to enjoy Mary all to himself.

The poets had been gone for four days when Mary presented Polidori with a gift. It was wrapped in paper and tied with a blue ribbon.

Polidori was astounded at such kindness. "For me?"

"For you," Mary smiled. "But pray don't open it until you return to Diodati, and when you do, pray regard it with respect."

"Of course... but why –?"

"It is a book, as I'm sure you know by its shape and feel. I wish you to read it, Poli, because when you do, I believe you will understand many things that you do not understand now."

"My dear Mary," he said, beaming with pride, for he was certain that it was her finished manuscript of *Frankenstein* and she had chosen him to be the first to read it. Not Shelley – but *him* – John Polidori.

Returning to Diodati and his room, he untied the blue ribbon and carefully removed sheet after sheet of her brown wrapping paper ... slowly revealing to him that the gift inside was not large enough to be her manuscript, for he had seen her writing on large foolscap pages. And then at last ... there it was ... her gift to him – *Alastor, or The Spirit of Solitude* – a newly published collection of poems by *Percy Bysshe Shelley.*

In a red-faced rage he furiously threw the book out through the open window. How could she do this to him? How could she cast such a blight on his hopes of future happiness? It was to get rid of Shelley he wanted – not to *read* him!

Some time later, when he had cooled down, he went out to the garden to retrieve the book. He would need to read *some* of it, of only to be able to answer adeptly if Mary questioned him.

In the salon, flopping down in one of the armchairs, he opened the book and flicked through the pages, choosing a poem at random: '*Mutability*' which caused him to smile in a sneering way. So Mr Shelley had written a poem about life's ability to keep on changing from good to bad and good again. How very clever!

Yet as he read, the sneer faded from his lips as he discovered that Shelley's poem was not only insightful, his language was excellent. By the time he reached the last two verses, Polidori was biting his lip jealously.

We rest.—A dream has the power to poison sleep;
We rise.—One wandering thought pollutes the day;
We feel, conceive or reason, laugh or weep;
Embrace our woe, or cast our cares away.

It is the same! – For, be it joy or sorrow,
The path of its departure still is free:
Man's yesterday may not be like his morrow:

Naught may endure but mutability.

Oh yes, that was true – one bad dream could spoil a good night's sleep. One miserable thought could ruin a fine day – so shove it away – shove the damned thought away!

It was a good poem, but hopefully there were worse ones – poems he *could* sneer at. He turned the pages, but the more poems he read, the more beauties he found.

Chapter Twenty-Six

~~~

The weather was calm, the lake tranquil, and the sun had returned ... but for how long?

After the near disaster of the previous day, Maurice had expected to receive an order from the two Englishmen to take them straight back to the safety of their houses and gardens.

Instead they had come down to the shore, in good cheer, ready to sail on.

Disappointed, Maurice scowled. He was not happy with the Lake Léman this year. It was an unusually bad summer, and the Léman knew it, throwing up its furious waves in bad humour.

As usual, when Mr Shelley questioned him, he ignored Shelley and made his reply direct to Lord Byron.

In return, Byron did the same, answering all Maurice's questions with an answer to Shelley.

"Where now, milord?" asked Maurice.

Byron looked down at Rousseau's book, read a line or two, and then gave his answer to Shelley: "Clarens."

Shelley looked to Maurice. "Clarens."

A few hours later Maurice landed them on the shore at Clarens.

"Clarens – sweet Clarens, birthplace of deep love! Thine air is the young breath of passionate thought," Byron wrote in his notebook, for this was Rousseau's territory.

The two poets happily explored, jotting down this and jotting down that, always writing on the spot; and then, at last, walking in the Elysian garden near the edge of the lake where, in Rousseau's novel, Julie had walked with her lover, St Preux.

Shelley walked with reverence among the paths of the vineyard overlooking Julie's garden, saying in a
~~~

wondering tone to Byron: "A thousand times I ask myself, did Julie and St Preux walk along these paths, looking towards these mountains, treading on this ground which I now tread?"

Incredulous, Byron smiled. "My friend, they were never real, except in Rousseau's mind. It is a novel of his own creation."

Shelley was not so sure. "Does not all fiction spring from some reality known to the author? If not, then Rousseau has made his lovers more real than reality."

"True," Byron nodded; but as they walked through "*Julie's Wood*", Shelley felt himself compelled, in the presence of Byron, to suppress his tears of transport, which it would have been so sweet to indulge in – now that he was *here* in this beautiful place which he had visited so often in his imagination.

Later, some of the villagers proudly pointed out "*le bosquet de Julie* " telling them many tales of the sweet girl, delighting Shelley, who turned to Byron with an accusing look of reprimand.

"At least the inhabitants of this village are impressed with the idea that the persons of that romance *did* have an actual existence."

Byron shrugged. "Perhaps they did exist after all. Who knows with Rousseau."

"I know," Shelley said, as they sat down on stools by a haystack to eat some of the villagers' bread and honey. "I know Rousseau to be a man of the sublimest genius, who can write a story so wonderfully peopled, and so at once familiar, that he makes the false appear real, and casts a shade of falsehood over that which we call reality."

Byron agreed, because he was so fond of Shelley, even though he was beginning to suspect that Shelley might be a touch mad.

~~~

Stepping back into the boat, Maurice again ignored Shelley and addressed his question to Byron. "Where is
~~~

next, milord? Lausanne? I have many friends in Lausanne."

Again Byron consulted Rousseau's book, and then gave his answer to Shelley, "The Château of Chillon."

Shelley looked to Maurice. "Chillon."

The mood in the boat became subdued when they reached Chillon and caught sight of the Château for the first time – gloomy and stark and solitary – a grey Castle of a place, standing on a small rocky peninsula of land between the border of Switzerland and France, and surrounded on three sides by water.

Maurice was scowling again, not understanding why the Englishmen wanted to go such a place, for its history was dark and terrible, having once been a prison for political dissidents and religious heretics.

Maurice and the second boatman and even Mr Berger remained on board; while Byron and Shelley were landed to walk across the drawbridge and enter the huge empty Château through a large iron gate.

A solitary Castellan, the caretaker of the place, charged twenty napoleons to unlock the doors and apprise them of the prison's history and past occupants.

The Castellan led them through the Knight's Hall to a narrow staircase that led up to the towers and torture chamber where Shelley gazed around, appalled at such "cold and inhuman tyranny."

In his novel, Rousseau had mentioned a prisoner named François Bonivard; a patriot who had rebelled against the Duke of Savoy and had been incarcerated for years in this place.

Byron asked their guide about Bonivard.

"Bonivard?" The Castellan pointed downwards, to the dungeons.

Many narrow steps down, and a maze of internal corridors led them down to the execution cell. Across the arches of the ceiling was a beam, now black and rotten, on which prisoners had been secretly hanged at night.

Shelley had never seen an example of human cruelty

more terrible. Only his devotion to Rousseau kept him going onwards, book in hand, determined to see this revolting nightmare through to the end.

They finally came to a long and lofty dungeon, supported by seven stone pillars, whose branching capitals supported the roof. This was the dungeon where François Bonivard and others had been kept chained to the separate stone pillars. It was a horrific place. Dark and damp, and with no sound but the continual swishing of the waters of the lake against the outside walls.

The Castellan held his candelabra high so they could see the black iron rings fastened into the pillars where the men had been chained.

"And this is how the noble Dukes of Savoy once treated their citizens?" Shelley said in disgust.

Byron said not a word, nor gave any opinion, holding his own candle high or low as he slowly walked around the dungeon, staring at every inch of the walls, every crack and crevice, while listening to the words of the Castellan.

"How many men were confined in this dungeon?" Shelley asked.

"Seven in all," said the Castellan. "Three were brothers."

Byron turned his head and stared: "*Three* brothers from the same family? Chained in here together?"

"*Oui*. Bonivard and his brothers."

"How young or old?"

"*Vingt-six,"* said the Castellan. "François Bonivard was the oldest of all seven."

"The oldest – at twenty-six?"

Shelley had opened his book at a particular page. "In *Novelle Héloïse"* he said to the Castellan, "Rousseau describes Bonivard as *'a Savoyard who loved liberty and toleration.'* What more do you know of him?"

"Of Bonivard?" the Castellan shrugged. "I know all there is to know. I am the Castellan of the Château. It is my duty to know."

Walking close to the rocky walls, Byron continued listening to the voice of the Castellan while estimating that the floor of the dungeon was below the lake – judging by the swishing sounds of the water against the walls; and also by the air outside the small barred window high in one of the walls.

Byron suddenly noticed a cleft in the wall, as if it had been paired away by someone to make a footing.

Curious, and glancing over his shoulder to see the Castellan occupied in conversation with Shelley, he put his own good foot into the cleft and, using his hands to pull himself up, smiled when he saw that the cleft allowed him to rise high enough to peer through the bars of the glassless window. The cleft in the wall had been paired away by a prisoner, eager to get up and glimpse the world outside again.

His descent back to the ground was more clumsy, due to his strong foot being in the cleft and therefore forced to land on his weak foot, half-toppling over but quickly recovering.

When he eventually inquired about the level of the lake, the Castellan agreed with his estimation – only the ground of the dungeon was below the surface of the lake – "Making it so cold in the winter when the ice comes. Freezing cold."

The Castellan waved his hand around the dungeon. "Water below and surrounded by walls of stone. No warmth in stone."

"Did Rousseau come here in person, down to this dungeon?" Shelley asked.

The Castellan smiled. "Rousseau died over thirty years ago. If he came here it would have been so long ago, and I have no knowledge to give you."

Byron was inspecting each of the seven stone pillars in turn, looking at the iron rings and the remnants of chains hanging to the ground.

"Which of these pillars was François Bonivard chained to?"

"*Le cinquième pilier*" said the Castellan, pointing to

it. "Bonivard was lashed to the fifth pillar."

Shelley had more questions to ask, and while he did so, Byron wandered off until he was standing by the fifth pillar, holding his penknife and carving his name into the stone.

"No, there is no hope of escape," he could hear the Castellan telling Shelley, "because there is an opening to the lake, by means of a secret spring-lock, connected to which the whole dungeon would be quickly filled with water before the prisoners could possibly escape."

Shelley had heard enough. He looked around searchingly for Byron, and found him standing with his head resting lightly against the fifth pillar, his eyes shut.

"Are you tired or bored?"

"Neither," said Byron, opening his eyes. "I was listening. These walls echo every sound."

The Castellan nodded: that was true. "That is why I do not speak too loud down here, so you will not think I am shouting at you."

Maurice was again shouting at his second boatman when they had reached the drawbridge, and then instantly changed into a pleasant manner when he saw his lordship approaching.

"It was bad in there, yes?"

Shelley nodded. "Very bad."

Maurice looked at his lordship. "And now we go – ?"

It was still very early in the afternoon, so Shelley said abruptly –"To Lausanne. And a hotel with comfortable rooms. I need to get the stench of that foul place out of my nostrils."

Byron did not speak, nor look once at Shelley nor anyone else while the boat glided over the lake in a cool breeze, his eyes fixed on the distance while his mind still brooded on the dungeons of Chillon, imagining how it must have been, how it must have felt, to be chained to a pillar for years, half dead, half alive, yet surviving, while your brothers and comrades died one by one at your side.

~~~

Due to a headwind, it took longer than expected to sail the fifteen miles to Lausanne, and so the evening was coming on when they landed and checked into *l'Hotel de l'Ancre* in Ouchy, to the south of Lausanne.

Inside the hotel, Byron made some quick and vague excuse to Shelley and went straight up to his room, and did not appear again for the rest of the evening, leaving Shelley to dine alone, and then wander indolently through the gardens.

Occasionally Shelley glanced up to the window of the room occupied by Byron. The drapes were drawn shut, as they had been all evening, even when it was still light outside. He wondered if Byron had immediately gone up to his room due to feeling ill?

In his room, by the dim light of one thin candle on the desk, and surrounded by the darkness of the rest of the room, Byron was writing.

Mentally he was not in a hotel, not in a room – his mind and soul was back in that dark and damp dungeon, using his pen to write words in the voice of François Bonivard, telling the world about the long years he had lived as *The Prisoner of Chillon.*

My hair is grey, but not with years,

Nor grew it white

In a single night,

As men's have grown from sudden fears:

My limbs are bowed, though not with toil,

But rusted with a vile repose.

For they have been a dungeon's spoil,

And mine has been the fate of those

To whom the goodly earth and air
~~~

Are banned and barred – forbidden fare.

We were seven — who now are one.

The tapered candle had flickered out. He quickly lit another.

There are seven pillars of Gothic mould,

In Chillon's dungeons deep and old,

There are seven columns, massy and grey,

Dim with a dull imprisoned ray,

And in each pillar there is a ring,

And in each ring there is a chain;

That iron is a cankering thing,

For in these limbs its teeth remain,

With marks that will not wear away,

Till I have done with this new day,

Which now is painful to these eyes,

Which have not seen the sun so rise

For years — I cannot count them o'er,

I lost their long and heavy score

When my last brother drooped and died,

And I lay living by his side.

They chained us to each column stone,

And we were three — yet, each alone;

We could not move a single pace,

We could not see each other's face,

But with that pale and livid light

That made us strangers in our sight;

And thus together — yet apart,
Fettered in hand, but joined in heart;
'Twas some solace in the dearth
Of the pure elements of the earth,
To hearken to each other's speech,
And each turn comforter to each
With some new hope, or legend old,
Or song heroically bold;
But even these at length grew cold.
Our voices took a dreary tone,
An echo of the dungeon stone.

Lake Leman lies by Chillon's walls:
A thousand feet in depth below
Its massy waters meet and flow;
Thus much the fathom-line was sent
From Chillon' snow-white battlement,
Which round about the wave inthralls:
A double dungeon wall and wave
Have made — and like a living grave
Below the surface of the lake
The dark vault lies wherein we lay:
We heard it ripple night and day;
And I have felt the winter's spray
Wash through the bars when winds were high
And wanton in the happy sky;

The verses rolled on and on throughout the night, as if Bonivard himself was speaking in his ear; telling him all about how it had been, in that place which he himself had seen. And Rousseau, of course, had told him some, but the Castellan much more.

The brightness of morning must have appeared beyond the window-drapes, for Mr Berger had entered the room carrying his tray of morning tea, which was ignored, as was he.

Later, Mr Berger told Shelley that his lordship was writing, and must have been writing all night, for he was still in his day clothes, the same clothes he had worn the day before. And Mr Berger knew, if Shelley did not, that his lordship never wore the same clothes two days running, not unless they were still spotlessly clean.

"But I'm not so good at the sponging and pressing of his clothes as Mr Fletcher is," Berger lamented to Shelley. "Being Swiss, I was employed for my knowledge of Geneva and the Genèvese and my fluency in French, and also my way with the horses; but not as a valet."

By mid-afternoon there was still no sign of Byron, so Shelley went exploring on his own, climbing up hills and collecting rare flowers to take back to Mary to dry and press inside her journal – a memento of his time away from her.

Forgetting that he had often done the same himself, Shelley was beginning to think that Byron must be a touch mad to sit writing night and day. But then Byron himself was like Night and Day, sometimes cold and abrupt in his manner — something which Claire and even Mary had remarked upon — but mostly full of lightness and laughter and friendship.

"Still," Shelley wondered, "what the damnation was he writing? And writing *now* — instead of getting on with their tour of Rousseau's world."

Shelley returned and entered the hotel to be met by Mr Berger, who handed him a manuscript of pages, along with his lordship's plea for forgiveness at deserting his friend so suddenly and for so long.

"Lord Byron" said Berger, "says that as you were with him yesterday, in the dungeons, he wishes you to read the pages, in your own time and at your leisure, so that he may eventually benefit from your valued opinion, and advice on any necessary changes. He says to warn you that it is only a rough first draft."

"And where is Lord Byron now? Does he intend to join me for dinner?"

"He would like to join you, yes, but unfortunately he has now collapsed into his bed. He says to tell you that he will hold on to Maurice for an extra day, to make up for the lost day of the tour."

Shelley was content with that, the extra day to make up for lost time. And faced now with something possibly interesting to read, and not feeling at all hungry, he forfeited dinner; ordering a simple repast of two slices of bread and a pot of tea to be brought up to him in half an hour's time.

Sitting by the window in the brightness of his room, candles aglow everywhere, Shelley slowly began to feel a cold and imaginary darkness seeping around him as he read page after page of *The Prisoner of Chillon*.

He had never read any other poem like it, and yet it was written in true Byron style, masculine and candid in all of its detail, brutal in parts, tender in others, and Byron's voice mingling with Bonivard's words until you could not tell one from the other.

I said my nearer brother pined,

I said his mighty heart declined,

He loathed and put away his food;

Not because it was course and rude,

For we were used to hunter's fare,

And for the like had little care:

Shelley was startled out of his concentration when the

knock came on the door His tray of tea had arrived. He called for it to be left outside and he would collect it.

"Si vous voulez, Monsieur."

As soon as he heard the footsteps receding down the landing, his eyes returned to Byron's manuscript and the world of François Bonivard and his younger brother, the only two of the seven prisoners still living.

But why delay the truth? — he died.
I saw, and could not hold his head,
Nor reach his dying hand —
Though hard I strove, but strove in vain,
To rend and gnash my bonds in twain.
He died — and they unlocked his chain,
And scooped for him a shallow grave
Even from the cold earth of our cave.
I begged them, as a boon, to lay
His corpse in dust whereon the day
Might shine – it was a foolish thought.
But then within my brain it wrought,
That even in death his freeborn breast
In such a dungeon could not rest.
I might have spared my idle prayer –
They coldly laughed – and laid him there.

What next befell me then and there
I know not well — I never knew —
First came the loss of light, and air,
And then the darkness too:

I had no thought, no feeling –none –
Among the stones I stood a stone,
And was, scarce conscious what I wist,
As shrubless crags within the mist;
For all was blank, and bleak, and grey;
It was not night –it was not day;
It was not even the dungeon-light,
So hateful to my heavy sight,
But vacancy absorbing space,
And fixedness –without a place;
There were no stars, no earth, no time,
No check, no change, no good, no crime
But silence and a stirless breath
Which neither was of life nor death;
A sea of stagnant idleness.
Blind, boundless, mute, and motionless!

A light broke in upon my brain, –
It was the carol of a bird;
It ceased, and then it came again,
The sweetest song ear ever heard,
And mine was thankful till my eyes
Ran over with the glad surprise.
But then by dull degrees came back
My senses to their wonted track;
I saw the dungeon walls and floor
Close slowly round me as before,

I saw the glimmer of the sun
Creeping as it before had done,
But through the crevice where it came,
That bird was perched, as fond and tame,
And tamer than upon the tree;
A lovely bird with azure wings,
And song that said a thousand things,
And seemed to say them all for me!
I never saw its like before,
I ne'er shall see its likeness more:
It seemed like me to want a mate,
But was not half so desolate,
And it was come to love me when
None lived to love me so again.

And cheering from my dungeon's brink,
Had brought me back to feel and think.
I know not if it late were free
Or broke its cage to perch on mine,
But knowing well captivity,
Sweet bird! I could not wish for thine!
Or if it were, in wingèd disguise,
A visitant from Paradise;
For – Heaven forgive that thought! the while
Which made me both to weep and smile –
I sometimes deemed that it might be
My brother's soul come down to me;

But then at last away it flew,
And then 'twas mortal, well I knew
For he would never thus have flown –
And left me twice so doubly lone –
Lone as the corpse within its shroud,
Lone as a solitary cloud.

Shelley was unaware that tears were sliding down his face. That little bird singing his song to the poor lonely shackled prisoner ... And oh! what a revelation this was from Byron ... a side to his character the world did not know.

Wiping a hand over his eyes, Shelley read on ... through the fourteen stanzas, weeping again for poor Bonivard who, as the years passed by, had learned to accept his imprisonment. A hermit who had grown used to communing with no one but his own solitary thoughts. No longer wishing to be free, but dreading such freedom; for with no child, no sire, no friends, and no kin, he now believed that "*the whole earth would henceforth be a wider prison to me.*"

Eventually they had unchained him, but kept him locked up in the dungeon alone. Over time he had made a cleft in the wall, to give him a footing up – not to escape; no, all hope and thoughts of that had gone –

But I was curious to ascend
To my barred window, and to bend
Once more, upon the mountains high,
The quiet of a loving eye.
I saw them – and they were the same,
They were not changed like me in frame;

I saw their thousand years of snow
On high —the wide long lake below,
And the blue Rhone in fullest flow;
I heard the torrents leap and gush
O'er channelled rock and broken bush;
I saw the white-walled distant town,
And white sails go skimming down;
And then there was a little isle,
A small green isle, it seemed no more
Scarce broader than my dungeon floor,
But in it there were three tall trees,
And o'er it blew the mountain breeze,
And by it were the waters flowing,
And on it there were young flowers growing.

The fish swam by the castle wall,
And they seemed joyous each and all;
The eagle rode the rising blast,
Methought he never flew so fast
And then to me he seemed to fly;
And then new tears came in my eye,
And I felt troubled —and would fain
I had not left my recent chain.
And when I did descend again,
The darkness of my dim abode
Fell on me as a heavy load;
It was as is a new-dug grave,

Closing over one we sought to save, –
And yet my glance, too much opprest,
had almost need of such a rest.

At last men came to set me free;
I asked not why, and reck'd not where;
It was at length the same to me,
Fettered or fetterless to be
I had learned to love despair.
And this when they appeared at last,
And all my bonds aside were cast,
These heavy walls to me had grown
A hermitage – and all my own!
And half I felt as they had come
To tear me from a second home.

With spiders I had friendship made
And watched them in their sullen trade,
Had seen the mice by moonlight play,
And why should I feel less than they?
We all were inmates of one place,
And I, the monarch of each race,
Had power to kill – yet, strange to tell,
In quiet we had learned to dwell;
My very chains and I grew friends,
So much a long communion tends
To make us what we are: – even I

Regained my freedom with a sigh.

Shelley could not move, left in motionless awe by the power of Byron's genius. Yes, they were all there, everything that Byron had seen at Chillon; and Shelley knew he should have seen them too, or at least seen them with more attention – the small isle with three tall trees on it – the white walls of the distant town. The spiders here and there running along the dungeon walls. Not one thing had escaped Byron's eyes.

But even then – even before he had left Chillon, Byron must have known that he was going to capture and repeat it all in poetry. Was that why he had carved his name in stone on Bonivard's pillar? Shelley had no answers; not yet. All he knew for certain was that, in his humble opinion, in writing Bonivard's story in *The Prisoner of Chillon,* Byron had written a masterpiece.

~~~~~~~

*A staunch admirer of Byron, of his poetry and his politics in relation to France, *The Prisoner of Chillon* was one of the major influences that inspired Victor Hugo to later create the character of Jean Valjean in his own masterpiece; the novel – "*Les Misérables.*"
~~~~~~~

PART SEVEN

"The voyage around the lake was made in the society of Lord Byron, and the memory of that derives from the light of an enchantment which can never be dissolved."

Letter from Shelley to Thomas Moore
December 16, 1817

Chapter Twenty-Seven

~~~

The morning was unusually hot, relieved only by the cooling breeze that escorted them into the harbour.

It had taken the poets eight days to circumnavigate the banana-shaped Lake Leman from start to end; and now, as the boat docked in the small harbour at Montalègre, Mary came rushing from the house to greet them, joyous to see Shelley again.

Claire was absent, due to being off on one of her long walks.

Without pausing for tea or anything else, Byron set off on the path up through the vineyard to Diodati where, in the salon, he found Dr Polidori stretched out on the sofa, his eyes glazed.

"Are you drunk?"

"No." Polidori made to jump up alert but was unable, falling back down again. "I took some bad medicine last night. It has left me weak."

"Bad medicine?"

"For my stomach. It made me worse."

"Where is Fletcher?"

"Fletcher?" Polidori looked around him hazily. "He was here last night."

"You *are* drunk. Damn me if you're not. Well, that is your own concern," said Byron, going off to find Fletcher, and found him nattering in the back garden with the domestics.

"Fletcher?"

Fletcher turned, relief coming on his face. "Oh, I'm glad to see *you* again, my lord, mighty glad."

The domestics seemed to be glad too, for they all started clapping in welcome.

Byron frowned, wondering what had been going on in his absence.

Fletcher waited until they were alone in his lordship's
~~~

bedroom, telling him all the news as he helped him take off his coat.

"It's Dr Dori, my lord. He's been a tyrant with us all. But now I know what causes that occasional flowery smell up in his room."

Byron, due to his limp, and forced to climb up stairs one step at a time, rarely ventured up to the floor above, and so had no idea what Fletcher was talking about.

"Flowery smell? Perhaps he wears scent."

"Oh no, my lord, I doubt Dr Dori would spend his money on expensive scent – not when there's other things he can buy more cheaply."

"Don't draw it out, Fletcher. If you mean he prefers to spend his money on liquor then I –"

"No, my lord, not liquor – *hopium!* "

"Opium?" Byron shrugged. "So why all the fuss? Opium is in everything medical, and even in some of those desserts that Shelley hates so much."

"I knew it for sure when Mr Hentsch the banker called again to see you, my lord. The second time he came, and you were still away, he bade me to warn you about a rumour that's started going round Geneva that either you or your doctor is a bad hopium addict. But I assured him it was not *you,* my lord, it was Dr Dori and no mistake."

"Poli? An opium addict?"

Fletcher nodded and went on: "And I know it for sure because this morning, when he was stretched on the sofa unconscious, I went up to his room and I found his long pipe, and the base of the oil-lamp on which he heats his water-bowl. It was the same as the pipes and bowls the Turks used to smoke from when we was in Albania."

"He *smokes* it? Raw opium?"

"Aye, but he also has the purple pills and pellets and God knows what else up there.

Byron had to sit down on a chair. He had smoked opium himself in Turkey, on a few occasions, so he knew its effect. "*Sweet Poison*" the Turks called it. Yet if

Polidori was dosing himself with it regularly?

"Now it is all beginning to make sense," he said. "Polidori's frequent dizzy spells ... the sudden highs and lows of his nature ... But what am I to do? As his employer I am also his master, and therefore his health and everything else is my responsibility while he dwells in my house."

"Although," said Fletcher, "I do think chewing the pellets is no harm. I knew a man in Nottingham who used to go to the druggist's stall on market day every week, and he would always buy a penny-worth of purple hopium pellets to give to his wife when she was cantankerous with him. He swore by those hopium pellets – said there was nothing better for keeping women-folk quiet for a day or two."

Byron was thinking back to his days in London and those ladies he knew who also used opium on a daily basis. Lady Melbourne for one; she was always chewing on her opium pellets to case her rheumatism; Lady Caroline Lamb, Lady Holland – all seemed to believe they could not get through a day without a few opium "sweets" to chew on.

Byron stood up. "Well, there is no use in talking to Polidori now, not until he sleeps it off."

"He's been asleep on the sofa all night."

"Then make him some strong coffee and force him to drink it, or alternatively to go up to his bed. Either way I'll have nothing to do with him until he's clear-headed. Now I'm going for a swim."

An hour later he was dressed again, and inside the calèche, on his way to Geneva to see Charles Hentsch.

~~~

Upon his return, at five o'clock in the afternoon, there was no sun, only a pale silver blur in the sky.

Standing by the balustrade of the front balcony Polidori cheerily waved down to him, looking as fresh as a mountain spring.

"You look revived," Byron commented when he
~~~

joined him on the balcony. "What miracle has brought about this change in you?"

Polidori smiled. "Like you, I went for a swim in the lake. It was very refreshing."

"Indeed." Byron decided to broach the subject there and then.

Polidori was full of denials. "It is *not* an addiction, it is merely a habit – a habit I can give up any time I wish."

"It is a vice of the neurotic, not a habit of the normal. Why do you need it so regularly?

"Who says I need it so regularly?"

Half the apothicaires in Geneva say it. You have been to most of them, night after night – some even think you have been getting it for *me."*

"No, that is a lie! They know I am a doctor and buy it for my medical bag."

"In such quantities?"

"I use it to make up your laudanum vials."

"No, you don't. They are made up complete by the apothicaire. Just one *tincture* of opium in a tiny vial of wine. I would not trust that measurement to you or anyone but a skilled apothicaire."

"So why do *you* need even that? A *tincture* of opium?"

Byron stared. "Are you mad or just stupid? I was born with a lame foot and if I stand on it for too long I suffer severe pain in my leg – that is why *I* use laudanum, only for the alleviation of physical pain, and only occasionally – and it is solely due to my disability that I hired *you* as my doctor."

Polidori nodded. "I know, yes, I know, and I was obliged and grateful to be chosen for such a distinguished position, but ... my lord ... I have *my own* demons to fight ..."

Moments later he was crying his eyes out, his head lowered, sobbing and searching blindly in his pockets for a handkerchief.

Byron walked to the balustrade of the balcony, gazing

down upon the lake until Polidori's sobs had ceased and he was able to speak in a normal way again.

"Life has not been good to me. My father has been good to me, very good, but not *life*. My time in Edinburgh was bad ... I made few friends ... I was too serious ... I first smoked opium because it made me feel good about myself ... it gives me ... an *elevation*."

Byron sighed, knowing that smoking raw opium caused a state of high and wonderful euphoria, followed by deep lows of dark depression.

Polidori snuffled and went on: "It also helps me to laugh."

"To laugh ...?" Byron slowly turned around. "Now that reminds me of an incident last year, in London ... Coleridge introduced a young man to me, Thomas de Quincy, a shrinking kind of fellow, even though he had studied at Oxford. During the conversation the smoking of opium came up, due no doubt to poor Coleridge's obsession with it. But Dc Quincy stopped the conversation dead, shrinking even more into himself as he said, 'Nobody laughs long who deals much with opium'."

"Samuel Taylor Coleridge – the famous poet? He is *obsessed* with opium?"

"Yes, and it is slowly destroying him."

Polidori nodded, knowing it must be so. "Tell me what I should do," he begged. "Go away? Back to England and my father?"

"And what good will that do? Apart from distressing your father. This is *your* problem and your responsibility, and yours alone."

Polidori clasped the arms of his chair in a kind of despair. "What are you saying?"

Byron was about to answer when his eyes caught sight of Claire standing by the balcony door, The very sight of her irritated him, because Claire was one of those "sudden" people who suddenly appeared when least expected.

"My goodness, whatever is wrong?" she asked, staring

at Polidori's red eyes and tear-stained face. "Is the good doctor feeling sick again?"

"Our conversation is *private*," Polidori snapped; and Byron quickly moved forward to escort Claire back inside the salon.

"This is not a good time to call," he told her quietly. "I've been away for more than a week and now I have things to discuss with Polidori."

"You are sending me away? Why can't I wait here, in the salon?"

"I would prefer you did not. I don't know how long my conversation with Polidori is going to last, and as he said, it is a *private* conversation."

Polidori pricked up his ears, trying to listening ... Surely his lordship was not going to tell Claire Clairmont the subject of their conversation? Oh, surely not?

He could hear Claire's angry voice protesting all the way across the salon and down to the ground floor; although what she was actually saying to his lordship, Polidori did not care enough to listen more keenly.

"Now, if that was Mary," he found himself thinking, "and she had been the one to come along and walk in during a private conversation, Mary, with her refined softness of manner, would have immediately made her own excuse to leave and not have to be asked, like her presumptuous and over-confident stepsister.

He stood up and saw Claire walking hurriedly away from the house, down towards the vineyard – good – she had gone – he had sent her away – she would not like that – how he hated Claire and all her snide and vindictive remarks about him and to him.

Byron returned to the balcony, continuing the conversation as if it had not been halted. "Taking your problem home to your father is no answer, Poli. You must deal with it yourself, and quickly."

"It will be hard – it is a curse!" Polidori said, tears forming in his eyes again. "I *want* to be good, I want to do right ... *You*, my lord, must show me the right way."

"How the devil should *I* know?" Byron snapped. "For some people there is *no* right way in anything, and you seem to be one of those people. Damn it, Poli, why can't you just get some control and ... behave like a respectable doctor!"

"I will, yes, in future I will," Polidori nodded. "I will give up the opium and become a very respectable doctor."

"To be sure you must give it up, if your need of it is so extreme and excessive. If you can't, then go where you may but it will be out of my service. One more chance, Poli, that's all I can allow you, one more chance."

"Thank you."

Byron sighed and walked back indoors, wondering why he had given him any chance at all.

Inside the salon Fletcher met him with raised eyebrows. "Have you dismissed him? Is he going?"

"No, not yet –" Byron was now feeling angry with himself – "but one more disreputable incident, Fletcher, one more embarrassment to me, and I will not dismiss Polidori, I will *eliminate* him."

Chapter Twenty-Eight

~~~

During their tour around Lake Leman, Shelley had voiced only one regret – that Mary had not been with them at Clarens – for she, too, another devotee of Rousseau, would have loved to walk in '*Julie's Garden*' at Clarens.

"I will make it up to her," Shelley had told Byron one evening. "When we get back, a week or two after, I will take Mary on an expedition to see Mont Blanc. How wonderful will that be?"

And now Shelley and Mary were making plans for their trip together to the valley of Chamonix and the dramatic Mont Blanc; although their vitality and enthusiasm for the adventure was slowly being dampened by Claire's black moods.

Since the return from Lake Leman, Shelley and Mary were aware that Byron's renewed and continual rebuffs of Claire's company was the cause of her moody unhappiness ... but what could they do about it? They could not *force* Byron to welcome her into his arms.

Yet Claire persisted, refusing to take no for an answer as she badgered and hounded Byron around Diodati, until Byron's renewed indifference towards her grew into actual dislike.

He begged Shelley to speak to her, to advise her to stay away from Diodati, until Shelley was left with no alternative but to persuade Claire to accompany himself and Mary on their trip to Mont Blanc ... a persuasion that succeeded, but pleased neither Claire nor Mary.

Travelling overland, they took Elise and baby William with them; leaving Byron alone with Polidori – who was now seeking to wean himself off his addiction to opium by purchasing a large jar of opium seeds and liberally sprinkling the black poppy seeds onto every piece of bread, cake, or food he ate – a remedy suggested to him by a doctor at Ghenthoud.
~~~

"At least he is *trying* to help himself," Byron said to Fletcher.

Fletcher sniggered. "Should you not tell him though, about all the black specks on his teeth now when he talks?"

Byron sighed. "No, I have said enough on the matter. So *you* must tell him, Fletcher, and tell him today, otherwise this evening I will be too embarrassed to take him with me to Coppet."

As the Shelley group were absent, Byron decided to respond to Madame de Staël's daily notes inviting him to spend more time with her at the château, mostly because she had assured him there would be no parties or large gatherings, which enticed him – especially as he had now received a letter from his friend, Thomas Moore, sadly informing him that his wife, Lady Byron, was rumoured to be "dangerously ill".

He was sorry to hear it, despite their past enmity, although his main concern was for his daughter. If Annabella was at death's door, then he had no intention of leaving his little Ada in the care of his malicious former mother-in-law.

Yet he was unwilling to go up to Coppet and leave the hapless Polidori alone and free to avail himself of the nightly temptations of the opium apothicaires and grisettes in Geneva's 'red light' district.

"As soon as he is twenty-one," Byron said to Fletcher, "an age when he is deemed old enough – even by the *law* – to be responsible for himself, I shall send him on his way, and be glad to be rid of him."

~~~

The lamps all around the salon had been lighted, as they had in every other room within the Château d'Coppet.

Germaine de Staël was glowing as brightly as her home, delighted by the short note informing her that Lord Byron would be happy to visit her this evening.

Although she had not been quite honest with him in her many assurances that the château would be "empty"
~~~

if he came to visit, for she always had five or six male friends of some importance residing with her in her home, wherever she lived; a woman who thrived on the warmth of good company and good conversation.

Upon his arrival, Byron did appear somewhat perturbed by the sight of the other guests, all eager to meet him; but Madame's warm welcome forced him to relax into good manners and congeniality until supper was over. Then she palmed Polidori off onto her guests while she invited Byron to join her for some conversation in her private sitting-room.

"We can speak together more cosily in here," she smiled, leading him in.

Byron was gratified. If the rumour about Annabella being dangerously ill was true, Madame de Staël would know. She was a prolific letter-writer, and received tons of letters in return. No piece of gossip from England, no news about anyone, ever escaped her, not even here in Switzerland.

As soon as they were comfortably seated in armchairs, he spoke of his concerns about little Ada.

"You poor little *shilde*, so small, so defenceless, I know how you worry for her ... but as for your *wife,"* Madame tutted, "I should not worry so much about her."

Byron was confused. "Is she not, then, dangerously ill?"

"She is still making a fuss, still trying to make the world feel pity for her and hatred for you ... I am sorry now that I wrote to her asking her to consider a reconciliation with you."

Byron stared. "You wrote to her?"

Madame shifted in her seat uncomfortably. "I confess, yes, it was presumptuous of me, wrong, but then, you know, last time, when you were here ... you spoke to me so sadly about your shilde that I thought ..."

She shrugged with annoyance, "but since then so many letters have been sent to Lady Byron from those despicable women lodging at Hôtel d'Angleterre, telling her about white petticoats and you living wickedly with another woman at Diodati and –"

"And *is* Annabella dangerously ill? I know Tom Moore can often be righteous in his actions – but is he *right* in what he says?"

"Yes, *perhaps* she has been ill, but I receive so many stories, so many letters, but only a few I trust ... wait, let us have some brandy, then I will tell you those I trust, and what I know."

Byron held onto his patience while she poured a glass of brandy and placed it into his hands, before pouring another and seating herself down again, sipping from her own glass.

"That woman, I must say with truth, is beyond toleration, at least to all of your *true* friends. She presents herself to the world now as a semi-invalid, broken in health and nerves, suffering from heartbreak and weakness and attended upon by many doctors, and blaming it all on *you*. Yet, according to her London servants, when the doctors have gone she sleeps soundly and her appetite is excellent."

Madame de Staël sighed, and not without some disgust. "But then, so many of those wealthy English gentlewomen – and your wife is now very wealthy, is she not? – they have so much *time* on their hands, so much leisure and luxurious idleness, and so free from the need of any work or exertion, they are only too happy to seek comfort in the vapours and the constant attendance of doctors. *Oh, ces femmes!* Most European women have no time for such senseless things."

Byron did not know if what she was saying to him was true, but now he did not care.

"Although, you must know yourself that Lady Byron *is* a true neurotic," Madame insisted. "A neurotic who irritates all your friends with her continual bitterness and animosities. She is *determined* to be persecuted, always eager to be perceived as the victim, and takes every word of praise about you to be an indirect criticism of herself. Lady Holland, Lady Jersey, oh, they cannot stand her!"

"Enough about Annabella," Byron said quietly, having heard *more* than enough. "Now tell me something of my *friends*, some good news."

"Yes, but now first, please to tell me – all this *cruelty* they accuse you of against her? The latest I hear is that in the last six months of the marriage, you never once joined her for dinner and always left her to sit and eat alone."

"Alone? She was always accompanied at dinner by that evil governess of hers. But the *real* reason I could no longer stomach dining with Annabella, was due to her insistence on not swallowing any food in her mouth until she had precisely chewed each mouthful for *exactly* forty times."

"*Mon Dieu!*" Germaine burst into laughter, her arms opening in that French way. "Can you see if that was so at all my dinner parties – all my guests sitting silent and chewing for so long? No conversation? No exchange of news or laughter? Such a long silence would be *cruelty* to any host!"

"Indeed. Now enough," Byron said. "Some news of my friends – some *good* news, pray?"

Germaine de Staël smiled, still trembling with amusement as she sat back in her chair. "This news you will like ... your favourites, the Hollands and Lord and Lady Jersey, they will be arriving in Geneva next week, and Lady Jersey begs me to tell you that her door will be open to you from the moment she arrives. The Hollands also. "

Polidori knocked and popped his head inside the door, his expression curious; but before he could utter a word Madame de Staël ordered him in, told him to sit, and then placed a glass of brandy in his hands, before returning to her seat and continuing her news ... Lady Caroline Lamb had now been ousted from Melbourne House, forced to live at their country house out in Hertfordshire; and her husband, William Lamb, is said to be seeking a divorce from her.

"His father is now of such an old age," Madame said, "William Lamb knows that he will soon inherit his title and become Lord Melbourne, and he is determined also to one day become the Prime Minister, so he cannot continue to have such a mad and badly-behaved wife."

Polidori listened silently and avidly to all the news about people he had only heard of, but never met; all the upper-class gossip which fascinated him, and hearing enough details to make his journal for the publisher, John Murray, extremely interesting.

Yet, upon their return to Diodati, Polidori's brief entry was, as usual, scathing –

> "*Madame de Staël is better at home, those who know her say, than she is abroad. She talks much; would not believe me to be a physician. Ugly, but good eyes. Is writing on the French Revolution. Polite, affable; tells all to Lord Byron.*"

A few days later, Byron received a number of letters. One was from Shelley, in Chamonix, describing the beauty of the scenery and urging him to join them –

> "*I write in the hope – may I say so? – that we possibly shall see you before our return. No sooner had we entered this magnificent valley than we decided to remain several days. An avalanche fell as we entered it. We heard the thunder of its fall, and in a few minutes more the smoke of its path was visible. I wish the wonder of these 'Palaces of Nature' would induce you to visit them whilst we, who so much value your society, remain yet near them.*"
>
> *Claire sends her love to you, and Mary desires to be*

kindly remembered.

Yours faithfully, P. B. Shelley.

He opened another letter – this one from his sister Augusta – alarmed at all the reports about him living sinfully with *two* mistresses in Geneva. Annabella was furious about all the rumours and was presently out and about in London in the company of her mother.

Instead of replying to Shelley or to his sister, he decided to write a reply to Thomas Moore, finishing the letter with a wry P.S: –

Lady Byron, as you say, has been dangerously ill; but it may console you to learn that she is dangerously well again.

Chapter Twenty-Nine

~~~

Claire was now in utter despair. She had fervently hoped that her absence would have caused Byron to miss her; but since their return from Mont Blanc three days earlier, he had not only shown no interest in her, but had cold-shouldered her out of his bedroom, ignored her in his salon, and then walked out and left her alone in his house.

All her dreams of a life of love and happiness with him were shattered; all her plans to that end had gone wrong. She had been sure she could influence him back into her arms, but no ... and even worse, she had now lost all her former influence over Shelley.

Or had she?

She walked slowly through the vineyard muttering to herself, oblivious of the vine-dressers who watched her.

Finding a bench in her path she walked around it five or six times, still muttering, while the vine-dressers gawped at her in puzzlement as she kept circling the bench, unaware that she was lost in a world of her own cunning ... "No," she muttered, "not Shelley."

She had always charmed and seduced and got her own way with Shelley – and perhaps now Shelley would help her to get her own way again with Byron?

Upon entering the kitchen at Maison Chapuis, she saw Mary sitting in a chair by the fireside nursing baby William, and Shelley sitting at the table, head bent, engrossed in editing his new poem, *Hymn To Intellectual Beauty.*

She moved closer and whispered into Shelley's ear, "I need to speak to you alone."

Shelley looked up at her, and then at Mary, saying aloud, "Why should you need to speak to me *alone?"*

Mary turned up her eyes impatiently. "Oh, another of her little intrigues, no doubt."
~~~

"About Albè," said Claire.

Shelley shook his head. "No, I don't wish to get involved."

"But you *must* – I am begging you! Or do you also wish to abandon and *desert* me too?"

Mary watched silently as Claire persuaded Shelley to go outside with her for a short walk, resenting Claire and resenting Claire's constant presence in their lives.

She looked at Elise, who was standing by the window folding baby-clothes and sighing. Elise did not like Claire either.

"Two years ago," Mary said derisively, "Claire also accused *me* of attempting to abandon and *desert* her. But how could I be accused of attempting to desert someone I have never owned? We do not have the same father, we do not even have the same mother – and although in law we may be stepsisters – we have *never* been friends."

Elise thought it all very odd, but was too polite, in her Swiss way, to say so.

William had fallen asleep. Mary covered her breast, but then sat staring at his little sleeping face, for although she had never noticed it before, William now had suddenly reminded her of her sister, Fanny. In sleep, William had a way of pursing out his bottom lip, and in sleep so did Fanny.

"I have another sister," she said musingly to Elise, "an older sister, three years older, and she is more of a sister to me than Claire could ever be ... a *real* sister, in that Fanny and I were born of the same mother, Mary Wollstonecraft."

Mary did not mind sharing things with Elise, because Elise's understanding of English was quite poor, yet between broken French and English, they managed to understand and get on very well together.

Mary gently stroked William's head as she thought of Fanny, dear, sweet, quiet and modest Fanny, left behind in London, in that unhappy house in Skinner Street where she had always been forced to address Claire's awful mother as "Mama" and Mary's father as "Papa" ... How cruel it had been to leave poor Fanny behind, and how much better a sister and companion she would be now ... so much nicer than Claire.

"But you see," she said pensively to Elise, "Fanny was hopelessly in love with Shelley, and so it would have been cruel to bring her with us."

Elise frowned. "So why you take the other one?"

"Because Claire *forced* herself on us. Because she kept insisting that *she* was *not* in love with Shelley ... Also, she was only sixteen, and although she was her mother's pet, my father had never liked her."

Shelley returned to the kitchen alone, looking seriously disturbed. Claire, he said, had gone off for another of her walks.

"So what did she need to say to you in such privacy?" Mary asked. "Are you allowed to tell me?"

"No, not yet ... I *will* tell you later, Mary, although you will know soon enough – but first, I have been given the unenviable task of going up to Diodati to speak to Albè"

~~~

Claire had not gone off for another of her walks, as she had told Shelley.

She had gone no further than a clump of whispering trees down by the lake, just below Diodati, where she had a good view of the villa's balcony.

In answer to her plea for him to "put her out of her misery" Shelley had eventually promised that he would go and speak to Byron immediately, although he had been reluctant to do so.

She stood in the shadow of the trees, hidden, waiting impatiently, until she caught sight of Shelley emerging from the vineyard and walking very slowly towards the house, as if pondering, and still reluctant.

Not until he entered the villa did she let out a sigh of relief. Now Byron would no longer be able to ignore her.
~~~

Now he would be bound to her forever.

Inside Diodati's salon, Shelley nervously said what he had to say, and waited for Byron's response.

For a long moment Byron remained silent, but Shelley recognised all the signs of his controlled anger.

"Claire pregnant?"

"Yes."

"Are you sure?"

"She is quite sure."

Byron was not disposed to believe it – not the fact that Claire was pregnant, but that *he* was definitely the father. He knew that Claire had also slept with Shelley. And if Claire had not told him so, he would have known it anyway. He was a man of the world, and no fool. The only one who genuinely did not seem to know it, was Mary.

Yet he had no wish to embarrass Shelley, nor endanger their friendship. He knew Claire too well; she was a clever seducer.

Standing in the shadow of the trees, peering relentlessly up at the house, Claire stood alert at the sight of Shelley leaving the villa, walking as slowly away from it as he had earlier walked towards it.

She moved rapidly in her strides back towards Maison Chapuis in order to waylay Shelley as he came out of the vineyard.

"Well, what did he say?"

Shelley sighed, shaking his head. "He begs leave to think about it. He says he will send a note down to me later."

In the Diodati salon, Byron was fuming, so much so that he suddenly grabbed up a glass vase and flung it violently against the wall, smashing it to pieces.

Was he being trapped? Or had he trapped himself?

Later he sat down to write a letter to his friend, Douglas Kinnaird, the only one of his friends who had met Claire Clairmont – "*that odd-headed girl*" who had pestered them both in London when they had been on the committee of the Drury Lane Theatre –

But is the brat mine? I have reason to think so – for I know – as much as one can know such a thing – that she has not lived with Shelley during the time of our acquaintance.

He looked at the word *lived,* certain that Kinnaird would understand the euphemism ... But there was no word he could substitute to explain his repugnance for Claire Clairmont. Once again, she reminded him of his clever wife; certain that in holding the child, she now held all the power.

Chapter Thirty

~~~

The lake was quite dark now, and gloomy; no longer shimmering under the sun which had so recently sunk, making way for the pale moon that began to outline the dark hulk of the Jura mountains.

Elise was settling William down to sleep in his crib upstairs; while Mary sat alone at the kitchen table, writing an entry in her private journal:

> *Shelley and Claire go up to Diodati. I did not go for Lord B. did not seem to wish it.*

It was strange that Lord Byron should wish to exclude her, yet he must have stated so in his note to Shelley, but why? Had she been mistaken in believing they were friends and he liked her?

"Oh, I don't know," she said, blotting and closing her journal and pushing it aside. She pulled forward her essay book, deciding to continue her story about Victor Frankenstein. The trip to Chamonix and Mont Blanc had given her many new ideas, inspiring her to set part of the story in the beauty of those snowy mountain glaciers.

Yet she could not fully concentrate, due to her increasing mood of jealous irritation, for once again Shelley had left her to go off with Claire, while *she* was the one left sitting at home like the spinster sister.

~

Claire had been consumed by a passion to see the delight on Byron's face; to hear him speak tenderly to her; to feel the touch of his hand as he vowed to take care of her and the child. She was certain he would insist upon her moving into Diodati immediately, where his servants would be able to guard her every move and
~~~

serve all her needs.

But now there were stinging tears of disappointment in her eyes as she sat listening to Byron speak in such a calm and neutral tone to Shelley.

"I did not seek her out. She knew my destination and she made sure she was here when I arrived. She knew what she was about, and I knew too. Why should I take responsibility for her now, and allow her to become a fixture in my life? I do not love her. I have never even *pretended* to love her, I took her on *her* terms, and she knows it."

Shelley was floundering. "Yes, but now that she knows she is pregnant –"

"There will be a child at the end of it. And if she is certain the child is mine, I will do my duty and take full responsibility for it."

"Of course the child is *yours,"* Claire snapped. "What a thing to say!"

"Then I will financially support you and the child for the next twenty years or so. Isn't that how it goes? What a man must do in this situation?"

Shelley muttered something about that being fair; at least, the best one could expect. After all, he reminded Claire, although legally separated, Byron was *still* married.

It seemed to Claire that the beating of her aching heart could be heard in the silence as she stared at Byron.

"You intend to abandon me? Leave me all alone in the world? I cannot look after a child on my own. No, I *cannot.* And think of the shame to my reputation – an unmarried girl with a child!" She turned her glare on Shelley. "I am *not* like Mary, you know, I do *care* about my reputation."

Byron watched Shelley, who seemed to be crumbling under the embarrassment of it all.

"In that case," Byron said to Claire, "may I make a suggestion that will secure your reputation from all rebukes?"

"Pray do," Claire said hopefully ... and then listened in disbelief as Byron suggested that if Claire was certain she would not be able to look after the child herself, it could be put into the care of his sister Augusta.

"She loves children, has four of her own, so one more would cause no extra trouble to her."

"No, no –" it was Shelley who protested first. "The child cannot be put into the care of a stranger."

"A stranger? If the child is mine it would be going into the care of my *sister,* so she would be the child's *aunt*. And that fact alone would cause Augusta to adore it."

"No, I could not allow it," Claire said, standing up to join Shelley. She stared beseechingly at Byron as she hastily came up with her own suggestion –"Once the child is born, would *you* not agree to care for it and have it live with you in your household, bring it up as your own?"

When Byron did not answer, did not refuse, Claire persisted, "And I could visit the child regularly. I could pretend to be its aunt or cousin or something like that."

Byron regarded her archly. "And *who* would I say was the mother?"

"Oh, some Swiss girl ..." Claire shrugged in desperation. "I have always believed that a child should be brought up by at least *one* of its parent, at least until the age of seven."

When Byron still did not answer, Claire pushed on: "You would be able to house and pay for nursemaids to take care of the child so much better than me. And you never hesitate to rescue and care for any strange *animal* that crosses your path, so *why* should you be so uncaring now about me and our child?"

Byron was sick of the subject, and truly sick of Claire. During the rest of the conversation she made her demands, and he made his.

Shelley was quite saddened by it all, returning to Maison Chapuis to tell everything to Mary, while Claire marched straight up to bed.

"Pregnant?" Mary was flabbergasted, and yet selfishly relieved. "And will Byron now accommodate Claire?"

"No, not for a minute. Their agreement is that when Claire gives birth to the child, she will care for it for as long as she can; and when she feels that she no longer can, he will take the child into his care. In the meantime he will financially support her throughout, but he will only do so, on the fulfilment of one condition."

Mary could not hide her disappointment when Shelley told her of Byron's condition – "His *one* and only demand ... that Claire be kept away from Diodati from now on, as he never wants to set eyes on her again."

"Oh." Mary sat back, shaking her head, not knowing what to think about it all.

"He may change his mind about Claire," said Shelley, "but I don't think so. He is convinced she set out to trap him, and it's all too soon after the end of his marriage and his heartbreak over the child he has already."

"Too soon ...?" Mary calculated, and nodded. "Yes, less than six months ago."

"Only five months, according to Byron. He says he signed the Deed of Separation in April."

"Madame, *s'il vous plaît* ..." Elise entered the kitchen holding a note and looking very annoyed.

"Madame, the other one ..." she handed the pencilled note to Mary, which was from Claire, asking Elise not to sing any of her songs to William in the morning, as she wished to sleep late.

Mary nodded, for Elise's songs in the morning sometimes did have a lot of querulous yodelling sounds in them.

Yet Elise's objection was apparently nothing to do with her singing, but her name – pointing to the word "Elise" written on Claire's note.

"*Ce n'est pas correct, madame.*"

"Not correct? But your name *is* Elise?"

"*Oui, madame.*" Frustrated, Elise lifted Mary's pen on the table and slowly wrote her name ... Louise

Duvillard.

"Ah ..." Mary said. "Your name is *Louise*."

"*Oui*" said the girl, and pronounced it the Swiss way, "*EL-eese.*"

"Yes," Mary agreed, "*Elise* ... it is only the spelling that is wrong?"

"From the tragic to the trivial," Shelley said tiredly, turning to leave the room – stopping dead at the sight of Claire standing in the open doorway, her hair down and her eyes glaring in rage. "Trivial? How dare you?"

Shelley was dumbstruck, capable only of raising his hand to point towards Elise and her note by way of explanation.

"How could you allow him to abandon me so easily?" Claire demanded. "But then *you* would, wouldn't you, Shelley? *You* who abandoned your own wife and child – and poor Harriet was *pregnant* with your second child when you left her to run away with your dear sweet Mary!"

Claire's rage was like the eruption of a volcano, hotly spitting out all of Byron's sins and Shelley and Mary's sins and every damned thing they had ever done wrong – in a torrent of tears – blaming everyone for her pregnancy except herself.

Not understanding much of what Claire said, but seeing her tears, Elise was moved enough to put her arms around Claire to try to calm her in the soothing tones she always used to calm baby William, "*S'il te plaît, mademoiselle, calme-toi s'il te plaît ...*"

Elise succeeded in guiding Claire out of the room and up to bed with the promise of a glass of warm milk. Claire allowed herself to be led tearfully out of the kitchen, leaving Shelley and Mary behind her, shrouded in their own guilt.

Shelley had no words to say, and Mary was close to tears. She knew that Shelley's wife blamed her for stealing her husband, and now that she was a mother herself, Mary understood Harriet's pain.

And now she, too, lived with the occasional dread

that Shelley might one day abandon her also, and sometimes she was certain that if he did, Claire, ultimately, would be the cause.

Shelley silently left the house, deeply hurt, and found himself wandering back up towards Diodati. Women could be the very devil to contend with, as Byron would say. Byron was in the same situation as himself. He, too, knew all about unsuitable wives and the misery of domestic tyranny.

Byron put down his pen when Shelley wandered into the salon, not at all surprised, for Shelley now had a habit of wandering in and out of Diodati whenever he pleased.

Shelley wandered over to the bookcase, perused the books, lifted one out, and walked over to a chair by the fireplace and sat down to read it.

Byron dipped his pen in the ink and continued writing.

Later, when Byron had set down his pen and was blotting his page, Shelley turned his head to look at him and ask, "Were you ever happy in your short marriage to your saintly wife?"

"Rarely," Byron replied. "Much of the time I hated that still, quiet life."

"Did you know it was going to be like that?"

"I think I knew I was making a mistake even on the morning of my wedding – at the last moment I would have retreated if I could have done so."

"Still, the end of the marriage –"

"The end of the marriage," Byron said, pushing back his chair and standing, "may have been my fault, but it was her choice."

"Why a legal separation though? Why not a clean divorce?"

"She did not want a divorce. And the only clue I have as to why she did not, is her statement in a letter to my friend, Francis Hodgson, insisting that a legal separation would *not* preclude a reconciliation in the future."

“Did you not think of seeking a divorce yourself?”

“How could I? Do you not know our laws, Shelley? In England we can only seek a divorce on the grounds of *female* infidelity. And as you say, my wife is a self-proclaimed saint.”

"Do you think your wife was surprised when you suddenly upped and left England? It *was* sudden, wasn't it?"

Byron shrugged. "When things are so bad, there is only one way, and that is to move on. I *will* go back, if only to see my little Ada."

Fletcher came in, asking if Byron wanted the fire lit in his bedroom now?

"No, leave it, Fletcher, don't bother." Byron gave a small wry grin "I have a suspicion that Mr Shelley wants to sit awhile and talk."

"I do," said Shelley dolefully. "I bloody do."

And talk they did, until after three in the morning, about marriage and children and mistresses and mistakes and none of it was their fault. After all, they were poets.

"I once knew a man," Byron said, "who resorted to a plea to the House of Lords to grant him a Bill of Divorce. His reason was that he could not get one otherwise, as he had no legal grounds against his wife, who would be the perfect wife for any man, but she was a disaster for him.

"'Why so?' he was asked.

"'Because I am a writer, my lords, and she does not understand a writer's passion or his need for solitude and concentration. She talks prettily, my lords, but she is driving me mad'."

Shelley was laughing. "And did he get his divorce?"

"No, he was frog-marched out of the place by the guards."

Byron grinned. "Although *I* would have granted his appeal on the spot."

~

Shelley finally left around four o'clock, making his way home in the darkness through the narrow paths of the vineyard. Byron instructed his dog to accompany him, knowing he would bark if anything untoward occurred.

"Good boy, good boy," he said when Leander returned. "You are my hero, do you know that?"

"I do, yes," Leander replied in his barking way, and then padded tiredly past him towards the bedroom and sleep.

Byron was not in the mood for sleep. All the talk about marriage and wives and women had somewhat depressed him. He sat on the balcony and gazed at the weakening moon, thinking not of his wife, or Claire, but of the only girl he had ever truly loved ... the only girl he had truly longed to marry ... Mary Chaworth.

Dear Mary ... gentle, fragile Mary, he had not seen her since her mental breakdown ... and too late he had learned that she had not, as he had thought, returned to her abusive husband, Jack Musters, but – according to Nanny Marsden – she had heard Mary telling Musters about her "love for Byron" and he had immediately left her again at Annesley and rejoined his mistress in Yorkshire.

If only he had been told? If only servants in Nottingham had stopped talking amongst themselves and had talked to the people to whom their gossip was relevant.

And according to Nanny Marsden of Annesley Hall, who had told Nanny Smith of Newstead Abbey, who had eventually told him – that on the day the *Morning Chronicle* had announced Byron's marriage to Miss Milbanke, the effect on Mary Chaworth was terrible. Even Reverend Nixon, the Vicar of Hucknall Church, had spoken about Mary's lapse back into a terrible illness ... her "mental darkness" as he called it.

So, now Mary was mad, and he was miserable, and yet it might have all been so different ... *The whole tenor of my life might have been different if I had married Mary Chaworth ...*

And yet, looking back now to that time of love and longing, it all seemed like an unreal dream.

~~~

The dawn sky was the colour of smoke, a light grey. Maurice the boatman was already up and in his boatyard, preparing to set out on the lake to try and catch some fish when, to his shock, Lord Byron wandered into his boatyard.

"Milord?"

"Can you take me out on the water?"

"To where?"

"Anywhere."

Maurice was about to protest about the early hour – he had fish to catch for his family's breakfast – but stood dumb when his lordship thrust a bag of money into his hands.

"Three hundred Napoleons. Will that be fare enough to take me?"

Maurice almost fainted. For three hundred Napoleons it would be fare enough to take his lordship anywhere he wanted until midnight; but then these English had little understanding of Swiss money. Few knew the difference between a louis and a napoleon, which all made Geneva such a happy place in the summer – for the Swiss.

Maurice lifted two fishing rods with nets and placed them in the boat, presuming his lordship wanted to fish. All Englishmen liked to fish.

As soon as they were out on the silent lake, Maurice lifted a fishing rod to hand across to milord; but Byron ignored him, taking out a notepad and pencil from his pocket and beginning to write.

And so the time passed, hour after hour, while Maurice sailed his boat and milord kept writing rapidly as if Maurice was not there.

Maurice did not mind, having already decided the young milord was a little crazy – yet why should he not love him as much as he did. Thanks to Milord Byron,
~~~

when the cold winter came, the lake frozen over, and no work for anyone in Geneva, he would not have to go to Paris like so many Swiss men did, to work as waiters or porters in the Paris hotels.

Now Maurice would not be forced to go to Paris, but he would be able to stay leisurely at home by a warm crackling fire in Sécheron with his family. And all because of the young milord, who had made him famous. *Oui! – un célèbre* – because now the English wanted no boatman for them but Maurice. Some came from all over Geneva, just to sail out on the lake with Maurice – and once seated in his boat, all wanted to know only the same thing – "What did Lord Byron say to you? What did he speak about?"

And Maurice, being a good and honest Calvinist, always answered the truth. "He did not speak to me. He never speaks to me."

But they did not believe him, and kept asking questions; some even came back to go out in his boat again and again, believing he had taken an oath of secrecy and they were determined to break it. Maurice always laughed, because there was no oath, no secrecy, but if they wished to keep coming, and keep paying money for his boat ... A sudden cold breeze blew across Maurice's face, making him shiver, for it reminded him of the cold autumn and freezing winter soon to come.

All visitors left Switzerland in the autumn, all work slowed to an end. And in the depths of winter, when the land became as cold as death, Sécheron was a starving kind of place.

"Where were you?" Fletcher asked when Byron returned to Diodati. "It's almost noon and you gone missing, your bed untouched. Leander is out looking for you.

"I went sailing. And *now* I'm going to bed."

In the bedroom Byron took out his the notepad and placed it on his desk. It contained the long poem he had been writing in his head for years, since his youth in Nottinghamshire, about Annesley, about Newstead, about his love for Mary Chaworth. Now it was written down on paper, now it existed in the material world and not only in his mind. He had titled it *The Dream*.

Now he could go to sleep.

Chapter Thirty-One

~~~

"*Go forth, Christian soul,*" cried one of the two bonneted Englishwomen standing by the open door.

"Go forth and return to your home in England," the other chimed, *"and atone to God for all your wicked sins."*

Mary shut the door against them with a slam. She returned to the kitchen, quite shaken, and wishing Shelley had not gone out to the lake to try and catch some fish.

When Shelley returned from the lake she told him about the two women. "I did not know what to say or do. What would you have done?"

"What I always did when women like that accosted me in England – just stare and tremble – that always pleases them."

Mary could not shrug it off so lightly. She may have gone against all the norms of society in living with Shelley, but she did not see herself as wicked.

And even if she and Shelley *had* sinned, they had been well and truly punished for it ... Shelley had been disowned by his father, and his yearly annuity of £7,000 which was legally his by right since he had reached the age of twenty-one, had been slashed to one-seventh by his father, and the full amount and his father's forgiveness would not be returned to Shelley, until he had returned to his wife Harriet.

And she, too, had been shunned by all friends, disowned by her father, barred for ever from the house in Skinner Street, and even her sister Fanny was banned from writing to her. Some might also say that the loss of her first child, little Ianthe, was also a punishment sent to her, but if there was a God, she could not believe he was that cruel ... as cruel as mere humans.

And now Claire ... she could not blame Claire for
~~~

loving Byron, so perhaps from now on she should try and think more kindly about Claire.

Up in her room Claire was no longer very troubled, and back to her usual self, convinced that she could find a way to surmount all obstacles to her desires. Byron had treated her badly, but she would ignore it, as if it had never happened. The less said, soonest mended.

And her first task was to write an eye-lash-fluttering letter to Byron.

> *Dearest –I would come tonight if I thought I could be of any use to you. If you want me I am sure Shelley would come and fetch me. Can you not pretext the copying? It would make me happy to finish 'Chillon' for you.*

Later, when her letter had been ignored, she sent up another note:

> *It is said that you expressed yourself last night so decisively to Shelley that it is impossible to see you at Diodati. Is that true? When you had such bad news to announce, was it not cruel to behave so harshly in the day? If you will trust 'Chillon' down here, I will take the greatest possible care of it.*

Less than an hour later, Mr Berger came down from Diodati with two letters in his hand. Claire was the first to grab the letters from him, but they were not addressed to her. One was addressed to Shelley, and the other to Mary – two letters which Mr Berger had collected from the Geneva post office along with Lord Byron's letters.

Mary was out with Elise and William, picking flowers in the nearby wood. Shelley opened his letter, emitting a groan as he read it. The letter was from his lawyers, stating that his case to fight for his legal inheritance from his grandfather had run into difficulties, which necessitated his return to London.

Mary, who was now feeling much brighter in mood, returned to the house carrying an armful of pale lilac and yellow Alpine flowers. "Are they not beautiful? I do believe that some of the most beautiful flowers in the world are to be found here in Switzerland."

Shelley handed her the letter from his lawyers. "I could go back on my own and sign whatever they need me to sign and have notarised. It would take less time if I went alone, and cheaper."

"I suppose so," Mary muttered. She was distressed, disappointed, and annoyed with Claire for so eagerly agreeing with Shelley.

"It makes sense, Mary. We have limited money. And although we will be two women alone, I'm sure Byron will watch out for us and keep us safe."

Mary ignored her, opening her own letter.

Now Claire was alert and excited. With Shelley gone, Byron, as a gentleman, would be duty-bound to allow herself and Mary to visit his villa, and also make regular calls down to them to ensure that all was well.

"Mary! What's wrong?" Shelley exclaimed.

He stood up, shocked to see Mary change so drastically before his eyes and become so crumpled and wilted and small, silently stricken.

"Fanny," Mary whispered. "My dear sister Fanny ... she has committed suicide."

~

During the twenty-four hours that followed, Claire was outraged at the suggestion that they all must now return to England. She had never been close to Fanny, and she felt no guilt whatsoever. If anyone was to blame it was Mary, for leaving Fanny behind with Mary's awful father.

"If anyone is to blame," Mary countered, "it is your awful mother – for always favouring you and treating poor Fanny like a servant."

Shelley took control of the situation and arranged for them *all* to return to England, including Claire.

Elise was sad to hear from Mary that they were leaving Switzerland, and then she readily agreed to go to England with them and continue as William's nursemaid.

Shelley had informed Byron that he and Mary would take care of Claire in England until her child was born. Byron assured Shelley that he would immediately instruct his accountants to commence regular payments for Claire's upkeep.

Heartbroken, but not without undaunted hopes for the future, Claire sent another letter up to Diodati.

> *"Dearest – we go in two days. Are you satisfied? Remember how very short a time I have to tease you, and that you will soon be left with your dear-bought freedom. Tell me one thing else – shall I never see you again – not once again?*

On the morning of their departure from Maison Chapuis, Shelley ran up through the vineyard to collect a number of manuscripts which Byron was entrusting to him to deliver to his publisher, John Murray.

"Canto III of *Childe Harold's Pilgrimage,* and *The Prisoner of Chillon,"* Byron said, "and tell Murray that I explicitly insist that *you,* Shelley, should read and revise the proofs before publication, and be paid the usual fee for doing so. They are mainly all about Switzerland, so you will know better than anyone what I intended to achieve with them."

He then handed Shelley his manuscript of *The Dream.* "I have written out the fair copy myself. Take good care of it."

Shelley nodded. "I'll write and let you know how it goes. And if you move on from here, or return to

England in winter, you will keep me informed of your new address?"

Byron nodded, sad to see Shelley go.

A short time later, from his view on the Diodati balcony, Byron could see the Shelley party's calèche trundling along the road towards Geneva.

The following day, another letter from Claire was handed to him, which she must have posted at the Geneva post office, on their road out.

Dearest – when you receive this I shall be miles away. Don't be impatient with me for writing again; I don't know why I write unless it is because it seems like speaking to you. Indeed I should have been happier if I could have seen you once and kissed you once before I went, but now I feel as if we had parted ill friends.

You say you will write to me, dearest. Pray do, and be kind in your letters; my dreadful fear is lest you might quite forget me – I shall pine through all the wretched winter months – whilst you, I hope, may never have one uneasy thought.

He paused at that last line, recognising a touch of Claire's sarcasm.

One thing I do entreat you to remember – beware of any excess in wine.

And now she was nagging him like a *wife*. The only difference was that his former wife regularly entreated him to give up writing poetry, or as she termed it – "the abominable trade of versifying."

> *I make no account of Mary and Shelley's friendship, so much more do I love you. Now don't laugh or smile in your little proud way, for it is very wrong for you to read this merrily which I write in tears. I am fearful of death, yet I do not exaggerate when I declare that I would die to please or serve you with the greatest pleasure.*
>
> *Farewell then, my dearest, dear Lord Byron. I shall love you to the end of my life and nobody else.*

He slowly put the letter down, feeling far from merry. Regret, remorse, guilt ... but had she not forced herself on him? Had she not hunted him down in London, at the Drury Lane Theatre?, At his apartment? And then again here in Geneva?

He should not have weakened to Claire in the first place, and now he was determined never to be soft and weaken to her again.

But as guilt-inducing as her letter was, it also reminded him once more of his wife; for she, too, had written similar letters, all wanting to please and serve him for his greater happiness, yet within weeks of the marriage she was doing her utmost to get rid of all his friends, blatantly showing her disregard for them, and making them feel not at all welcome in his house.

To separate a father from his child was beyond forgiveness, but to try and separate a man from his lifelong friends was the act of a fiend, and the final straw.

PART EIGHT

"I am sure of nothing so little as my own intentions."

BYRON

Chapter Thirty-Two

~~~

At Cambridge University they had been a coterie of inseparable friends: John Cam Hobhouse, Scrope Davies, Charles Matthews, and Lord Byron.

Matthews had tragically drowned one Saturday morning when swimming in the River Cam at Cambridge; and now Byron was in self-exile in Switzerland – a place as far away as death, if one did not have the urge or the money to travel.

John Hobhouse and Scrope Davies had both the urge and the money. In London they had stood at Byron's side during all the uproar against him during the break-up of his marriage; and they had accompanied him all the way down to Dover when he had decided to leave England. A sad farewell that had left them standing silently on the dockside staring after Byron's ship, until it was finally gone from view.

Now they were in Lausanne and Scrope Davies wanted to delay for a few days, to seek out any good gaming clubs, but Hobhouse insisted they push on.

"You have no time for card games, Scrope. We need to reach Geneva before the summer vanishes."

Scope smiled to himself, knowing that Hobby's urgency was less to do with a vanishing summer, and more to do with his fear of a vanishing Byron.

"You know what I have always said about him, Scrope – he's as unreliable as a woman, as fickle as the wind, and all his promises are as uncertain as tomorrow's sun."

"Oh, very well," Scrope agreed amiably. "We will leave as you please, after breakfast in the morning."

"Thank you," said Hobhouse; and then went up to his room to drop his bags and freshen up for dinner; but not before he had taken out his Diary and made a worried entry: "*Lausanne – no letter from Byron.*"
~~~

During dinner, Hobhouse again voiced his worry to Scrope. "Why do you think Byron sent no letter to us? He promised he would send instructions for the best and quickest route from Lausanne to Geneva. He could be ill, or he could be *gone* – off to somewhere else and forgetting all about us."

Scrope remained relaxed. He was good-natured and sympathetic and rarely became impatient with anyone; and did not now with Hobby, whose anxieties he understood.

For the past ten years, ever since their Cambridge days, Hobhouse had been known to all as '*Byron's Bulldog'*, due to his self-appointed role as Byron's bodyguard. In those younger days, Hobby had got Byron out of many scrapes; admonishing him when he acted foolishly – such as becoming enamoured in London with a young prostitute named Caroline Cameron and getting engaged to her – until Hobby had cautioned and protested and eventually persuaded Byron back to common sense, and back to Cambridge to secure his degree.

In truth, Scrope knew that although Hobhouse was not a homosexual, nor had any tendencies in that direction, yet he adored Byron, and would readily risk his own life to protect him.

As soon as they came out of the dining room, Hobhouse wrote a quick note to Byron, and then gave it to the hotel's manager to be sent post-haste to the Villa Diodati at Cologny:

> *Lausanne – We are so far on our way to join you at your godsend villa; and I put these few lines in activity to give you that important intelligence. – H.*

At last, they were finally travelling along the road to Sécheron, rolling through Nyon and then passing Coppet before reaching Ghenthoud, where they left their carriage, shaking the cramps from their legs, and then embarked into a boat which would row them over the lake towards the vineyard below the Villa Diodati.

~

Byron had not yet received the letter from Lausanne. He was strolling leisurely along the lake's shore with his dog when he saw the boat on the water. He could see two boatmen rowing and four passengers seated in the boat which appeared to be weighed down with trunks and bags.

More English visitors on their way to the Hotel Angleterre!

He moved to saunter on, and then suddenly paused and turned to stare ... and stare hard ... for one of the men in the boat had a familiar side-profile. He was looking straight ahead, but that beak of a nose was *unmistakable.* There was no other in the world like it. In London, Hobhouse's nose had once been described in shape as "exactly like Cockspur Street."

He walked back to the little wooden jetty below Diodati; sitting down on the edge of a boulder to wait and watch as the boat veered towards Cologny. As it drew nearer he stood up and waved, and was answered by two of the men standing up in the boat and excitedly waving back to him.

The first to step ashore with a wide grin on his face was Scrope Davies – Scrope of the *"fierce embraces"* who had made conquests of so many women – now laughingly caught Byron in a fierce embrace, delighted to see him again.

Hobhouse was more bashful, quickly assuming an aggrieved and bored expression, as if all this travelling just to visit Byron was a great nuisance.

"We thought you might have gone," he said huffily. "You sent no letter for us to Lausanne."

Byron smiled, knowing Hobby so well. "And yet here

you are – without any guidance from me."

"With *every step* of guidance from you," Scrope corrected. "Why do you think Hobby insisted you put every detail of your own journey in your letters? So we could follow it step by step and at every turn. He even insisted that we view every church and spire that you had viewed, and stay at the same inns or hotels."

Byron looked archly at Hobhouse, who shrugged. "I can't agree with you about Rubens and his florid canvases though. You were right, Byron, when you said you knew *nothing* about art."

Byron laughed. "Same old Hobby! Come on, let us go up to the house."

Chapter Thirty-Three

~~~

As Hobhouse and Scrope Davies had both brought their valets with them, it was decided that the four remaining empty bedrooms on the first floor should be allotted to each of them.

Polidori was not pleased. He had become used to having the first-floor landing all to himself, but now it would be crowded with strangers – and even worse, two *servants.*

And these two servants, he discovered, were almost as upper-class as their masters. The one called "Joseph" – Mr Hobhouse's valet – insisted he was *not* a valet, but a "gentleman's gentleman".

"What is the difference?" asked Polidori.

"A *great* difference," said Mr Davies' man. "A valet attends solely to clothes, but a gentleman's gentleman is also a butler who not only oversees his master's food menu, but serves it."

"Like Fletcher then? His lordship's servant. Does that mean all three of you will be buzzing around the table at dinner?"

"No, indeed, no. One does not buzz. And one does not wish to infringe when in another man's house," said Joseph. "We shall, of course, be standing nearby ready to assist Mr Fletcher, if needed."

Polidori returned to his room, annoyed and miserable at the prospect of his first-floor landing being crowded with toffs. Descending into self-pity, he finally allowed himself one opium pellet to dull his dissatisfaction.

And yet down in the salon, Byron's delight was increasing by the minute. To be with two old friends – especially *these* two true friends, whom he had known for so long, and who had stood loyally by him throughout the bad and the worse, was like coming in from the freezing cold to the comfort of a warming fire.

Friends ... what did some wise old sage say about the
~~~

importance of good friends? ... *Friends are the siblings God never gave us.*

"And as for our friend, Beau Brummell," Scrope was saying, "you will *weep*, Byron, when I tell you his news. But I will save that until later this evening, after dinner and nearer to bedtime, in case you prefer to weep privately into your pillow."

Byron was intrigued, but Scrope had moved on, relaying the latest news about Webster and others, making Byron laugh so much that Hobhouse sat back with ease, and sighed with contentment.

Life in London had been so dreary these past months, and the one thing Hobby had missed so terribly was Byron's laughter ... that peculiar laugh of his ... merriment occasionally mingled with scorn.

"Shelley and I – *Satanists!* Robert Southey said that? In the *Courier?"*

Byron's laughter was as Hobby expected, amusement mingled with scorn. "I thought Southey had more intelligence. And as for Shelley, the only object of his worship is the glory of Nature."

"Still," Hobhouse said with a note of caution, "associating with Shelley has done you no favours back home."

"Why so?"

"He's a notorious rabble-rouser, always preaching Revolution."

"*Non-violent* Revolution," replied Byron. "So hardly a rabble-rouser."

"And your life here, Byron?" Scrope asked. "Has it been good? Peaceful?"

"Peaceful?" Byron rolled his eyes. "Far from it. Gossips have made my stay here a nightmare. There is no story so absurd that they have not invented it at my cost. I have been watched by binoculars on the other side of the lake, and by binoculars too that must have very distorted optics. I have been accused of every sin, including the corruption of all the grisettes in the Rue Basse – even though I have not been anywhere near the

Rue Basse. And every day they gather in small crowds around my front gate trying to get a glimpse of me, as if I was some kind of man-monster."

"Damned outrageous!" said Hobhouse, his anger rising.

"But these are the English – and all strangers that I have never met and never knew. Unlike the Swiss, I hasten to add, who are far more polite, and many of whom are now my friends."

He told them about Charles Hentsch, De Bonstetten, Madame de Staël. "I receive hospitable invitations from the Genèvese almost every day."

"Madame de Staël?" Hobhouse was very surprised. "She is here in Geneva?"

"She is. And now I owe much to Notre Dame de Coppet. She has been extremely kind to me here, and has always made me very welcome."

During dinner Polidori was bright and cheerful, talking non-stop, but he soon slumped; silenced by the continuous baffled frowns of John Hobhouse, who did not seem to understand a word he was saying.

"Is he sane?" Hobhouse asked with some bewilderment, after Polidori had excused himself to go into Geneva to visit a Dr Odier.

"He's an embarrassment," Byron replied quietly, "but I have not yet had the heart to dismiss him." He looked at Hobhouse. "Will you do it, Hobby?"

"Dismiss Polidori?"

"Yes. You know how to do these things without causing any pain. Find a viable reason that will not dent his very high self-esteem."

Hobhouse considered it. "Perhaps he could return to England with Scrope."

"No, pray, no," Scrope insisted. "I like to do my travelling quietly, with either a good friend or a good book. I can't stand continuous prattle."

Byron stared at him, "You are going back before Hobby?"

Scrope shrugged a smile, "You know how it is with

me, By. My life is regulated by the calendar. So, yes, my time with you will be quite short."

"You travelled all this way – "

"Just to see *you,* my friend – and to drink some of your excellent wines."

Byron sat back in disappointment ... But yes, he knew how it was for Scrope Davies. He was not as free as Hobhouse who was preparing to be a politician and so had little to do. Scrope, on the other hand, was a Fellow at King's College, Cambridge where his duties included the supervision of studies and teaching, so he would have to be back in time for the Autumn term."

"So what is the news of Beau Brummell?" asked Byron. "Why will I weep?"

"Ah, poor Brummell," said Scrope, and looked sad enough to weep himself. Beau Brummell had been one of his close friends, and over the years they had become two of the most successful professional gamblers in England. When Scrope was not teaching in Cambridge, he was at the races with Brummell, and making his own very clever computations on the odds of each horse.

And when there was no racing, Scrope was down in London with Beau Brummell in the Gaming clubs, playing cards, and each amassing a fortune. The yearly stipend which Scrope received from teaching at Cambridge was merely small change.

For years, clever and skilled gambling had always been Scrope's main source of income; and the *sole* income for Beau Brummell.

But now, it seemed, Brummell had lost every penny that had taken him years to win.

"He was foolish," Scrope said, "joining Lord Alvaney and the Marquess of Worcester in investments that would show no return for years, if at all. He should have stuck to the cards and the horses."

Byron and Hobhouse unconsciously leaned forward to listen, for gamblers were notoriously secret about their computations, methods, and especially their *investments*, but Scrope Davies was not prepared to reveal anything more, other than his amazement at the sheer decorum and *style* of George Brummell in everything; even in disaster.

"He held an exquisite dinner party in his apartments," Scrope said, "inviting all and only his favourite friends. We sat down at a table of beautiful china plate and crystal glasses; the usual excellent food and wines; and Brummell as cool and as witty as always. No one suspected the collapse of his fortune. No one knew that this dinner with his friends was one of farewell.

"Yet not long after everyone had left his apartment, " Scrope went on, "Brummell also left, slipping into his carriage and travelling through the night down to Dover, where he had chartered a boat to take him over to Calais. It was not until the following day that his departure was discovered, when the bailiffs reached his apartment in Mayfair and were greeted by a paper tacked onto his door stating simply – *'Gone To The Continent'."*

"He did right to go," said Hobhouse. "At the worst he would have ended up in a debtors' prison, and at the very least, forced outside respectable society – the same society of which he had been king."

Byron was not sure if he wanted to laugh at Brummell's audacity, or cry for him. He was also puzzled. "But how do you know all this, Scrope? His secret journey through the night down to Dover?"

"You can thank me for that," said Hobhouse. "Having travelled to France in the past, en route to Paris, I knew that an Englishman may be beyond English law in France, but he could not travel beyond Calais unless he held a passport."

"And the odds," said Scrope, "against Brummell managing to get a passport in so short a time were not good, so we calculated that he was probably still in Calais."

"So when *we* arrived in Calais," Hobhouse continued, "we searched for him there, and we found him, staying at Dessin's Hotel, just off the Place des Armes. He was surrounded by English, all fawning over him, the famous Beau Brummell, although none of them knew that he was there on the run, because all of them were travelling *back* to England."

"And how was he?" Byron asked.

"Oh, calm and fine and as amusingly droll as always," said Scrope. "He must have held a secret stash of money back, to be able to stay at a hotel as plush as Dessin's."

"All I know about Dessin's Hotel," said Byron, "is that it was once the home of Laurence Sterne, the author of *Tristram Shandy*."

"Brummell has a nice room there, and we sat with him for a time in Dessin's large garden. He asked about you, Byron ..." Scrope helped himself to more wine. "And now that Napoleon is imprisoned on some rocks on the edge of nowhere, Brummell said that he now views this year of 1816 as the year of the downfall of three great men – Bonaparte, Byron, and Brummell."

Byron shrugged. "If I have fallen, the descent has not been very deep. Unlike Bonaparte, I am free to go or stay anywhere I choose. And unlike Brummell, I hold a passport and can return to England whenever I wish."

"Still, I was apprehensive abut him being *forced* to stay in Calais, well, really, for the rest of his life. He can't move forward into France, and he certainly can't go back to London."

Hobhouse nodded. "Surely the change must be unbearable? To go from the greatest city in the world, to a small French seaport – and be stuck there!"

"Yet Brummell is very philosophical about it," said Scrope, "and gives all credit to his own temperament. I asked him if he did not find Calais a melancholy place in comparison to London. 'No,' he answered, 'not at all. I draw, read, and study French; and there are some pretty French actresses here. In truth, I have never been any place, in my life, where I could not be tolerably happy and amuse myself'."

The following morning Scrope amused himself practicing pistol-shooting in the woods with Byron; while Hobhouse preferred to sit quietly by the lake fishing.

Polidori returned from Geneva and joined Hobhouse by the lake. Hobby looked at him in alarm as he sank down on the grass "Good grief, you look ill. Did you get drunk last night in Geneva?"

"I did, alas," Polidori sighed. "Dr Odier, you know, is a man who likes his liquor too much." He turned his head to look back towards the wood. "What is all that gunfire?"

"Pistol practice. Scrope and Byron. Those two have always loved guns. One day they will probably shoot each other."

"Do you mean, by accident?"

"Of course I mean by accident." Hobhouse glanced at the doctor as if once again wondering if he was quite sane. "They would never *deliberately* harm each other."

"No, I suppose not." Polidori lay back languidly on the grass. "I am a very good shot, you know. Is Mister Davies a good shot?"

"Scrope's best shot has always been when he shoots the roll of a dice. He knows exactly how to make the throw."

"But you prefer to fish?"

"When I'm not shooting game in the hunting season, but unlike those two, *I* don't need to practice my aim."

"Are they not very good?"

"Byron has always been an accurate wafer-splitter, but then he's been practising pistol-shooting since a boy. Damnit, wait, yes ... I think I've caught something ... yes ... yes ... Oh, good grief ... *why* would anyone throw a dirty old bag into a beautiful lake!"

"Is she dead?"

"A *handbag,* you fool."

Polidori laughed, turning his head at the sound of a loud calling whistle, and saw his lordship and Mr Davies strolling back towards the house.

"They are back." Polidori stood up. "But how did you expect to catch any fish, Mr Hobhouse, with all the noise of gunfire in the air?"

"All fish are *deaf,"* Hobhouse grunted. "Everyone knows that. They use their lateral line system to detect the movement of other fish or obstacles in the water. This lake may look calm on the surface to you, but underwater the fish are surrounded in their own world by the noise of wave currents and – "

Polidori had strolled off, eager to pretend to his lordship that hc had returned home late last night.

Byron and Scrope were already seated on the balcony when Polidori joined them. Fletcher carried in a tray of coffee and cups. "Some coffee for you, Dr Dori?"

"How refreshing," the doctor replied. "When Mr Shelley was here, it was always tea we were served ... *green* tea."

"Now this afternoon," said Scrope, "if we can get Hobby away from his fishing ..." He paused and looked enquiringly at Polidori: "Are you skilled in any way at tennis, doctor?"

"Tennis? No, not really. All that running here and there ... it affects my balance."

"Oh, that's a pity."

Polidori did not like the look of disappointment on Mr Davies face, and took umbrage. "I am a good shot with a pistol though. I can meet any man in a duel. I once called out Mr Shelley, but he refused and took flight."

"That is not true," Byron corrected. "Shelley is sworn to non-violence, and therefore on principle, will refuse any call to a duel with guns."

"Quite right too," said Scrope. "Guns are solely for protection, and duels should always, and only, be the last resort of gentlemen." He drank back his coffee and stood. "I'll go down and see if I can persuade Hobby to some tennis later."

When Scrope had left the balcony Byron sat back looking at Polidori. "I hope, Poli, that while he is here, you will never consider threatening Scrope to a duel."

"Why? Because he can't shoot?"

"No," Byron was laughing gently, "because his first shot is always bang on target."

Polidori said nothing; and Byron went on: "A few years ago, in London, in a gaming club, words had passed between Lord Foley and Scrope Davies, words of insult that Scrope did not believe he could allow to pass, so he called me in as his second in a duel with Foley. Scrope always chose me as his second, because I knew how to mediate between two men bent on carnage; and if that did not work, Scrope knew how to step in and end the matter ..." Byron paused to take a drink of his coffee.

"What happened?" asked Polidori. "Did Mr Davies win?"

"No, because on the morning of the duel, I got Foley to make an apology, and I got Scrope to take it, and then left them to live happy ever after. Both were fond of high play in the clubs, and although Foley is a titled peer, Scrope is a gentleman in every sense of the word, and that I can swear to. Although very mild, he is not fearful, and so dead a shot, that, although Foley is the thinnest of men, Scrope would have split him like a cane, if it had come to the test."

Polidori swallowed. "But you stopped him."

"As a second, that is my first duty. Afterwards, both men conducted themselves very well, and I'm certain Lord Foley never once insulted Scrope Davies afterwards."

"Yes, well ... that is good," said Polidori uneasily, "but why, I wonder, do you tell *me* this?"

Byron shrugged. "Just a warning, Poli, about that tongue of yours. Keep it tight."

Chapter Thirty-Four

~~~

In England, Mary's father, William Godwin, was not only furious, but also shamed by Fanny Imlay's suicide. It was the act of an ungrateful stepdaughter. Buried in an unmarked grave, her death was to be kept secret. Relatives and neighbours had been told that she had gone to Ireland. Later they would be informed that she had died over there, after suffering from a severe winter cold.

In the privacy of their household, and renouncing all guilt, Godwin and Mrs Clairmont blamed the girl's death on Shelley, and only Shelley, insisting he had infatuated and led on all three girls, and then had shunned poor Fanny who had been hopelessly in love with him.

Mary was outraged, blaming Claire's mother for always spoiling her own daughter while continually neglecting Fanny. "Poor timid Fanny, whom *you* always treated like a servant! I had my father, Claire had you, but poor Fanny had nobody. To both of you, she was always the *unwanted daughter."*

Mary was racked with regrets. wishing she had not left Fanny behind; telling Shelley, "I feel so guilty. We *should* have taken her with us and offered her a happier and more proper asylum."

"Asylum? With him?" declared Claire's mother derisively. "Did his own father not try to get him locked up in an asylum when he was sent down from Oxford? Did he not seduce and run away with you – even though he had a wife and children? Did he not mesmerise my little girl into going abroad with you too – and now everyone knows about your brazen *ménage à trois* – everyone!"

They abruptly left the house in Skinner Street and also left London. Shelley's only determination now was
~~~

to keep Claire's pregnancy a secret; something they could not do in London, where they were all known. Once the child was born they would say it was the child of a sick relative, whom they were fostering.

They headed west, deciding the city of Bath would be as good a place as any; renting a house at 5 Abbey Churchyard, near the centre.

Mary felt sympathy for all unmarried mothers, knowing how hard life would be for her if she did not have Shelley to care and provide for her. Yet she found it hard to feel any sympathy for Claire, who now seemed to have cemented herself to Shelley as her caretaker.

The house was pretty and roomy, with a large secluded garden at the back; yet as soon as they had moved in, Shelley was preparing to head back to London. He had business to attend to. A publisher to call on in Albermarle Street. John Murray was now *the* leading publisher in England. Any book published by Murray immediately led to keen interest and large orders.

He said to Mary: "When I deliver Byron's manuscripts to Murray, do you think I should also take the opportunity to show him *Queen Mab* and some of my other poems?"

"Oh, yes, *do*," said Claire, before Mary had a chance to answer. "Show him just how very talented you are and he will *beg* to be allowed to buy your copyrights."

Shelley smiled. "I'm grateful to know you have such faith in me, Claire, but ... well, we will see."

Chapter Thirty-Five

~~~

In Switzerland, following the exact route of Shelley's itinerary, Byron and his friends, accompanied by Polidori, made the same journey to Chamonix and Mont Blanc.

Standing and staring up at the towering Mont Blanc it was hard for Byron not be impressed at the grandeur of the mighty scene. From the top, gazing down below, all humans must look as small as pinheads scattered at its base.

Mont Blanc is the monarch of mountains,

They crowned him long ago

On a throne of rocks, in a robe of clouds,

With a diadem of snow.

Gazing around him in awe at the huge glaciers and snowy mountains, Byron had not noticed another small group of tourists standing nearby, until one of the women said loudly to her companions:

"If you ask me, it is all rather rural. Have you *ever* seen anything more rural?"

Byron turned to his friends in stunned amazement. "Rural?" he said. "As if this was Highgate or Hampstead or Hayes or Basingstoke – rural! Rocks, pines, torrents, glaciers, clouds and summits of eternal snow far above them – and *rural!*"

Turning to make their way back down, they saw another lady sitting on a small bench, fast asleep.

Again Byron looked at his friends in amazement. "Here we are – in the most *anti-narcotic* spot in the world, with the constant sound of ice and snow crashing down in avalanches – and she is asleep. Excellent!"
~~~

Hobhouse gave Scrope Davies a wide grin as Byron walked on in disgust. "I would say our friend is now back to his old sarcastic self again."

Scrope grinned and agreed. "Excellent!"

Ten days later they returned to Diodati laden down with mountain crystals, agates, and necklaces for Scrope to take back to England from Byron. Some were gifts for Augusta and her children; the crystal necklace was for Byron's own child, Ada.

Upon their entering Diodati, Fletcher was horrified to see that Byron had also brought back a new dog – an ugly small dog that looked as if it had been neglected, and worse – it had no tail.

"My, but he's a sorry-looking hound!" Fletcher said. "Would it not have been kinder to drown him?"

"I think I would prefer to drown you," Byron said flatly. "Look closer, Fletcher, and you will see his beauty."

Fletcher moved closer and stared at the dog, shaking his head "No, I can't see it, my lord; he still looks an ugly little brute to me."

Polidori giggled.

"And what good is a dog with no tail?" Fletcher asked, mystified. "How will we know if he is happy or not with no wagging going on?"

Byron closed his arms around the pup, holding him tighter to his chest. "Pay no attention to him, Mutz," he said comfortingly to the dog. "Fletcher is a cruel barbarian whom you must bite at every opportunity."

"Mutz?" Fletcher said. "What kind of a name is that?"

"*Mutz* is a perfect name for him, because it signifies 'no tail', Byron said. "Now, as to his breed ... I would say he is a cross between a German Shepherd dog and a Swiss mountain dog."

Fletcher was so annoyed about the addition of another dog, he almost forgot to give Byron the two letters that had arrived for him that morning.

Two letters marked on the outside 1, 2, from Claire

Clairmont, from her new address in Bath ... Shelley had gone up to London, but his ambitions there, on his own account, had not been successful.

We had a letter from him today, wherein he mentions having called on Murray with your new Canto of 'Childe Harold'. He says Murray complimented him on his poem, which shows what a mean-spirited paltry soul Murray is, and fit for nothing in this world but to give you heaps of money. I know I would not spare him.

I am sure you will be sorry to hear poor Shelley has dreadful health – vile spasms in his head. This is all that vile nauseous animal Doctor Polidori's doing. He will do you some mischief, so pray send him away, and hire a clever steady physician.

Are you angry with me now dearest that I have told you all the news to please you. Perhaps it is my health that makes me so melancholy and peevish. I suffer from Rheumatism. Add to this the unhappy death of that poor girl. I passed the first fourteen years of my life with her & though I cannot say I had so great an affection for her as might be expected, yet she is the first person of my acquaintance who has died & her death so horrible too.

Your favourite Mary is nauseous enough to think it wonderful that you have kept your promises. I wonder if you ever think of me. I daresay not. I am melancholy and ill-humoured and so I won't write any more.

Ever affectionately,

Clara.

So, she had changed her name again, from Claire to Clara. He opened her second letter, which was more of the same – more grumbling and resentment. Shelley had returned from London.

"And so, instead of £1000, you are to have two thousand from Murray for your new Poems, which quite delights me who likes you to have money.

Shelley saw Kinnaird who told him that Lady Byron – usually called your wife – was in good health and in London on a visit to your sister, Mrs Leigh. So much for the gossiping of Coppet and its stock of old novel-writing ladies who pretend to faint when a handsome poet makes his appearance. I would have them all set to reap the corn, which could not fail to cure them of meddling in other people's affairs.

Godwin says he likes your 'Monody' which is everywhere with everybody. Good Heavens! with such a reputation, how happy you ought to be! My dearest Albè might be the happiest of creatures if others would let him alone. You should have a nice house to live in; my little girl (I hope it will be a girl) to educate; the friends you love best to visit you; and we should have nice poems written by you and copied by me to improve this vile world, which always reviles in proportion to its envy. If I could only think this would be the case.

Mary has been musing how to send you her message. She says "my love" is too familiar, and so it is changed into "remembrances." Kinnaird told Shelley that you told him I was an atheist and a murderer. You see the stupidity of people, so be chary of my name. A fine character I shall have among you all, when I am nothing more than an innocent quiet little woman, very fond of Albè –

He threw down the letter, unwilling to read any more. Her pompous way of talking to him was an insult in itself.

His face was tight with anger ... How dare she think she could so quickly replace his infant daughter with talk of her own "little girl" and a nice house for them to live in where he would write nice poems.

He would never live anywhere with her – not even in *Paradise* if he ever got there! He would generously support her child, but that is all he would do. He would prefer to go to damnation, than to ever be forced to see Claire Clairmont again.

~

While Byron had been reading his letters, Scrope Davies had gone up to his room to pack, and Hobhouse had gone up to his room to rest.

It had been an enjoyable tour of Chamonix and Mont Blanc, for the most part; but unlike Byron and Scrope Davies who had travelled together, Hobhouse was mentally exhausted, due to being forced to share *his* carriage every day with Dr Polidori.

Only when they were riding their horses in single file along the narrow mountain passes did he get some relief from the doctor's childish prattle and his claim to be an expert geologist, lecturing Hobhouse at yawning length about the formations and elements of every mountain they saw.

And if the doctor was not praised and agreed with, or he suspected some doubt or impatience in his listener, his mood would abruptly change, sitting sulkily silent and stony-faced, refusing to speak or engage in any further conversation.

Hobhouse turned sideways on his pillow, but sleeping in the daytime was not usual for him. Sighing, he got up off the bed and sat down at his table to update his journal, jotting down his bafflement about the strange doctor, Polidori.

> *Dr Polidori – He does not answer to Madame de Staël's definition of a happy man, whose inclinations must be squared with his capacities. Poor fellow! He is anything but amiable, and has a most unmeasured ambition, as well as inordinate vanity; – all the true ingredients of misery.*

After dinner that evening, it was Byron himself who dismissed Polidori. He did it kindly and gently, and without any malice.

Polidori felt close to tears, but what could he say or do? His lordship had kindly thanked him for his service, and had paid him double the amount of wages due to him, and also the cost of his voyage home.

"Scrope leaves tomorrow," Byron said. "And in a week or so, Hobhouse and I will be moving on to Italy.

It is a country I have long wished to visit."

"Where in Italy?"

Byron shrugged. "From here ... across the border into Como, and then onto Milan."

"Milan? You intend to lodge there?"

"For a week or two. Ludovico di Brême has sent me an invitation to call at his home if I go there."

"Yes ... Signor di Brême ... he was a nice man ..."

Sick with grief, Polidori sat down on the chair by his desk. He did not want to go back to England. His time in Lord Byron's houschold had been the happiest time in his entire life. Even when he had been censured by his lordship, the resentment had never lasted long. And even when he had hated Shelley, he was still happy to be who he was, and where he was ... And now he must go? Back to being a nonentity in England? And never to see or speak to Lord Byron again?

"My lord," he said, looking up ... but Lord Byron had gone from the room.

Polidori jumped up from the chair and went in search of him, and found Byron standing alone on the balcony, his back to him, his hands on the balustrade, looking down on the lake.

"My lord, I confess to you, I am dismayed and shocked! I cannot comprehend why my employment with you has now ended – or why it has lasted such a short time?"

Byron looked over his shoulder, gazing back at him silently, still unable to comprehend why Polidori's employment with him had lasted so long.

Returning to his room and the chair at his desk, Polidori sat immovable for some time, pale and listless, until eventually he managed to indolently lift his pen and write a letter to his father.

> *Lord Byron has determined on our parting, – not upon any quarrel, but on account of our temperaments not suiting. I believe the fault, if any,*

has been on my part; I am not accustomed to having a master, and therefore my conduct was not free and easy.

Getting drunk, drugged, involved in brawls and being arrested – Polidori knew his conduct had always been *too* free and easy – but he had no intention of allowing his father to know that.

Nor had he any intention of going back to England and never seeing Lord Byron again. The cut was too sharp, too swift. too intolerable. There had to be a way of rectifying the situation. Perhaps if he was to offer to behave better, more sedately, more studiously? Perhaps if he was to offer to work for free?

No ... that would not persuade him, he cared so little for money. Only yesterday he had received a letter from *'Le Pastor De Cologny"* begging for help for the poor of Switzerland in winter, and had responded by sending a draft on *Monsieur Hentsch & Co Bank* for the sum of three hundred francs. Polidori had thought it was much too much, but of course he could not say so. One did not tell Lord Byron what to do – nor could he be persuaded to change his mind, as he had just sought to do on the balcony – as always, he had responded with a mildness in his voice, but his decision had been made.

No, there was nothing now to be done to change things, yet how could he stay here another day – in this house, this life – knowing he would soon no longer be a part of it anymore.

No, he could not bear even the thought of it, nor would he be able to say goodbye to Lord Byron without weeping tears. He was a man one got attached to, God knows why, for even at the best of times he was a reserved enigma. He had hoped to become his friend, but he had remained an employee; yet even that was a gift that he had not appreciated to the full.

Something inside him disintegrated and broke apart, rendering him heartbroken and weeping silently and copiously. He could not bear to say goodbye to Lord Byron, truly, as some said, "the greatest poet that England had ever known, apart from Shakespeare." No, he could not stay here, not now. He would hide his tears and run away.

~~~

That same evening, Byron and Hobhouse said their farewells to Scrope Davies who needed to reach the gates of Geneva before they closed at ten o'clock. The following morning at dawn, when the gates opened again, Scrope would be inside a coach making his journey back to England.

Sad to see him go, Byron told Scrope he would see him again – "In England, in the spring."

Scrope looked at him. "In England, in the spring? Do you promise?"

Byron nodded. "I have to go back occasionally, if only to see my daughter."

"Then God bless Ada!" Scrope said smiling. "How old is she now?"

"Nine months. You will make sure Augusta passes on my gifts to her from Mont Blanc?"

Scrope nodded, and then hesitated. "I wish I could have stayed longer, but unfortunately – "

"Unfortunately," Hobhouse said airily, "Newmarket speculations on horses call you homewards by certain days not recognised in our calendar. We know, Scrope, we know, but that does not mean we forgive you deserting us for the racing nags."

"What else is a professional gambler to do?" Scrope laughed, climbed into the carriage and shut the door behind him. Once seated, he dropped down the window and looked seriously at Byron. "Don't forget, my friend," he said, "we will meet again, in England, in the spring."
~~~

PART NINE

~

Pray continue to like Shelley – he is a very good – very clever – but a very singular man – he was a great comfort to me here by his intelligence and good nature.

Byron to Douglas Kinnaird
Diodati, September 29th 1816

Chapter Thirty-Six

~~~

"Dr Dori is gone," Fletcher told Hobhouse the following morning. "He must have set off before dawn. Mind, he does not have much to carry, just a few clothes and his medical bag."

"Gone?" Hobhouse was surprised. "But he knew that he was free to stay here until we *all* leave and the house is closed up."

Fletcher shrugged. "That's Dr Dori for you. I suppose since Lord Byron had given him his pay, he saw no reason to stay."

When Fletcher carried in Byron's morning tea, his attitude had changed from happy to anxious. "Am I the next to be sent home, my lord?"

Byron turned sideways and looked at him with half-shut eyes. "Would I be able to cope without you, Fletcher?"

"I doubt it."

"Surely in Italy I could find someone more agreeable and less annoying than you?"

"I doubt that too."

"Do you? Oh well then ..." Byron turned away, "pray close the door behind you and allow me to go back to my dreams."

"What about your tea?"

"Give it to Mutz."

"Mutz? Is it tea for him now? After all the roast turkey he was fed last night. And not just scraps but the *best* and thickest slices. Next you will be ordering me to fill his water dish with champagne!"

"Fletcher, if you don't scram and quick, I will shoot you dead."

"Even Joseph, Mr Hobhouse's valet, was shocked. He said no dog should be coddled in such a way," Fletcher went on. "And *Leander* was not too pleased either,
~~~

because he only got half as much. And as for poor little Jade – would it please you to know that Mutz also lapped up most of her milk?"

At the breakfast table, Hobhouse got a jolt when he heard the gunshot. He jumped up and ran towards Byron's room, slowing as he saw Fletcher coming out carrying a tray.

He stared at Fletcher. "What happened? I thought it was a gunshot I heard."

"Aye, it was." Fletcher shrugged. "But he always fires high above my head."

"You see now, Byron," Hobhouse remonstrated later, "why some people say you are mad."

"And bad, and dangerous to know," Byron said laughingly. "Well, let them think so, if it keeps them far away from me."

"To be honest, I am more concerned about Fletcher. That's a dangerous game you two play."

"Dangerous? No. As soon as Fletcher sees my hand reach for the pistol by my bed, he always ducks down, and I always fire high – but it gets him to shut up and scram, and that's the purpose."

"What about the holes?"

"What holes?"

Hobhouse frowned. "Surely you don't intend to leave Diodati with bullets and holes in your bedroom wall?"

"Certainly not. And the holes are not in the *wall*, because no matter where we live, I always fire straight into that line of join between the wall and the ceiling."

"Wall or ceiling, a bullet-hole is still a bullet-hole."

"And Fletcher always deals with it." Byron finally poured himself some tea. "Whenever we are preparing to vacate an establishment, off he goes to my bedroom carrying his little wooden lathe and tub of plaster, and then up he sits on his ladder making the holes vanish and smoothing over his work with some matching paint. He is very skilled at it, a master in fact. In my opinion, as I have told Fletcher many times, he is another Michelangelo, or an undiscovered Leonardo da Vinci, in potential."

"And what does Fletcher say when you tell him all that?"

"He agrees."

Hobhouse sat back and sighed. "He once told me in Albany that you fire him every month, but I didn't realise he meant with a gun."

Mr Berger came in carrying a letter. "Milord, the messenger at the door says it is urgent and he has been instructed to wait for a reply."

The letter was from Madame de Staël, and the words caused Byron to smile with delight. "Tonight, Hobby, we are begged to go to Coppet, because many of our old friends from London will be there ... Lord and Lady Jersey, the Hollands, the Rawdons ... and all wishing to see us."

"And the Baroness von Holstein de Staël *begs,* does she?"

Byron nodded. "She does ... 'I beg you to come ... and pray bring your sarcastic and obnoxious friend Mr Hobhouse with you'."

"She does *not* say that –" Hobhouse reached over to snatch the letter from Byron's hand – crestfallen as he read the note himself: "She does not even mention me!"

"She probably thinks you returned to England with Scrope Davies."

"Of course, that must be why," agreed Hobhouse with relief. "If Madame de Staël knew that I was still here, she would undoubtedly be most keen to see me again. The last time she and I met in London, she introduced me to someone as 'my dear friend'."

Later that evening, when Germaine de Staël stepped out to the courtyard at Coppet to welcome Lord Byron and John Hobhouse, she could not help thinking what an odd-matched pair they looked – Byron, the handsome pale and slender *homme fatal*, taller than average – and John Hobhouse, short and stocky and strong; and every bit the formal and proper English gentleman.

"*Mes amis ...* " she welcomed one as warmly as the other; and she was glad Mr Hobhouse had come tonight, because to him she would give the latest news from London – news she had received in a letter only that afternoon – cruel news which she felt would be kinder passed on to Byron by a close friend. *She* did not wish to be the one to tell him, and none of the English here knew that news yet, but they too would be angry when they learned of it.

Within minutes of entering the salon, Byron was enclosed in thc dclighted circle of his English friends, surrounding him like a prince, and all trying to get their words in at once.

And while they were doing so, Madame de Staël took Hobhouse's arm and walked him away to the library. "You and I, a little talk, yes?"

Inside the library she poured two brandies, and then saw the alarm on Hobhouse's face as she told him her news.

"But why?" said Hobhouse, his anger mounting. "I know she is a cold and vindictive individual, but why would she do this? And why *now?"*

Madame shrugged. "All those gossips writing letters from the Hotel Angleterre. Oh, so much mischief, and so many scandals! He should not have become so friendly with the atheists – to them that was his biggest crime."

Hobhouse nodded. "Even before I left London, Lady Melbourne was very concerned, and asked me to find out if any of the gossip was true."

"Lady Melbourne – the aunt of his wife?"

"Yes, but she has nothing to do with her niece now and declares Annabella's behaviour to be unforgivable."

"Tell me something – do you know? – Why did Byronn marry that plain and prim young woman?"

Hobhouse confessed that he still did not know. "All I know for certain," he said, "is that on the same date he responded to one of Miss Milbanke's numerous letters to inquire politely about the level of her interest in him; he also wrote to me by the same post, asking if I would go on a journey to the Continent with him, saying he was resolved on going to Italy the following week."

Madame's grave expression changed to one of confusion. "What are you saying? I don't understand."

"*She* replied by *return of post* – accepting his marriage proposal – but his letter had contained no proposal of marriage; yet as she had read it as such, how could he withdraw without losing his honour, or damaging hers?"

"Did he not tell her she was mistaken? What did he do?"

"What could he do? She lived up North, and he had met her only *twice* in London, before she started all her letters to him. He was exasperated and annoyed at the misunderstanding, but he was loath to hurt her. So he resigned himself to a fate he could not control, and spent the next two months convincing himself that, judging by her letters, she was a kind and virtuous young lady who would undoubtedly make him a very *good* wife, and provide him with some peace and domestic refuge from all the female fanatics constantly at his door."

"*Mon Dieu!* Was he such a fool?"

"Personally," said Hobhouse, "I lay a lot of the blame for the marriage at Lady Melbourne's door. She was like a mother figure to Byron, always advising and guiding him, and always extolling the virtues of her *niece*. I think she and Miss Milbanke were conspirators. Also, as it turned out, Miss Milbanke was not a rich 'heiress' after all – her father was stone-broke and up to his eyes in heavy debt. So Lord Byron's estate at Newstead Abbey must have been very appealing for the money it would fetch, if sold."

"We need another brandy!" Madame reached for the decanter. "But you see," she said as she poured, "that is the big difference between the French and the English. We marry for love, but for the English it is always about money."

Hobhouse was indignant. "Byron got no money out of

it! He still hasn't been paid her measly dowry."

"And now the marriage is over ..." Madame de Staël shrugged her disgust. "Still, it is Byronn's own fault for being such a fool. A young man who loves roses should not have married a field flower, not under any circumstances."

In the salon, Byron was having a wonderful time with his London friends, enjoying every minute of seeing them again.

Throughout the rest of the night he hardly saw Hobhouse, apart from across the table at dinner, when he noticed poor Hobby was being bombasted with the opinions of Wilhelm von Schlegel, a dogmatic little man, who seemed to be always at Madame's dinners.

"Von Schlegel," Hobby whispered to him later, "who the deuce is he? What does he do?"

"He translates Shakespeare for the Germans, which is very tolerant of the Germans."

"I prefer De Bonstetten."

"So do I, but his English is very poor. On my last visit here he insisted I tell him about Greece, and now he thinks '*Piraeus*' is a friend of mine."

"Piraeus, the seaport?"

"Exactly."

In the boat back across the lake to Diodati, Byron was in such high cheer and good humour; Hobhouse did not have the heart to spoil it for him by passing on bad news.

The following day another invitation arrived for Byron, from Lord and Lady Jersey who had taken up residence at Maison Verte in Geneva.

"Byron looked up from the letter. "We are begged to go."

"Tonight?"

"No, this afternoon. A garden party."

"And do we go?"

"Lady Jersey says the party is in my honour, so I suppose we must. She says some of my Genèvese friends such as Charles Hentsch will be there."

And so the socialising went on. Two evenings later it was Charles Hentsch who held a dinner-party at his villa of *Mon Repose*.

Everyone knew that the summer was coming to a close, and soon the autumn would set in. And when the autumn came, all the visitors would be gone, and Geneva would become dull and empty again.

Chapter Thirty-Seven

~~~

Almost six days had passed since his conversation with Madame de Staël at Coppet, and still Hobhouse had not had the heart to apprise Byron of the cruel news.

Perhaps he had delayed in doing so, he told himself, because he was hoping it was not true. Who could know for sure these days, when the world seemed to be spinning on unfounded gossip most of the time.

Or perhaps, he reflected honestly, that his heart had been all for himself and he had dreaded the upset the news would cause. Since he had arrived in Geneva, going here and there and everywhere with Byron, it had been like old times in London again, and he had been enjoying himself most entirely; and although not wishing to tempt the wrath of fate, he had even dared to write down in his journal that he was happy.

But poor Byron would be devastated when he was told ... anger or tears ... it would be one or the other ... so perhaps he had been right to adopt the policy of *delay, delay, delay* in saying anything at all, just to keep the sun shining and the laughter going for as long as possible.

Yet later that day, during luncheon on the balcony, when Fletcher handed Byron a letter which bore his lawyer's seal, Hobhouse realised his policy of waiting for "the right time" had been a terrible blunder.

Now the news would hit Byron like a brick in the face, and he had not been warned that it was coming. After all, in retrospect, had that not been the reason why Madame de Staël had told *him* – so that he could warn Byron, and prepare him – so that he would not be caught off-guard?

As Byron opened the letter, Hobhouse quickly sat forward and opened his mouth to speak, then sat back slowly and resumed his silence, gravely watching his
~~~

friend while he read the letter.

"God damn..." Byron put the letter down, appearing to be utterly stunned.

"What is it?" Hobby asked, his face reddening with guilt.

"A new piece of vengeful treachery ... one I had never thought of."

"What?"

Byron told him – his wife had made his daughter a ward of the Court of Chancery.

Hobby rubbed a hand against his cheek. "There *is* something you can do. You can write back to Hanson and instruct him to –"

"No! I will not write to Hanson, not yet!" Byron moved quickly and stood, his eyes now blazing with anger. "First, I will write directly to her – *Lady Bitch!"*

In his bedroom, at his desk, he could hardly hold his pen, his hands now trembling with his rage. He inhaled a deep and slow breath for calm, and then began to write with a steadier hand.

To Lady Byron.

It was generally understood that all legal proceedings were to terminate in the act of our separation. To what then, am I to attribute the news of which I am apprised? The object is evident – it is to deprive me of my paternal right over my child. You and yours might have been satisfied with the outrages I have already suffered – if not by your design – at least by your means.

Now I am made aware that our daughter is to be the entail of our disunion – the inheritor of our bitterness.

If you think to reconcile yourself to yourself – by accumulating harshness against me – you are again mistaken – you are not happy nor even tranquil – nor will you ever be so – even to the very moderate degree that is permitted in general to humanity.

For myself I have a confidence in my good fortune which will yet bear me through – the reverses which have occurred – were what I should have expected – did not every thing appear to intimate a deliberate intention of wilful malice on your part.

However, I shall live to pity you one day or another – if I live – and if not – then time and Nemesis will do what I would not. You will smile at this piece of prophecy – do so – but recollect it – it is justified by all human experience. No one was ever the cause of great injury to others – without a requital – I have paid and am paying for mine – so will you.

BYRON

To Mr John Hanson
Lincoln's Inn Chambers
London.

Dear Sir – I request you to get me the best advice on how to proceed in Chancery, because I am determined to reclaim the child to myself – as her natural guardian – in consequence of the Milbankes' recent conduct. I have done what I could to avoid extremities, but this shall not deter me from asserting my right – now I authorise and desire you to get this Chancery Bill – answer it – & proceed upon it. I shall apply to have the child, and to assume the care and personal charge of my daughter – in short, as they have begun – I will go on – I will return to England directly if necessary.

BYRON

"Of course, that is what she wants," Hobby said, "for you to return."

Byron looked at him, frowning. "Why would she want that?"

"To keep open the possibility of a reconciliation or to bring you back to the battle – either would suit her, in my opinion."

"Again, pray answer – *why* would she want to do either?"

"Because without you there as the leading man in her public drama, she is *nothing* – as she *was* nothing before you married her and brought her to London and the attention of the press and public."

"Hobby ..." Byron was astounded at the outburst, but Hobhouse's anger against himself and against Miss Milbanke was spiralling.

"What was she? – a country bumpkin from the deserted wilds of Durham who rarely saw a stranger, and did nothing all day but sit and read books and say her nightly prayers! Now the fame of being Lady Byron has gone to her head and she wants to remain centre stage, but the lights are dimming and the curtain is coming down, because without *you* there, she is becoming a person of no importance again. Even the press are tired of her. To them she is an old story now – a six months old story – but you go back and fight her in court and *out* they will all come again, like hungry vultures!"

"I have to fight for my child."

"Of course you do, but don't give her the satisfaction of dragging you back to be mauled again by the press – let your *lawyers* do all the fighting on your behalf. Hire the best, pay them well, and for God's sake get *rid* of John Hanson."

"Hanson?" Byron was indignant, shaking his head. "No, I could never get rid of John Hanson. He has looked after me and my interests since I was a boy of ten years old."

"Yes, and now he's getting old, and he's getting slow, and the Milbankes will wipe the floor with him."

"*He* will not be advocating in court on my behalf – a barrister will."

"I know that, but make sure Hanson instructs a good one – a first-rate King's Counsel of the Silk – accept nothing less."

Later, when Byron had gone for a walk along the banks of the lake with his two dogs, Hobhouse remained on the balcony, regretting his outburst, and even more bitterly regretting his advice to Byron.

He had come here directly from his home in London and he had heard all the gossip about Byron's *'Satanic league of incest and orgies'* with the atheist Shelley and his two immoral females.

All nonsense, of course, but there *had* been a girl in a white dress who was seen going up to the Villa Diodati late at night, and then was seen again near the lighted windows of the villa's salon. And that same girl had stayed as a resident at the Hotel d'Anglettere; and no doubt the proprietor of the hotel had been able to supply her name, from the register, to any investigator who might have called there on behalf of the Milbankes.

There were even reports circulating around London

of Byron, seen in high frolic, running after the girl across the villa's lawn on numerous occasions – which showed just what little truth the gossips actually knew or spewed about Byron – a man born with a lame foot, who could only walk with a limp, and had never in his life been able to *run* anywhere.

But all the rumours had no doubt stirred Annabella into a jealous rage and set her heart on exacting even more revenge. She had never forgiven Byron from the day she realised he did not love her as she loved him; certain he did not love her at all, and so she had been determined to destroy him.

Hobhouse moved to his feet to stand by the balustrade and looked out, still thinking of Miss Milbanke, for he never could think of her as anything else but *Miss* Milbanke.

He had been Byron's best man at the small private wedding in the Milbanke's drawing-room – arranged so quickly by Annabella herself that Byron was given little time to change his mind and withdraw.

And as well as being the groom's best man, he had also been the only guest at that strange wedding on that freezing-cold January morning ... Why that bitter month? And why the rush to seal the match? Their child was not born until eleven months later ... and Byron had been unhappy for almost as long as that – until his daughter was born – and seeing his love for the child, Annabella had even accused him of loving the child more than her.

Hobhouse looked up at the low hovering clouds which threatened rain ... In his opinion she was an evil woman in many respects, despite all her show of religious virtue; and no doubt the pantomime of the poor wronged wife would now begin again, and all the world would rally to pity her ... especially as Lady Melbourne had told him that she now kept a wound constantly open on her bandaged arm, underneath which leeches regularly sucked on the blood, leaving her with a pale and wraith-like appearance. No wonder

Byron was blamed and *she* was pitied by so many.

And knowing all this, *he* had advised his friend to hire the best King's Counsel that money could buy?

Foolish, foolish, *foolish* advice – because with all the gossip, and some of it provable; especially about the immoral girl in the white dress – not even a first-rate Kings Counsel of the Silk could win a custody case for Byron now.

Chapter Thirty-Eight

~~~

"Stay for me in Italy," begged Madame de Staël. "Will you stay for me there, in Italy, until I join you?"

"Of course we will wait for you," Byron assured her, without any intention of doing so.

"And after Italy, the three of us, we can go down the coast and sail over to Greece."

"Ah, Greece ..." Byron smiled and placed a hand over his heart.

"You still want to go back?"

"I do, if only to get away from men like Pictet and Von Schlegel who, for all their talk about Greece, have *no idea* just how oppressed the poor Greek people are, and will remain so, unless they rebel against the Turks."

"But not while *we* are there," smiled Madame de Staël. "No fight for freedom while we are there, eh? Just blue seas and golden sands, yes?"

Byron smiled again, but there was a sadness in his eyes; and when she reached up to put her hands on his shoulders and kissed his face on each cheek in farewell, he held her for a moment and then kissed her face also; something he had never done before, and it brought a glaze of tears to her eyes as she said quietly, "*Mon cher Byronn, mon Byronn ...* "

In the boat on the lake heading back to Diodati, Hobhouse was still perplexed. "Were you serious, about us waiting for her in Italy?"

"No."

"Then why say we will?"

"To be kind."

"How, pray? By lying to her?"

"She will not be coming to Italy, Hobby, and she knows it." Byron's gaze moved slowly around Lake Leman. "She has come home to Geneva to die."

"What?"
~~~

"Home to her father's château, where they both lived long ago. She once told me he was the only man she ever truly loved."

Hobhouse was startled. "To die? How do you know? Did she tell you?"

"No, but I know it, and she knows it too. She has had an eventful life, but now she is very tired. Her talk of joining us in Italy and going to Greece is only a dream. It would be foolish to wait for her."

Hobhouse was stunned into a silence, not knowing what to think; but then Byron had said intuitive or prophetic things like this in the past, and they had always proved true.

~~~

In the Hotel d'Angleterre the following morning, Monsieur Dejean was up in the attic room, peering through his telescope and not liking what he saw. "*Mon Dieu!*"

Rushing down the stairs, he barged into his wife's sitting room to tell her the bad news. "He is going – leaving us – Milord Byron!"

"No!" Madame Dejean could not believe it. "Are you sure, Jacques, are you sure?"

"*Oui!* His carriage and two calèche – all are being packed by the servants. Even the two dogs are now on board one of the calèche – and then I saw a servant carry out a small animal in a cage – the little black cat I think? The one he brought here."

"*Mon Dieu*!" Madame' Dejean's hand went over her mouth. This was terrible news. "But we still have *guests,* Jacques, and all they want is to see him – the famous Lord Byron!"

Jacques suddenly stood still. "We need not tell them, if they do not know ... We can pretend he is still there, if they do not know."

"How could they know – it is not yet the breakfast
~~~

hour. Not for one more hour."

"*Nous ne dirons rien.*" Jacques put a firm finger to his lips. "We will say *nothing*, and say it well."

~

Hobhouse's love for Byron was as deep-rooted as a tree. No scandal could shake it. His friendship knew no sacrifice beyond his capability. His aim was to protect Byron at all costs, and in every way.

Mr Berger, the Swiss servant, who was now also going to Italy, did not know that; and so he wondered what quarrel had caused Mr Hobhouse to leave the villa two hours earlier, dressed for travelling in hat and gloves, walking off briskly towards Geneva's main road.

"Why so?" he asked Fletcher. "M'sieur Hobhouse, he does not come with us to Italia?"

"Certainly he is coming with us." Fletcher hefted the last portmanteau up onto the back of the caleche. "That's why he has gone on ahead, to lead the way."

"Walking? On foot? To Italia?"

"Aye."

Berger looked around him, bemused. How could the Swiss understand these English? They were all a little mad. On the lake Monsieur Shelley had refused to allow his lordship to save him from drowning if the boat capsized in the storm. And now Monsieur Hobhouse was *walking* to Como.

"He won't be walking *all* the way," Fletcher explained when all the baggage was boarded. "But you see, these English gentlemen, especially the friends who were with his lordship at Cambridge – all are great walkers. There was one time – the day after his lordship's twenty-first birthday at Newstead Abbey – Mr Hobhouse and Charles Matthews walked all the way from Nottingham to London, more than a hundred miles."

Berger was even more puzzled. "Why did they do that?"

"I dunno." Fletcher shrugged. "All I *do* know, from

the talk I heard from his lordship afterwards, is that they had a quarrel halfway there, Hobhouse and Matthews, and so they walked the last fifty miles to London on opposite sides of the road, and not another word was spoken between them – not until they reached Highgate when one finally apologised and the other accepted, and so they continued on into London the best of friends."

Fletcher grinned. "That's gentlemen for you, Mr Berger. They're not like us, no, not like us."

"Did they have no carriage to take them? A calèche or a char-à-banc?"

"No, not back then. And it's said that when they got on the road, both men discovered they had not enough money between them to board a stagecoach *and* also pay for their beds at the inns, so they chose to sleep at night and walk in the day. Mr Davies always disagreed and said there was a bet in it somewhere, the long walk, a wager, but I don't know if that was true."

Mr Berger put on his hat. "And now M'sieur Hobhouse is *walking* again. Another wager, you think?"

Hobhouse was walking because he loved exercise, and could not bear to be trapped inside a carriage for long periods.

Byron also loved exercise, but he fulfilled that need with his long daily swims in the lake.

The two friends had travelled lengthily together in the past, through Portugal, Spain, Malta, Turkey and Greece; and Hobhouse knew that walking for long periods caused Byron great discomfort. Poor fellow, his afflicted foot often made him painfully lame if he walked too far and too long; and attempting to walk at the same speed as his friends was impossible.

Fortunately, in Greece and elsewhere they had done most of their travelling on horseback; but now with all the luggage to convey, only carriages would do.

So Hobhouse had devised a plan that would suit them both. Each day he would set out two hours earlier than

Byron to walk, until when Byron would catch up and collect him in the carriage. That was Hobhouse's plan, and he would brook no disagreement.

"You are treating me as if I am a lame cripple," Byron had complained.

"No, not in the slightest, but I don't see why you should have to march all over the country just because I spent a year in the Army."

"In the militia."

"Oh very well – the militia!"

"In Ireland, where the land is flat."

"Ireland or England, army or militia, bumpy or flat, one still learns to march – do you *always* have to argue about such trifling things?"

"Then when you walk, I shall walk with you."

"No, pray don't. My bent is to walk alone so I can philosophise my thoughts."

"Then go on, bugger off," said Byron smiling, knowing that Hobby was just trying to make life easier for him.

"Charming," said Hobhouse, pulling on his gloves. "Did they teach you to speak like that at Eton?"

"Hardly, considering my school was Harrow, not Eton."

"Oh damn, yes ... it was Scrope that went to Eton."

"While *you*, poor thing, went to neither."

"True," Hobby agreed, lifting his walking cane. "My father absolutely *refused* to allow me to join the aristocratic riff-raff at those two suburban dens of dunces, choosing instead the more *selective* Westminster."

The banter went on until Hobby had gone out the door and had started walking. Byron had watched him go, thinking how damned lucky he was to have such a good friend as John Cam Hobhouse – eldest son and heir to one of the richest men in England, who had luckily *not* gone to Harrow or Eton.

To have known Hobby when he was a pedantic and brainy schoolboy would have probably been quite unbearable.

~

All the doors of the villa were locked, and Byron was on the point of leaving when a postal messenger on horseback delivered three letters.

Two of the letters were from Shelley, which Byron opened and read inside the carriage:

My Dear Lord Byron, – I have just seen Murray and delivered the next episode of "Childe Harold" to him. He was exceedingly polite to me; and expressed his great eagerness to see the Poem. I shall call on Mr Kinnaird tomorrow. Murray tells me that Lady Byron is in London, and her health has materially improved.

I shall write to you again soon – at this moment I am suffering from a spasmodic headache that does not allow me to connect two ideas. Let me hear from you, and let me hear good news of you. The deep interest I feel in everything that concerns you leads me to expect with eagerness the minutest details.

My dear Lord Byron,

Your sincere friend, P. B. Shelley.

Poor Shelley. Byron could not help agreeing with Claire's statement in her last letter – Dr Polidori was the cause of Shelley's headaches.

He recalled again how shocked he had been, and how angry, when he had discovered that Polidori had persuaded Shelley to take some prussic acid to cure a headache. Prussic acid was a *deadly* poison. Yet Polidori had insisted that poison it was, in a substantial quantity, but a few small drops worked wonders in curing headaches, and no harm done."

Thank God Polidori was gone – but poor Shelley was still suffering from his hapless medical ministrations.

He opened the second letter from Shelley.

My Dear Lord Byron, – You have heard the arrangement that has been made about "Childe Harold". You are to receive 2,000 guineas. I hope to soon inform you that I have received the first proof.

I saw Kinnaird and had a long conversation with him. He informed me that Lady Byron was now in perfect health – and that she was living with your sister.

I felt great pleasure from this intelligence, as I consider the latter part of it as providing a decisive <u>contradiction</u> to the only important charge that ever was advanced against you. On this ground at least it will <u>now become necessary to the world hereafter to be silent.</u>

And yet it was Annabella herself who had made the accusations against himself and Augusta which had stirred up all the outrage – that was the most galling thing – and now she was in London *living* with Augusta! What was that devious woman up to?

Kinnaird spoke of some reports which he says Caroline Lamb propagates against you. I cannot look on these calumnies in the serious light that others do. They appear to be innocent from their very extravagance, if they were not still more so from their silliness. They are the sparks of a straw fire, that vanish when their fuel fails.

Shall we see you in the spring? How do your affairs go on? We are now all at Bath. Claire is writing to you at this instant. Mary is reading over the fire; our cat and kitten are sleeping under the sofa; and little William has just gone to sleep. We are looking out for a house in some lone place; and one chief pleasure, which we will expect then, will be a visit from you.

You will destroy all our rural arrangements if you fail in this promise. You will strike a link out of the chain of our lives which, esteeming you as we do, and cherishing your society as we do, we cannot easily spare. Adieu.

Your sincere friend
P. B. Shelley

The third letter was from Claire.

Oh! noble, mighty, grand young gentleman! Wonder of the age! Can you guess where that comes from? Why, Lady Caroline Lamb's book about you. And so you are addressed in it! Well, I have read it all through. You wretched creature, to go about seducing and rebelling and then to make even the chickens and hens of Belfont run after you! I really am ashamed to hold communion with you.

"Then *don't!"* he said irritably, tossing the letter aside and not reading any more of it.

Not until the carriage was some way along its journey and before it reached Hobhouse, did he casually pick up the letter again to continue reading it:

We have been gone from Geneva these six weeks and not one word of news have we heard from you. You might be ill, and I who love you so much am as ignorant and neglected by you as if you had never heard my name.

My darling Albè, I know what you will say: "There now, I told you it would be so – I advised you not.– I did everything I could to hinder you – and now you complain of me."

I don't complain, dearest Albè, and would not if you were thrice as unkind. Indeed my dearest dear, if you will write me a little letter to say how you are, and above all if you will say you sometimes think of me without anger, and that you will love and take care of me and the child, I shall be as happy as possible.

So, at least she remembered that he had warned her, and repeatedly tried to put her off. He had never been cruel, but he *had* been unkind to her, such as the night she had come to him at his bed where he was laying comfortably and reading a book, her hands reaching out to embrace him, her words gushing love, and looking up from the book he had said to her tiredly, "I wish you would go away. Pray do."

At least he had never been dishonest with her. And now her continual insistence upon his personal care of her and the child, when it was born, puzzled him. He had already arranged a substantial regular allowance for her and the child, so what more could he do?

And he had arranged it with Shelley, who had volunteered to be Claire's guardian and keep her living in his household as usual. She had come from England with Shelley and she would return to England with Shelley. That was the arrangement. So why was she continuing to demand more of him now?

> *"Be kind and good to me, dearest. Write me a nice letter beginning, not with those scanty words "Dear Claire" but "My dearest Claire" and tell me that you like me and that you will be very pleased to have a little baby of which you will take great care."*

He already had a little baby, or had she in her own self-obsession forgotten that?

Chapter Thirty-Nine

~~~

The scenery on this route through Switzerland was new to Hobhouse, who was truly enchanted by all the magnificence around him, the rocks higher and more impending, all of which Rousseau had found so savage in winter.

"I do not find it savage at all," he said to Byron. "Although it *is* getting rather cold now."

Stopping at the little inn at St Gingolph, Byron pointed across the lake to where the boat carrying himself and Shelley had almost capsized in the storm.

"No risk of anything like that happening this time," Hobhouse said confidently. "Travelling overland is much safer."

Leaving the carriage to follow behind, they walked on together and met a tall, pleasing-looking man dressed like a farmer who seemed to wish them to stop and talk.

"*Vous êtes anglaise?*"

"Yes, English," Byron replied, and the farmer kindly replied in English.

"In my youth, I killed many English," he said. "Now I regret it, for it gained me nothing."

Hobhouse moved to walk on in a huff, but Byron was interested. "May we know your name, sir?"

"General Duppa." He had fought in the French Revolution. He had known Napoleon well. He looked towards his wife, who was killing chickens in the farmyard.

"Formerly," said the General, "I commanded divisions, now I command nobody but my wife. I have no steward, and am my own servant."

Hobhouse stood mute as Byron asked some questions about Bonaparte, but the ex-General's main theme was his own woes.

"I lost 75,000 livres of annual income because of
~~~

French politics, and now I am about to lose four hundred more, and all for the reason that I did not choose to be naturalised in France."

When he finally shut up, and they had walked on, Hobhouse grunted with disgust.

"If an Englishman told so much to two men he had never seen before, and was never likely to see again, he would be thought mad."

At their next stop, after Hobhouse had gone to his room at the inn, Byron called him out again to look at something urgent.

He rushed down the stairs, wondering what was wrong, only to find Byron sitting back on a bench and tracking the path of the moon above the far side of the lake.

"It has been rolling slowly up the side of that mountain, but now it seems to have stopped to rest on the top. Do you see it, Hobby, the way it is just resting there?"

Inwardly furious at being called out for something so trivial, Hobhouse looked up at the yellow moon resting on top of the mountain ... and yes ... he had to concede, it was near the full, and ... "most beautiful," he murmured.

"Does it not make you wonder, when looking at the moon," Byron said thoughtfully, "the importance of the number seven."

"What?"

"Well some *do* believe that seven is a heavenly number. Others, such as gamblers like Scrope Davies, believe it is a lucky number.

"Honestly, Byron, for a man who claims to believe in *nothing,* how can you even think of a mere number being heavenly or lucky!"

"Well, consider it, Hobby ... the moon is almost at the full, because it changes its cycle every *seven* days."

"True."

"And the Biblical references to the number seven are numerous. God created the world in *seven* days. In the

Book of Revelations there are *seven* churches, *seven* seals, *seven* trumpets, and *seven* stars."

"And there are *seven* days in the week," Hobby said. "Who decided that?"

"The Romans had *seven* deities, from whose names they chose the names of the days of the week."

"Only the names, the *seven days* were already there, long before the Romans."

"And in Christianity," Byron added, "there are *seven* sacraments, and *seven* deadly sins."

"And now I come to think of it," said Hobby, sitting down on the bench, "the number seven is very important to the Freemasons."

Byron looked at him archly. "Are *you* a Mason?"

"No, but my father is. I once happened to see his apron, and it had *seven* tassels hanging down each side of it."

"Meaning what?"

"I don't know. He would not tell me. Mind, I was only a boy of nine at the time. But I've since learned that seven is considered a *sacred* number to Freemasons."

"Well, if the Freemasons like it, the number *must* have some significance in our world's cosmology."

Hobhouse folded his arms. "You are right, you know. In almost every system of antiquity there are many references to the number seven. The Arabians had *seven* Holy Temples."

Byron nodded. "They still do."

"King Solomon was *seven* years building his Temple. And he dedicated it to the glory of God in the *seventh* month, in a celebration that lasted *seven* days."

And so it went on, until the coldness of the night air began to chill them and finally sent them indoors to the warmth of the inn.

The following morning Hobhouse rose at six, only to find Byron had risen at four, and was now sitting by his window writing rapidly with a pencil, as if his mind could not contain all the unexpressed images inside.

"More poetry?" Hobhouse asked.

"No, my laundry list."

Whatever Byron was writing about, it was not to be shared. The most Hobby managed to see was the title of the poem – *Manfred.*

In the following days they left the monotony of the carriage and rode on horseback to St. Maurice, where the scenery became even more glorious.

Looking up, they saw a Swiss shepherd on the opposite hill; and seeing them also, he began to play on his pipe, which they could hear distinctly, as well as his shouts of laughter which reverberated from every hill.

Mr Berger hallooo-ed up to the shepherd, calling for him to sing the *Ranz des Vaches,* which the shepherd sang, or rather shouted out – and all the scattered cows on the hills rose up from their leisure positions and began to move in an ambling herd towards the shepherd.

"Oh, I had forgot, and should not have asked him to sing that tune!" said Berger remorsefully." It is the tune that calls together the cows at the end of the day."

Fascinated by this scene of Alpine life, Byron sat on his horse, gazing all around him as he observed that the peaceful green pastures, with the cottages and the cows on these heights, was like a dream. "Something too brilliant and wild for reality."

"Yet, it is not always so," Mr Berger told him. "In winter, life here in Switzerland is very hard for the people. From October to April the valleys are usually blocked up with snow, so that horses cannot travel, and only with difficulty can men cut a way through from cottage to cottage. And enough food to eat is not easy, so each family salts a cow and a pig, which, cut in sparing slices, adds a flavour to their green soup, which subsists them for the winter."

"So what do they do for all those winter months?" Hobhouse asked. "The men, I mean?"

Berger shrugged. "The men attend to the cows and goats; but as for any other work, there is not more than one month's labour in six. It is hard, that is why the young men go to Lausanne or Paris in the winter to work as hotel porters or cleaners. And that is why, here in Switzerland, the hotels need to greet as many paying visitors as possible in the summer."

~

In Sécheron, Monsieur Dejean was feeling glum. There was no more pretending ignorance to the guests now, no more hiding from the truth. Because all had seen it for themselves through their binoculars or the telescope – the Villa Diodati was empty, the green shutters closed on all the windows – Lord Byron was gone from Geneva.

"*With every day that passed, I loved him more,*" wrote Dejean in a letter to his brother in Ouchy. "*Milord Byron came to us like a prince, and left us more wealthy than we had ever been. So many visitors, all hoping to see him. Now we can see our winter come with no worry.*"

Madame Dejean was not so content, worrying about the future in her womanly way. "But what of *next* year, Jacques? We are five miles outside Geneva, in the environs. We are not so easy to find, and the English are so lazy. What will bring them out to us *next* year?"

"The Alps ... Lac Léman?"

"*Tch!* They can see those from everywhere. No, we need to keep Milord Byron with us ... every summer ..." She suddenly stood up swiftly onto her feet. "*J'ai une idée!*"

Jacques though her idea to be an excellent one, and worked quickly to put it into operation, and in every possible way – on the hotel's letter-paper on which visitors would write home to England – and in the hotel's spring newspaper advertisements which would go out in April – but, most important of all – on the brass plaque that Monsieur Dejean would proudly place above the hotel's entrance in time for the coming summer:

Hotel d'Angleterre
Sécheron
The Residence of Lord Byron
1816

Chapter Forty

~~~

Riding their horses along the valley of the Simplon, with a view of the glacier and the huge Dent du Midi looming overhead, they came to the famous waterfall of the *Pisse Vache* – a name which Hobhouse was too embarrassed to pronounce, when Fletcher asked him.

"It's a waterfall. Why do you need to know its name!"

"Oh, because ..." Fletcher was fascinated by this particular waterfall, moving over to Byron on his horse and looking up at him. "Do you see what I see, my lord? It's an uncanny likeness. Almost a portrait ..."

Byron stared in puzzlement at the great body of falling water. "A likeness to what?"

"To old Reverend Becher's wig – you see how the spray is falling in waves in an arch – just like Becher's long white wig used to fall."

Byron smiled as he remembered their old pastor in Nottinghamshire, but before he could agree with Fletcher, he saw a beautiful rainbow forming above the waterfall. "I suppose he must be dead now. He was old enough back then."

"Aye, and with his wig here, and that rainbow now glowing over it," Fletcher said, "I suppose that's him letting us know he is up in Heaven now."

Byron nodded. "He was a good soul."

Hobhouse stared. "Wigs in water and signs from rainbows! You're as bad as *he* is, Byron? Every bit as juvenile!"

Byron laughed. "No more than a grown man who is too shy to say the Swiss word – *Pisse."*

Arriving at the inn at Sion, they were given clean rooms with good beds and offered a decent dinner.

Settling himself down comfortably at the table, Hobhouse might have enjoyed the food, were it not for the waiter who carried on a long conversation with
~~~

Byron about bears.

"I had my own bear once," Byron told him. "Bruin was his name. The most adorable bear this world has ever known."

"No, no..." the waiter shook his head with warning. "There is no thing in the world as a bear adorable. None are to be trusted."

Hobhouse would have *liked* to have been able to eat his dinner in peace, but the waiter still chatted on, telling Byron a story of a bear and a man who met in the mountains, where they wrestled each other fiercely, until both rolled over a precipice, and in the fall, the bear being undermost, was killed; but the man above was saved."

"Look here," Hobhouse interrupted. "Is it always so damned cold at this time of year?"

"Cold, yes," said the waiter, "and soon all will freeze."

The following day was even colder. They rode through a desolate village of closed doors and smoking chimneys, and finally reached the Simplon Pass.

"It's the carriage from now on," Hobhouse said, shivering. "It's too cold for horseback."

Byron agreed, pulling his cloak tighter around him, but before dismounting he turned his horse around and sat looking back at Switzerland ... the wild land of mountains and rocks and snow that had inspired so much artistic creation ...

Mary's *Frankenstein* had been created here; as had Shelley's tribute to Rousseau, *Hymn to Intellectual Beauty*. And also too, so many of his own works ... *The Prisoner of Chillon; The Dream; Darkness;* the continuation of *Childe Harold's Pilgrimage*; and even *Manfred* had been conceived here, if not yet finished. Never before, nor anywhere else, had his writing been so prolific, as here in Switzerland

"Byron, get down and come *on*," Hobhouse called. "Or do you want to freeze to death?"

The inside of the carriage was almost as bitterly-cold as outside, so they arranged themselves on the opposite benches of the carriage and each covered himself in a warm blanket of merino wool.

The carriage rolled on through a dreary stone valley up to the wild country of the Sierre and the Simplon-Napoleon Road, and then downhill to a Roman bridge, and then uphill again ... if they could have travelled as the crows fly, straight across, the journey would have taken a tenth of the time, but as the only road was up and around a huge mountain range before coming down again, there was little to do to but endure the monotony.

As darkness began to fall, reducing the scenery outside to dim shadows, Byron said, "Now, if I was in the company of the Shelley party, they would insist upon us telling stories to pass the dullness of the long journey – preferably stories of the blood-curdling *Fantasmagoriana* kind."

"All nonsense," said Hobhouse, folding his arms over his blanket. "Monk Lewis was the same. He was always telling horror stories. I remember one story he told me that was very strange."

"Strange?" Byron said with interest. "How strange?"

"As I said, *very* strange."

"Blood-curdling?"

"Not if you have good arteries."

"So tell it?"

"A man, visiting a friend who lived on the outskirts of a vast forest in Germany, lost his way. After wandering for some hours through the trees in the darkness, he suddenly saw a light in the distance, and so made his way towards it, hoping that he would find a path out of the forest. However, on approaching the light, he was surprised to discover that it came from a monastery, now in ruins, and overgrown with weeds. Puzzled by this, the man thought it wise to peer through a window before making his presence known, and so made his way towards the nearest wall.

"It was then that he saw an extraordinary sight: a dozen cats were assembled around a small grave, four of whom were at that moment letting down into the grave a coffin upon which rested a crown. The man, startled by this sight, and imagining that he had stumbled upon a coven of witches, turned and hurried away as fast as he could without looking back.

"At dawn, he was fortunate to arrive at his friend's house, who had been waiting anxiously for his arrival. 'I will tell you why,' replied the man, 'although I know you will not believe me', and so told him what he had seen at the monastery. No sooner, however, had he mentioned the coffin with the crown upon it, than his friend's cat, who seemed to have been asleep by the fire, leapt up, saying, 'Then I am now King of the Cats!' and ran out the door, and was seen no more."

After a long silent moment of incredulity, Byron said, "Well, if nothing else, Hobby, you have spared me a sleepless night. I will not be staring stark-eyed at the moon over *that* story."

Hobby grinned. "I told you it was strange. Still, the telling of it has helped me to forget the cold for a while. God knows how we would cope without these warm wool blankets."

They sat for a time in silence listening to the clop-clopping of the horses and the rolling wheels of the carriage, until they finally fell asleep.

Mr Berger and Fletcher, accompanied by the two dogs and Jade the cat, were asleep in one of the calêches, the roof up and locked tight to keep in the warmth, and both men also wrapped in warm wool blankets. The other servants, including the Swiss cook, who had all refused to leave Byron's service, were also wrapped up and asleep in the second caleche – all tired out from the five days of travelling. Even the drivers were drifting off in their seats, but the strong and noble horses kept on going throughout the night.

How long he had slept, Byron did not know, but when he awoke it was to the sight of bright sunshine and, magically, the world felt warmer.

He reached over and shook Hobhouse awake. "Hobby, I think we must be in Italy."

"What?" Hobhouse sprang awake like an excited boy and peered through the window. They passed by two villages in the distance and then burst upon green pastures and meadows populous with white villages whose white churches dotted the plains of the woody hills.

The road forward was perfect, and driving through one of the white villages, for the first time they saw ripe red grapes growing on the trellises in vineyards.

Dropping down the window, they both began to wonder aloud if it was just their imagination – or was the breeze softer, the sky more blue, the houses more white, the pastures more green ... They had been planning to travel together to Italy for years, and two years earlier had been only a week away from leaving England to do so – until Miss Milbanke's accursed letter accepting a proposal of marriage that had not been made to her, intervened.

Yet their uncertainty existed until the carriage stopped at an inn for a change of horses, and they were able to walk in a sunny garden where the walls were covered with oranges and lemons; and the perfume from the lime trees, which the warm breeze wafted towards them, was delicious.

It seemed as though they had passed, in one short night, from a northern autumn to a southern summer. Here, they had travelled down to a lower level and warmer climate than Switzerland; and all looked so totally different to everything they had seen on the other side of the Alps.

One of the inn's waiters approached them in the garden, spoke to them, bowed and walked away again.

"He spoke Italian, *real* Italian!" Hobhouse was delighted. "You can speak Italian, Byron, so what did he say to us?"

"Signori, iI tuo tavola da pranzo è pronto. Benvenuto in Italia ... Sirs, your dining table is now ready. Welcome to Italy."

Ω

To Read the First Chapter of Book 6, turn to next page ....

BYRON

Another Kind Of Light

A Biographical Novel

Gretta Curran Browne

SPI

Seanelle Publications Inc.

Prologue

Italy
December 1816

In her father's house at Filetto in Northern Italy, seventeen-year-old Teresa Gamba, escorted by her maid, slowly made her way down the long staircase of her father's house dressed in a simple gown of white silk to indicate her purity.

She was the second of Count Ruggiero Gamba's five pretty daughters, and the most attractive. Like many Italians from the northern parts of the country, Teresa's colouring was light; her hair fair. She possessed a kind of classic grace, for she had been well-tutored in all matters lady-like, so necessary to the daughter of a Count.

Yet she was not happy, for she had just come home from school, having spent most of her life in education at Santa Chiara's Convent at Faenza, returning to her family only for a few short weeks during the summer holidays and at Christmas.

And now, she had thought, she would have all the time in the world to spend at home in the company of her brother and sisters; and the nuns and the strictness of their education would belong to the past.

Reaching the dark oak door of her father's study, her maid swiftly inspected Teresa's appearance one last time, and then knocked on the door, waiting for the call to enter.

A moment later Count Gamba called *"Accedere,"* and the maid opened the door for Teresa to enter.

Teresa took a step inside the room, and suddenly came to a halt, incapable of moving any further, her face white with shock.

Standing next to her father was a young man of

twenty-two – her brother Pietro – and next to Pietro stood a tall elderly man with greying red hair and whiskers.

Her father came and took hold of her arm, walking her into the room. "Teresa, this is L'Conte Alessandro Guiccioli. He has asked to meet you."

Almost without thought, so well had she been trained, Teresa curtseyed silently to Count Guiccioli, and then lowered her eyes to hide her disappointment.

It was evening; the room was well lit, yet Count Guiccioli lifted a candle and began to walk in a circle around her, inspecting her from head to shoe. Not that he needed to, for he had seen Teresa Gamba on one occasion before, although she had not noticed him. He had studied her then, and liked what he saw. Most of all he liked the fact that she was the daughter of a Count, and so a worthy choice for him.

"Teresa," her father said, "has been educated to a degree of excellence. The Abbess of Santa Chiara's has claimed her as a prize pupil of the school. She can talk to you of Dante and Petrarch and has studied all the classics of our literature."

Count Guiccioli was not impressed. "The Church does not approve of Santa Chiara's methods of educating girls as if they were boys. The Church believes that too much learning is damaging to women."

"And yet Teresa is not damaged," answered her father with a proud smile. "To me, she is a perfect daughter."

Count Guiccioli passed a finger over one eyebrow. He was a clever man, skilled at making bargains, always ensuring that he got the best of it. He never allowed himself to appear eager, just mildly interested.

"I have conditions, to which she must agree," he said quietly, and then beckoned to his manservant who was standing like a mute in the corner of the room.

"Read, Paolo."

Paolo unfolded a square of paper and began to read aloud: – "Let her always determine to be a solace to me, and never a trouble. She should therefore always be cheerful with me, annoy no one in the house, ask politely for anything she wishes, but accept in silence any refusal."

Teresa glanced at her father who merely shrugged, saying to the Count: "That is no more than any husband would ask."

Paolo continued reading: – "Let her be true and frank, so that she will have no secrets from me, but let her be prudent in handing on my confidences to others.

"Let her be docile and ready to execute all my directions. And let her be faithful and beware of any appearances to the contrary."

Teresa waited for Paolo to read out the conditions for Count Guiccioli's side of the contract, but nothing further was said.

"Teresa, you may leave us now," her father said, and Teresa obediently curtseyed again and left the study, closing the door behind her.

"*Così*?" her maid inquired anxiously and Teresa collapsed into her arms. "Rosa, he is *old*! Older than my papa!"

Moments later she was surrounded by her clamouring sisters who dragged her into the sala where her mother sat smiling, ready to congratulate her.

"You should be happy, my child. You have been chosen by one of the richest men in Ravenna."

"But Mama, he is *old!"* Teresa protested. "At least eighty years old!"

"He is younger, barely sixty. A man of experience. So he will know how to look after you. L'Conte Alessandro Guiccioli is held in great respect in Ravenna."

"Si-ixty?" Teresa stammered. "More than forty years of life between us!"

"So he will die a long time before you do, and then you will inherit his great fortune. You must do so, Teresa, for your family. We have four more daughters to secure, but with L'Conte Guiccioli as your husband, we will know your financial future is safe."

"I don't know," Teresa was still stammering. "I – am

afraid – to marry – such a man."

Countess Gamba glanced around at Teresa's sisters with a commanding look in her eyes, and they all immediately obeyed, exclaiming how lucky Teresa was to have caught the eyes of such a wealthy man.

"You will be a Countess!"

"You will have so many servants, Teresa, and all dressed in fine livery!"

"You will have your own box at the Opera!"

"A fine house all your own to rule as mistress!"

"And a carriage with *six* horses!"

Her mother interrupted. "Teresa, what special qualities did the nuns teach you at Santa Chiara's?"

"To be noble and self-sacrificing – but Mama, they teach that because they are *nuns* – and have sacrificed all to become a bride of *Cristo* – not the old Count Guiccioli!"

All protests were futile. It was the Italian way. The parents arranged the marriage and the daughter obeyed.

The two men remained in the study debating and wrangling over all the details, until the arrangement was finally agreed and concluded. The marriage would take place in three months. The contract was signed.

Count Guiccioli had driven a hard bargain. In return for her care and shelter, and the huge fortune that Teresa Gamba would one day inherit as his wife, her father, Count Ruggiero Gamba, had agreed that Teresa's dowry on marriage would be the amount of scudi 45,000.

A large amount; and one which Count Alessandro Guiccioli needed quickly, to pay off his increasing debts.

~~~

By the time Teresa had returned to her bedroom she had worked herself into a rage, tears streaming from her eyes. Despite all the efforts of the nuns at Santa Chiara's, she was not noble nor self-sacrificing, she was
~~~

proud and vain and had imagined that her husband in the future would be young and handsome.

"I cannot endure it, Rosa! To be married to a man more than forty years older than I! And twenty years older than my Papa! Even to think of it is more than I can bear!"

"Cara, *cara ..."* Rosa gathered the girl into her arms and soothingly hushed comforting words to her; but even as she did so, she was afraid for her master Count Gamba if the marriage did not proceed as agreed.

Rosa knew a lot about L'Conte Alessandro Guiccioli of Ravenna, more than she liked to know; but all of it was whispered gossip, and she had often wondered how much of it was true?

All the whispered gossip had been confided to her by Fanny Sylvestrini, her aunt, who lived in the household of the Count at the Palazzo Guiccioli in Ravenna, and had served as a maid to the Count's first and second wife.

Rosa glanced at Teresa now sitting alone at the window of her bedroom, staring out at the darkening evening and weeping silently, her hand constantly wiping at her face.

Had she been told that she would be Count Guiccioli's *third* wife?

Just the thought made Rosa shiver, for although they did not know it here in Filetto – in Ravenna there had been many whispers and rumours about the sudden deaths of both those wives.

Count Alessandro Guiccioli's first wife had been the Contessa Placidia Zinanni –"an ugly woman" – according to Fanny Sylvestrini, who was thirty years Guiccioli's elder, but she made up for her age by bringing him a large dowry, which made Guiccioli as rich as the highest ranking families in Ravenna.

During this time there were rumours of mysterious assassinations of any man who stood in his way, usually by dagger in a dark street at night. Not to be proved, no finger could point, but many had their suspicions.

"The sudden death by dagger one night of Domenico Manzoni," Fanny had said, "a rich landowner from whom the Count had bought a lot of land, and then not paid, still caused rumours in the salas of Venice to this day."

The Gamba family, here in Filetto, would know nothing of this, and Fanny had bound Rosa to an oath of secrecy on the Gospels that would lead to Hell and Damnation if she ever broke her sworn oath.

"During his first marriage," Fanny had said, "Guiccioli seduced many of the maids and then dismissed and replaced them with others. Only to one maid did he stay true, Angelica Galliani, and she stayed true to him also, providing him with six illegitimate children before his wife found out and complained. So he sent his wife to a lonely country house, and did not allow her to return to her rightful place in the Palazzo, until she had made a will in his favour, leaving all she possessed to him. Soon after her return to the Palazzo, came her death.

"Oh, so many whispers of 'murder' and 'poison' from his enemies," said Fanny, "but he met all of them with a high head and spoke with honey on his lips about the sad loss of his wife, until all were silenced.

"Soon after," Fanny had said, "he married Angelica Galliani, legitimised his six children with her, although many scorned him for marrying a servant – and now Angelica has suddenly died!"

Again Rosa glanced at Teresa sitting at the window, her heart throbbing with fear, because now Count Guiccioli was already seeking a new wife – a young lady of wealth and rank this time – but why oh *why* did he have to choose one so young and innocent as her beloved Terasina?

Rosa began to weep, and then wail, until Teresa rushed to her with love and tried to comfort her.

"Don't cry, Rosa. I know I cannot disobey Papa, but I have thought, and L'Conte Guiccioli is very old, so I will be good and kind and will regard him like I do my grandfather, until he dies, which Mama thinks will be soon."

Rosa stared at the girl in utter pity. Had she been taught *nothing* useful to woman by those nuns at Santa Chiara's? *Mio Dio* – what use would books and Italian literature be to the girl when she found herself locked inside a bedroom with an old murderer? No use at all.

~

Venice

December, 1816

Some two hundred miles north of Filetto, at Fusina, having left their carriages and horses stabled at the inn, two young men, Lord Byron and John Hobhouse, stepped into a gondola to be rowed over to the island of Venice.

It was pouring with rain, so they had selected one of the larger gondolas, a *battello*, six-foot wide, which could accommodate six to eight people, and had a large black-wooden cabin built onto it, which was more comfortable than it looked, like sitting down in a small floating drawing-room.

Inside the cabin, which they were told was called a *felze,* the brocade upholstery of the sofa-like seat was red and soft and luxurious to sit on.

"This seat is almost as comfortable as the one in your carriage," Hobhouse said, and was even more gratified by the small window on either side of the cabin, also draped in curtains of red lace. He pulled aside the curtain on his side and peered through the window. "I can't see Venice, not yet, not through this rain."

"How long," Byron said, "did he say it would take to get over there?"

"I didn't ask how long, but I know it's as far as five miles across."

"Oh well then, if there's nothing to see but sea ..."

Byron settled himself in his seat, leaning back against the cushions, and closed his eyes, enjoying the gentle swaying motion of the gondola as it glided over the water.

The door of the cabin was open, and yet the only sound in the silence on the sea was the splashing of the oar and the gentle swishing of water against the sides of the gondola.

Tired out from all the travelling down from Milan and Verona, Hobhouse also settled himself back in the seat and closed his eyes, drifting into a gentle doze, until some time later the echo of the oar became louder and Byron opened his eyes, saying: "We must be under a bridge."

The gondolier, who was standing at the back of the boat behind the felze, on a raised deck, banged on the roof and shouted, "*Rialto!*"

Shortly afterwards they were landed under the canopy of the *Hotel della Gran Bretagne* on the Grand Canal – the Hotel of Great Britain – which lived up to its name when the hotel's manager greeted them in perfect English.

"Oh, thank God for that," Hobhouse murmured to Byron. "Unlike you, *I* don't speak Italian."

"And I speak it more fluently than accurately," Byron said. "But no matter. I'm told the Venetians use their hands a lot when speaking, so we can do the same."

"At first sight," Hobhouse said, "Venice to me looks like Cadiz or some handsome town – flooded."

Byron smiled. "You knew it would be so."

"Yes, but one has to actually *see* it, to believe it."

As soon as the manager of the hotel inspected the two passports, and saw the name of the youngest of the two Englishmen – Lord Byron – he waved away the Bell-boys and personally escorted the two men up a magnificent staircase to their rooms of gold gildings and painted silks.

"My lord ..." he said, and once again John Hobhouse noticed that Byron was given the best room, the largest and most opulent – and yet this very fact caused a stirring of uneasiness in Byron.

Years before, as an unknown student at Cambridge, he had loved going down to London just to stay in the hotels; but since his fame as a poet, and his recent experience in the Hotel d'Anglettere in Geneva when he had been watched and followed and spied upon at every moment during his stay there, he now had a horror of all hotels.

"I shan't stay here long," he said later to Hobhouse. "My main reason for coming to Venicc, this out of the way place where few English tourists come now, was to enjoy some privacy for a change, to become anonymous and be able to enjoy life again."

"We have to stay here." Hobhouse was disturbed. "Have you forgotten that my brother and his wife will be joining us here in a few days, in *this* hotel, and by *my* arrangement. I can't just wander off now to somewhere else. Besides, that manager was not kow-towing to a famous poet, because I daresay no one in Venice has ever heard of you. He was merely being obsequious to your rank and title, nothing more."

"Are you sure?"

"I am certain."

"Oh, well then ..." Byron smiled and relaxed; until half an hour later when there was a knock on his door. He opened it to a stranger ... a white-haired Englishman with a delighted smile on his face and holding out a card.

"Ah, pray forgive my calling, but I was so excited when the manager gave me your room number. My name is Lansdowne, and I have come to introduce myself to the first poet of England."

After a pause, Byron looked cynically over his shoulder at Hobhouse who had been busily writing a letter. "Lord Byron, it seems you *are* known in Venice, because you have a visitor."

"What?" Hobhouse stared in confusion, and then, realising what prank Byron was playing, blurted out the first thing that came into his head – "Can't you see that I am *writing!*"

Byron looked at the stranger with an expression of true sympathy. "His lordship is very temperamental, and hates to be disturbed."

"I merely wished to see ... if I could be useful to him in any way," stammered the Englishman, and after two or three silent fits, took his leave.

Byron closed the door. "You do no favours to your reputation, Byron, not with pranks like that," Hobhouse said irritably. "And it was rather cruel of you, because now he will be following *me* around the hotel, thinking I am you."

"Ah, not so certain and blasé now, are you?" Byron grinned. "Not now the shoe is on the other foot."

~

London

December 1816

In the dull murkiness of England's winter, Percy Bysshe Shelley was looking back on that long tranquil summer in Geneva with Byron as if it had been a dream, now over.

Now there was no tranquillity, no careless days boating on the lake, only misery. England was in a terrible state, the poor and starving were increasing by the day, and young people everywhere were committing suicide. The ruling Tory Government, as usual, cared nothing and did nothing to alleviate the situation.

Mary's sister, Fanny, had committed suicide by overdosing with opium, leaving behind her a sad suicide note – although her death and burial had been hushed up with the explanation that she had gone to Ireland. Later it would be announced that she had died in Ireland from a severe chill.

Her stepfather, William Godwin, had been outraged at Fanny's rash act, and fearing people might attribute the cause of her deadly depression to life in his household, had insisted upon silence.

And Shelley, being the son of a Baronet, had behaved like the perfect gentleman throughout, following all instructions and never speaking of the matter. Fanny was in Ireland, that was all he knew.

Fanny's death had brought one benefit, as tragedies often do, because now William Godwin was prepared to reconcile with his daughter Mary, whom he had coldly disowned for running away at sixteen to live unlawfully with Shelley, a married man.

Yet now, needing Shelley's help and the public support of his daughter, Godwin had offered to welcome Mary back into his good graces.

Not that Mary had moved back into her former home on Skinner Street in London, forced as she was to stay in the lodgings they had rented over a hundred miles away in Bath, in order to hide and care for Mary's other half-sister, Claire Clairmont, who was now heavily pregnant – a state that would lead to more outrage, not only from Godwin, her stepfather – but all decent society.

Shelley hated all these domestic disputes, and was now in London for only one reason, to try and get a publisher for his poetry.

John Murray, of John Murray Publishers, to whom he had personally delivered the new manuscripts of poetry which Byron had written in Geneva, had agreed to read Shelley's new poetry also, and after doing so, expressed praise for it, but made no offer to publish.

He had then sent his latest poem *Hymn To Intellectual Beauty* to Leigh Hunt, one of the two brothers who published a liberal monthly magazine, *The Examiner*.

Leigh Hunt had now replied by return of post, stating his admiration for the work, and his desire to publish it, but first he begged a possible favour of help from the author – "a loan, not a gift"– to be repaid with interest; to help a cause in aid of prison reform that he was organising.

Shelley did not even pause to wonder if the loan requested was actually a bribe, so delighted was he at the news that his work would be published and reviewed favourably in a liberal journal – so much *better* than the gossipy newspapers that preferred to publish nothing more than trivial gossip, unfounded lies, and the latest lauded activities of the vile Prince Regent.

Shelley immediately wrote a cheque made out to Leigh Hunt for fifty pounds – an amazingly large sum, considering the rent on Shelley's house in Bath was that amount – fifty pounds a year.

The fact that his contribution to a worthy cause might also be seen as a bribe on his part, did not occur to Shelley.

Nor was he given time to consider it, for the very next day another crushing blow fell – this time not on the Godwin family, but on Shelley himself – when his friend, Thomas Hookham, informed Shelley that his twenty-one-year old wife, Harriet Shelley, had committed suicide by drowning herself in the Serpentine River in Hyde Park.

"Everybody will blame you as the cause, for deserting her," Hookham said. "So if I were you I would go back to Bath and stay there. At least for a while."

Shelley had no intention of doing such a cowardly thing. He had left his marriage and Harriet two years earlier, so why the suicide now?

He went immediately to the Westbrook's house in Grosvenor Square, where a maid told him Mr Westbrook was too grieved to receive anyone; but Harriet's older sister, Eliza Westbrook, was quick on the scene – a spinster of thirty-three, and a virago of a woman, whom Shelley had always blamed for her continual interference which led to the eventual collapse of the marriage.

"I don't know how you have the *nerve* to show your face here today!"

Shelley was distraught. "What of my children?"

"What of your children, pray?"

"I have never failed to financially support them, and now that they have no mother, I must be allowed to take care of them."

"No – No! You abandoned them along with your wife, so you should be rejoicing, Mr Shelley – because now you are free to marry your atheist whore! Get away from this door!"

The door slammed in his face.

Normally, it would have been Shelley's way to turn and walk away, but today he felt a violent need to fight for something precious to him.

He banged on the door furiously, his shouts becoming shrill ... but no matter how long he stood there banging, the door was firmly locked against him. And now he knew that it would never be opened to him again.

Eventually he turned and walked away, now convinced that Harriet had *not* committed suicide; or, if she had, then she must have been *driven* to self-murder by her hateful sister.

The following day Shelley visited Thomas Hookham in his bookshop and questioned him about Harriet.

"She was only twenty-one," Shelley said, "with two small children, and most of her life still before her – so why should she want to commit suicide?"

Hookham thought Shelley somewhat disingenuous, after all he had left Harriet and the two children for another woman, but then – "*Judge not, lest ye also be judged.*"

"I believe she *was* sent out of her house by her sister, solely to hide her advancing pregnancy from the wrath of her parents, due to her attachment to a groom named Smith. She left her children in the care of her sister and took lodgings in Chelsea, near the barracks, under the name of Harriet Smith. And now, according to her landlady, who spoke to the police about Harriet's solitary depression, she went out one night over a month ago, and was not seen again until her body was eventually found floating in the deepest reaches of the Serpentine.

"Harriet was pregnant?"

Hookham's face was red with embarrassment. "Some say by you, others say by Smith."

"Not by me – how *could* it be me? – I left England nigh on eight months ago!"

"That's what *I* said, but Eliza has her suspicions. She said you visited Harriet before you left."

Eliza – Harriet's sister! Now Shelley was not only traumatised, but incandescent with rage.

He left Hookham and went straight to Mr Longdill his solicitor, who greeted him with sympathetic condolences.

"Poor Harriet! Her body must have been in the water for almost a month. Strange that no one went looking for her, when she had disappeared for so long a time. No one at all. And, of course, *you* were abroad. So how could you know?"

"I need to recover the custody of my children from that house – from the Westbrooks," said Shelley, and I need you to do it for me, legally."

Mr Longdill was not so confident. "Are you still associated with Miss Godwin?"

"Yes. And we have a child, a boy."

"In that case, Mr Shelley," said Longdill, "if you were to legalize your union with Miss Godwin, in marriage, making her the lawful stepmother of your children, then your legal custody of the children would almost certainly be a matter of general routine."

For the first time in days, Shelley managed to smile.

Arriving back at his lodgings, he wrote a letter to Mary:

It seems that Harriet, the most innocent of her

abhorred and unnatural family, was driven from her father's house in order to hide her illegitimate pregnancy by a man named Smith.

There can be no question that the beastly viper her sister Eliza, unable to gain profit from her connection with me – has secured to herself the fortune of the old man – who is dying – by the murder of this poor creature.

Shelley was beyond the capability of allowing himself to believe, even for a moment, the possibility that Harriet had killed herself willingly. She had been a gentle creature, and yet this was not only an act of violence against herself, but also her two children. He *had* to get them back into his care, and so he would marry Mary. They had been living together like a married couple for more than two years, so it would make no difference to their daily life.

I told Longdill that I was under contract of marriage to you; and he said that in such an event, all their pretences to detain the children from me would cease."

A week later, distressed and anxious, his assurance destroyed, he wrote another confidential letter, this time to his friend, Lord Byron; knowing he would sympathise. Of all the poets, Byron was truly the most political, and he was famous for those beliefs, which were the same as his own – libertarian, anti-monarchical, and free-thinking. Byron also knew all about hateful in-laws.

I write to you, my dear Lord Byron, after a series of the most unexpected and overwhelming sorrows.

My late wife is dead. The circumstances which attended this event are of a nature of such awful and appalling horror, that I dare hardly to avert to them in thought. The sister of whom you have heard me speak , may be truly said (though not in law, yet in fact) to have murdered her for the sake of her father's money.

The sister has now instituted a Chancery Court process against me, the intended effect of which is to deprive me of my unfortunate children, now more than ever dear to me; and to throw me into prison, and expose me on the pillory, on the grounds of my being a REVOLUTIONIST *and an* ATHEIST. *It seems whilst she lived in my house she possessed herself of such papers as to establish* these allegations.

The opinion of Counsel is that she will certainly succeed to a considerable extent, but that I may escape entire ruin, in the worldly sense; though I am given to understand that I could purchase victory by recantation of my sympathies and beliefs; this I will not do before their tribunals of tyranny.

So here is an imperfect account of my misfortunes. I have no other news to tell you, but I often talk, and oftener think of you. In poetry I still feel the burden of my own insignificance and impotence.

Faithfully yours, P. B. Shelley.

~

Venice

December 1816

Still in the *Hotel della Gran Bretagne,* Byron passed through the spacious main hall into the foyer, and came face to face with Lady Francis Shelley, a nice-looking woman in her early thirties, and a friend of his sister Augusta. She was accompanied by her husband, Sir John Shelley, and both appeared very surprised to see him.

"Lord Byron. we were told you were here, but we thought it was just gossip."

"Lady Shelley." Byron bowed and warmly shook Sir John's hand. "You have just arrived?"

"No, we are just leaving," said Lady Frances. "We have been here a full week. You do not use the dining room?"

"No, but my friend Mr Hobhouse and his relatives do. Have you not seen them?"

Lady Frances looked at her husband. "I don't think we know a Mr Hobhouse, do we?"

Byron smiled. "You would certainly know if you did. He and his tribe have just left for Rome. I intend to join them in a few weeks."

During the polite conversation that followed, Byron was anxious to know any news of his sister from Lady Frances, and agreed to take tea with the Shelleys in the tea-room, which was quite empty. They sat in a secluded corner where Lady Frances shook her head negatively.

"We have been touring all over the place. I believe we missed you at Geneva. So no, I have heard nothing at all from England."

"Which reminds me," said Sir John, "Madame de Staël begged us, if we met you in Venice, to give you her *amour,* and to remind you that she intends to join you and your friend in Italy very soon."

Byron smiled, but did not respond, knowing Madame de Staël would never arrive in Italy; and disappointed that Lady Frances could tell him nothing of his sister.

Still, she made up for it by telling him all that she knew about the mode of life of the society in Venice.

"You have not yet been to the Salon of Madame Albrizzi?"

Byron smiled a supercilious negative. "They say she is the Italian Madame de Staël, but I doubt there could ever be a fair copy anywhere else in the world."

Sir John seemed to agree, but Lady Frances felt bound to say, "Although Madame Albrizzi is very *nice,* very welcoming, and I'm sure you would also find her so. Two nights ago, we left her salon at half past ten, intending to return to our beds to sleep, but then our friend the Marquis of Cigognera took us on to the salon of Madame Benzoni, where we *also* met a really very agreeable society of Venetians and strangers from all nations. All the Venetian ladies were escorted by their *cavalier serventes* but two or three actually brought their husbands."

Byron was puzzled. "*Cavalier servente?"*

"Their lover," said Sir John. "They are really quite open about it, and very different to all the bam and hypocrisy in England where that kind of thing is every bit as bad."

Lady Frances voiced her objection, and Sir John glibly apologised. "Yes, Frances, it was wrong and rude of me to say such a thing about our countrymen and women in London society – and the more so for it being true."

Byron smiled. "Truth is a strange thing, isn't it? Very few people seem to like it. I once escaped a duel for writing the truth about a very bad and stupid actor, who had ruined an entire production and yet did not seem to realise he had done so. Two lines only, a couplet, but the truth – for which I was furiously called out to a duel to the death."

"My goodness," said Lady Frances, "what was the offending couplet?"

"Not to be hissed delights the dunce,
But who can groan and hiss at once?"

Sir John laughed. "And who won the duel?"

"No one. He did not show up at the appointed time or place."

Lady Frances was smiling "So he was not so stupid after all."

"What *is* stupid though," said Sir John, "are the damnable late hours they keep here in Venice. Truly exhausting. The theatre does not begin until nine o'clock and the casinos open at midnight. The salons and the *converszationes* can go on all night, and many of the coffee houses stay open all night. Very few go to bed before three in the morning."

"And staying up with them is exhausting," said Lady Frances. "But this I have learned about the life here from Madame Benzoni. A Venetian lady's day is thus passed – she rises about twelve o'clock, and accompanied by her *Cavalier servente,* attends daily Mass. She then takes a few walking turns on the Piazza San Marco for her health. She lunches between three and four, and then undresses and goes to bed completely. At about eight o'clock she arises, and then spends until three or four o'clock in the morning at the theatre and casino, or, in the summer, in the cafes on the Piazza."

"So no different to the English ladies in London then?" Byron grinned. "At least the ones *I* knew."

Lady Frances looked at him judiciously. "You have read Lady Caroline Lamb's book about you – *Glenarvon*?"

"Which cannot be true, and certainly could not be an accurate portrait of me, because I did not sit long enough for the painter."

Lady Frances nodded. "She is quite mad of course. And just as vindictive as Lady ..." her face began to redden as she realised what she was about to say, and to whom.

Byron spared her blushes by asking Sir John about Shelley. "My friend in Geneva, Percy Bysshe Shelley – is he a relative of yours?"

"A very *distant* relative," Sir John replied quietly. "I'm afraid the Shelley family don't talk about Percy Bysshe any more. Not since he was sent down in disgrace from Oxford, and then ran off with the daughter of a wine-merchant to marry her in Scotland. Even his own father, Sir Timothy Shelley, has disowned him for being a radical and an atheist."

"Is he still in Geneva?" asked Lady Frances.

"No, he has returned to England."

"And so, regrettably, must we," said Sir John, looking at his fob-watch. "Still, it has been a pleasure, Lord Byron, a pleasure."

Byron escorted them out to the steps of the hotel and their gondola, which was packed with their luggage and waiting.

As she was about to step down into the gondola, he said quietly to Lady Frances: "When you see her, you will give my love to my sister Augusta, and tell her that I am well."

She nodded. "I will – and it will be the *truth* – because to my eyes you look better than I have ever seen you look. Your time in the peaceful Swiss Alps must have done you great good."

"And you will tell her so? You know how she fusses and worries."

Again she nodded, and added, "Truly, if this gondola did not await us, I'm sure we would be happy to stay another day or two, if only to introduce you to the society of the Countesses Albrizzi and Benzoni."

Byron answered good-naturedly. "I have already received invitation cards from both of them. I shall go, but in my own good time."

"Pray may I ask," said Sir John, "why you did not go to Rome with your friends?"

"Because I hate hotels, and Rome will still be there in the future, but as I intend to stay in Venice for a while I need the time to find myself a good private apartment."

"Well, good luck to you then, Lord Byron," said Sir John, and then added warningly. "And you mind yourself in this beggary place. Venice may be beautiful in its way, but it's also full of starving beggars that would not hesitate to kill a decent-looking man to get a few *scoldi* to buy food."

Byron considered that to be a typical English exaggeration. He had seen the beggars, and they had held out their hand, and he usually dropped in a few coins, but none looked as if they would kill. Or maybe he was just being naive? He would give it some thought.

He watched as they boarded the gondola, and as it began to glide off down the Grand Canal, both waved back to him, with Sir John calling out – "Cheerio, Lord Byron! Cheerio!"

Cheerio, indeed. The meeting had unsettled him, for it reminded him too much of his former life in England. But, dammit, the world was bigger than England – that tight little island, with all its hypocrisy and its cold climate and chilly artificial women – so why the deuce was he feeling homesick?

A sensation of the moment. Nothing more. It would soon pass.

~

Italy

January 1817.

Inside the Palazzo Gamba at Filetto, Teresa Gamba had always enjoyed Christmas with the delight of a child, and then looked forward to the coming new year, wondering what unexpected miracle or what new happy times it might bring.

But this new year held no wonder for her, nor any of the years after that. The long road of her future on this earth was to be filled with unhappiness and the servile meekness of a wife complying with all orders from her husband ... *"Let her determine to always be a solace to me and never a trouble. Let her be docile and ready to execute all my directions."*

Yet she could not speak out, could not complain, nor defy, for now she understood that her father was not only asking her to do her duty to her family, but also to her country.

"God first, the family second, Italy third. The three sacred duties for all Italians," her Papa had said. "And that applies to you, Teresa, as well as to Pietro, and I know I can trust you to do your duty to all three."

She had felt very honoured and very grown up when her father had explained to her the realities of Italy outside the world of Santa Chiara's convent.

"After the defeat of Bonaparte," he had said, "the British handed Italy over to the Austrians – as a gift. Now we are ruled by the Austrians, and they rule us hard. And now our hearts and minds are determined on only one acceptable destiny – the freedom of Italy."

Teresa had trembled when she heard her father say the word *"Carbonari"* – the secret army of men pledged to rise and reward the Austrians in blood for their theft of Italy.

"But not until the time is right. Not until we are big enough and ready," her Papa had said. "And so you, Teresa, must be a good daughter, by being a good wife, and then come and tell your Papa everything that you see, everything that you hear, in the house of your husband, L'Conte Alessandro Guiccioli."

"Why? Is he a bad Italian?"

Her father had shrugged. "He was a friend to the French, and now he is a friend to the Austrians. He goes wherever the smell is sweetest. We in the Carbonari know that, but Guiccioli is not aware that *we* know."

Her father then stood up from his desk and presented her with the Family Bible, reached down and placed her hand on it. "Now, Teresa Gamba, in the name of God, and in the name of the Gamba family, swear your oath that you will never breathe a word of what I have said to you this day."

Teresa obediently swore her oath, and knew she

would never break it.

Later that afternoon, Teresa's maid, Rosa, found her alone in her bedroom, sitting in an armchair and silently weeping.

"Terasina, why are you crying?"

Teresa lifted the book she had been reading and showed it to Rosa – the story of Paolo and Francesca, by Dante.

"It is so beautiful," Teresa said, "and in the past, when I have read the part where the love between Paolo and Francesca grows as they read a book together about Lancelot and Guinevere, my heart used to beat with excitement ... but now it makes me sad."

And Rosa knew why, and felt like crying herself, and she still could not understand why Signor Gamba had agreed to such a marriage. How bad it was, and how hard it would be, for a pure young maiden in her teens to be married to a hoary old sinner.

Yet she said encouragingly, "L'Conte Guiccioli is still a handsome man, stands tall, a man of power and respect, even to the Austrians."

Teresa nodded. "I know. And I also know that he is twenty years older than my papa."

Which reminded Rosa of why she had entered the room: Teresa had been summoned again to her father's study.

Teresa laid down her book. "Do you know why?"

Rosa shook her head. "How would I know? Your mother is in there with him, so it must be important."

"Then I must go quickly."

Teresa rushed downstairs and entered her father's study with increasing uneasiness. She curtsied before her parents, and then looked at her father with dread.

Ten minutes later she came out of the study and found Rosa waiting for her as usual.

"*Che cosa?"*

Teresa's face was flushed and her eyes glowing. "A miracle!" she whispered; and then beckoned for Rosa to come up to her room.

Once inside, she told Rosa the good news. "The priests of the Church have stood against him. They say it is not good Catholic practice to marry so soon, and he must wait for a year after the death of his last wife before he can be married again by the Church."

Rosa clapped her hands. "So, it is not to be?"

"It is still to be. The contract is signed," Teresa said quietly, and then she smiled again. "But not for almost a year, and perhaps another miracle will come to me before then?"

"*Per favore Dio!*" Rosa prayed.

~~~
~~~

Thank You

Thank you for taking the time to read ***'A Man Of No Country'*** the fifth book in the *Lord Byron* Series. I hope you enjoyed it.

Please be nice and leave a review.

*

I occasionally send out newsletters with details of new releases, or discount offers, or any other news I may have, although not so regularly to be intrusive, so if you wish to sign up to for my newsletters – go to my Website and click on the "Subscribe" Tab.

*

If you would like to follow me on ***BookBub*** go to:- **www.bookbub.com/profile/gretta-curran-browne** and click on the "*Follow*" button.

Many thanks,

Gretta

www.grettacurranbrowne.com

Also by Gretta Curran Browne

LORD BYRON SERIES

A STRANGE BEGINNING

A STRANGE WORLD

MAD, BAD, AND DELIGHTFUL TO KNOW

A RUNAWAY STAR

A MAN OF NO COUNTRY

ANOTHER KIND OF LIGHT

NO MOON AT MIDNIGHT

***

LIBERTY TRILOGY

TREAD SOFTLY ON MY DREAMS

FIRE ON THE HILL

A WORLD APART

***

MACQUARIE SERIES

BY EASTERN WINDOWS

THE FAR HORIZON

JARVISFIELD

THE WAYWARD SON

***

ALL BECAUSE OF HER
A Novel
(Originally published as GHOSTS IN SUNLIGHT)

RELATIVE STRANGERS
(Tie-in Novel to TV series)

ORDINARY DECENT CRIMINAL
(Novel of Film starring Oscar-winner, Kevin Spacey)

Printed in Germany
by Amazon Distribution
GmbH, Leipzig